KIDNAPPED IN THE SOUTH PACIFIC

by

Robert Prince

Published by Robert D Prince

Robertprince67@bigpond.com

This is a work of historical fiction set in Queensland, Australia, 1870 to 1915. Names, characters, places and incidents are the product of the author's imagination or are used fictitiously.

ISBN 978-0-9944708-8-1

Cover art and design: Glen Holman www.glenholman.com

Editing and interior design: Philip Newey http://www.philipnewey.com/All-read-E

Other books written by the author to recreate Australia's colourful past: *The Farrier's Son, Shadows of the Mountain*

To all the South Sea Islanders and their descendants who have contributed to building the Australian nation

PREFACE

No matter how history is rewritten, the undeniable truth is that some of the 62,000 South Sea Islanders brought from Melanesia to Australia during the latter 1800s were kidnapped and held as slaves, while many others were duped into slave-like bondage by a system of indentured labour designed to secure a cheap work force. Since the days of colonial rule in Australia, argument has pitched back and forth regarding the morality and legality of what became known as the 'Labour Trade'. Although slavery was abolished in the British Empire in the 1830s, pockets of the practice continued in the West Indies.

Following cessation of the cheap labour of the convict era, colonists, particularly those in the colony of Queensland, turned to procuring South Sea Islanders to fill the shortfall. The burgeoning sugar industry of coastal Queensland, in dire need of manual workers to clear land and grow sugar cane, became the major importer of Islanders from the 1860s to 1900.

During the early years of the trade, slavers raided island villages, nabbed young males and the occasional female, stuffed them into the holds of sailing ships, transported them to Queensland and sold them to the sugarcane planters. However, before long, those of the Abolitionist Movement of Britain together with moralists in Australia brought the trade to notice, claiming the practice to be illegal.

To cover themselves, members of the Queensland colonial parliament, a legislature well represented by sugar planters, devised the 1868 *Polynesian Labourers Act* as a means of circumventing the Imperial ban on slavery. Under the guise of a system of indentured labour, Islanders were brought to Australia and effectively enslaved for a term of three years. The scheme flourished, with more than a thousand recruited each year and put to work for nearly no pay and in conditions that were often considered wholly inadequate. The legislation, with its deficiencies and associated corruption by government officials, allowed for shiploads to be brought to the mainland and sold to the highest bidder. The bickering between the landed class, the politicians and the moralists continued till the turn of the century, with increasing restrictions on the procurement of Islanders and improvements in their working conditions.

With the formation of the Federation of Australian colonies in 1901 came the *White Australia Policy*, a racially based policy to exclude non Europeans from entering Australia, restrict employment opportunities for those in the country and, in particular, forcibly repatriate South Sea Islanders to their islands of origin. Between 1904 and 1908, 7,000 of the 9,000 Islanders then resident in Australia were returned home, and those that were allowed to stay, mainly the elderly and infirm, were placed under severe employment restrictions in a bid to protect white Australian workers from cheap labour.

Though the trade had been abolished, racism continued well into the twentieth century, with people of South Sea Islander descent being marginalised. While a few sprang to fame on the sports field they remained, in the main, social outcasts. Only since the 1990s have they been recognised as an ethnic minority. The Commonwealth Government formally recognised them in 1994, and the State of Queensland gave belated recognition in 2000.

While much has been written and continues to be debated about the merits or otherwise of the 'Labour Trade' there are, within the Australian South Sea Islander community, groups actively campaigning for the advancement of their people. The debate on this matter is not closed and, with descendants of these Islanders now educated and holding prominent positions within Australian society, much more is yet to unfold.

Kidnapped in the South Pacific shines a light on this dark chapter of Australian colonial history. The story follows the journey of Princess Marcella, a beautiful young mixed-race Islander girl who is kidnapped from the island of Lifou, shackled in the captain's cabin and brought to Australia. As a slave girl she faces an uncertain future, fearing all manner of privations. From ship's cabin to country estate, and then a sudden move to a remote sugarcane plantation, Marcella is led on an odyssey. Racism and servitude are never far away, with the Islander labourers being bought and sold and living in fear of reprisals from the planters.

The author, a Queenslander with seventy years of close association with the sugar industry and an understanding of the role the Islanders played in its establishment, sets to capture the essence of the Islanders' experience and bring due recognition for their valuable contribution to the development of Queensland.

CONTENTS

Princess Emile, a pearl of the South Sea, stood in the moonlight, with the sea quietly lapping the shore. According to custom, this eighteen-year-old maiden daughter of King Jacques, a tribal chief of the island of Lifou, would one day be united with a warrior chosen by the King and bear children.

Captain Mark Richards, a young and ambitious sea merchant, had set foot ashore only three days prior and now stood before her, reaching for her outstretched hands.

During the 1800s Spain, France and Britain tussled for control of the South Pacific. Some engaged privateers to harass and intercept ships flying flags of opposing colours. No seafaring merchant could consider himself safe; only the daring or those lusting for the treasures of the South Sea Islands ventured into these waters. French and British warships scoured the seas of New Caledonia, the New Hebrides and the Solomon Islands for buccaneers engaged in the slave trade.

In the winter of 1853, Captain Mark Richards stood on the foredeck of his schooner *Fearless* as his helmsman navigated the passage between reefs that led to Lifou, an island of the New Caledonia Archipelago. When past the treacherous outcrops of coral and entering a tranquil lagoon the captain signalled to reduce sail. The days before had been difficult, battling high winds and wild seas, with the crew manning the rigging by day and night. They now stood at ease, appreciating the vista before them. The water, deep blue and crystal clear below, turned to aquamarine in the shallows by the beach. From a distant bluff on the port side, sand dunes swept the full length of the cove to a coral cay protecting the southern extremity. The lush tropical jungle beyond the shore added another jewel to the crown of this island hideaway. Spirals of smoke, drifting from a grove of coconut palms, confirmed they had located the village. Mark had not previously traded with this island but, from reports received, he expected to reap a handsome reward from trading sandalwood in return for much wanted European goods.

He dropped anchor in three fathoms of water and then, as was the routine, waited to be spotted by the community. Children playing on the beach scurried off at seeing the ship, and soon a tall native, naked except for a grass tie about his waist, appeared. He watched curiously for a few moments and then placed a conch shell to his mouth and sounded a series of blasts. Return calls drifted from far corners of the cove; everyone had now been alerted to the arrival of the white trader. Women and children crowded the beach, while men and a few young women dragged outrigger canoes to the water. The waving of hands and the smiles of those paddling the canoes greeted the crew with a disarming welcome. The men responded, delighted to make contact with members of an ancient culture. Fortunately for everyone, the Islanders spoke South Sea Pidgin, a language developed over a century of whalers, *bêche-de-mer* fishermen, traders and other stopovers visiting the islands.

Mark, dressed in white calico shirt and trousers and with his sandy hair tied in a ponytail, beckoned them aboard. He reached to assist one. Other crew members began to help, heaving warrior-like men up and over the gunnel. Princess Emile, a young bare-breasted female, sought Mark's help when her canoe slid from beneath her feet, leaving her dangling by the side of the ship. He took her hands and gently lifted her to the deck. The fine lines of her body caught his attention, and when they locked gazes the radiance of her broad smile and bright eyes captured him as no woman had before. The trading items assembled on the deck were inspected with nods of agreement, confirming that a deal would be done. When the villagers returned to their canoes, Princess Emile, wearing only a skimpy grass skirt that bared her thighs with every move, cast Mark a longing look to which he replied with a knowing smile.

The next morning, Mark and the crew loaded a whaleboat with the items to be traded and rowed ashore where villagers helped carry the goods to the village. King Jacques, as he had been coined by previous French traders, beamed with delight at the dozens of items spread before him: steel tools, spear tips, knives, cooking pots, rope, cord fishing lines, fishing nets, soap and candles and, for the women, mirrors, coloured beads and trinkets. So pleased was he that he invited Mark and his crew to join with his people for a celebratory feast. During the remainder of that day and the next, the villagers, including Emile, helped the crew ferry the sandalwood to the schooner, fill the ship's holds and lash the surplus to the deck.

At daybreak the following morning, the men rowed ashore with golden shimmers breaking across the water with each stroke of the oars. When ashore, children gathered around and took them to the village where preparations for the feast were already underway. Emile, with a dainty Tiaré flower behind her ear, a frangipani lei about her neck, a grass skirt and a shark-skin anklet, greeted Mark by presenting him with a lei that complemented the one she wore. Throughout the morning and into the early afternoon she waited on him like a handmaiden. She then asked if he would come and bathe with her in the creek behind the village. When he declined she went alone to prepare herself for the night of her dreams.

The women of the village moved about carefree, some wearing grass skirts, and others nothing more than a girdle of fresh leaves. With sprigs of flowers tucked into their fuzzy hair, they laid flower petals at the base of totem poles, swept inside and outside their grass huts with palm-frond brooms, collected fruit from the forest and dug yams and taro from the garden. In the early afternoon they prepared the vegetables and seafood for cooking. All this time their laughter and cheery calls, from one group to another, could be heard filtering through the coconut grove.

During the day older men collected firewood, while the younger men fished an inshore reef and returned with canoes laden with turtles and fish. All of this, together with village pigs and fowls, provided an abundance with which to feed the tribe of two hundred. Some lads dug a pit-oven where hot stones would cook the meal. A medicine man, who the tribespeople believed possessed special powers, ceremoniously lit a fire in the pit and later placed the food on the bed of hot stones and sealed the top with leaves and sand. Hosting a feast for their newfound friends, the white traders, brought fresh meaning to their spiritual understanding. Some believed the friendly crew to be the incarnation of good spirits.

That night they feasted by the light of a full moon rising above the ocean and, when the moon rose above the palms, the drummers set to, pounding a resonating beat that summoned all to the village common. King Jacques, bare chested and wearing a loin cloth, strode through the crowd, ascended a platform decorated with palm fronds and sat on a carved chair. The young women, including Emile, formed a semicircle before his stage and, to the rhythm of the beat, carried the night forward with island song and dance. At the conclusion of the *sing-sing*, Emile, wearing only a light grass skirt and a mother-of-pearl medallion that hung in the cleavage of her breasts, came to Mark's side and held his hand. The lure of the South Pacific, with its seductive charm, took them aside to a place where time was their own. Without thought to consequence, each surrendered, fulfilling their desires and whispering words of love.

When the first rays of morning light sheeted across the calm sea they walked hand in hand to the beach where they sat, each with dreams of the future. While Emile imagined life with Mark, his thoughts were otherwise. The cargo of sandalwood had yet to be delivered to Canton where it would fetch a fortune as incense for the rich.

Emile rested her head on his shoulder and asked, 'You will come back?'

Mark, not wanting to let her go, replied, 'Yes, as soon as I sort a few things.'

The uncertainty in his voice caused her concern. She turned in the sand, faced him and pleaded, 'Promise?'

Her gaze, as it had before, left him defenceless. He kissed her, took a silver broad-band ring from his finger and held it before her.

Emile took this to be a marriage vow. She leant forward and pressed her lips to his for moments, before leaning back and wiping tears from her eyes.

'Yes, my love, it's for you,' he said lovingly. He twirled the ring in his fingers to catch the light and read aloud the inscription engraved on the inside, 'Mark Richards 1813.'

Emile pointed to the ring and, having learned his name since he came ashore, asked, 'Your name Mark?'

'Yes, I was named after my mother, whose name is Marcella.' He explained that, as a seaman trading the high seas, he could lose his life at any time, and if this were to happen the ring would identify his remains by his name and year of birth.

Emile, upset at such a thought, drew back and sat on her haunches. Mark captured that moment with the sun behind her, creating a golden aura about her body and teasing through the curls of her hair. He reached for her hand, placed the ring in her open palm and clasped her fingers closed. That surreal moment would stay with them both, no matter how the future unfolded.

Four of the crew rowed a whaleboat towards them. When it was near the shore, Mark lifted Emile to her feet and hugged her. She walked into the sea with him, and when he boarded and the oarsmen pulled away she stood, sobbing and distraught.

After his departure Emile took herself to the beach every day where she sat, gazing seaward, waiting for him to return. Each time a sail ship appeared on the horizon her heart leapt, only to be thrust into despair when it passed by. As the summer months became hot and oppressive, her expectation of his return faded, and by the time she gave birth to their baby daughter, whom she named Marcella, all hope had been dashed.

Unknown to Emile, Mark faced great danger on the voyage to Canton. His schooner, though robust and well manned, was not suited for such a long voyage. While other schooner captains took their cargo of sandalwood to Sydney to be loaded onto large, square-rigged sailing ships, Mark, lusting for riches, wanted to exclude the middleman. The *Fearless* made good headway till a wild storm in the Philippines shipwrecked her on a remote island, leaving the crew stranded for months. Upon his return to Sydney, Mark had no ship, no money. He captained ships, but none that traded with Lifou, Emile's island home. If he knew that she now cared for his child perhaps he would forfeit everything and go to her side.

PART ONE
Held Captive by a Sea Captain

Shipload of South Sea Islanders arriving in Queensland during the 1800s

CHAPTER 1

'Grandpa! Grandpa! Come out and see.'

'What?'

'There's a ship in the bay.'

'What sort of ship?'

'The biggest ship I have ever seen. A square-rigger flying the English flag.'

King Jacques rose up from his mat bed, pulled a loin cloth about his waist, hobbled to the door, shaded his aging eyes against the glare and asked, 'Who is it?'

'I don't know. I've never seen the ship before.'

Marcella, now sixteen years of age, took him by the hand. 'Here, Grandpa, hold my hand.'

Villagers left their huts, and others came from the forest as Marcella and Jacques crossed the village common. When partway across, Marcella stopped to adjust her sarong. She unwrapped the colourful fabric from her slim body, revealing the beauty of her maidenhood, and then covered herself again. During this brief moment Jacques dwelt upon her fair complexion and wondered if Mark would ever return. Marcella took his hand again and led him to the beachfront.

The ship, two hundred yards from shore, rocked slightly as the crew, high in the rigging, furled and secured the sails. Captain Oliver Morgan, owner and master of the cargo ship *Trade Winds*, stood on the quarterdeck, shouting commands to the first mate, who relayed the instructions to those aloft and those working on the deck securing the anchor. In between shouts Morgan, middle aged, corpulent and with long, curly locks and a black beard, watched the activity gathering on the shore.

Outrigger canoes were being dragged from the shade of coconut palms, slid across the soft sand and pushed into the water. Men and a sprinkling of women piled in, four and eight at a time, hurrying to be first to reach the ship, hoping they might be handed a gift—anything from a plug of tobacco to a glittering piece of glass jewellery. The more enterprising carried coconuts, yams and curios, hoping to get more by trading. Some, unable to find room in a canoe, clung to the sides of the wooden boats, while those seated paddled towards what many thought was mana sent by the gods. Some even swam after them in their excitement to be part of a ritual where ships called and traded flour, rice, hand tools and trinkets for copra which, during the past decade, had replaced sandalwood as the mainstay of their island trade. They climbed rope ladders lowered over the side and clambered to the sun-scorched deck. When thirty or so were assembled, Morgan descended from the quarterdeck and, as he approached the eager villagers, gave the first mate the nod to bring samples of the trading goods from the cargo hold. Jacques and Marcella watched from the beach till the canoes began returning and then walked, hand in hand, back to the village. Jacques would have his turn tomorrow with the captain approaching him as chief of the tribe. Jacques's princess granddaughter, Marcella, the only part European on the island, would be co-host.

Next morning the captain, accompanied by the first mate and four other crew members, arrived at Jacques's hut where huge turtle shells stood each side of the doorway. They presented themselves as a motley crew, with the captain, a formidable-looking man, wearing a battered three-cornered hat, a red kerchief about his neck, grubby cotton shirt and trousers, no boots and a revolver tucked beneath a broad belt. The others, also barefoot, looked scruffier, with their hair hanging in rat tails from beneath sweat-rag hats and wearing threadbare shirts and trousers made from ship's canvas.

Jacques, clothed simply in a loin cloth and wearing a whale-tooth necklace, spoke first, greeting the men in South Sea Pidgin. He then introduced Marcella, who wore a revealing sarong and a lei made of frangipani flowers. Marcella, being young and having met English mariners before, spoke some English and extended the welcome.

The captain, wanting to establish rapport, sent the four crewmen to watch the boat and oars while he and the first mate inspected the coconut plantation. Jacques, partly crippled by stiff joints, readily agreed and watched as Marcella led them past some huts and into a nearby grove. They wandered for a couple of hours, following the coast, going from one to another of the coconut groves where men could be seen climbing trees, falling clusters of nuts and carrying them off to the village. Back near the village, Marcella showed them men husking and cracking the nuts, and women prising the copra from the shell, breaking it into pieces and placing it on trays in the sun to dry. The strong smell of coconut oil, mixed with smoke coming from a smouldering pile of discarded husks, twitched the sailors' noses. Marcella woke Jacques from his afternoon nap, and together they went to the thatched storeroom, where the captain opened and inspected several sacks of copra. He then lifted each to gauge its weight while counting them. They settled in Jacques's hut, sitting in a circle on a large thatched mat and drinking kava, while discussing what each had to offer. After agreeing to a deal, freshly cooked crayfish, garnished with lemon, was served. The captain had commented earlier in the day on the beautiful silver ring that Marcella wore on her left hand. Now, sitting next to her, he again referred to its exquisite beauty. When Marcella lifted her hand for all to see, he took it in his own and kissed the ring. The show of affection reminded Jacques and Marcella of Emile, the love she had shown to them as daughter and mother, the story behind the silver ring and her untimely death at an early age. The first mate thought that the captain's attention to an attractive mixed-race Islander was more than courtesy. The moment of reflection soon passed, and Marcella, enjoying the company of the two men, stayed on, drinking kava till late. As a parting gesture, Captain Morgan took Marcella's hand again, kissed it and then asked her father's name. Marcella, excited by the prospect that Morgan might know him and make contact, quickly replied, 'Mark Richards. He's a sea captain.'

As arranged, the captain brought whaleboats ashore early the following day. Jacques inspected the one loaded with barrels of flour, sacks of rice, tobacco and clay pipes, tomahawks and knives, fishing lines and hooks, gardening and hand tools and tea chests filled with cheap print calico, mirrors, ornaments, jewellery and other trifles. After a quick perusal he nodded approval. The crew then took the sacks of copra to the boats. Just before departing, the captain again drew attention to Marcella's ring. He said he had a tray of similar rings in his cabin and invited her to come aboard and choose one for herself. Jacques, without question, readily agreed to Marcella's request and, after giving Grandpa a hug, she set off with the captain and crew in a whaleboat bound for the mothership.

After they boarded, Captain Morgan and Marcella watched the crew stow the copra into the holds.

Once done Morgan called to the first mate, 'Set sail!' to which the first mate replied, 'What about the girl?'

Morgan ignored the comment, took Marcella by the hand and led her to the quarterdeck where he opened the lid of the hatch above his cabin, descended the steep stairs and beckoned her down. Marcella, drawn by the promise of a ring, followed. Morgan pulled a drawer full of glittering trash from a cabinet, set it on a large chart table strewn with charts and said, 'Here, sort through this. I'll be back soon.' He then climbed the stairs without looking back.

Marcella, sensing something wrong, called after him. She asked him to wait for her, but her words were silenced when the lid of the hatch closed with a thud and the latch was locked. Realising the implications, she scrambled up the stairs but, hard as she tried, the lid remained fixed. She pressed her face to the wooden slats in the side of the hatch and cried out for help. Sailors heard, with some in the rigging casting a glance towards the quarterdeck.

The villagers, assembled on the beach to watch the square-rigger sail away, became aware that their princess was in trouble when they saw the whaleboats being winched aboard and men ascending the rigging. Within moments, the conch shells sounded a distress call, summoning everyone to the beach. Their shouts and rallying calls echoed through the palm grove and across the water as men, women and children raced to the foreshore.

Warriors tossed their spears and clubs into the largest of the outrigger canoes, swept them across the sand, launched them and then paddled with fury towards the ship. Younger men and some women and boys took to the smaller crafts, with tomahawks, sticks and stones lying at their feet. These people knew how to wage war. A thousand years of territorial fighting to protect scarce food resources against invasion and pillaging from those of other islands meant that a call from one was a call to everyone.

Marcella peered between the slats, watching Morgan standing only a few feet from her and shouting commands with increasing urgency. Against the blue sky she saw men scrambling to unfurl the sails.

On the deck seasoned sailors took to their allotted tasks. The capstan winch creaked as the heavy anchor was lifted from the water. Those manning the yard lines let the ropes race through the pulley blocks as the sails unfurled. Others lashed loose items to the masts and gunnels, securing the ship for the open seas. The helmsman, tall, bronze and strong, glanced towards the captain, awaiting instructions.

The water churned as the warriors leading the charge dug their paddles deep into the surf, skating the canoes across the water. Their piercing shouts and blood-curdling war cries were heard by all on board. The sea, now a writhing mass of advancing and hostile natives, put fear into the crew. Morgan, asserting his authority over that of the first mate, took full command. The roar of his voice reached every able man, threatening them with retribution if their station failed its duty.

Still the natives came, slicing through the water with speed that would surely close the distance before the *Trade Winds* set sail. More canoes had been launched behind those manned by the young men, the women and the boys. This third flotilla, manned by the old and infirm, when amassed with the others at the ship's side, would amount to one hundred souls prepared to sacrifice their lives as their forefathers had done when their island or its people came under attack.

The sails, now fully open, lay lifeless in the stillness of the morning. Morgan, doubtful of setting sail on an almost becalmed sea, ordered that muskets, shot and gunpowder be brought to the deck. Men hurriedly took the weaponry from the armoury and, by the light of day, tipped gunpowder from powder flasks down the barrels, followed by lead balls, and then tamped the charges with ramrods. Morgan contained himself till the first flotilla came within range and then ordered warning shots to be fired. The sound of the overhead shots crossed the bay, echoing in the palms. Undaunted, the tribe's people continued their advance, paddling even more furiously, trying to reach and board the ship.

The first mate, now in a panic, called to Morgan, 'Shoot to kill! Sir, give the order!'

Morgan, for reasons unknown to the crew, shouted back, 'No killing! Warning shots only!'

The first mate relayed the order to the marksmen. 'Warning shots only!'

When within spear-throwing distance, some warriors stood and hurled spears that pitted the wooden deck as they struck. The second and third flotilla came alongside and, as a naval brigade, they launched an assault. To an age-old war cry they swarmed the ship like an army of black ants with the intention of rescuing Marcella, the chief's daughter, plundering the ship's stores and devouring the flesh of the invaders. Some hurled spears, sticks and stones while others tossed light-weight anchors over the gunnels as grappling hooks. Agile men, shiny black under the tropical sun and bristling with vengeance, took to ropes, pulling themselves upwards.

The first mate, fearing that the ship would be lost, again called to Morgan, 'For Christ's sake, give the order to shoot!'

Morgan wavered in indecision and then ordered the crew to cut the boarding ropes and defend the gunnels with oars. Fifteen to twenty ropes had been secured and the crew, dodging spears and stones, hacked the ropes with machetes, sending climbers to the water. Those that managed to bridge the gunnels were prodded with oars and forced to dive overboard.

The flurry of spears, sticks and stones continued and men tried to scale the gunnels till a slight breeze put a belly into the sails. Only a draught, but enough to bring hope that clear water would soon separate the ship from the canoeists. Crewmen took their chances, exposing themselves to being killed or wounded while pulling the sails as tight as possible to make best use of every breath of breeze.

The ship, now fully rigged to sail, began to move, with the helmsman holding hard to port to steer the ship seaward. The hull of the turning ship pushed against canoes, wrecking outriggers and capsizing some. Although the natives' assault had been foiled they followed, hoping that the vessel would strike a reef and be holed in its rushed attempt to tack through the maze of reefs leading to the open sea. Jacques, too crippled to man a boat, stood on the shore watching till the ship cleared the reefs and disappeared from sight. Bewildered and distraught, he wept inconsolably at the thought of never seeing Marcella again.

Marcella witnessed what she could of the melee through the side slats of the hatch, and when Morgan again appeared on the quarterdeck and approached she slid down the stairs and huddled on the floor in a far corner of the cabin. In silence she watched as the sunlight filtering between the slats became shadowed when Morgan moved close and peered down. Her thoughts were numbed. Never in her wildest dreams could she have envisaged being taken captive and locked in the hull of a sailing ship. When Morgan lowered himself through the hatch, blocking out all the light, and the cabin became dark, a feeling of dread swept over her. Thoughts, previously unimaginable, swept her mind, reducing her to a mire of confusion and fear. When Morgan stepped to the floor and the light returned she watched intently as he moved to a cabinet, took a large bottle of rum and poured a hefty draught into a pewter mug. His nervousness showed as the corner of one eye twitched. He ignored Marcella till the last of the rum was gone and then moved to where she lay. He gazed down at her momentarily without speaking a word before crossing the floor, climbing aloft and securing the hatch.

During the remaining hours till sunset Marcella heard him shouting instructions to the crew from his position on the quarterdeck. As night descended, Morgan returned with two bowls of food that he placed on the chart table before lighting a whale-oil lamp. Marcella cringed in terror when he turned, stepped to her side and indicated that she should take his hand. Being a compliant and defenceless child, she lifted a hand, which he clasped. His firm grip sent shivers through her body. When he lifted her to her feet her anxiety gave way to tremors.

He then spoke for the first time, saying quietly, 'Marcella, you must eat. Here, sit with me at the table.'

By the wavering lamplight she took a seat opposite and, during the time it took Morgan to eat his meal of fish and beans, she remained downcast without lifting a spoon or uttering a word. He tried to make conversation, telling of the islands they would visit in the coming weeks but, try as he did, nothing would prise her lips open. His disappointment became apparent when he ceased talking, clasped his hands together on the table and lowered his head. During his moments of absence, Marcella looked at him and began to wonder.

When Morgan turned his attention her way again, she engaged his eyes and, though still fearful, saw what she thought was a softness in his gaze.

Midst the confusion playing in her mind she asked, 'Where are you taking me?'

Morgan replied, 'One day at a time.'

He rose to his feet, came to her side and, with a gentle touch, took her by a hand and led her to one of the wooden bunks fixed against the wall. Marcella became petrified, fearing that her thoughts only moments before were untrue, that he was about to rape her there on the bunk. She tried to pull away.

'No.' He tightened his grip about her slender wrist. 'Please stay calm.'

She pulled back again, jerking harder, but his seaman's grip held tightly with one hand while he slid open the compartment beneath the bunk and withdrew an iron wrist cuff attached to a length of chain.

Marcella fell to the floor, but he followed her down and pinned her wrists to the deck. Now helpless, she stared up at him in the pale lamplight, utterly confused as he shackled the iron cuff to her wrist. He rose to his knees and, heaving for breath from the struggle, fixed the loose end of the chain to a metal ring attached to the bunk. Marcella, caged and chained, wept and pleaded to be spared. Morgan lifted himself to his feet, took the lamp from the table and put it on an upturned cask by the bunk. He hauled Marcella to her feet and, while still holding her hands, said, 'This is for the safety of us both.'

Before she could comprehend what had been said he scooped her up in his arms and lay her on the mattress of the bunk. Shocked and in disbelief, she lay there listening as he explained that the shackle was only for night time to prevent her from doing anything silly. She became further perplexed when he said, 'Goodnight, my sweet,' before stepping away and pouring himself rum.

The night remained one of torment for Marcella. She watched him sitting at the table drinking, wondering if, when he had consumed his fill, he would come to her bunk. As he became more inebriated he murmured and mumbled to himself. When he finally stumbled to the bunk set against the wall next to hers and fell asleep his snoring shook the panelling of the cabin.

On deck, the men on night watch spoke amongst themselves. They had witnessed Morgan kidnap or hoodwink Islander males and take them back to Australia to be sold but never a young female. While the captain claimed that the payments received were 'commission', the crew knew that the amount received for each sometimes equalled a seaman's yearly wage. To this they added comment about his considerable wealth and the country estate he owned in the hinterland of his home port of Brisbane.

The early morning sun, shining through the fixed-pane windows at the stern of the ship, woke Marcella, delivering her from the nightmares that had plagued her during her few hours of sleep. She heard the sweep of the ocean against the hull, the captain's breathing that had steadied, and, when she sat up, the rattle of the chain. Soon, sunlight shafted through the overhead vents of the hatch, followed by a call, 'Breakfast served.' The captain, hearing the call, woke, propped himself up on one elbow and called for the meal to be brought down. The galley cook, with a tattoo of a mermaid on his bare chest and an earring, came inside, placed the food on the table and, as he left, glanced at Marcella and the shackle. Morgan, foggy from his binge, washed his face in a basin, removed the wrist iron and said, 'Marcella, it's breakfast time.'

Still shocked by the events of the last day, she took a seat opposite him at the table where two plates of smelly pickled herrings and corn bread lay amongst the charts that Morgan had been studying the previous night. She picked at the food while Morgan ate and cleaned his plate with a crust of bread.

When finished, Morgan offered an explanation. 'We'll be at sea for weeks, so make yourself comfortable.'

He left the table, placed his three-cornered hat on his head, went aloft and locked the hatch behind him.

For three days and nights Marcella remained confined to the cabin, lonely, heart broken and fearful of what might come next. Morgan remained civil and, on the fourth morning, seemed cheery when he took her to the deck above, explained that it was the quarterdeck reserved for himself and the first mate, and that under no circumstances was she to venture to the main deck or speak with anybody except himself or the first mate. At night time she remained chained to the bunk while Morgan drank heavily.

For the next few weeks, Marcella spent her days on the deck, brooding, longing for home and hoping that by some miracle she would be returned to Lifou and her people. The galley cook continued bringing the meals and, of late, had been making comments, some of which were suggestive. Marcella, not familiar with the ways of men, listened and, one day, he coaxed her into the cabin with talk of a special meal. No sooner had they descended the stairs and he had placed the plates on the table than the first mate appeared at the open hatch and called the cook aloft. From the heated exchange, Marcella surmised that the cook was being threatened with a lashing.

Morgan made calls at several of the New Caledonia and New Hebrides islands to trade copra and now sailed north towards the Solomon Islands. When natives were invited aboard at these stops Marcella was confined to the cabin with the hatch secured. With her view through the slats of the hatch being limited, she kept watch through the glass panes at the rear of the cabin, taking note of the natives who canoed behind the ship. She noted their dress and customs, and from tales and folklore told by elders she pieced together that they were following a chain of closely linked islands. At times they anchored for three or four days and, while thoughts of diving overboard and escaping came to mind, they were soon dismissed when she recalled stories of headhunters cutting off the heads of strangers.

Marcella's young and submissive mind came to accept Morgan's company in the cabin and being chained to the bunk at night. Mornings continued much the same, with Morgan releasing the wrist iron, sitting with her during breakfast, going aloft and leaving her to tidy the cabin and attend to her personal care. The cabin, though small, had become her refuge, a place where, strange as it may seem, she felt secure from the outside world. Even the wrist iron provided comfort, a sense of attachment to the surrounds. She became increasingly reliant on Morgan. Later in the mornings she would make her way to the quarterdeck where the breeze played in her hair, bringing reminders of her village and thoughts of family. Painful as these recollections were, they gradually eased and, with time, became less worrisome. She often found lunchtime disconcerting when the grubby cook brought food to the cabin and, if the captain was absent, made remarks that only a whore would appreciate. After lunch, when the deck burned hot from the sun, Marcella would stay below. Here, she either rested on her bunk or watched through the fixed pane windows, following movement of the seagulls as they dived for small fish that came to the surface in the wake breaking from the ship's stern. When evening drew close she would return to the deck to enjoy the closure of the day with its brilliant sunsets and cool breezes.

She began to look forward to the evening meal when she would again sit with Morgan as company, her only company. Though she had often seen and heard him shout abuse at the crew during the day, he never brought his troubles to the dinner table. They shared freely, passing morsels of food to one another, engaging in conversation and exchanging the occasional smile. After meal time, when Morgan studied his maps and charts, Marcella went aloft to study the stars. Though she could not read paper maps, she, like all the other Islanders, could read the constellations with accuracy equal to anything on paper. She knew their position in relation to Lifou and, with intuitive orientation, could navigate back to her island. With nightly sightings she had plotted the ship's course in her mind and knew that, since leaving Lifou, the captain had steered a course to the north. In the early weeks, soon after leaving Lifou, she had yearned for an immediate return but now, having become accustomed to life at sea and feeling a sense of adventure, much of that longing had been dispelled. At bedtime, Marcella would lie on her bunk with her sarong as a cover, waiting for Morgan. Sometimes she waited for an hour before he came across and put the clasp about her wrist. He had taken to giving the back of her hand a pat before turning away and, unknown to him, Marcella enjoyed the warmth of his touch. Later in the evening, Morgan would pour a rum, take a small ukulele from the compartment beneath his bunk and sit at the table to play and sing. His voice, soft and estranged from that which abused crew members on deck, filled the cabin as she watched him from her bunk. He would pick for a while, striking a chord, and then strum and sing island songs with melodies that Marcella could relate to. His drinking had eased in recent times and, instead of getting inebriated and mumbling to himself as he had done in the past, he satisfied himself with a few rums, a few songs and then retired to his bunk.

Marcella had been on the deck earlier in the morning and now lay in her bunk, dressed in a sarong and having a nap before lunch. She snapped from her doze when she felt a hand touch one of her breasts.

To her horror, there before her stood the cook, leering down at her.

'Not a word,' he said as he reached with the other hand and undid the knot holding her sarong snugly across her breasts.

Marcella froze with fright when he pulled the garment aside, bent over, and suckled her breasts.

Her thoughts became chaotic when he stripped the remaining folds of the sarong away, leaving her naked, and then slid a hand to her crotch.

She pleaded for him to stop, to go away, and when he persisted she shrieked a piercing scream that was heard on the deck.

Crewmen stood aside as the captain raced from the forecastle of the ship, back to the cabin, and disappeared down the open hatch.

The cook, hearing the commotion erupting aloft, tried to cover Marcella with the sarong but was too late. Morgan had seen and leapt over the stair rail when halfway down.

In his rage he charged the cook while shouting abuse.

The cook, lean and with age on his side, stood his ground.

Punches flew both ways, each hammering the other with blows that would down many a hardy seaman.

Marcella, now wholly panic stricken, huddled in the corner of her bunk.

The first mate, who had been high up in the rigging, saw Morgan's mad dash and now joined the fray.

They pounded the cook into submission. When he lay struggling on the floor Morgan became manic, kicking into him with his bare feet.

Those on deck knew better than to interfere and crowded the main deck, listening to the shouts.

None of them were surprise when Morgan and the first mate dragged the cook from the hatch and to the deck where they were gathered. The brutally beaten man, hardly conscious, fell to his knees when the men released their grip. Morgan, in a fit of rage, drew his revolver from his belt and took aim.

Marcella stayed below, and when she heard three shots in quick succession, she sat with the sarong pulled about her shoulders and sobbed.

Within an hour Morgan appeared at the hatch again. When partway down the stairs he paused in the eerie stillness. A shaft of light streaming through the hatch lit his dishevelled profile. Without his three-cornered hat perched on his head he looked much older than his age of two score years and ten. His hair, spilling recklessly about his shoulders, told of his maddened state. Sparks of glimmering light lit the frayed ends of his thick beard. His eyes, sharp as those of a roving petrel, cast about as he took a few more steps, bringing him closer to the cabin floor and to Marcella. The kerchief about his neck, tightly knotted and damp with sweat, hung from his neck like a dead man's noose. Bloodstains, not there before going aloft, streaked his trousers. As he stepped to the floor and came closer Marcella saw the twitching of one eye and a tremble that shaped the corners of his mouth. Her mind raced: *Does he think I encouraged the cook? Will he seek revenge?*

Still sitting on the bunk, Marcella gathered the sarong tightly about her body as a show of virtue. Her long, wavy hair that she had inherited from her father framed the anxious look on her face. With frightened eyes she watched as Morgan came within a few paces. When no more than a pace away she hung her head in shame, hoping she would be forgiven for any perceived misconduct and be spared the fate dealt to the ship's cook. She was prepared to sacrifice everything of herself to Morgan if it meant a stay of execution.

Morgan now stood within hands' reach, with his bloodied trousers looming large before her eyes.

Marcella, quivering with fear, let go of the sarong bunched about her breasts, letting it fall to her lap and leaving her naked to the waist.

Morgan for the first time saw the fullness of her beauty and reached out, placing his hands on her shoulders.

Marcella closed her mind to his touch, ready to accept what she thought would be the inevitable.

Morgan, after feeling the warmth of her shoulders for a few moments, moved his broad hands to the back of her head and drew her face closer.

Marcella, having committed herself to what she thought were his wishes, pressed a cheek to his shirt and put her arms about his waist.

Morgan neither gazed on her nor felt for her breasts. Instead, he continued looking ahead while running his fingers softly through her hair.

Marcella accepted the attention and, when Morgan cupped a hand under her chin, lifted her head and said, 'You're safe,' she slowly rose to her feet while holding the sarong about her waist, searching his eyes for the truth. 'Yes, he's gone,' he answered.

Marcella, believing this, and now seeing Morgan as a saviour, let go of the sarong, wrapped her arms about his body and lay against his chest.

Morgan held her close in his arms. He let go first, and when Marcella lifted her head he kissed her on the forehead before stepping back. A voice from the crow's nest on the main mast had called 'Land ho!'

By evening the *Trade Winds* had anchored at their first port of call in the Solomon Islands. Morgan, having washed and changed his clothes on deck and being satisfied that preparations were in place for the night watch, helped himself to food from the galley and proceeded to his cabin where he laid the plates and his loaded revolver on the table. He then called, 'Supper is served.'

Marcella, feeling safe for the first time since the attack, left her bunk and joined him at the table by the lamplight. She ate little, sat quietly and again wondered about Morgan as she watched him shovel food into his mouth. This Englishman from over the sea, with his unpredictable ways, had fascinated her since she first came aboard. After he had taken her into his arms earlier that afternoon and kissed her on the forehead, she had thought about what the future might hold.

Morgan set aside his usual routine of studying his charts and, instead, took a cask of rum and a tin pannikin from the compartment beneath his bunk, poured a big slug and swallowed it in a few gulps. Then another and another and another until he began to sway on his chair.

Marcella retired to her bunk and lay awake till late, listening to the ship creaking on the ocean swell and seeing shadows from the lamp moving about the cabin. Her last recollection before falling asleep was Morgan muttering something about 'Next time, next trip, more boys for the plantations …'

She woke in the wee hours of the morning to find the lamp doused. In her drowsy state she imagined that she had been unshackled but soon realised she had slept through the night unchained. The only light, a filtering of moonlight through the stern windows, showed Morgan unconscious and slumped over the table with the revolver by his hand and snoring with a rasping breath. To appreciate the fullness of being free, Marcella crept across the cabin, climbed the stairs and stepped to the quarterdeck. The yardarms of the masts, with their sails furled while anchored in the bay, rocked back and forth before the ghostly moon. On the deck below, the three men of the night watch stood almost motionless by the light from a single lamp. The dark silhouette of the nearby island with its native inhabitants lay in slumber. Marcella looked further out, across the expanse of the ocean from whence she had come. Thoughts of home came to mind; recollections of earlier times and all that had happened during the past six weeks at sea. With mixed feelings she tried to sort the emotions that dragged her back to the past and those that encouraged her to embrace an unknown future.

When the first glow of sunrise appeared on the horizon, she slipped back to the cabin and into bed so as not to be missed. Morgan, who had remained asleep, woke when the first mate called and delivered breakfast. He pushed his plate of food aside and sat morose and insular while Marcella ate. When finished, Marcella, almost with a sense of guilt, held up her arm to show that she had remained unshackled throughout the night. Morgan heaved a big sigh and then, with a note of resignation, said, 'Marcella, there will be no more chains. No more.'

Marcella, breaking into a youthful smile, replied, 'Thank you, Sir.'

Later in the morning she went aloft, and when she returned the chain and shackle had been removed, never to be seen again.

While navigating by the stars at night when the *Trade Winds* departed from the islands, Marcella noted a significant change in the ship's line of travel. What had been a north-westerly course switched to southerly. This confounded Marcella because there was nothing in her folklore to indicate land in that direction. *Where are we headed? Will we sail off the end of the earth?*

After three days of sailing the open ocean and with no islands having been seen, she overheard a conversation on the main deck. Reference was made to 'Australia'. Casting back she remembered English visitors to her island saying that they were from Australia, the Great South Land. *How far? How long? What to expect?* These thoughts occupied her mind till, twelve days later, the ship dropped anchor off Moreton Island, the gateway to Brisbane, the capital of the young colony of Queensland.

CHAPTER 2

Marcella's anticipation deepened as she stood on the deck, watching the crew prepare for landing and seeing ships coming and going.

Morgan had been jolly all morning and now spoke to Marcella on the quarterdeck. 'Marcella, we'll be going ashore soon, to your new home. You need to go below deck and prepare.'

She followed Morgan down the ladder and watched curiously as he took a pair of scissors from a drawer. She was astonished when he handed her the scissors and said, 'I want you to cut your hair off, short as possible.'

'My hair?'

'Yes.'

'Why?'

'Never mind. Just do as I say.'

Marcella, now confused, remained silent as Morgan threatened, 'I'll be back soon, and if it's not gone then I will chop it off myself.'

When Morgan left she turned to the mirror on the wall and gazed at her reflection. She drew the long, soft tail of the hair forward across her shoulder, letting it spill down to her waist. *How can I cut my hair? It is me, and with its light colour and fine texture sets me apart from other island women. It identifies me with my lost father, the man who, one day, will come and find me.* With that thought she took a handful of hair and snipped. With a lingering sadness and misty eyes she tucked the precious strands into a small calico bag. In between whimpers and more thoughts of her father she proceeded hacking till all the hair had been cropped. In dismay she stood before the mirror, thinking she looked more like a boy than a girl.

When Morgan returned to the cabin he made only a passing comment about the treatment of her hair. He seemed unmoved by Marcella's changed appearance or how she might feel. That evening Marcella stayed reclusive, talking little and retiring to her bunk early. Morgan sat at his table till late, pouring over papers and drinking heavily.

Early the next morning the first mate gave the order to weigh anchor and set sail for the river mouth. The muddy approach to the river, with its fringe of mangroves, gave way to a sparkling river course that opened into open forest where first settlers had cleared patches of land and built slab huts. River traffic increased as the square-rigger made its way upstream towards Brisbane, the only major port on the Australian east coast north of Sydney. After sailing a few miles, Brisbane town appeared.

On the north bank lay the commercial centre of the town. People dodged horses and carriages as they made their way along dusty streets between business houses built of timber, stone and brick. The very rich, those with endowments of money from the mother country or entrepreneurs who had made good, lived in two and three-storey mansions that towered above the billets of the less fortunate. The women's factory, a large stone building where female convicts of earlier times were imprisoned and forced to work under slave-like conditions, captured the eye of every new arrival.

On the south bank vessels of all sizes lay at anchor or moored to jetties. A scattering of workshops and residences fringed this bank, and beyond, across the cleared landscape, men and women worked in the fields of their small holdings. Free settlers and pardoned convicts worked shoulder to shoulder, eking a living from the fertile soil of this new-found land.

With the population of Brisbane and nearby settlements now approaching 25,000, and the government offering more incentives to investors, the future for Brisbane and the colony of Queensland looked promising.

The *Trade Winds* docked at Queens Wharf where bales of wool, hauled along rough bush tracks from pastoral properties beyond the Great Dividing Range, were being unloaded from horse-drawn drays and rolled into cargo nets. Further along, dozens of barrels of tallow, fresh from the boiling-down works, stood in rows, awaiting shipment to England.

Marcella witnessed what she could of this through the side slats of the hatch. Morgan had taken her below to his cabin when they entered the river and told her that she must not come aloft.

He now stood before her in the cabin, stuffing her personal items into a duffel bag while explaining, 'Later today men from the government will come on board to check the cargo, and if they find you they will take you away in chains. So, for your own sake I want you to keep watch through the slats of the hatch and when they come aboard hide in the empty compartment beneath your bunk.'

He then left without any further explanation and later met three customs officers when they stepped from the gangway to the deck. The officer in charge read the ship's manifest and then said, 'I see you have copra on board.'

'Yes, fresh from a trip to the islands. All went well with a two-and-a-half month turnaround.'

'Anything else to declare?'

'No.'

The officer asked further, 'And the crew, all safe and well?'

'Mostly. We lost a man at the Solomons. He slipped his footing and fell to the deck. A hell of a mess and he died instantly.' He added, 'We gave him a decent burial and I will make enquiries about next of kin.'

'What's his name?'

'Clive Robinson. Not sure if I can trace his family. Seemed to be a wanderer with no near family.'

'Hmm,' murmured the officer before turning to his assistant and saying, 'Make a note of that.'

They walked around the deck, checking the rigging for safety, and the officer in charge, knowing of Morgan's interest in procuring slaves, enquiring deeper into the ship's movements. When done he gave instructions to his assistants. 'Verify the cargo and then check the crew's sleeping quarters for illegal imports. The captain and I have more to discuss.'

The customs official then addressed Morgan, 'You seem to have covered the islands extensively. I'd like to see your charts.'

Morgan responded, 'They won't show much. I don't mark them, just chart the course as I go.'

'I appreciate that but, all the same, let's look at them so I can get a clearer idea of the route taken.'

Morgan, with a hint of reservation in his voice, said, 'No problem. The charts are in my cabin.'

Morgan lifted the hatch cautiously, checked that Marcella was not in sight, and then invited the inspector inside.

The inspector entered, looked about briefly and then asked to see the charts. As Morgan explained the route taken and the stops made the officer became suspicious. The chairs at the table, one across from the other, drew his interest. Where Morgan sat was obvious, with the charts arranged for him to see, but who occupied the other side? With a practised eye he cast about thinking: *The cabin is too tidy for a man like Morgan. He must have someone else keeping house.*

Morgan, in an effort to divert attention, said, 'I must get back on deck and check on the men.'

The seasoned inspector, following his suspicion, ignored Morgan's request and, instead, began a thorough search.

Morgan placed a hand on the revolver tucked under his belt and thumbed the hammer. If Marcella was discovered and he was convicted of kidnapping the consequences would be dire. In the event of her being found, Morgan would first try to buy himself out of the situation and, if that failed, he would attempt an escape.

While rummaging through a pile of rolled charts, the officer came across a lady's pendant. 'Hmm, where did this come from?'

Morgan, recognising the pendant as one he had given to Marcella, sought to cover himself. 'Oh, it's a trinket. I have boxes of them that I hand out to the natives. It is a good introduction, especially when making contact for the first time.'

Morgan's words hardly registered with the government agent as he held it close for forensic clues. 'It's tarnished on the back. Hardly what I would call new.' He then looked at Morgan directly and asked, 'Do you want to declare this item?'

Morgan, with a quick tongue, replied, 'No, as I said, it's one of many. Old stock that's not worth handing to them. Will probably give it to the street kids that beg at the wharf.'

The officer slipped the pendant into his pocket and then glimpsed something of interest on the floor—long strands of hair showing clearly in the sunlight spilling through the rear windowpanes. He knelt, picked up the strands and examined them closely. 'Where did this come from?' He held the hair for Morgan to see.

Morgan, holding his composure, replied, 'It's from the islands. It's one of the small pleasures available to sailors on long trips.'

'Which island?'

'Not sure now. I nailed a couple. I'd say it was a young one from the New Hebrides.'

The officer, disbelieving Morgan and becoming agitated, threatened him with, 'I'll tear this place apart if need be. What's in the compartments under the bunks?'

'Only clothes.'

'Then you won't mind if I have a look?'

'Go ahead. I have nothing to hide.'

The officer, having noticed Morgan toying with the grip of his revolver, stepped back and said, 'Better you open it.'

Morgan sheepishly opened the compartment under his bunk to reveal the innocuous-looking duffel bag. The officer then pointed to Marcella's bunk and Morgan, realising that this would be the end, went to draw his revolver but was stymied when the officer drew a handgun from his pocket, pointed it at Morgan and said, 'If you please, just do as you are told.' Morgan, with no option but to comply, bent over and slowly opened the lid. To his profound astonishment he found the compartment empty!

The inspector, still not satisfied, ordered a full search of the ship. Others from customs were called in and the crew interrogated but, as the officers knew, sailors were sworn to the seaman's code of silence and would deny any knowledge. They ransacked every hold, upending sacks of copra and searching for hidden compartments, but found no trace of a stowaway. With reluctance a halt was called to the search and the customs officials left empty handed.

Morgan, confounded as to how Marcella had managed to escape both him and the customs officers, swallowed half a pannikin of rum, climbed from his cabin to the quarterdeck and scanned the busy wharf for Marcella. Dozens of people milled about on the wharf, making it difficult to distinguish one person from another. The only person he recognised was Rusty Leghorn, a retired sailor and busybody who sat hunched on an upturned cask with a pipe in his hand.

Morgan's mind searched for an answer. *If Marcella has gone ashore, where is she? Has she already been taken into police custody and questioned? Should I disband the ship before I am arrested for kidnapping?* He spoke to the first mate, and between them they conducted a fresh search, probing every crevice of the ship. After an hour the first mate reported to Morgan, 'Nothing. Not a sign. She's vanished. Must have jumped overboard?'

Morgan returned to the quarterdeck where he tried to fathom how Marcella could have escaped unnoticed. He remained there, deep in thought, until, suddenly, he caught sight of movement under a canvas hatch cover shoved against the gunnel. He cautiously stepped towards the canvas, knelt and lifted a corner to discover a frightened little girl. Her eyes, terror stricken, blinked in the bright light as he pulled the cover aside to reveal her trembling in her sweat-soaked sarong. He gazed at her momentarily, marvelling how nobody had thought to look under a piece of crumpled canvas lying on the exposed deck, and then put a hand on her shoulder and said quietly, 'I've been looking for you.'

He scanned the wharf again and, thinking all was clear, lifted Marcella to her feet and helped her to the cabin. When asked why she had hidden there she replied, 'I too frightened to go under the bed so I peeped out and when nobody was looking I opened the hatch and crawled under the canvas.'

Morgan wrote a note to be delivered to the manager of his country estate. The note simply requested that the estate manager come at ten o'clock the next day and be prepared for two passengers.

At nine o'clock the following morning, Morgan approached Marcella as she stood by the stern windows dressed in her sarong. He handed her a sailor's shirt and trousers and said, 'We're leaving the ship soon. I want you to change into these.'

'Why?' asked Marcella, taken aback.

'No questions. Just do as I say,' he replied unapologetically.

Marcella reluctantly took the clothing and, when Morgan returned to the deck, she slipped from her sarong and gingerly pulled on the sloppy sailor's clothing. Nothing fitted, and with her hair cropped she felt embarrassed and ashamed about going ashore where she would be seen by others. She sat sad and forlorn, waiting for Morgan to return.

Morgan spoke to the first mate, confirming the arrangements about shipping the copra to Sydney, and then returned to his cabin. After checking that Marcella was suitably dressed and having pulled a rag hat tightly across her forehead, he led her to the deck and across the gangway to be greeted by the estate manager.

The manager, a Caucasian named Seamus in his mid-thirties, shook Morgan's hand and acknowledged Marcella with a nod and a 'Hello'. Though the manager must surely have wondered about the presence of Marcella he knew better than to ask.

'This way,' he said, pointing to where the wharf accessed Queen Street, the main thoroughfare leading from the dock.

Morgan shepherded Marcella, keeping her between himself and Seamus, while watching for customs officials and police. Some who knew Morgan nodded; others looked elsewhere or looked at him with disdain. Morgan had led a chequered career and made some enemies on the waterfront.

A sudden call of 'Cap'n!' came from near the Mariners Inn, a place Morgan frequented while ashore. Of the many voices it could be, Morgan recognised it clearly. Not wanting to engage, he moved forward, only to recoil when he heard, 'I see you have contraband.'

Morgan propped, signalled to Seamus with a clenched fist, and then turned to confront old Rusty the busybody. Seamus, being Morgan's minder, also turned, bringing Marcella around with him.

The little old man, with sun-bleached hair, a beard and moustache tinged with ginger, and a hunch back, met Morgan's glare with a piercing look. They had clashed in the past and, although Rusty appeared infirm, the tone of his voice told that he was still a match for his former captain.

Morgan stepped close and, almost in a whisper, asked, 'What do you want?'

Rusty, a man known for reserving his words, nodded towards Marcella and held out an open palm.

'No you don't,' warned Morgan. 'She's legal. I've got the papers to prove it.'

Rusty, with his hand still outstretched, replied, 'The cops can sort that.'

Some passers-by took notice, while those who knew of the animosity between the pair took interest.

Seamus, intent on a quick resolution, came to Morgan's side but was stayed by Morgan's hand.

Rusty, a shrivelled weasel of a man, held his ground unnervingly till Morgan drew a chamois pouch from his pocket and placed a gold sovereign in his hand. As Morgan drew the drawstrings of the pouch, Rusty indicated for more with a flick of his fingertips. With the attention from onlookers growing and the likelihood of Marcella being recognised as a kidnap victim increasing, Morgan begrudgingly placed another sovereign into Rusty's hand. Rusty, not wanting to press his luck too far, accepted the coins, left Morgan belittled and entered the Mariners Inn where most of his life's earnings had been spent on alcohol, tobacco and bad women. Those who knew the pair well recalled how Morgan had sent Rusty and others aloft during a raging storm to furl the sails and how, when descending a ratline, Rusty lost his footing, fell and landed on his back, leaving him a cripple and unable to work again. Since that day, Morgan had disowned Rusty and, as revenge, Rusty had followed his movements and blackmailed him whenever an opportunity presented itself.

The harnessed mare fidgeted as Seamus unhitched her from the rail, and then kicked out as Morgan put a foot on the step to mount the sulky.

'Where's Bessie?' asked Morgan, pulling himself up by the rail.

'She's home spelling. I got this young one at an auction. Still green, but with some training should be fine.'

Marcella, having never before seen a horse, stood back till Morgan reached out. 'Here, take my hand.'

Marcella came forward timidly, glanced warily at the animal, and then mounted. At the direction of Morgan, she squeezed between him and Seamus on the leather seat.

'The street's busy today,' commented Morgan as they left the wharf and began to drive up the incline of Queen Street.

'Yes, it's getting busier by the month. It's the gold strike at Gympie that's bringing them. Business is flourishing with the arrival of newcomers.'

'How's Nellie, Thruppence and the farm going …' continued Morgan, turning his mind from the sea to his bushland estate located westward of the town.

'Good. Since you were last home we have sold twenty goats, harvested the crop of corn and supplied fifty bushels of wheat to the Brisbane market.'

Marcella paid little attention to the conversation. Her thoughts were occupied by the streetscape unfolding before her eyes. The transition from the grass huts of Lifou to the stout buildings lining the dusty street held her in awe. This new world, this never-before-imagined way of life, spilt all about her like a fantasy land, difficult to comprehend. Nowhere in her folklore had an existence of this kind been described. Stories told by sailors visiting in their tall ships had been many, and while she had conjured thoughts of faraway places she could never have conceived the likes of what she saw unravelling before her eyes. The fair skin of the sailors had always fascinated her and now, seeing hundreds of them mingling, she wondered how many more there were and where they lived. Her mind scrambled to cope with all she saw unfolding before her: Impressive two-storey structures with shingle roofs, dominating the smaller building set in between. Awnings, stretching from the front of the more progressive business houses, providing shade for those walking the earthen pavements. The street traffic, all horse drawn, cluttering the roadway, providing needed services to this, the main street of Brisbane.

As they moved further along Marcella observed many shops, including a drapery, chemist, shoemaker, hardware, bookshop, crockery shop, grocery store, the Imperial Hotel and Mrs McCoy's boarding house. She dwelt on the gold lettering of a window that announced William Stirling, Barrister at Law, but, unable to read and never having seen such things before, Marcella remained mystified.

When they were midway along the street a wagon, pulled by six horses, approached, loaded high with barrels of drinking water to be delivered to the shops. Seamus' mare, unaccustomed to street life, baulked at the barrels stacked four high, and when one fell from the load and began rolling down the street towards her she shied and leapt to one side. Seamus, taken by surprise, grappled to draw rein as the mare mounted the pavement. Pedestrians, equally startled, jumped aside as the mare, with a sulky wheel firmly wedged in the deep, stone-pitched gutter, struggled to be free. The jolt dislodged those in the sulky, with Morgan and Marcella tumbling to the pavement and Seamus jumping clear to take control of the floundering mare. Marcella sprang to her feet to find bystanders crowding about. They all seemed to be staring at her, causing her to panic. She wanted to run, to escape, but to where? She knew no one, no place to hide. She stood stock still like a frightened animal. The fear that Morgan had put into her mind—that she would be taken away in chains—consumed her thoughts.

Morgan, aware of the implications if Marcella was exposed, lifted himself from the earthen pavement, stepped quickly to her side and grabbed her by a wrist. This show of overt restraint drew an immediate response from an onlooker who shouted, 'Let her go!' Further back, a gentleman dressed in a frockcoat and top hat whispered to his wife, 'She'll be a slave girl.' At hearing this, the wife wanted to intervene but took heed when her husband cautioned her. 'It's a matter for commoners.' While talk of South Sea Islanders being kidnapped and held as slaves was commonplace within closed circles, the consequences of an abduction being witnessed in broad daylight on the main street of Brisbane could be explosive.

Morgan, mindful of this and the scrutiny from the bystanders, set to defuse the situation. He let go of Marcella's wrist, took her by the hand and said loudly, 'Darling, it's all right. We'll be out of here as soon as Seamus frees the horse.'

The sound of Morgan's voice, the one she had become accustomed to, struck a chord. She turned his way and offered an awkward smile. Morgan seized upon the gesture, calling to Seamus, 'All's well here. How's the mare?'

'Fine. Once I get the wheel clear we'll be on our way.'

With the help of a couple of brawny men, Seamus soon untangled the mare and sulky and made ready to leave.

With Marcella still trembling from the ordeal, Morgan helped her to the sulky seat, climbed aboard himself and signalled to Seamus to proceed.

No sooner had they departed than those gathered there dispersed, but not without thoughts of kidnapping foremost in their minds.

CHAPTER 3

The mare settled into a steady gait after leaving the busy town and entering the bushland. The clopping of her feet on the earth, the clinking of the leather harness against her hide, the smell of freshly dressed leather and the sunlight glinting from the brass harness fittings sharpened Marcella's senses, bringing the sights and sounds foremost to her mind.

While the men chatted, she leant forward, eager to see beyond the next bend. Each turn, each new twist in the road, brought to life more of this rich new land. The carriageway, no more than a track that had been carved by convicts in chains, weaved its way between stands of tall gum trees, crowned with leaves shimmering silver in the summer sun.

A teamster, tired and haggard, bearing the toll of a 190-mile round trip to the inland to transport bailed wool, paid them little attention as they passed by.

A wild dingo, drawn by the sound and then smell of man and beast, watched keen eyed from a nearby thicket, unaware that Marcella, with her piercing brown eyes, had him firmly in her sight.

At Crystalbrook, also known as the six mile, Seamus halted the young mare midstream and held the reins loosely while she drank. Here, Harry Fritz, a displaced farrier who operated from a calico tent, made ends meet by shoeing travellers' horses in return for rations and rum.

The mare, refreshed from the spell and knowing that a few more miles would see her home, lengthened her stride. They whisked along and passed a lagoon, where the sight of a shepherd tending a flock of sheep captivated Marcella's imagination.

This strange land, this rugged but glorious landscape, reached out to her, warming her heart and relieving her anxiety.

Morgan had switched his persona from seaman to one of the landed gentry by swapping his captain's three-cornered hat for a bowler hat and dressing in Wellington boots, gabardine trousers, linen shirt and a blue cravat. Contrived as this was, his awkwardness when riding in a sulky revealed his pretence to passers-by. For, in reality, he was a seaman-cum-businessman, suited eminently better to urban life than as a man of the land. Many people surmised that his country lifestyle was a front, a ploy to distract attention from his main business of procuring South Sea Islanders to work as cheap labour for the colonists. Few had been invited to the property, encouraging speculation that it could be a place where things or people were hidden from sight.

At a road junction known as the ten mile, Seamus reined the mare to the right, heading towards hilly, upland country. The track narrowed, with bird and animal life becoming more abundant in the virgin woodlands. Settler's 'runs', with boundaries marked by blaze marks on trees and slab huts with bark roofs a measure of their success, became fewer the further they went. Marcella had no idea that these open spaces, where large tracts of virgin bush could be leased for a few pounds a year, was a place where hardships thrust members of the aristocracy and the yeomanry together as equals. However, disputes did erupt, mainly over boundaries and livestock, and while most were settled without violence, some were resolved by gunshot or traces of strychnine.

Although the leather seat of the sulky was well padded, the ride, travelling over rutted roads, deep gullies and around cross-country detours, made Morgan's backside pucker. Marcella felt more jolts than ever before. They were thankful when Seamus pointed to a blaze mark on the trunk of a towering ghost gum that marked the entrance to Morgan's property, a hideaway he named Sorrento after a lost love. As the mare swung into the carriageway leading to the homestead, a big buck kangaroo and his harem of grey females stood high on their haunches. After a moment of recognition, they hopped to one side, allowing them to pass.

Morgan stretched to relieve his cramped body and then patted Marcella on a knee. 'You'll be pleased to sleep in a comfortable bed after weeks at sea.'

Seamus caught a glimpse of her coy smile and drew a conclusion, rightly or wrongly, as to what might have happened while they were on board ship.

The mare, anxious to be home, unbridled and fed, lifted her head and whinnied to her mates.

'The mare shows promise,' said Morgan, reconsidering his earlier thoughts when she nearly upended the sulky in Queen Street. 'Which reminds me, I will be going to town a few times this stay, so make sure the grey horse is shod.'

'I've already done that. Expected you home about now so put on a new set of shoes earlier in the week.'

'Good man.' Morgan could rely on Seamus for everything from overseeing the farm to being his minder when needed.

A yodel from a nearby brook drew their attention to Thruppence who managed the goat herd at Sorrento. Without Thruppence there would be no herd. With no boundary fence on the 640-acre selection, the goats would run wild across the hills, never to be seen again. Thruppence, a twenty-year-old scrawny simpleton, named after a three-penny coin, together with Jock, a smart sheepdog, shepherded the goats. Thruppence, orphaned since birth, had come to Sorrento five years earlier when Seamus found him wandering a lonely track, brought him home to the stables and bunked him down on a cowhide stretcher with a sheepskin cover. After a few months of restless behaviour and a few psychotic episodes, he accepted Seamus as the boss, took an interest in the half dozen house goats and had since expanded the numbers into a commercial herd.

At seeing the buildings, Marcella sat upright, crowding the men for space on the sulky seat. Seamus shot her a glance, the first since leaving Brisbane, and felt the warm glow of her soft South Sea expression.

'You'll like it here,' he said by way of a welcome.

Morgan let the comment pass and introduced Marcella to the property by pointing out the homestead with its white-picket fence, the smokehouse for curing meat, the blacksmith shop, stables and work sheds built with pit-sawn timber. Also the goat yards, where the goats were penned at night to protect against attacks by dingoes and hungry travellers who were none too shy of stealing a goat.

'Whoo,' called Seamus, bringing the mare to a half-halt and then a stop beside the water trough. He jumped from the seat and held the mare while the others dismounted. Morgan, with his big belly, struggled to find the step before easing himself down. He held out his hands to assist Marcella, cupping them under her arms. She accepted his help readily, falling into the grasp of his big hands and trusting he would not let her fall.

While Morgan and Seamus unhitched the sulky, Marcella wandered about, trying to comprehend all the trappings that she thought made for a complicated life. She touched the saddles and harness, stepped into the worker's kitchen where Seamus and Thruppence ate, peeped into their living quarters, furnished with timber bunks and pegs in posts to hold clothing. Across the way, near the goat pens, she puzzled at the milking bail and butter churn. Further around she came across a large store of shelled corn and trickled the dry kernels through her fingers as though they were nuggets of gold. Upon hearing Morgan call her name she hurried from the shed and accompanied him to the house with its weatherboard walls, shingle roof and brick chimney.

Unknown to Marcella she had been watched from the kitchen window of the house and now, with she and Morgan walking towards the picket gate, light fingers slowly drew the curtain to obscure the view.

Nellie, Morgan's housekeeper of seven years, knew of his dealings in human cargo, but to bring home a female native? *Trouble a plenty*, she thought, stroking creases from her ballooning skirt that reached to her slippers. On hearing the latch of the garden gate, she drew breath and opened the back door to greet Morgan and his new 'procurement', a term she had often heard him use when referring to his South Sea Islander trade.

Yes, it's a woman, but what of the disguise? Surely Oliver hadn't the audacity to smuggle her ashore and take her through the streets of Brisbane and not expect to be noticed?

Oliver's boisterous voice interrupted her thoughts. 'Hello, Nellie, we're home,' and, without offering an explanation, he added, 'Marcella is going to stay with us.'

Nellie had been taken by surprise, and to buy time she fiddled, adjusting the flour-bag bonnet covering her head and drawing the collar of her old crinoline dress high about her neck. She then stepped forward to meet the guest, 'Pleased to meet you Miss—'

Oliver cut in, 'Marcella. She goes by the name of Marcella.'

'Oh, and where are you from Marcella?' asked Nellie, trying to be civil to someone she took to be a savage from the islands.

'Lifou, I come from Lifou,' replied Marcella in a timid voice.

'Lifou?' asked Nellie, stern faced and pressing her point.

'Yes. It's in New Caledonia,' said Marcella, more clearly and with a hint of pride.

'Well, we'll see,' asserted Nellie with a note of indignation.

Oliver, as usual, paid little heed to Nellie's complaints and, instead, asked if she had a meal prepared.

Nellie had received the messenger's note telling of Oliver's arrival and, in anticipation, Seamus and Thruppence had killed and dressed a goat that would keep them in fresh meat for three days. Fortunately, Nellie had roasted a leg, and together with freshly dug potatoes, greens from the garden and cream from the goat dairy, there was plenty to serve the three of them. Oliver, knowing Nellie to be a good cook and clean housekeeper, had no complaints and, upon whiffing the roast meat through an open window, suggested they move inside.

Marcella hesitated at the doorway, not apprehensive about entering a white man's hut but in awe at the enormity of the dwelling and the extent of the contents, much of which appeared to her as curiosities. The polished floors, high ceilings with decorative cornices and, in the dining room, a massive dining suite to seat ten, and a pair of ornate crystal candelabras. The kitchen, though less extravagant, still carried the hallmarks of the love Oliver held for Ivana Sorrento, the woman for whom he had built the home. Ledges on the walls filled with ornaments Ivana had collected; a spacious pantry; racks and hangers to store pots and pans; a kitchen table with a marble top; and a cooking hearth crafted by the best stonemason in the colony. All of this he had assembled for Ivana who, sorrowfully, was killed in a sulky accident when returning to Sorrento one summer's night. Beneath a ghostly moon the horse had taken fright when a night bird flew into its path, causing it to bolt pell-mell along the shadowy roadway and, with Oliver too drunk to keep control, the sulky crashed into a gully, leaving him stunned and his loved one dead by his side. He buried her at Sorrento and struggled with the loss for months, till finding solace in the whorehouses of Brisbane.

Oliver gobbled his food as usual and then, with a pile of correspondence awaiting him in the office, he excused himself, leaving Nellie to introduce Marcella to the colonist's way of life. Nellie, believing that every Islander needed a good scrub, particularly if sleeping in *her* house, enlisted Marcella to help prepare a tub of warm water. Marcella, having bathed with island women in the past, had no hesitation when Nellie undid the top button of her shirt and asked her to undress. Nellie then stood aside while Marcella bathed herself and turned back when she stepped to the floor mat. She dwelt on the chafe marks around Marcella's wrist and, knowing they were shackle marks, felt pity.

Without notice she asked, 'Did the Master touch you while on board?'

Marcella, though a virgin, knew what was meant and replied, 'No, he has been good to me.'

Nellie, believing her but having difficulty accepting that Oliver would withhold, searched for an answer while drying Marcella's back. When done, Nellie handed her the towel, told her to cover herself, and led her to Ivana's old sewing room. The room, where Ivana had spent many pleasurable hours, displayed shelves stocked with a variety of colourful fabrics, a stack of dress patterns, rolls of braiding and ribbon, and dainty boxes filled with sparkling sequins, needles, thread and thimbles.

'Here, Marcella, drop the towel and I'll measure you for a sarong,' said Nellie, shaking the creases from a piece of light material.

Marcella, enjoying the attention, held the cloth shoulder high while Nellie pinned the length and then drew it about her waist to measure the width.

'I'll cut and hem this and have you dressed in no time,' she said, picking up a pair of scissors from the desk.

Marcella, interested in her personal appearance, watched as Nellie cut the cloth to size and set to stitch it on a treadle sewing machine. With Nellie treadling the machine with her feet and feeding the hem expertly between the bobbin and moving needle, Marcella wondered why Nellie did not dress nicely instead of wearing old garb that covered her from head to toe. What of the wrist-length sleeves that could easily catch fire when cooking? Surely they could be trimmed to the elbow. The floppy flour-bag bonnet that sat cockeyed on her head? Surely she could sew something more becoming. Perhaps the disfigurement of her left cheek, an ugly teardrop burn mark from cheek bone to jaw, had shattered her pride to such an extent that she dressed drably to hide from the world. In spite of this, Marcella saw strength of character in the strong lines of her face, enough, she thought, for Nellie to dress nicely and engage with others.

'Here,' said Nellie cheerfully as she held the garment for Marcella to try. 'Put it on and see how it looks.'

Marcella, overjoyed at receiving such a lavish gift, held the sarong behind her back, drew the corners around, pulled them firmly across the bridge of her breasts, and then made a twist before tying the ends together behind her neck to make a halter. She then moved to the full length mirror and twirled around, showing the graceful moves of island dance.

At seeing the grace and beauty of this mixed-race Islander, Nellie commented, 'You look like a princess.'

'I am!' replied Marcella. 'My mother was Princess Emile and my grandfather is chief of my tribe! I am Princess Marcella of Lifou!'

'And your father?'

'Yes, he's from your land.'

'Oh, and do you know his name?'

'All I know is that he owns a boat and is called Mark Richards.'

'Have you met him?'

'No, he promised to return to my mother but it's too late. She died a few years ago.'

Nellie, presuming that Marcella had been kidnapped, digressed, not wanting to dig too deeply. 'Here, choose a colour you like and we'll make another one.'

Oliver entered his office and, after moments of reflection, took a letter opener and sliced open the envelopes, paying attention to some wax seals and blithely ignoring others. He then read the notes written by Nellie, sat and began replying to the correspondence.

Most of the letters were about shipping arrangements and, with a flourish of pen and ink, he replied, drawing on memory for names and dates. A letter from the Lands Office, announcing that a government inspector would call the following week to audit the improvements made to the property, drew his ire. He despised authority, especially that of government and, rather than upset himself, he set it aside for Seamus to handle. To be fair, Oliver had leased the land from the Crown under the provisions of the *Land Act*, and as a condition of the lease certain improvements of fencing, building and cultivation had to be undertaken. The inspector, a low-paid civil servant, would do no more than visit on horseback, confirm that adequate improvements had been made and, in return, expect a cup of tea and maybe lunch. Oliver would have none of this. Seamus would receive the official, grant him the minimum access needed and send him on his way without tea or lunch. This ingratitude had been noted in reports by previous inspectors, and Oliver should be careful that the officer, as retribution, did not demand to inspect the inside of the house and, in the process, discover Marcella.

Having dealt with the correspondence, he now addressed another overdue matter. With one sweep he pulled a Persian carpet away from a cast-iron chest the size of a coffin. The heavy chest that took four men to lift into position held a trove of valuables that only Oliver could access. After closing the office door, he took a key from a hollowed curtain rod end, inserted it into the brass lock of the chest, and fiddled till the lock clicked free. He bent low and heaved open the weighty lid. As always, the sight of his real wealth, thousands of pounds worth of gold bullion and nuggets, Spanish gold coins, British currency, promissory notes and trays full of quality pearls from the Torres Strait, brought a gleam to his eyes. Following this moment of avarice, he took a set of gold scales and a handful of nuggets and set them on the desk. The quarterly payment of £25 in gold that he was about to weigh and later deliver to Angus Buchanan, the government's chief immigration officer, would guarantee him immunity from prosecution under the *Polynesian Labourers Act*. The trade, with up to 250 islanders being brought to the mainland each voyage and sold for £12 a head, proved so lucrative that the graft passed down the line to licensed recruiting agents and government inspectors. Oliver had, in the past, often grumbled about paying for protection, but the returns from this *black trade* were almost as good as striking it rich on the Gympie goldfield! He weighed the gold, giving not a penny more from his pocket and not a penny less to the man who held the key to the continuation of the trafficking.

Since the payment would be made in the coming days, Oliver simply tucked the pouch of gold under some papers in the top drawer of the desk. While doing so he spotted the revolver he kept there in case needed and took it in his hands. He also had loaded weapons stashed elsewhere around the house in case an intruder managed to cross the perimeter of Seamus' and Thruppence's watchful eyes by day, and the Rottweiler watch dogs that roamed the property by night. As usual Oliver spun the chamber, removing the cartridges one by one, and then reloaded before returning it to the drawer. His habit or, as many would say, his addiction, to alcohol was never far away. A crystal decanter of colonial rum, nestled among the papers on the desk, gleamed at him, beckoning he partake. Without hesitation he pulled the stopper free and poured a draft of rum into a glass. After a sip and then a swig, he turned his attention to the unread newspapers. Though Oliver was primarily a seaman who spent most of his time at sea, he was also an avid reader, and within minutes he found himself immersed in the recent news. He followed shipping intelligence reports carefully, informing himself of ship movements both in Australian waters and the South Pacific. He knew most of the big traders, the names of their ships and, by a process of deduction, could anticipate their plans and, in many instances, had clipped their intention by undercutting their bids.

He scoffed aloud as he read a *Letter to the Editor* where the correspondent claimed that the government indenture system of procuring South Sea Islanders amounted to slavery. That the governing legislation was a sham, and the so-called indentures, where 'X' was placed on a piece of paper as a signature, was a fraud. That, in the absence of the fraught *Polynesian Labourers Act*, these shysters would be prosecuted under the *Imperial Emancipation Act*. The writer cited cases where, without the cover of the deficient *Polynesian Labourers Act*, the perpetrators would be jailed. The contributor berated members of parliament, accusing them of pandering to the sugar planters and pastoralists in exchange for their votes. Oliver again scoffed with a guttural laugh because the public expression of concern only added to his image of himself as a scurrilous rascal, a villain that could outwit the law; either on the high seas or ashore. He had positioned himself with a fast ship, hardy crew and contacts within government. He believed he was untouchable and that he could conduct his business with impunity. After indulging in the papers, and having reaffirmed his belief that he was a man of wealth and repute, he locked the iron chest and closed the door behind as he left the office.

He swaggered down the wide hallway and entered the kitchen to find that Marcella's hair had been neatly trimmed and Nellie teasing it with her fingers.

He watched on approvingly till Nellie finished and then asked Marcella to accompany him to the stables. The crisp grass gave way before the hem of Marcella's new sarong and under her bare feet as they walked to the goat yards and farm sheds where Thruppence and Jock were mustering the herd to secure them for the night. Jock darted this way and that, sometimes at Thruppence's command and other times of his own accord when a wily goat broke from the herd.

'Fetch 'em. Swing 'em. Here boy—back—back …' Thruppence bellowed, with his voice sweeping across the pastures as the herd of white goats pushed up the slope. At the entrance to the night compound, some goats, objecting to being herded and penned, ducked back through the mob in a bid to escape, only to be turned back by Thruppence wielding a stick or Jock snapping at their noses.

'He's doing well,' said Oliver to Seamus when he and Marcella met Seamus by the yards.

'Sure thing,' replied Seamus. 'Without him and Jock the herd would be torn to bits by the dingoes. They've been particularly bad of late.'

After Thruppence had chained the gate, he and Jock skipped across the railed yards to greet the Master and the new girl. As he approached, Marcella was drawn by his rugged appearance and agile movements, but the moment he opened his mouth and said with a lisp, 'Please ya meet ya,' she realised that he had an impediment. It caused her to stall for words, and before she could reply Thruppence, taking this to be a rebuke, added 'S'pose ya Pi'gin talk.'

'No-no-no,' stammered Marcella, caught off guard and unconsciously mimicking his broken speech.

Before Thruppence could hit back, Oliver intervened. 'I see there are a few more kids on the ground. At this rate we will soon double the herd. Well done, Thruppence!'

While Seamus sorted the goats, mothering the kids with the nannies, Thruppence spread pails of corn into troughs. The sight of the nannies with their young, some only days old, soon had Marcella in the yards, learning how to 'feed out', as it was called.

That evening, Oliver, Nellie and Marcella ate heartily in the dining room, passing around pleasant conversation by lamplight. When finished, Oliver complimented Nellie on the meal and retired to his office, leaving the women to attend to the kitchen. They washed the dishes, tidied the benches and then, by candlelight, Nellie led the way to what was to be Marcella's bedroom. When Nellie put a hand to the brass knob of the door Marcella tried to imagine but had no real idea of what lay beyond the heavy oak panelling. With what was almost reverence, Nellie turned the knob and slowly opened the door to a large bedroom. Marcella waited as Nellie crossed the room and lit three lamps and then, as she turned the wicks high, Marcella's intrigue turned to surprise.

Nellie beckoned Marcella forward and explained, 'This was Oliver's bedroom, the one he shared with his wife before she died. This was before I came here but, from what Seamus has told me, neither Oliver nor anybody else has slept in it since that day. It's been left exactly as it was as a shrine to Ivana.' Nellie paused before continuing, 'He has asked that it be your room, which makes you very special.'

Nellie took Marcella's hand, squeezed it, and then in a soft voice said, 'Here, let me show you around.'

Everything, all that had been in place at the time of Ivana's passing, lay as a stark reminder of her presence. Doilies on either side of the Tudor duchesse—one with the word 'Oliver' and the other 'Ivana'—had been embroidered by Ivana and evidenced that she truly cared for this man. With a blink of the imagination one could imagine Ivana sitting on the stool, dressed in a negligee and brushing her hair before the mirror, while Oliver changed into a nightshirt. A large four-poster bed with turned columns, lace curtaining and drapes that could be drawn for privacy, stood against a wall. Marcella stood in awe of the surrounds. Never could she have imagined such luxury. She gazed at the bed in disbelief till Nellie drew her attention by opening the doors of a wardrobe filled with ladies' clothes.

They sifted through the garments, with Nellie holding up those of interest. When Marcella held one against her body and turned to see herself in the full-length mirror, Nellie commented, 'You're the same size as Ivana.' Upon realising this resemblance, she thought that Oliver might see Marcella as a substitute for his lost love. When finished with the rack of clothing they crossed the carpeted floor to a writing bureau where Nellie rolled back the concertina lid to reveal a polished desk top that featured a mother-of-pearl inlay at its edges. Marcella recognised the shell immediately and traced the inlay with her fingertips, recalling the magic powers her people believed the opalescent shell possessed. Finding it here, in what would be her room, gave a sense of connection, and in the excitement of the moment she beamed with delight. 'This is the magic shell from my island!'

'Magic?' asked Nellie, showing interest in island folk law.

'Yes, spirit of the sea. See the colours, all the colours of the sea. They bring island people good luck.'

Nellie, realising that this small remnant of island life might provide comfort, smiled fondly and nodded.

She placed a lamp on the desk top and slid open the drawers, giving more insight into Ivana's personal life. Some drawers contained loose papers and cards, while others were neatly stacked with official-looking letters and scrolled documents tied with ribbon.

As the written word meant nothing to Marcella, she soon closed the drawers and turned to a nearby dresser filled with everything from evening finery to nightwear. The girls indulged themselves, raking through the garments, playing a game of fantasy, with Princess Marcella trying on this and that at Nellie's direction. After a thorough scavenge they chose a revealing nightdress that Marcella would wear.

With that sorted, they moved across the room and opened the tall French windows to the veranda.

'That's better,' said Nellie after taking a few deep breaths. 'We'll leave the windows open to be rid of the stuffy, camphor smell.' She followed with, 'Mind you, Thruppence does the gardening and I have caught him peeping, so be careful. He's a good lad in his place, but I dare say he could be a pest with a young woman like you.'

Marcella listened while Nellie explained more, telling how Thruppence sometimes roamed the property at night with the Rottweiler guard dogs. 'You can never be certain where he'll be.' She added, 'The dogs are kept in kennels behind the shed to avoid contact with people. This way they stay savage and are more likely to attack strangers. The dogs don't even know me except they would have smelt my scent while prowling at night. They are chained all day and let loose at night to free range the property. They're vicious, and God help anybody who visits at night.'

'Will they come inside?' asked Marcella, somewhat nervous.

'No, not unless someone leaves the gate open. They won't jump the fence, but if the gate is left open ...' Nellie hesitated and then added, 'Under no circumstances are you to go outside the fence at night. Oliver tells people they are to protect the goats from dingo attack, but the real purpose is to guard against intruders who might have a grudge against him, or even a police raid.'

Hearing this, Marcella became unsettled and, to reassure her, Nellie turned the bed down, helped her change into her nightie, tucked her under the sheets and, after saying goodnight, doused the lamps and left.

CHAPTER 4

Within a few days Marcella began to settle into her new life. With patience and understanding, Nellie introduced her to the household duties, beginning with the kitchen and extending to the other rooms, except for Nellie's and Oliver's bedrooms and Oliver's office, all of which she forbade Marcella from entering. So insistent was Nellie that Marcella wondered what lay behind the doors, always closed or left ajar just enough to catch a draught of breeze. When Seamus and Thruppence were away she ventured to the sheds, exploring and figuring the use of some items, and marvelling about other strange contraptions for which she could see no use. Most of all she loved the goats and soon found herself helping to yard and feed them of an evening. She nurtured kid goats with their nanny mothers, picking them up, walking through the herd and encouraging them to suckle. When done with the goats, she bathed in a tub and, at Nellie's insistence, brushed her hair and dressed nicely for dinner. Oliver did likewise, presenting himself well dressed and conducting himself in a gracious manner. Nellie, always with the excuse of being busy preparing the meal, remained in her drab clothes till later in the evening when she bathed and dressed in secret by candlelight. Some nights Marcella stepped over the low sill of the open French window of her bedroom to the veranda and then crossed to the garden, where she studied the stars and thought of those left at home. When woken during the night, she lay on the satin sheets, listening to the call of night birds—some near, others afar.

Three weeks after Oliver and Marcella arrived home from the sea voyage, Oliver went to Brisbane, timing his visit to coincide with the *Trade Winds'* return from Sydney. He woke to the crow of roosters and had stoked the kitchen fire by the time Nellie entered. To Marcella's surprise, Oliver had almost finished stuffing breakfast into his mouth when she presented herself still in her nightdress.

'I'm off to Brisbane,' he stated with a note of anticipation in his voice.

Marcella, detecting this, asked, 'How long?'

'Oh, probably a couple of days. Have some business to attend and the first mate is expecting me back at the ship anytime now. '

'Are you sailing away?'

'Lord no. I wouldn't do that without telling you. Here, give me a hug before I go.'

The invitation of a hug, the first since arriving at Sorrento, drew Marcella to his side where she wrapped an arm about his brawny shoulders and kissed him on the neck.

When done with the early morning chatter, and eager to be on his way, Oliver went to his room, packed and soon returned, dressed in his best town clothes. Though somewhat rough in manner, he did pride himself on his looks and stood with a bag of clothes in one hand and a small leather case containing papers, various forms of currency and a revolver in the other. The girls had to admit that he looked posh in his pressed linen shirt, white moleskin trousers, silk cravat and shiny Wellington boots. They wished him well as he took his bowler hat from a peg by the door and whisked away towards the stable.

Seamus had drawn the grey horse to harness and stood by its side, ready to give Oliver a heave up when he put his foot onto the metal step of the sulky. Oliver did enjoy his food, eating to excess and suffering the consequence of being extended about the middle. However, it would be a mistake to underestimate his ability if engaged in a brawl.

Seamus tapped the grey on the rump and bid Oliver goodbye as he gathered the reins between his gnarled fingers; a legacy from dragging at heavy rigging lines since he first went to sea as a fifteen-year-old. Oliver had done the hard yards, working his way to become captain of a ship and then buying his first boat and upgrading through a series of vessels till he eventually purchased the square rigger he now commanded.

Oliver enjoyed the journey to and from Brisbane: the blue sky, fresh country air, the twitter of song birds and, most importantly, time alone to think. Often he left Sorrento with a plan in mind and arrived at his destination with a revised but more effective means of negotiating the business claiming his attention. As he came closer to Brisbane, the stringy-bark shacks occupied by new chums gave way to the established landholders who lived in weatherboard dwellings with tin roofs. The grey horse, having travelled this road many times and keen to be free of the harness, needed no encouragement from Oliver to swing into Hanson's Livery Stable located on the outskirts of Brisbane. From here he took an enclosed coach rather than an open cab for the purposes of making a discreet approach to the government offices situated in George Street, where he had arranged to meet with Angus Buchanan, his go-between. The offices, a fortress-like precinct, built of sandstone and with a single public entrance that opened into a courtyard, never sat well with Oliver. The rough-hewn stonework and the wasted space in the courtyard left him wondering how much the government had paid for what he considered to be a monstrous architectural blunder. No doubt money had changed hands and, by the amount of sandstone set in place, Oliver surmised the quarry man must have had influence in government circles. Indeed, the quarry might have been owned by a politician or senior public servant.

Angus, a lanky, drawn prune of a man with a personality equally as dry had secured the appointment as chief immigration officer through the decisiveness of his actions. 'If in doubt, ask Angus,' was the mantra in the hallways of the Immigration Department, over which Angus presided. Although his initial appointment of three years was by the minister responsible for the department, his service thereafter had been extended simply by a memo raised by the minister's secretary.

Angus readily communicated with members of the public, granting audiences in his office and making himself available to address groups, whether they be the poor with grievances about life in the colony, or others with more immediate concerns, like a shipload of South Sea Islanders having docked without the necessary paperwork to allow them entry into the country. Whatever the problem, Angus, most times, found a ready solution, and for this he was held in high regard. Few members of the public stopped to question his methods, let alone his integrity. To the outside world he conducted himself as a true servant of Her Majesty's service. However, inside the halls of parliament and inside the stone walls of the government offices he was seen as a fixer, a man who, for a price, would use whatever means available—lawful or not— to bring about a preferred outcome. With the majority of the elected members of parliament coming from the sugar and pastoral industries, parliament condoned any measures that would bring manpower to their labour-starved properties. Angus had recognised this early in his tenure and had quietly acquired wealth under the guise of a protector of the colony.

Oliver understood this and, as his contribution to the protection racket, took the pouch of gold from his leather case and slid it across the desk to Angus.

'You'll find it's correct,' said Oliver, having attended to the first matter of business.

'No need. You always pay to the penny,' replied Angus, while stashing the bounty behind papers in a drawer of his desk.

A preamble then ensued during which Oliver outlined his movements since his last visit to Angus' office. He reported that, apart from profiting from the copra exchange, he befriended those of the islands visited and could easily 'persuade' 120 healthy males from New Caledonia, the New Hebrides and, if short, the Solomon Islands. He made no mention of having brought Marcella with him on his last trip, or whether he would visit Lifou on the next voyage.

Having listened to the detail, Angus leant forward, cocked his head slightly to one side as was his custom when plotting mischief, and laid out a plan.

'I have requests from plantations at Mackay for 150, and more later. The planting begins in April so, to get the best price, it's best that delivery is made by then.'

'What are they paying?' asked Oliver, as though enquiring about the auction price of livestock.

'That depends on the delivery time and the quality of the stock. Last year started at £12 per head at the start of the season and fell away to £9 by November. If you get in early and sort them into lots then you should offload them for an average of £10 to £12.'

'Is the 150 head guaranteed?' asked Oliver.

'As far as can be expected. These planters are on my books, and while they are not bound to it, they know the benefits of dealing through me. If you agree to deliver them by the start of April I'll ask them to hold off buying elsewhere. They've kept their word in the past, and with your reputation for supplying quality stock I can't see any problem. At the worst we can offload them elsewhere at no less than £9 a head.'

'Who else might want a slice?'

'There's Rufus of the *South Pacific Venturer*, Red Harry of the *Sea Dog*, Dalziel Henning who commands the *Ruby*, and a new player who I've not met. Apart from these, there are only a few other schooners that are of no concern.'

Oliver grunted, showing his disdain for the other traders. According to Oliver he should have the pick of the trades and entered fierce competition if challenged. With a flash of anger creasing his forehead he declared, 'I'll take the deal. Those schooners won't be able to handle the heavy seas of the cyclone season, particularly with human cargo being tossed about in the holds. Apart from that, my man-o'-war can outrun any schooner on the open sea and they know it. Tell them the contract is mine and not to go looking for trouble. As for the planters, give them my guarantee that I will berth by the first of April.'

'I'll pass that on. I'll also advise the government inspector stationed at Mackay. He's on my books also, so there will be no problem with auctioning the cargo and the paperwork. We'll complete the permit form while you're here, and I guess you'll need some more indenture forms.'

After the permit to transport South Sea Islanders to Australia had been completed and signed by Angus, he reached to a shelf and handed Oliver a wad of single-page indenture forms.

Oliver begrudgingly looked at the pile, fingered the top page and bemoaned the burden the *Polynesian Labourers Act* imposed on ship captains bringing island natives to the mainland. 'Not like the old days when we just loaded them into the holds, brought them across and sold to the highest bidder.'

'True,' agreed Angus, 'but this way we get around the *Imperial Slavery Act*. Without the *Polynesian Labourers Act*, debauched as it is, there would be no trade. At least this way the trade can continue, albeit under the guise of this Act.'

Angus reached to the shelf again, took a bound document, handed it to Oliver and said, 'Here, take this. It's a submission recently prepared by an anti-slavery advocate and presented to parliament.'

Oliver reluctantly took the document and put it in his case. He longed for the old buccaneer days when a ship's master took what he wanted. However, those days were gone, and he accepted the new regime of bogus laws and government corruption.

When the meeting concluded, Oliver clinched Angus' hand, more by way of sealing the deal than bidding his operative farewell. Once free of the sandstone building that reminded him of the old convict prison down the road, he continued down George Street, turned into Mary Street and headed towards the river. At Claudia's, a small but fashionable brothel, he stepped into the alcove and, with a tremor of excitement, turned the brass knob of the door and entered. Everything seemed the same: the spacious reception room with an open harpsichord that had never sounded a note since being installed, a full-size bronze of a naked women carrying a Parisian scarf in her hand, vases of artificial flowers and a bookstand filled with magazines for clients to peruse while waiting. An insipid little man sat in a plush lounge chair in the far corner, stargazing while waiting his turn in one of rooms. He seemed possessed by fear, as though expecting his mother to come through the door and drag him away. He looked so shaken and miserable that Oliver thought he would need a hand to get started. Another, with a thin moustache, showed signs of impatience, tapping his feet and twiddling his thumbs. A burly man from the Gympie gold diggings, with a gold nugget hanging from his neck, had trouble concealing the bulge in his trousers. A fourth, hardly dressed well enough to gain admittance, lay back comfortably on a sofa, signalling that he was a regular and, in spite of his scrappy appearance, would be served, albeit in one of the cheaper rooms.

'Hello, Oliver,' called Claudia, drawing his attention away from the customers in waiting.

A beaming smile that clearly showed Oliver's anticipation spread wide as he came to the counter, put his luggage down and tipped his hat.

Claudia did like Oliver. They shared similar personality traits: free from inhibition, giving little credence to moral codes, prepared to do and say whatever they liked, irrespective of whether members of the public or the law condoned their behaviour. As to risk, each had the ability to push to the limit and beyond. When in trouble, Oliver depended on his revolver and connections, while Claudia surrounded herself with pimps who kept her informed and police accepting free services in exchange for protection. Both had accrued wealth, with Oliver holding stocks of gold and investments in shipping and property. Claudia had battled her way up from being a sixteen-year-old street-walker to now owning a well-patronised brothel in the upper-class district of Brisbane. While conspicuous in this respect, few knew of the hidden trove of jewellery she held in a safe deposit at the bank, much of which had been gifted from undisclosed members of the gentry—politicians and leaders of commerce. Many were the proposals, promises to leave their wives, to buy her a mansion, to treat her as a lady, but little did they know that she had led them astray with no intention of succumbing to a subservient life under the control of a loveless and disloyal male. No! Never would Claudia bow down. Yes, open her legs for a share of their wealth, but nothing further. The only guarantee she gave was that word of their interludes would never escape her lips. Oliver understood this and conducted himself accordingly, always respectful of her independence. He enjoyed her charm and caress, always feeling renewal after an engagement. For Claudia, Oliver brought daring, a release, a sense of freedom and, if the truth be known, she would happily accommodate him free of charge. With this understanding, Claudia ushered him to her suite where they wiled away the afternoon. When parting, Claudia kissed Oliver on the lips, a privilege she seldom offered to a man.

Oliver breathed easily on the short walk back to Queens Wharf where he saw the *Trade Winds* docked in the distance. With the sun setting, he thought it best to bunk down at the Mariners Inn for the night and meet with the first mate in the morning. Though somewhat squalid, the inn served the mariners and dock hands well by providing cheap, sly grog that had been smuggled on ships and hidden in the cargo sheds that lined the dock. Police raids on the inn and other dockside drinking houses proved fruitless due to a subterranean network of informants keeping the publicans posted. When stashes were found in warehouses, the investigation almost always concluded that the crates had been planted there without the owner's knowledge and hence no charges could be laid. Fanny O'Leary, the owner of the Mariners Inn, acted as a banker for the trade, arranging deals and skimming a hefty margin from all transactions. She was an old friend of Oliver's and greeted him with gusto.

'Good afternoon, Sir,' she boomed, with her loose breasts bobbing.

Oliver admired Fanny, not just as one of his own criminal ilk, but as a dependable friend. Once, when the police were searching for Oliver, she stripped off, took him to bed with her and berated the police when they entered her bedroom. To their question of 'who is sharing the bed' she named a senior police officer and threatened to lodge a complaint with the commissioner of police. The policemen, though not believing her story, dared not pull the sheet aside for, if it were the officer mentioned, their positions in the force would be in peril.

'Jamaican?' she asked when about to pour a slug of rum.

Oliver raised two fingers to indicate a double nip and fiddled in his pocket for coin.

Business looked to be as usual, with patrons scattered about in the dingy bar room and bawdy barmaids engaging them with titillating talk while serving drinks. Though Oliver was well acquainted with most present he preferred to chat with Fanny. After all, she could give a more reliable account of the latest dockside shenanigans.

As evening fell and the room was lit with the light of oil lamps, some of the earlier patrons staggered off to go home to starving families, while others, tossed out of home or living a lonely bachelor's life, took refuge amongst the stacks of cargo on the wharf.

When the number of patrons swelled for the evening session, Fanny and Oliver moved along the bar where Fanny sat on a stool with her back to the wall and one leg cocked up. Oliver sat opposite with his bag and case by his feet.

Over a plate of beef stew they shared more of the gossip, telling of the latest criminal activity and digging deep into people's personal affairs. Johnny Knox sat in a corner, brooding over a fight he had lost last week. Enoch, the Jewish money lender, became embroiled in a rowdy confrontation when Freddie the tramp denied owing him £5. Captain Wishart of the second regiment prided himself in arm wrestling and stood ready to challenge all comers. A barmaid, aptly named Rosebud, had finished her shift and touted for business at two shillings a time.

Fanny withheld from drinking, keeping to her routine of once a week. The surgeon had said, 'Fanny, there is no point in dying as the richest whore on the waterfront. Best you restrict your indulgence to once a week.' Fanny had followed his advice, felt healthier and in return gave him a discount for the service she proffered his way once a month. She now sat with her skirt pulled up to her thighs, splashing more rum into Oliver's glass each time he took a couple of gulps.

Fanny suddenly slipped a hand across the bar, touched Oliver on the wrist and whispered, 'Don't look around but Rusty the hunchback is watching from the door.'

Oliver sat upright, braced himself and if it had not been for Fanny's restraint he would have confronted Rusty and maybe given him a hiding.

'Better not,' advised Fanny. 'He knows you brought an island girl ashore and that could mean trouble.'

'How do you know?' quizzed Oliver.

'It's common knowledge on the dock and the police are aware. They were about asking questions soon after you set foot ashore.'

'He's been a thorn in my side for years and should be put down,' said Oliver, referring to Rusty.

'Yes, I agree, but not now. Best that Seamus attends to it while you're at sea.'

Oliver accepted her counsel and, at her suggestion, picked up his bag and case and followed through the rear entrance of the bar room. With Fanny in front holding a candle they went down the narrow corridor to the bunk rooms where men and occasionally women lay on beds festooned with bed bugs, and often linen soiled by previous occupants.

Fanny placed the candle on a small bedside dresser, turned to Oliver and asked, 'How are you situated?'

Oliver, knowing Fanny well, answered honestly, 'I've spent the afternoon with Claudia.'

Fanny, still making herself available, quipped, 'Then maybe first thing in the morning.'

'Maybe, but the first mate is expecting me on board early.'

Fanny, not in need of a shilling or two, had made the offer more as a gesture to a friend. She hugged him goodnight and, when leaving, said, 'Maybe tomorrow night.'

When Oliver was aboard the *Trade Winds* the next morning, the first mate reported on the ship's movements since Oliver and Marcella had disembarked. He had delivered the copra to Sydney and forwarded it to London on a ship registered to the East India Company. He also managed to secure a back-loading of building materials with more to come.

Oliver thanked him and then told about the deal to deliver 150 Islanders to Mackay by April. When asked from which islands Oliver replied, 'We can start with Mare Island and work north from there. It doesn't matter so long as they are young and fit …' Consideration then turned to planning, pulling together a crew suitable for the expedition and provisioning the ship. Oliver finished by saying, 'Till then, shipping materials from Sydney will keep you busy.'

For lunch they ate leftovers of scrambled eggs and salted beef in the first mate's cabin. During the meal the mate reported how immigration officials had enquired about the sighting of an island girl leaving the ship. He added, 'Old Rusty saw her and won't let the matter alone.' Oliver grunted a short reply, signalling that Marcella's whereabouts was not open for discussion.

Oliver returned to the Mariners Inn just before dusk and settled at the bar with Fanny, whose pale breasts, bursting from her tightly laced bodice, competed for his attention. Being Friday night, gambling night, and the bar expected to be packed, Fanny's security guard, a tall mulatto who had jumped ship years ago, stood with his back to the wall watching every move. He had been born into slavery in Trinidad, where negroes and their offspring were treated as chattels; bought, sold and often beaten to death with no recourse to justice. Following emancipation he sought revenge, returning to the plantation of his enslavement and beating the old master to death with a shackle chain that had held him and his father in bondage. He escaped to sea and sailed the world in tall ships and, by a turn of fate, eventually sailed into Brisbane in a sinking ship. Since his status was that of a declared British subject under the *Emancipation Act* he had the same rights as Oliver and Fanny, able to come and go to any dominion in the British Empire. He looked Fanny and Oliver's way often, but not so much as to be intrusive. Many patrons knew the story of his enslavement, the retribution he had dealt to his former master and the rumour that he had beaten to death a drunkard who threatened Fanny. Although the body of the drunkard had never been found, some believed it lay beneath the paving stones in Fanny's cellar. A police investigation into the matter fell short of laying charges because the chief magistrate of the colony owed Fanny a favour. The magistrate's nephew had been accused of illegally importing opium but avoided conviction based on Fanny's false testimony that the accused, a regular patron of her inn, was drinking in the bar room of her establishment at the time of the alleged offence. Even a request for a search warrant to dig up the foundations of the cellar failed to get approved.

Oliver liked to pitch himself against those on the poker table as much as he did others he confronted in life. With his notion of being invincible, he swigged another rum and made to the gambling den at the rear of the inn. He swaggered into the room where men's thoughts were shrouded with greed and soon found himself engaged in a high-stakes poker game. Those present were a remittance man spending his quarterly allowance, and beside him the son of an English duke who had inherited an estate. Across the table sat a retired army general noted for bragging about his heroic actions in the Crimean War, and a wool merchant who commanded a chain of investments from wool on sheep's backs in the colony to the wool mills of Lancashire. During the following hours Oliver lost, by his reckoning, £100. With his notes and coin gone and nobody prepared to take a promissory note, he made a daring move. He groped into his leather case and placed in excess of £150 worth of gold nuggets on the table and then wagered the full amount against the total of what each of the others had skinned from him. With Oliver's contribution far in excess of that which any of them had taken from him, they readily shoved their share to centre table. All agreed that the wager was to be determined by a simple cut of the cards, with the highest score taking all. Those playing on nearby tables became excited when they realised the enormity of the bet and crowded around to witness the spectacle. One after another the five men cut the pack, took the top card and held it against their chests. When done, Oliver showed his card first. Then followed the others. The onlookers gasped when Oliver held the winning card and watched incredulously as he held open his case and raked in the winnings.

When this sobering moment passed the five of them, now more determined than ever, resumed play. By lamplight and the smell of cigar smoke they continued till, in the early hours of the morning, Oliver sensed that he was being watched, a creeping sensation that distracted him. He began to cast about, catching shady glimpses of those at the other tables and the few bystanders. Nothing seemed amiss until, through the blur of cigar smoke, he saw what appeared as an apparition standing in the dark by the rear door. His curiosity deepened and, time and again, his focus was drawn away from the game and to the figure whose image waxed and waned behind the cloud of smoke. He began to lose, one hand then another, and, thinking his luck had run out, called it quits and made ready to leave. As he rose from the table the mystery figure approached to reveal itself as Rusty the hunchback. Oliver, heeding Fanny's advice, decided to ignore the wretched scab of a man and, after nodding to those at his table as a courtesy, he prepared to leave by the doorway to the bar.

'Not so fast!' sounded a call that carried an inference of menace.

A hush descended over the room as the players and onlookers turned their attention to the ghostly figure now holding a post to support his ailing body. A barmaid left her tray of glasses and slipped to the bar room. Oliver could crush the bent-over weasel with a single blow but, with several witnesses present, this was not the time or place. He set to appease Rusty by taking two sovereigns from his pocket and holding them out as an offering.

Rusty, who had been watching the play, dismissed the offer by calling loudly, 'One hundred pounds. Nothing less!'

While some of the patrons knew of Rusty's hold over Oliver, the outsiders had no idea of the extortion demand. Those at Oliver's table had witnessed his blustering manner during the evening and expected he would simply ignore the demand as nothing more than a bleat from a defenceless cripple. They were all surprised when Oliver, with case in hand, went to Rusty and spoke to him in a low tone. Although their murmured exchange could not be clearly heard, it soon became apparent that Rusty would not accept anything less than his opening claim. Oliver's temper frayed. He began to point and then prodded Rusty, threatening him with violence. The crowd remained divided, with some sympathising with Rusty and others caring not if Oliver beat him to death there in the room. They began to whisper among themselves, exchanging views and speculating on the outcome. The army general, with his ire stirred by memories of bloodshed, toyed with the handgun in his pocket. The wool merchant, having accrued his wealth by shrewd negotiation, thought Oliver should, for the sake of shaking this rat from his back, offer £5 and not a farthing more.

Oliver's self-control flagged. His voice became menacing and his demeanour more threatening and, when it seemed he was about to swing a punch, Rusty shouted, 'Kidnapper!'

This public disclosure took all consideration of a financial settlement off the table. Oliver grabbed Rusty by the scruff of the neck, pulled him from the post and dragged him towards the back door. Rusty fought back as best he could, scuffling on the floor, grabbing at Oliver's legs. Oliver's intention was thwarted when a shadowy figure slipped around him and blocked the doorway. The mulatto, with the whites of his eyes showing in the semi dark, confronted Oliver's blind rage by shoving him backwards. Oliver, incensed by the rebuff, let go of Rusty, spat racial slurs into the mulatto's face and braced himself for a fight. The mulatto, catching sight of Fanny from the corner of his eye, staved off Oliver's first punch and then a second before Fanny could come between them.

With her hair tossed rough like a common wench and her breasts heaving she took Oliver by the chin, squared his face to hers and said, 'No, Oliver, not here. There's too much to lose.'

She spoke on, as a seasoned pub woman would, calming the moment with a view to defusing the disturbance. Her familiar voice, and memory of the light moments they had shared together, found a way to Oliver's heart, quelling his wrath sufficient to allow her to turn him away from the pitiful bundle now lying on the floor and usher him to the bar room.

With most of the patrons now gone, the barmaids preparing to close for the night and some lamps burnt dry, Fanny and Oliver sat together having a nightcap. When all except Fanny and Oliver had departed, Fanny lit a candle, took Oliver by the hand and led him to her room. By moonlight streaming through the window they caressed and then undressed, leaving them naked, with Fanny's full breasts, her crowning glory, yearning to be touched, and Oliver's throbbing phallus ready to deliver. They lay on the bed entwined, giving and taking, making the most of what each had to offer till overtaken by exhaustion and then sleep. They woke to the sound of street traffic and, thoroughly satisfied by the night's romp, robed themselves and made to the kitchen, where staff hurried about preparing breakfast for guests. As old friends they sat at a small table, drinking tea and discussing last night's events and plans for that day. Fanny thought she would take herself off to a salon to have her hair coiffured and nails manicured, while Oliver spoke of buying gifts for the two girls at home. At mention of the girls Fanny asked after the island girl.

'No, I haven't bedded her yet,' replied Oliver by way of an idle comment.

Fanny, not caring who Oliver bedded but interested to know the details asked, 'Is she special?'

'No, just an island girl I picked up along the way.'

'And Rusty?' asked Fanny, pulling her open robe across her breasts. 'Is that what last night was about?'

'Yes, he's pestered me since I brought her ashore.'

'Be careful, darling,' she cautioned. 'He'll do anything for a handful of silver.'

They spoke on in confidence, with Fanny saying she would keep watch and, maybe, the girl should be moved on.

'Maybe,' replied Oliver, not wishing to dwell on the subject.

Oliver bathed, dressed and, when he was ready to leave, Fanny said, 'Darling, if you need anything you know where to find me.'

Oliver, sharing the moment, took a nugget of gold from his pocket, put it into her hands and closed her fingers in a show of gratitude.

Oliver settled the bill at the livery stable with cash and rode the journey home in a mixed state of inebriation and emotion. Much had happened during his brief stay, particularly the incident with Rusty and Fanny's advice to be rid of the girl. While it might sound simple for a man of Oliver's brash personality, he stumbled on the thought of severing himself from Marcella. In her own, quiet way she had made her way into his heart and, if possible, he wanted her by his side into the uncertain future. Through the fog of his clouded thoughts he imagined Marcella to be Ivana, and with that thought he decided not to let her go.

Everyone welcomed Oliver's homecoming. Seamus had butchered a goat, Nellie had baked a cake and now had a roast meal and gravy in the oven warmer. Thruppence, though often moody, always found that the sight of the grey horse and sulky coming over the ridge lifted his spirit and reaffirmed his belief that Sorrento had saved his life. Marcella, expecting Oliver's arrival, had paid special attention to herself, bathing that morning, dressing nicely, tidying her nails with Ivana's manicure set and, for the first time, applying Ivana's favourite perfume that Oliver would surely notice.

The girls watched as Seamus helped Oliver from the sulky and took charge of the horse. They then waited in anticipation as Oliver lumbered up to the house carrying his luggage and a parcel. He looked forward to arriving home and receiving a warm welcome. At the bottom step he called for Marcella to come and take his heavy bag, leaving him to carry his case and the brown paper parcel. In the kitchen he presented Nellie with her gift and watched as she unwrapped a new cast-iron skillet. Nellie held it high for both Oliver and Marcella to admire and thanked him for being thoughtful. He then took a small jewellery case from his pocket and placed it in Marcella's hand. Marcella, having no idea what it might contain, fumbled to open the lid. On seeing the jewelled pendant tears came to her eyes. Oliver, moved by her emotion, took the necklace, hung it about her neck and then kissed her on the lips. Like a child who had received a special gift, Marcella returned the kiss and then stood speechless till Nellie spoke.

'That is beautiful, truly magnificent,' she said, stepping forward to hold the sparkling jewel in her palm and turn it to capture the best light. After further compliments and a word of praise to Oliver she suggested Marcella go look in the mirror. The reflections in the mirror, moving from one to another of the facets as she turned the gem in her hands, held her in awe. No one had ever before bestowed on her such a treasured gift. She released the pendant, letting it settle against her cleavage. A feeling stirred within, a desire to hold Oliver tightly, to share and give to him all she had. In a whirl of thought, fantasies almost too bold to imagine took hold, whisking her away on a fairytale journey of true love. *He loves me. He must love me!*

After breakfast the next morning Oliver recalled the parliamentary submission that Angus had handed to him and set to read it in the comfort of his office. The report, well documented and apparently prepared by a member of the Abolitionist Movement, was scathing of the *Polynesian Labours Act* and its flagrant abuse by the South Sea Islander traders and government officials alike. It read as an exposé of those involved in kidnapping and, although Oliver's name did not appear, he knew most of those so named. He took particular note of the following passages.

The French Governor of New Caledonia gives a different version of the voyage of the *Sir Isaac Newton*, and complains to the French Government of certain kidnapping operations of that vessel on more than one occasion at Isle of Pines. It is a striking fact, too, that the Governor of New Caledonia complains of the kidnapping operations of two other vessels of Mr. Crossley's, the *Fanny Nicholson* and the *Spunkie*, both of which vessels were engaged in the Queensland trade. Applying Mr. Crossley's remarks to his other vessels, it will be found that the *Spunkie* arrived at Sweers Island, Gulf of Carpentaria, on September 17th, 1868, with 150 South Sea Islanders; at Brisbane on June 2nd, 1868, with 138 (this was the trip on which the girl Nnguinambo was abducted from Tanna by Ross Luin); at Brisbane on February 29th, 1868, with 148; at Bowen on the 3rd December, 1868, with 138 natives. The *Fanny Nicholson* arrived at Bowen, Port Denison, on the 8th July, 1867, with 201 South Sea Islanders, of whom a very large number were kidnapped from Isle of Pines. At the latter place she narrowly escaped being captured by French troops ...

The Queensland 'Polynesian Labourers Act' regards kidnapping as a venial offence, punishable by a pecuniary penalty of £500, and classifies it as a crime of no higher degree than a breach of the ordinary regulations. This may be a very startling statement to make, but the clause proves the fact. The bond required of masters of vessels has not prevented kidnapping. If we take, for instance, the case of a vessel like the *King Oscar*, which brought 270 Islanders, and if it was proved that the people had been kidnapped, and the penalty was enforced, the speculation would still be a profitable one. The proceeds of a cargo of 270 men, at say £9 a head, would be £2430, which, after the payment of the penalty of £500, would leave a balance of £1930 to be divided, after deducting expenses, which in such a voyage are very small, among the parties engaged in the traffic.

Oliver, as he had done in the past, scoffed at what he read and, in a way, wished his name had appeared so as to claim a share of the notoriety. With sailor's wages being less than £1 a week, the profit, apart from any sinister claim to fame, spurred him and others to run the gauntlet of French and British naval patrols in the islands.

CHAPTER 5

A fter busying himself about the property for a month, Oliver gave notice of his intention to visit Brisbane and rose early on the morning of his departure. He set off soon after sunrise and arrived at the Mariners Inn, where Sassy, the redhead barmaid with a body shape that master mariners would proudly display as their ship's figurehead, greeted him with a comely smile.

'Is my sweetheart in?' asked Oliver after downing his first rum.

'Sure thing,' quipped Sassy. 'I'll let her know.'

Though Oliver had left Fanny with a nugget of Gympie gold after his last visit he wished to thank her in a more personal way, and by eight o'clock they were seated on the balcony of The Forester, the most exclusive of the riverside restaurants. They dressed suitably for the occasion, with Oliver sporting a dapper style and Fanny flaunting expensive jewellery. Nothing but French wine would do, and after being served the best by an obliging waiter they sat by candlelight, savouring the wine till the host brought their roast dinner—piping hot and garnished with lashings of peppered gravy. They stayed on, enjoying the river breeze and the show of light from the gas street lamps that lit the pedestrian way below and reflected on the water's edge. This special something between them—their spirit, character or personality—held them closely engaged till Fanny began to fidget and cast looks towards the river.

'Are you cold, darling?' asked Oliver, leaning forward and taking one of her hands.

'No. I'm all right,' she replied with another visible flinch.

'I'll ask for a shawl.'

'No, really. I'm all right.'

'Then, what is it?' quizzed Oliver, clinching her hand more tightly.

Fanny paused and then whispered, 'I think we're being watched.'

Oliver straightened in his chair and, without looking about, asked, 'Who, what?'

'There's two men hanging around on the street. I noticed them an hour ago and since then they've kept reappearing.'

'Sure?'

'Yes.'

'Maybe they're interested in someone else.'

'No. Guests have been coming and going but they keep looking our way.'

Oliver let go of Fanny's hand and leant back in his chair to steal a look. Yes, two shady characters wearing felt hats stood in the pale light from a street lamp below.

'Any idea who they are?' he asked, turning back to Fanny.

'Not sure. The tall one looks familiar but I've not seen the other before.'

'Maybe you have it wrong. Their business could be otherwise.'

'No. I sense trouble.'

'By who?'

'Not sure, but since your altercation with Rusty I've had an uneasy feeling.'

'What, about the ruffing up?'

'Not only that. He now knows what you carry in your case.'

They sat for a while longer till Fanny suggested they leave. Oliver paid the bill and ordered a horse cab. On the way home he comforted Fanny with an arm around her shoulder and, when in her bedroom, he helped her undress before stripping off and joining her in bed.

At breakfast the following morning Fanny raised the matter again, expressing her concern and asking of his appointments.

'Oh, the usual. Visits to the shipping agent, Lands Office and my banker.'

'And the drink?' asked Fanny, knowing Oliver's habits.

'No. No drink till I am safe back here,' he promised.

The shipping agent, having done well from Oliver's past business and always feeling refreshed after hearing of Oliver's exploits, greeted him with a hearty handshake and the offer of a cup of tea. The agent, in a pokey, two-room rental on the waterfront with a small shingle out front that read 'Reg Brixton. Shipping Agent', was the preferred agent for those engaged in the

Islander trade. Many a shifty deal had been schemed across his desk, and before long he and Oliver were laying plans to procure the 150 South Sea Islanders that Angus Buchanan had spoken about.

The visit to the Lands Office brought less joy, with a senior officer taking him to task about the reception his inspector had received during his recent visit to Sorrento. The junior officer, who arrived on horseback, became pedantic when Seamus made no offer of a cup of tea or lunch and, being spiteful, demanded he be allowed to inspect the inside of the homestead. Seamus, towering over him with a threatening stance, bruised the officer's ego when he was abruptly shown the road. In retaliation the officer lodged a report that resulted in a 'Show Cause' notice being issued to Oliver. Oliver, with a history of contempt for the Lands Office, restrained himself as best he could while agreeing that Seamus' behaviour was inappropriate and that in future the inspector would be welcome.

The bank manager always gave priority to the bank's wealthy clients and, with Oliver having brought much business their way, the manager treated him as royalty, offering him a tipple of fine malt whisky. They spoke of many things: the influx of immigrants to the colony, the local economy, plans to increase the coinage in circulation, strife with the poor making demands that the rich be stripped of their wealth, and the women's movement pushing for property rights.

Oliver concluded the conversation by saying, 'While the increase in population and coinage are welcome we'll have to hold back on the business of more for the poor and women's property rights. It's men like us who will build the colony.'

The manager concurred wholly, thanked Oliver for the visit and said he looked forward to another visit in the near future.

As promised, Oliver returned to the inn before dark. With Fanny attending to a full house he sat at the bar where Sassy and two other barmaids scooted about serving drinks and raking in cash. 'No IOUs' said a bold sign on the bar wall. Fanny knew how to make money and loads of it. Sassy served him a meal at the bar, heaping his plate high with roast lamb and vegetables, one of Oliver's favourites. With business brisk and Fanny unable to leave the kitchen, Oliver, contrary to his promise to be careful, decided to take himself to the Colonial Club, a posh, members-only men's club situated on Albert Street.

Sassy, having been told of the sighting the night before and Fanny's concern, tried to persuade Oliver to stay in-house but, in the grip of a need to gamble, he asked her to pass on to Fanny that he had gone to the club and would be home before the inn closed at midnight.

The doorman at the club, knowing Oliver by sight, ticked off his entry with a nod and, in return, Oliver put a sovereign into the pewter cup that stood on a marble pedestal by the man's side. *Cheap security*, thought Oliver, especially with more than £1,000 of various forms of currency in the case he carried. He passed through the well-lit bar and dining rooms, down the hallway beside the billiards room and into the gambling den where men of means pitched themselves against others in what was essentially a game of bluff. Two security guards, dressed nicely but conspicuous by their mannerisms, stood watch in case of trouble. The play manager, a shark from way back, soon found Oliver a place playing with three strangers. Hands were won and lost, players came and went, and at midnight Oliver, doing so well, decided to stay for another few hands.

Fanny had slogged all evening cooking, cleaning and restocking the bar, and when midnight chimed and Oliver had not returned she began to worry. She sat in the dark, having a nightcap with the mulatto and, when he set to leave, she asked if he would go via Albert Street and shadow Oliver when he left the club. The mulatto, with the stealth of a will-o'-the-wisp, disappeared into the shadows as she closed the front door.

When Oliver went to leave the club the doorman apologised for not having a cab waiting and assured him that if he were to wait one would arrive within the half hour. Being already late and anxious to be home to Fanny, Oliver decided to walk the few blocks back to the inn. By the gloomy light from the gas lamps he walked along Albert Street and down Elizabeth Street to the waterfront. The lamps there were out, so, by the light of a mellow moon, he walked the riverside towards the inn.

When he was almost there, two men, armed with sticks, appeared as if from nowhere. Without any warning they hit into Oliver, and when he fell to the ground, one kicked his body while the other tried to drag the case from his grip. He fought back, kicking and striking, and just as he thought his life was about to end a shadowy figure appeared from behind the attackers. With a mighty whack from a policeman's nightstick the mulatto cracked the head of one of the assailants, and when the other saw his accomplice fall to the ground he dashed off with his boots clattering on the wharf decking. Though battered and bruised, Oliver managed to get to his feet and, with the aid of the mulatto, they went to the rear of the inn and tapped on Fanny's bedroom window.

Fanny, awake and anxious, leapt from the covers of her bed and within moments unbolted the back door. With the mulatto assisting, they lit a lamp and sat Oliver at the kitchen table. Though groggy and in pain about the ribs, he managed to tell the mulatto that he 'owed him'. Oliver seldom used these words, but on occasions when he did it sealed a lasting friendship. After discussing the incident over a cup of tea the mulatto excused himself, leaving Fanny to help Oliver to bed. The night proved to be long, with Oliver groaning from the pain in his chest and Fanny by his side, wondering if he would survive.

As Sassy opened the front doors of the inn the next morning she caught sight of two policemen coming around the corner from Queen Street. Having been told of the assault and attempted robbery she shut the doors, dropped the security bar in place and rushed to Fanny's bedroom. She knocked, called loudly and then opened the door to find Oliver under the blankets and Fanny standing naked and about to pull on a robe.

'The police are here!' she blurted.

Fanny replied with urgency, 'Quick, you go and head them off while I hide Oliver in the cellar.'

Sassy needed no further instruction. As a street-smart lass with a history of dealing with police she whisked back along the corridor, composed herself in the bar room, and then opened the front doors.

'Good morning, gentlemen,' she greeted with an engaging smile. 'Early drinks?'

Sergeant Briley, the senior officer, nearing retirement age and with rounded shoulders and a drooping moustache, declined. His associate, a scruffy policeman with a pock-marked face and showing signs of suffering delirium tremens, said nothing but needed a drink.

Briley asked for permission to enter the premises.

'Why?' asked Sassy, stalling for time.

'A murder was committed on the wharf last night and two suspects were seen heading for the inn,' he replied while stepping forward.

Sassy pushed the door half closed and with a steely voice asked, 'Where's your search warrant?'

'Never mind. Step aside or I'll break the door down!'

Sassy, picking up on the line, hit back, 'Forced entry without a warrant …'

With the to and fro that ensued, Sassy managed to hold the officers at bay till Fanny, dressed in only a robe, came to her side.

Briley, seeing Fanny half naked and knowing her to be promiscuous, suddenly changed tack. He became affable and quietly explained, 'A body was found on the wharf this morning and we are doing a search …'

Fanny, thinking he could be easily swayed, invited him and his side-kick inside and closed the front doors behind them.

Following a brief discussion, Briley turned to the constable and said, 'You stay here and keep watch while I search.'

Fanny led the way and showed him through the inn, beginning with the kitchen and storeroom and progressing to the accommodation rooms. Nothing of interest was found, and when the search seemed complete Briley asked to see the cellar. Fanny hesitated briefly but then took a box of matches from a nearby table and said, 'This way.'

Briley kept close behind as they descended the narrow stairway in the near dark and then stood as Fanny opened the creaking door to the cellar. She struck another match and trembled as she reached up to light a lamp attached to the wall. Briley, noting her anxiety and guessing she had something to hide, drew his revolver, held it before her and said, 'Should I investigate?'

Fanny knew what he meant and, for the sake of her lover, brushed her hair back then slowly undid the tie of her robe, letting the front gape open.

By the flickering light Briley moved close and took her by the crotch. Fanny closed her eyes to hide the shame as he molested her further, groping all over and penetrating deep with his fingers. She stood still and let him have his way because to do otherwise could see Oliver accused and convicted of murder and hanged. After an eternity he stripped Fanny's robe from her back, dropped his trousers and rubbed himself against her body. Fanny shuddered, not only because of the naked indecency but because of the violation of her as a woman. With some effort, Briley managed to raise his aging dick and, when set, turned her around and forced her to lie across a barrel. He fumbled, trying a second and third time to make entry, and when he finally found his way, he held her hips with his big hands and thrust hard, scrubbing her breasts against the barrel with each stroke. Oliver, from his hiding place behind a rack of bottles, could see all and hear the 'slop, slop' of Briley's thighs slapping against Fanny's buttocks. He wanted to grab the oaf of a man and bash him to death but, suspecting that other police were close by, he stayed hidden. Briley ground away for ages, rising and falling, trying desperately to prove himself. Fanny, terrified of the repercussions if he were unsuccessful, worked her crotch and thighs, squeezing hard, bringing him on. He adjusted to the rhythm, strengthened more with each stroke until, with a final thrust, he gushed and unloaded into her.

While Fanny distracted Briley, Sassy engaged the other grub of a man in conversation at the bar. The long-time bachelor, with a predisposition for alcohol and fancy women, made the best of his time, downing free drinks and enjoying the titillating talk till, eventually, Briley returned and, after a quick rum each, they left by the front door. Sassy watched to be sure they would not double back, and when they disappeared around the corner into Queen Street she bolted the door and ran to the cellar where she found Fanny in a terrible state with Oliver bending over, trying to console her. Fanny sat naked on the cold paving stones, sobbing and quivering, unable to speak a word. The ordeal had shaken her to the core, not only because of the abuse she sustained but also the embarrassment she felt from Oliver having witnessed her bring on the vilest of men. Sassy, guessing what had happened, knelt by her side, wrapped the robe around her to give some dignity, and held her in her arms, hugging her and whispering words of reassurance. Fanny's composure slowly returned and, when she regained enough control, Sassy and Oliver helped her to her feet and assisted her to her bedroom.

Fanny, looking wretched and still crying, put a hand to Oliver's face and begged him to leave, to save himself. Oliver responded by taking Fanny into his arms and hugging her as best he could with his cracked ribs. He refused to leave her side and said, 'No, my darling. What you did for me is beyond anything a man could expect. If I only get one shot it will be to drop that mongrel who raped you.'

Sassy, seeing them entangled in an emotional spill and unable to think clearly, left them on the bedside and hurried away.

Word of the bashing incident soon spread the length of the waterfront and, as was the custom, members of the waterside fraternity closed ranks. They tied the police in knots, giving false witness accounts that varied from denying any knowledge of the assault to asserting that two policemen had been seen bashing a stranger with their nightsticks. This code of solidarity and the contempt shown towards police riled the law enforcers, making it imperative that Oliver be smuggled out before a new wave of police descended upon the riverside and revisited the inn. Sassy sent a messenger running, and within the hour Conrad Huxley, cartage contractor and a man known for his loyalty to the wharf traders, appeared on the wharf decking with his two draft horses pulling a half-laden cart. He reined in by the front of the inn and, after a brief word with Sassy, manoeuvred the cart, with the horses taking the strain on the pole shaft and backing the cart into the alley beside the inn. Sassy, together with some patrons who were in the know, crowded about, lifting empty barrels to the wagon. When nearly done and upon a signal from a lookout man, Sassy brought Oliver from the inn and, with the help of a couple of strong men, they lifted him, together with his bag and case, into the cart. Within moments of his being loaded, a tarpaulin was lashed securely across the load. Conrad then set the wheels of the cart turning, rolled across the wharf decking to the junction with Queen Street and continued along that street, passing a contingent of armed police heading towards the river. The evacuation, so quick and clever, escaped the attention of Rusty who had been prowling the wharf, hoping for a sighting or a snippet of information.

The boss of Hanson's Livery stable helped Oliver board the sulky and then, as he brushed his hand across the grey's forelock, said, 'Good to see you have the grey. With this storm approaching it could be a rough ride home.'

The gathering storm, building against the mountains of the Great Divide, blanketed the sun, creating an eerie feeling of abandonment. The tall gums, usually bright and majestic beneath the summer's sun, stood dull and listless in the calm before the storm. Kangaroos took refuge in sheltered rifts of the landscape while birds of many colours took flight to faraway places. At the Crystalbrook crossing Harry Fritz had secured his tent with additional stays and ropes. Oliver's condition had worsened as the hours passed and, if he had seen Harry, he would have asked for sanctuary. He considered the option briefly but then, at the insistence of the grey horse champing at the bit, he decide to take his chances and press on, hoping to reach Sorrento before the storm struck. Each time the sulky's wheels crashed into a deep rut or rocky washout the bump shot searing pains across Oliver's chest, causing him to let go of the reins and hold his chest. Blinding lightning strikes and deafening claps of thunder closed in, sending shivers of fear through the spines of both man and beast. When halfway to Sorrento, the storm struck with ferocity seldom witnessed, battering Oliver and the grey with hailstones that cut into the flesh. Oliver, crippled from the pain of his injuries and the cutting blows of the ice, dropped the reins and huddled on the seat. The grey, though stricken with fear, stood by his master, pressing through the blinding hail with his head down and, when the rain followed and the road washed with torrents of rushing water, he picked his way safely through the flooded crossings.

By the time they reached the turn into Sorrento the storm had passed, leaving in its wake sodden earth, grass laid flat and debris strewn across the carriageway leading to the homestead. The grey, spotted with blood stains from the biting hail, lengthened his stride and, when the homestead came into sight, whinnied loudly, alerting all to their arrival. Seamus, hearing the familiar whinny, left the forge where he had been shaping a ploughshare and stood in his smithy's apron ready to greet Oliver with a hearty welcome and to groom Oliver's favourite horse—the dappled grey. Thruppence, up to his ankles in mud and squish, left off sorting the goats into their pens and stood high on a rail and waved. Marcella, who had been bottle feeding a kid goat, forgot her mothering for the moment and turned her attention to Oliver's homecoming. Nellie came to the veranda and, upon seeing Oliver slouched in the seat, murmured a silent prayer before lifting the hem of her long skirt above the wet grass and crossing to the stables.

'No, not drunk,' replied Oliver when Seamus asked the obvious question.

All gathered around and, upon realising that Oliver had been bashed, a sombre mood replaced the joy of moments ago. With help from Seamus, Oliver lowered himself from the sulky and hobbled to the house with Nellie and Marcella by his side. The evening took on a sullen mood, with Oliver brooding over a cup of tea, Nellie watching him anxiously and Marcella wondering what the future might hold. Soon after they retired to bed, Marcella heard groans coming from Oliver's bedroom, intermittent but agonising enough to hold her from sleep. She lay there till the chimes of the clock struck midnight and then, with thoughts of Oliver lying alone and maybe dying, she did the forbidden and crept along the dark hallway towards his bedroom. The show of light from a candle inside cast an eerie glow that filtered through the partly closed door and spilt to the hallway floor. Marcella, dressed in a flimsy nightdress, held her hand to her heart as she approached barefoot. If she were discovered spying on the Master in his bedroom, would she be punished, receive a flogging, and be sent away? She dared not think. At the door, with the light showing her front, she craned her neck and peeped inside. To her shock and bewilderment she saw Oliver lying bare chested, propped up on pillows, and Nellie sitting beside him on the bed, sponging his forehead. Marcella knew that Nellie cared for him but had never seen any indication of intimacy, no suggestive words, no touching. Seeing them now, with Oliver lying there with his eyes closed and Nellie caring for him tenderly, she wondered whether they were secret lovers, lying together at night and deceiving outsiders by day. When Oliver lifted a hand and Nellie clasped it in hers, Marcella felt a pang of jealousy. Her lips tightened, tears began to well in her eyes and, to shut out painful possibilities, she took one last look and then turned and crept back to her bedroom.

At breakfast the next morning, Oliver sat at the table and spoke about his sore ribs but made no mention of Nellie having assisted. Nellie, dressed in the same garish crinoline that she wore every day, went about her kitchen duties as though nothing had happened during the night. The more Marcella pondered the situation, the more possessive she became.

CHAPTER 6

Messages had passed to and fro between Oliver and Angus Buchanan, the shipping agent, and the first mate, finalising preparations to sail to the South Pacific islands to procure a shipload of Islanders. With this voyage promising to yield a handsome profit, Oliver decided to visit Brisbane to check that all was in order. While Nellie and Seamus knew the purpose of the trip, Thruppence and Marcella had not been informed. Thruppence had only deduced that the Master was going to sea and would be away for a long time. Marcella, being a member of the household, had gleaned more, and although scant on detail she knew that the planned voyage was to the islands and involved Islanders.

Nellie packed Oliver's bag, and when he was about to leave the house she touched him on the shoulder, wished him well and watched as this man who had provided her with security and shelter for many years walked to the waiting sulky. Marcella, concerned for Oliver's safety, wanted to give him a hug for good luck, but with a kid goat between her knees and a bottle of milk in her hands she settled for calling, wishing him well. Seamus gave Oliver a leg-up to the sulky and said, 'Make sure the livery man gives the grey the best stall.' Thruppence stood by the brook, watering the goats, and when he saw the grey break into a trot he waved his hat as a goodbye to the Master.

Though Oliver had said little about the beating he suffered when last in Brisbane he had brooded about it and, once on the road, alone and heading back to the scene of the strife, he, for the first time he could ever remember, became unsure of himself. He had been in threatening situations before, even having looked down the barrel of a gun, but for some lurking reason the altercation on the wharf left him unnerved. The whole fracas—the confrontation, the mulatto bashing a man to death and Fanny's rape at the hands of a perverted officer of the law—left him wondering about the near future, let alone the long term. As he approached Brisbane his mind turned back to the purpose at hand, and by the time the grey horse had been stabled and he caught a cab to town, these nagging thoughts had been set aside.

Sassy spotted him first and rushed to tell Fanny to give her time to dress, brush her hair and apply powder, rouge and lipstick. Oliver, with his bag and case, entered the open doors to the bar room, plonked his baggage on the bar and ordered a rum. Fanny, as bright and vivacious as ever, soon appeared and, with unabashed glee, swung her arms about Oliver's neck and planted a smoochy kiss on his lips. This brought relief because, of all the concerns that Oliver had about the bashing incident, Fanny's recovery and frame of mind remained the most important. After a few rums, he and Fanny retired to her bedroom suite to reengage and strengthen bonds. At Fanny's insistence, Oliver stayed in her room and slept under her watchful eye.

The next morning, Angus Buchanan extended a warm welcome, and before long he and Oliver were conniving, not only about the forthcoming trip to the islands, but also planning further trips to capture the labour market while the planters were keen to buy and had the cash to pay. The avarice could be clearly seen, with Angus leaning forward with an ear cocked and Oliver, equally engaged, speaking in a low tone so as not to be overheard by some honest member of the Crown who might have an ear to the door. More gold passed hands and, when leaving, Oliver commented, 'You look after the law and I'll handle the trade!'

Reg Brixton, the shipping agent, shuffled around in his grubby office, making room for Oliver when he arrived unannounced. All had gone well with the shipping of building materials from Sydney and, from what Reg said, this fill-in work between trips to the islands would last indefinitely. Money, money and more money rolled before Oliver's eyes as he and Reg schemed how best to schedule operations for the next twelve months. Neither made any mention of the government announcement that restrictions on the 'Island Trade' were to be tightened. They pursued their aim of maximising their gains while the *Imperial Slavery Act* could still be circumvented. After a second cup of tea and a plan set in place, Oliver bid him good day. Oliver then, as a security measure, took a cab directly to the wharf, where the *Trade Winds* lay berthed.

The first mate, having been advised of Oliver's visit, bristled with excitement as he told of the success of the recent voyages to Sydney. Then, with the departure to the islands only days away, final arrangements were made for provisioning the ship for a two-month voyage and the employment of hardy sailors who could keep their mouths shut if interrogated by the authorities. While on board, Oliver stowed the papers that he would have to complete upon acquiring the natives. When closing the compartment beneath what had been Marcella's bunk his thoughts turned to her and something he intended doing before leaving Sorrento.

Fanny, still fresh and wanting, smiled when Oliver returned to the inn, sober and before dark. That night he broached the subject of her having been molested by that monster of a policeman and in reply Fanny said, 'Darling, let's put it aside and enjoy the night.'

Before leaving the next morning, Sassy called Oliver aside and told him that within an hour of his escaping the police had raided the inn.

Oliver, not realising the matter had gone this far and not wanting to implicate Fanny, replied, 'She's not responsible for this. I'll go and talk with her.'

'No, please don't. She will only worry more. I'm here to back her, and believe me I have enough on the police to blow the local cop shop apart. If it's trouble they want then they haven't seen anything till Sassy Maloney cuts loose.'

Oliver, seeing the fire in her eyes, the flash of her teeth and her flaming red hair toss about as she spoke, thought there was no room for argument and agreed to let the matter rest.

When departing, Oliver hugged Fanny dearly to show that he truly cared and, as he turned to leave, declared, 'I'll be back from the voyage as soon as I can. If things get out of hand send a message to Seamus. He'll sort the rats in this place.'

Fanny, knowing what this waterside talk meant and drawing some solace from the assurance, watched as Oliver mounted the cab. On the journey home, Oliver again fell into a melancholy mood, not only about his previous concerns but now more so about Fanny and her safety. Upon arrival he made jolly, greeting the men and hugging the women. As usual Nellie served a delicious roast dinner for the evening meal, and afterwards they sat together by the hearth, enjoying a toddy before retiring for the night. Marcella tossed long into the night, romancing about Oliver and how she wanted to make love with him before he left for the islands in four days' time.

Marcella had taken an interest in a pile of fashion magazines that Ivana had stashed in the bottom of a cupboard. She often thumbed the pages, amazed by how well society ladies presented themselves. She gloated over the pictures of the crinoline and satin, ribbons and bows, bodices and bustles, together with stylish coiffure and glittering accessories that distinguished the ladies of the courts of England and Europe and, in more recent times, the theatres of Sydney and homes of the gentry in Brisbane. In secret, Marcella had tried on most of the garments that lined the racks of Ivana's wardrobes, sorting what she thought to be most stylish and then parading before the full-length mirror with only herself as the private audience. Her hair, well-groomed and held in place with hairclips, would soon be long enough to style like the ladies in the magazines, and already her nails, rounded and polished, equalled anything she had seen in the books. All that remained was to impress Oliver and, to this end, she dressed elegantly for dinner on each of the three nights prior to his departure.

Nellie noticed and, realising that Marcella was fast becoming a woman, did nothing to discourage her. Oliver, stirred by Marcella's comely appearance, showered her with compliments. On the third night, when Nellie was in the kitchen dishing the sweets, Oliver leant forward and took the amethyst pendant in his hand. After holding it in his palm and gazing into Marcella's eyes longingly, he returned the pendant to her cleavage, leaving his hand resting against her bosom momentarily. Following dinner and the customary nightcap together, Nellie, sensing this to be Marcella's night, conveniently excused herself and went to her bedroom. Oliver moved close to Marcella, took her hand and, with kisses and nibbles, stole his way to her lips. Upon feeling his moist lips on hers Marcella surrendered, wrapping her arms around Oliver and squeezing him tightly. With the acceptance readily forthcoming, Oliver slipped a hand to her breasts, toying with both and fondling the nipples. With further stroking, and eventually a hand between Marcella's thighs, both knew there could be no turning back. Hand in hand, and with Oliver holding a lighted lamp, they passed quietly along the hallway and into Marcella's bedroom, the one that was once shared by Oliver and Ivana.

Marcella, having only an intuitive sense of what would follow, let Oliver take the lead. He turned her around, unlaced her dress and let it fall to the floor, leaving her naked to the waist. With loving kisses he made his way around till he took her breasts, one then the other, sucking hard, arousing her to heights that guaranteed she would not resist. Marcella, while kissing Oliver tenderly, stroked his shoulders and back, approving his intention.

With the lamp turned high on the bedside dresser and Marcella in full view, Oliver pulled her drawers part way down and then indicated for her to strip altogether. With love-light in her eyes, she bent her knees and removed the last of her clothing, revealing the magic of an island beauty. They embraced while Oliver stroked her buttocks and then slid his hand to her crotch, where he fumbled till gaining entry. Marcella opened her thighs, allowing for more, till the force of his fingers caused a sharp pain that made her flinch. Oliver murmured an apology, withdrew his fingers and, after more kisses and gentle fondling, edged her to the bed and lay her on her back in the lamplight. He then positioned himself so Marcella could see and proceeded to undress, removing shirt, trousers and underwear, leaving him fully naked. He stood, with his erection foremost, allowing Marcella to stare and imagine, to ignite the spirit that she thought would unite them for all time.

When Oliver stepped forward, she, though only sixteen years of age, held out her arms to accept him as a man about to honour her in the most profound way. As Oliver's body shadowed the lamplight and she felt his weight on her thighs, she thought that, in the next moments, her life would be made complete. There were no wild thrusts, just a gentle nudging until he began to penetrate. Even then he resisted any sudden move that could shock or cause undue pain, edging in and out to ease the way. When fully embraced, they kissed and murmured sweet words before Oliver began to engage further, with gentle stroking. Marcella took what was delivered, not without pain, but with love. She did not know what to expect and, for a fleeting moment, wondered how long it would take and how it would end. When the rhythm strengthened and she thought he could go no faster, she sensed a climax and, when he jerked and groaned, she took this to be the consummation of their love for one another. Oliver held his position till the urge subsided and then withdrew and lay on his back, panting, with his big belly rising with each breath. Marcella put her soreness aside and basked in what she thought would be a life together. Oliver lay for a few minutes, holding Marcella's hand, and then rolled over and kissed and fondled some more before picking up his clothes and leaving the room, naked.

Nellie rose early to prepare breakfast, and when Oliver and Marcella entered the kitchen soon after sunrise she greeted them with a knowing smile. While Oliver appeared nonchalant, his attentiveness to Marcella during breakfast revealed otherwise. Marcella could not contain herself and, after giving Oliver a passionate kiss and a lasting hug, she sat close by his side till a whinny from the stables reminded them that Seamus would have the grey harnessed and waiting. Nobody ever wanted to see Oliver go, not even for short trips to Brisbane, let alone two months at sea. With Oliver seated and Seamus at the reins, Nellie, Marcella and Thruppence waved as the grey found his stride, taking Oliver away into the unknown. Marcella, overcome with emotion, watched till the sulky disappeared into the woodland and then turned to Nellie for comfort. She buried her head into the folds of Nellie's dress and wept, while whispering about what had happened the previous night. When Thruppence lost sight of the Master he tried to cover his sadness by leaving their side and turning the goats out to pasture. When the crying settled to whimpers, Marcella stripped the sheets from her bed and took them to be washed. Nellie watched as Marcella struggled to carry large buckets of water from the well to the copper boiler in the garden. When she lit the fire beneath the boiler and began to load the linen, Nellie left the kitchen window and went to help. She took the soap from Marcella's hands, found the blood marks on the sheets and rubbed them between her soapy palms before the water became hot.

Oliver called at the Mariners Inn where he spoke to Fanny briefly while Seamus waited outside. Upon leaving, he gave Fanny a kiss on the cheek, asked her to think of him and then, with Seamus by his side, strode along the wharf like a man in command and boarded his ship *Trade Winds*.

CHAPTER 7

After a steam tugboat had towed the *Trade Winds* to midstream and the sails were unfurled, the helmsman manoeuvred the ship down the Brisbane River and to the open sea. Oliver loved the sea: the freedom, the challenges and the opportunity to exploit the riches of the new world. Of all the ventures he had profited from, the trade in human flesh held the most promise. With his man-o'-war, armed with four carriage cannons, a crew of men as tough as barnacles, and an assorted armoury, ranging from cutlasses and muskets to modern weaponry of rifles and revolvers, he rode on the high seas with seldom a challenger. Time and again seafarers had given way, all except Captain Scarface, the notorious buccaneer who pillaged the South Sea Islands and plundered ships less daring than he and the crew. Twice, he and Oliver had come into close-quarters battle with cannonballs smashing holes through hulls and grapeshot shredding sails. On the first occasion, when Scarface's crew tried to board from whaleboats, Oliver's crew blasted them while in the water, leaving only a few to abandon their boats and swim. The aggrieved Scarface swore vengeance and, upon sighting Oliver off Nouméa, launched an immediate attack, smattering the *Trade Winds* with cannon fire. Oliver, though undermanned and outgunned, fought back, vowing to fight to the last man and to scuttle the ship if all else failed. For two hours the battle raged, with puffs of smoke clouding the decks with each shot fired. Oliver, now out of cannonballs and facing imminent defeat, uttered a word of thanks to the Almighty when a French naval patrol appeared on the horizon. His men, now armed with hand guns and flashing blades of steel, also saw the French frigate closing the distance under full sail. They fired gun shots and fought hand to hand with cutlasses, trying to save the ship as Scarface's crew mounted

79

the gunnels. Oliver, having emptied his revolver, threw it to the deck and drew his sabre. He had lost three men, with more under dire threat, when a broadside cannonball from the French ship hit Scarface's vessel on the waterline, causing it to take water. Scarface, now in danger of sinking, recalled his men, manned the pumps and sailed away with his ship listing heavily to the port side. Though Oliver's ship had been saved, he knew that next time he might not be so lucky.

In spite of Oliver's shortfalls, he did play an astute hand when conducting business. His appetite for risk and shrewd dealings had, time and again, yielded returns that the common man would consider a fortune. He approached the procurement of Islanders with the same discerning mind—soft talk and deception rather than force and coercion. His reputation as a reliable supplier of cheap labour had grown and, by continuing with his practice of enticement, he hoped to double his annual trade. During the voyage where he had traded copra and kidnapped Marcella he had endeared himself to island chiefs by showering them with gifts. He also seeded the idea of taking tribesmen to the mainland where they would work for white planters for a time and then return, laden with riches. Some of the chiefs had agreed and, as binding tokens of trust, were each given a whale tooth talisman similar to the one Oliver wore around his neck.

The *Trade Winds*, a fine sailing ship, crewed by master seamen, reached New Caledonia in the near record time of seven days. With time costing money, particularly feeding the Islanders when taken aboard, Oliver dropped anchor at the island of Mare on the day of arrival. These friendly natives, who plotted time by phases of the moon and the seasons, had been expecting Oliver's return and greeted him with enthusiasm. They invited Oliver and a few senior crew members to an island *sing-sing*, and when Oliver strummed his ukulele into the night, playing South Sea tunes, some thought him to be a spiritual incarnation. The next day Oliver, together with his interpreter, explained the deal. At every turn Oliver spoke in glowing terms of life on plantations and assured them that they would be comfortably housed, well fed, have access to medical attention and that they would be returned to their islands with riches in hand. Once the recruits were convinced, gifts were offered to the chief and associates of the recruits to gain their approval. Within four days, fifteen males, aged sixteen to thirty, had agreed and planted 'X' on a document they did not comprehend and which carried only their name, estimated age and island of origin. This stopover was the most important because, at subsequent stops, this show of men on board would induce others to join what they thought to be an opportunity to better themselves and provide for their loved ones left at home.

From here Oliver navigated northwards, stopping at other villages of the Loyalty Group of islands. He dearly wished to visit Lifou but, fearing he would be murdered by members of Marcella's people, he sailed on to the New Hebrides islands. Here he stopped at the islands of Tanna, Erromango, Efate, Tongoa, Epi and Espiritu Santo, bringing his number to 140, which was 10 short of his target.

He then ventured further northwards to the Solomon Islands of Guadalcanal and Malaita in the hope of bringing the number of labourers on board to 150. From the reception he received, either he had been misinformed or recent traders had marred the relationship with the locals. At Guadalcanal, Oliver and his crew were ambushed when what appeared to be a group of friendly natives waved for them to come ashore, only to meet them with arrows raining down. One crewman was wounded, fortunately by an arrow without a poison tip. The landing at Malaita proved to be more treacherous, with the natives waiting till the landing party had stepped ashore and then showering them with a flurry of arrows from within a coconut grove. If it had not been for the crack of repeated rifle fire from the crew on the covering whaleboat, all would most likely have met their deaths there on the pearly beach.

After five weeks at sea and with 140 natives on board, the *Trade Winds* set sail for Port Mackay, a small frontier town 460 nautical miles north of Brisbane. While procuring the natives had been successful, there remained the challenge of delivering the cargo in good order and negotiating a high price. Space was scarce with 140 natives and 30 crew on board and, in addition to this, all had to be fed, bedded and, if possible, harmony maintained. The ship's galley alone kept six cooks fully occupied, preparing meals consisting of a basic diet of pickled pork, yams, rice and cocoa-nuts. With the ship requiring daily maintenance and three shifts needed to man the vessel, the crew had little time to spare. Oliver regularly stood on the quarterdeck, casting about and issuing orders.

Upon boarding the ship, each of the natives was issued with shirt, trousers and a blanket and given strict instruction that no disturbance would be tolerated. To reinforce this directive, an armed guard kept watch from the quarterdeck throughout the day and night. With intertribal fighting always a problem, the guard was instructed to shoot at his discretion in the event of riotous behaviour. Under no circumstance was he to go below deck to sort a dispute. The issued instruction was to shoot from the open hatch to maim the culprits.

With these precautions in place, the natives proved to be compliant throughout the voyage. Many looked towards the horizon with expectation of a better life ahead, while others took the fatalistic view that this was their destiny. The accommodation below deck remained cramped so, to alleviate this situation, many of the recruits slept on deck and, when sea spray showered across the deck, they covered themselves with tarpaulins. During the day, almost all spent their time on deck, engaging in talk about the Great South Land. When Oliver stood on the quarterdeck during the day, wearing his three-cornered hat, the 'boys', as they were called, were reminded of his authority. He often gazed down on those on the deck in a quixotic way, imagining himself as some sort of hero, risking all to provide barbarians with a better life. He dwelt on their shiny black bodies glistening under the burning sun, admiring their muscular strength, bold facial profiles and fuzzy hair. Some adorned themselves with arm and head bands, together with shell necklaces; others with feathers or braids in their hair. While some wore the clothes that had been issued, most wore loin cloths or the traditional waist girdle.

They made good time skating across the Coral Sea and arrived at the mouth of the Pioneer River in mid-March 1871. Oliver hailed a schooner operator who earned a living by ferrying cargo and passengers upstream to the fledgling port of Mackay. Yes, for five shillings, he would promptly deliver a message to the government immigration inspector stationed in the town.

The note read:

To: The Inspector of Immigration

Dear Sir,

I believe that you have been advised of my arrival with labourers for the sugar plantations.

I have 140 healthy men on board and wish to put them to auction.

The sooner the better, so please advise of the earliest suitable date.

I will stand-off in deep water at the mouth of the river till the due date.

Yours faithfully,
Captain Oliver Morgan,
Master of the *Trade Winds*.

Within a few hours Oliver received a reply:

Captain Morgan,

I have been expecting your arrival and have already advised the planters.

I have scheduled the auction for 11:00 am Friday this week and will immediately dispatch a notice to interested parties.

With the river being unnavigable for ships of your size I will arrange for four schooners to shuttle the men to the wharf on the morning of the auction.

Yours,
Arnold Hides

The hot, dusty streets and rough-hewn weatherboard buildings of the colonial settlement stood almost abandoned as the town's people crowded the wharf for a view. Even the butcher closed the doors of his sweat-shop butchery. The auctioneer, the local livestock agent, dressed special for the occasion, with his pressed shirt and trousers giving some respectability to an otherwise unscrupulous dealer. Four policemen stood at the ready in case of trouble.

Plantation owners from near and far arrived in river boats, sulkies and on horseback. They presented themselves as a varied assortment of landholders: The menfolk, dressed in everything from white moleskin trousers, vests, cravats and pith helmets, to the less haughty who wore gabardines, spurs and felt hats. The ladies accompanying their husbands took the opportunity to show their status by wearing fancy hats, lacey crinolines and, in one case, a full bustle.

The auctioneer's list of bidders included:

- Andrew Rushmore and his wife Atlanta of Rosewood plantation, who owned 1,280 acres of prime river land with a sugar milling factory and about 100 indentured island labourers.
- Louis and Antoinette Rousseau of Savannah plantation, the largest estate in the Pioneer Valley, regularly played host to members of the gentry visiting the district. They housed 130 indentured labourers and milled their own sugar cane and that of others.
- Barnaby Argent, Director General of the Lands Office. He and his son George recently purchased two adjoining selections on the south side with a combined acreage of 2,560 acres. George, the manager, boasted of big plans for the property.
- Jack Marshall, formerly of Jamaica, a bachelor man with a penchant for the company of black women.
- Timothy Randal, a remittance man from England with more money at his disposal than common sense.
- Rosette Thomas, a spinster with a vision of Utopia who cared as much about her indentured labourers as she did about her plantation.
- Rory Bullimore of Clarendon Estate, a small cane grower neighbouring Savannah plantation with an agreement for Savannah to mill his cane.
- Donald Fraser, an ambitious middle-aged man with a reputation for driving his workers like yoked cattle.

As each load of Islanders landed at the wharf they were quarantined to be sorted before allowing interested buyers to inspect. With Oliver supervising, they were matched by age and physique and, in some instances, tribal lineage, and then divided into groups of marketable size with the names of those in each group being noted. Once classified and given a final word about good behaviour, they stood in lots ranging from five to fifteen, ready to be inspected. With a blanket roll as their only possession, these men stood intimidated, frightened, humiliated and bewildered as the planters pointed and whispered as to their attributes and what they might fetch at auction. One lad, barely sixteen, burst into tears and had to be moved aside. Another, grieving for his family, pulled free and managed to swim partway across the river before being caught.

At sale time the auctioneer shouted, 'Saleo. Saleo ...'

He announced the terms of the sale and then called for Lot 1 to be brought forward. These men, once proud warriors, kings of the sea with families left behind on the seashore, stood in silence as starting bids opened for each Lot and quickly rose to £9, £10, £11 and, in some instances, £12 per head.

All Lots were sold, and at closure of the sale the purchasers signed for their stock and took the new recruits away by various means. Some found themselves transported upstream in punts, others loaded to horse-drawn wagons and ox carts, while the remainder trudged bush tracks for miles with white overseers riding on horseback behind to ensure their stock did not stray. These men, with their rights flouted and little recourse to justice, could only hope for benevolent masters.

The only upset during the auction occurred when Isobel Ruskin stepped forward, waved her parasol and shouted, 'Slavery! This is legalised slavery ...' As a strict Quaker and a member of the Abolitionist Movement of England, she pursued her mission to stamp out the practice of procuring Islanders by deception and thrusting them into slave-like servitude for the customary period of three years. Since taking residence in Mrs Smith's boarding house three months earlier, she had raised hackles by writing to the colonial secretary, complaining about the treatment of Islanders on Donald Fraser's plantation. The planters, seeing this as a threat to the viability of their businesses, approached the police with a view to having her silenced. To everyone's surprise they soon learned that this middle-aged spinster, who cared little about her appearance, had previously been a solicitor practising with a reputable law firm in London and had, in a few words, put the police in their place.

Oliver and the crooked immigration inspector stood at a bench in the inspector's office sorting the indenture forms according to which planter took which Islanders. They then commenced filling in details of the terms and conditions of what was supposed to be a contractual arrangement between the planters and the individual Islanders. The Islanders, with no knowledge of English law, only able to speak Pidgin and unable to read or write were completely ignorant of what the planters considered to be a commitment bound by law. Further, if an Islander did not conform to what Oliver and the inspector wrote into the indenture they could be found guilty of breach of contract and jailed. Such was the bogus means by which the planters, in collaboration with the Queensland Colonial Government, obtained cheap labour to work their fields.

During Oliver's absence from home, some spooky events occurred late at night.

Two nights after Oliver's departure, Marcella heard the distinctive clunk of the kitchen door being unbolted. *Opened from the inside*, she thought and presumed that Nellie needed to go outside. Moments later she heard the mumbled voice of a male and the door being closed. Marcella's thoughts raced, trying to fathom the situation. With only she and Nellie in the house it must be Nellie but who else? Who would Nellie unbolt the door for in the dead of night? The Rottweilers had not barked, leaving only Seamus and Thruppence as possible suspects. She imagined Nellie dressed in her frumpy nightdress and wearing that horrid nightcap pulled low over her forehead.

The silence returned as quickly as it had been broken, leaving Marcella baffled and curious as she strained to hear more. The eeriness became more maddening by the minute until, unable to resist anymore, she slipped from the bed cover, braced herself and, step by step, crept down the hallway. When in the dining room, a faint show of candlelight from the hallway leading to Nellie's bedroom drew her forward. Halfway along she stalled, feeling the guilt that comes from prying. She thought that to listen but not see would be only a half wrong and listened intently to the voices—that of Nellie and the other of an unknown. She promised herself that, if she could identify the male, she would leave them be and forget the whole thing. Easy to say, but when the bed posts began clicking and Nellie called for more, Marcella's resolve gave way. Feeling the pulse of the vibrations coming from within the room and the need to look, if indeed not participate, she sneaked the last few paces and peeped through the large keyhole. There he was, the man, stark naked, lying on top of Nellie and driving his buttocks as hard as he could. All she could see of Nellie was her nightcap covering her head, her nightdress pulled above her breasts and her legs high in the air. Marcella became engaged, entangled in the passion of the moment, and wished it were her lying on the bed. So taken, so consumed was she that she held her position on bended knee till the male lover reached a crescendo and then, with a violent burst of energy, jammed Nellie so hard that Marcella thought she would break in two.

They lay joined, locked together for a minute or so, and when the male rolled from Nellie's body and sat on the side of the bed Marcella wanted to reach for him. Never had she imagined that the polite Seamus could release such fury and passion. She could not take her eyes from his body, even after Nellie had risen and pulled her nightdress into place. What Marcella had witnessed and could still see roused her beyond her wildest dreams. He was younger, more agile and passionate than Oliver! When Seamus dressed and prepared to leave, Marcella stole back to her room, lay on the bed covers and fantasised about making love with Seamus.

In the weeks that followed, Marcella listened for the sound of the back door opening and closing. It occurred twice a week and, as before, she crept to the door each time and spied on them through the keyhole. While watching, she touched herself, sharing in the joy being felt by Nellie. What confounded Marcella most of all was why did Nellie not completely strip herself of her nightdress and cap to make a full offering?

Apart from Seamus' visits, another night was disturbed with nightmarish sounds coming from Nellie's room. Not wanting to interfere, Marcella held off from visiting her room till she could no longer ignore the screams. She then tiptoed to Nellie's bedroom and peeped through the keyhole.

At seeing Nellie she held her hand to her mouth to conceal the gasp. *Unbelievable*, she thought, adjusting herself on her knees and squinting for a better view of Nellie sitting on the bedside with her nightcap lying by her side. This view through the keyhole, though limited, revealed the naked truth of why Nellie always covered herself. To Marcella's horror, the back of Nellie's skull was hairless, with the scalp and nape of her neck severely scarred from burns. The sight, too grotesque to describe, held Marcella transfixed till Nellie put her head in her hands and began sobbing.

Marcella felt an urge to rush in and hug her, to provide comfort and an assurance that all would be right. Yet, she could not. Try as she did her hand refused to reach forward and open the door. She watched, stricken with pity as the women continued sobbing while murmuring something about her past. Marcella could faintly hear the garbled words spilling forth; something about 'Claude', about 'the drink', the 'kitchen hearth', her begging to be spared and then a tormented cry.

Marcella continued peering through the keyhole till she saw Nellie take the lighted lamp from the bedside and hold the hot glass close to her cheek. Thinking Nellie was about to self-harm, Marcella made a dash to save her. She flung the door open, raced to Nellie's side and, without notice, grabbed the lamp from her hand. This bold move snapped Nellie's hysteria. She became silent and sat staring at the blank wall until Marcella wrapped her arms around her and held tightly. When Nellie's anxiety eased and she began to look around, Marcella quietly reached for Nellie's nightcap and placed it on her head. This single act of kindness meant more to Nellie than anything and, in return, she hugged Marcella and said, 'Thank you, my darling.'

It was then that Nellie told Marcella the whole story: Nellie's former husband, in a fit of drunken rage, had taken a pot of hot fat from the stove top and tipped it over her head, causing disfigurement and mental trauma from which Nellie had not and would never recover. The scars would carry the memory and torment till the day she died. She had not been believed at the time. Her rag of a husband lied about the incident. An accident, he told those at the Horseshoe Inn. Self-defence when she attacked him with a fire poker, he told others. The police paid little attention to her complaint. She married a drunkard and so should bear the consequences, so the story went in police circles.

Vengeance also failed her, for when she later crept upon him in his sleep and crushed his skull with a hammer the police took this to be premeditated murder and charged her accordingly. With no legal representation and a bull-headed barrister as the prosecutor she crumbled in the witness stand, unable to provide any defence. The jury, left in a quandary due to Nellie's state of mind, tussled with the evidence for three days before issuing a verdict of manslaughter. The judge, having formed his own view of the chain of events, sentenced Nellie to only two years imprisonment. Upon release, Nellie, desperate for money to pay for food and lodgings, began walking the streets, prostituting herself for three shillings a time.

She met Oliver one night after he had left a vulgar dance hall where women undressed to music and offered themselves to the highest bidder. While staggering along the dock front he stumbled upon Nellie who, on the promise of being paid £1 for a night's service, accompanied him to Sorrento. All went well with them stripping by lamplight in the bedroom until Oliver, with little thought, insisted that Nellie remove her bonnet. She resisted, but, with a sweep of his hand, he swiped the bonnet from her head.

'No! No!' she cried, but too late. Oliver had seen the ghastly injury.

The revulsion of seeing an almost hairless women caused him to snap. He abused her, labelling her a 'whore' and a 'cheat'.

He then shouted, 'Go, get out of my sight!'

Nellie, fearing the situation would end in violence, quickly gathered her clothes and ran to the back door and, with no place to go, sheltered in the woodshed till morning. Oliver appeared early, expressed remorse and, having recently lost his previous housekeeper and because he was going to sea the next day, asked her to stay on to housekeep during his absence. Upon his return she offered herself to him but, still unable to stomach the prospect of laying her, he instead kept her on as housekeeper. This arrangement, now into its seventh year, worked well, with Nellie doing all except sharing Oliver's bed.

CHAPTER 8

After eight weeks at sea, the *Trade Winds* arrived home and berthed at Queens Wharf soon after sunrise. Oliver immediately sent a message to Seamus, and, when he arrived early in the afternoon, Oliver left the first mate to attend to the ship and set for home.

As they bumped along the pitted road towards Sorrento, Oliver told of the voyage, the number of natives secured and the prices received at the Mackay auction. Seamus listened, not only with interest but also with a sense of pride that his employer could command so many people. On approaching the homestead the grey, as usual, whinnied, alerting all to the homecoming.

'I haven't any gifts for the family. They'll have to wait till I go to town,' Oliver said by way of apology when Seamus drew rein at the water trough for the grey to have a drink. Thruppence saw them first and came running across the paddock, leaving Jock to watch over the goats. Marcella had swept the house while Nellie prepared pickled pork and vegetables for the evening meal. A sense of family and home drew them together, with Thruppence wringing Oliver's hand with a man's handshake. Marcella, dressed in stylish blouse and skirt, threw her arms about him and smacked a kiss on his lips. Nellie watched from the veranda, and when Oliver ascended the steps she came forward and put a cheek forward to receive his customary kiss.

During dinner, Oliver apologised again about the gifts and promised to make good when next in town. Marcella, with a mix of love and lust in her twinkling eyes, encouraged Oliver's attention whenever an opportunity arose. Nellie, happy for the couple, insisted on attending to the kitchen. With Nellie out of sight Marcella took a liberty, sat on Oliver's lap and snuggled close. Oliver slid the chair back to make room and, before long, had a hand on her breasts. Nellie smiled to herself when both called goodnight and announced they were going to bed. Keen to satisfy each other's needs, they went to Marcella's bedroom and, after a quick kiss and a cuddle, stripped and lay on the bed. Marcella, having learnt from her intimacy with Oliver and from watching Nellie and Seamus, obligingly spread her legs wide, and as Oliver lay on her she raised her legs high as she had seen Nellie do when she took Seamus' weight. They revelled in the lovemaking for minutes longer than last time and, when finished, Oliver, tired and worn, graciously excused himself and went to bed.

After breakfast the next morning, Oliver, keen to attend to his correspondence, excused himself, opened the French windows of his office and sat to sort the mail. A letter addressed to him with personalised handwriting and with no return address caught his attention. Upon opening it and seeing it signed by Fanny, he read the contents with mounting concern. The letter read:

Dear Oliver,

Much has happened since you went to sea.

Rusty has turned informant to the police, and between them they are after your hide.

For your own sake get rid of the Islander girl you have at Sorrento.

They know she is there and I am told they intend making a raid.

Briley has harassed me constantly for sex but I have resisted.

As much as I want to see you, please don't come to the inn. They have watchers everywhere.

Please burn this letter after you have read it.

Forever your darling,
Fanny

Nellie, who understood Oliver better than anyone, was the first to notice the change in his mood. He stayed in his office all morning and only briefly sat for lunch before disappearing again. Marcella remained oblivious to the change, attending to her looks and romancing about what she thought would be another blissful evening. Oliver stayed cloistered in his office throughout the afternoon, considering the contents of Fanny's letter. Fanny's words *for your own sake get rid of the Islander girl* worried him most. The affection that had been shown by Marcella burned deep, rattling his conscience and sense of decency. Time and again he picked up his pen to write to Reg Brixton, only to let the ink dry on the nib as thoughts of Marcella and her tenderness tumbled in his mind. Though little more than a child, she had found a way into his heart, and though he had turned away many women in the past, the thought of seeing her no more deeply troubled him. He knew what had to be done, but his hand froze each time he attempted to write. To blind his senses to the reality, he took a bottle of rum from a cabinet and drank, sculling the dark spirit by the mouthful.

Marcella, light and frivolous and full of expectation, presented herself in the kitchen well before dinner and busied herself helping Nellie prepare for what she thought would be another grand night. Nellie, having noted Oliver's reluctance to engage during lunch and his absence all afternoon, thought differently.

'Will I call Oliver?' said Marcella playfully when dinner was ready to be served.

'No, my sweet,' replied Nellie. 'Oliver is tired from being at sea. I'll go see.'

Marcella wanted to go too, but mindful that she had been forbidden from entering his office she occupied herself cleaning soot from the kitchen lamp. When partly done she heard Nellie call, 'Here, Marcella, quick!'

Marcella, shocked by the urgency of the call, let the lamp glass fall from her hands and smash on the table.

She rushed to the hallway to find Nellie staggering, trying to hold Oliver upright against the wall. Without any thought as to what might be wrong, she slipped under Oliver's other shoulder, and between them they managed to get him to his room and let him flop on the bed.

Marcella thought he was dying and, struck with fear, she backed away from the four-poster bed and stood horror stricken as Nellie straightened his body on the covers. All she had dreamed of—a future, a life together—now seemed lost.

She watched as Nellie, with practised hands, removed Oliver's boots and loosened his shirt and trousers. When Nellie turned and saw Marcella frightened and crying, she took her into her arms and explained, 'Oliver's drunk. Something has upset him. He'll be all right in the morning.'

Marcella wanted to watch over him during the night but, at Nellie's insistence, she returned to her room where she agonised all night. *Will he live or die? What has upset him? Will he still want me?* tossed in her mind till the brilliance of dawn and a cheerful call from Nellie eased her mind.

Oliver appeared mid-morning, morose and apologetic, and redeemed himself by thanking Nellie and, especially important to Marcella, giving Marcella a kiss on the forehead. Following a greasy breakfast of bacon and eggs, he pulled on his boots and went to the shed where he found Seamus repairing a harness. During their long conversation, Oliver handed Seamus two sealed letters, one addressed to Reg Brixton and the other to Fanny. Nellie, knowing something to be amiss and concerned for Oliver, watched from the kitchen window as Seamus saddled a horse and rode off towards Brisbane. Oliver returned to the house with a slowness to his gait and went to his office without saying anything further to the girls.

Seamus hitched his horse in front of Reg Brixton's office and entered to find Reg surrounded by a mountain of paperwork.

'I've always got time for Oliver,' replied Reg when Seamus asked if he could give Oliver's letter urgent attention. He would call again in a couple of hours to collect a reply.

Fanny welcomed Seamus with open arms before taking him aside, where they discussed the predicament surrounding the murder involving Oliver and what Fanny described as *that Islander girl*.

Seamus, roused by the situation, collected Reg Brixton's letter of reply and pressed hard to arrive at Sorrento with the horse in a lather of sweat.

Nellie looked at Seamus enquiringly when he handed her a sealed envelope addressed to Oliver. While the relationship between the two was close, it did not extend to Seamus divulging Oliver's business. Anything told to Nellie needed to come from Oliver who, so far, had said nothing about the predicament.

Oliver thanked Nellie with a nod when she handed him the letter in his office. The moment she left, he opened it and read:

Dear Oliver,

I understand what you say and, in fact, I have heard a snippet about the girl. She is now hot property with the police involvement and could be hard to place. However, I do have a client in Mackay who might be interested. The Rushmore family of Rosewood Plantation is wanting a housemaid, and from the description it has to be a young, presentable female.

They have a twenty-seven-year-old son who they want to marry off and I think this is what is behind the request. He is a malingerer with little chance of finding a white women, so they might well be interested in a mixed-race. Is she good looking and obedient?

If interested I can ship her out at a moment's notice, and if the Rushmores don't want her then, if she fits the description above, others will be interested. I know that Jack Marshall would take her on. He already has two or three living with him.

I'll await your advice,
Reg
PS What price range do you have in mind?

Oliver spoke further with Seamus when he received Reg's reply and said he would sleep on it and make a decision in the morning.

The evening meal proved to be sombre, with Oliver preoccupied with thought, Nellie's attempts at making conversation going nowhere and Marcella wishing Oliver's trouble would simply go away. Soon after the meal, Oliver excused himself and went to his bedroom.

Marcella, driven by desire, took a chance and asked Nellie, 'Do you think Oliver would mind if I went to his room.'

In reply Nellie said, 'My sweet, not tonight. Oliver has a lot on his mind.'

Marcella, exasperated at having to forfeit the night, went to her bedroom early, lay down and made make-believe love to Oliver.

Soon after breakfast the next morning, Seamus heard a cooee from Thruppence, closely followed by another and then another. Knowing this to be a signal that police were coming, Seamus raced out to see. With no one in sight, he returned two quick cooees for confirmation. There it came again: three distinct cooees from Thruppence.

Nellie also heard the calls and, knowing what the cooees meant, rushed to Oliver's office and spoke frantically, 'The police are here! Thruppence cooeed!'

With no police yet in sight and the confusion mounting, Seamus jumped on top of a water tank for a better view. Oliver scrambled to stash his paperwork in the chest while Nellie called to Marcella.

Seamus spotted them first, seven mounted police with rifles drawn, appearing from the cover of a thicket of trees on the eastern slope. The mounted troop broke into two, with three breaking into a canter and heading straight for Seamus at the shed, and the others making directly towards the homestead. Seamus, though unarmed, stood ready to defend himself against the British constabulary. *Ireland Forever* rang in his head as he recalled his father's last words before being gunned down in a back street of Belfast. His mother, who was subsequently found guilty of being part of the Irish Catholic uprising, was thrown into prison, never to be released alive. Never, while he could stand on two feet, would he submit.

When the first rider came within striking distance, Seamus reached to drag him from the saddle but was downed by a rifle barrel slamming him across the side of his head, leaving him unconscious.

Oliver clicked the lock of the chest closed and shouted, 'Nellie, where's Marcella?'

'Here with me in her bedroom,' came Nellie's panicked reply.

Upon entering Marcella's bedroom, Oliver quickly explained to them both, 'They've come for Marcella. They want to take her away!'

The women, shocked and dismayed, sought clarification. 'Why. Why do they want her?'

'Never mind. I'll explain later. You two clean up the room. Hide everything of Marcella's.'

Oliver then turned to Marcella and issued a firm instruction. 'When they come into the house, you hide in that cupboard.' He pointed to a heavy closet in the corner of the room. 'Pull the door shut and hold the latch. We'll let you know when they have gone.'

The other four troopers had reached the homestead and positioned themselves outside the picket fence, covering all sides of the house.

'Hurry,' urged Oliver, seeing the horsemen as he picked up Marcella's garments and stuffed them into drawers. When done, and after a quick glance around, he issued a final instruction to Marcella. 'Marcella, be sure to get into the cupboard. Nellie and I will meet the police and hopefully head them off.'

The police at the shed led their horses to the picket gate, hitched them to the fence and then entered the garden with rifles in hand and revolvers hanging from their belts.

After a short exchange of words between Nellie and Oliver, she went to the kitchen to busy herself as though unconcerned about the visitation. Oliver went to the door to greet the police with what courtesy he could muster under the circumstances. The police bypassed his attempt at appeasement, barged into the house and demanded he hand over the girl.

'What girl?' replied Oliver as though innocent of any wrongdoing. The senior sergeant, having been briefed and expecting a denial, brushed past Oliver and directed his men to search the house. While they searched, the sergeant began a detailed inspection of the dining room, noting the seating and cutlery setting for three. This find heightened his belief, leading him to Marcella's bedroom. Oliver, with a revolver tucked under his shirt, and Nellie, with a carving knife concealed in the pocket her apron, followed. If necessary, they would pounce on the officer who had foolishly separated himself from his colleagues.

The sergeant's interest deepened when he found oddments about the room that evidenced the presence of a young female. The duchesse, with an assortment of makeup and strands of colourful beads hanging from the mirror, girlish magazines lying in one corner of the room; all sorts of tell tales that he knew would not interest an old girl like Nellie.

He pointed to the cupboards and said to Nellie, 'What's in these?'

Nellie, managing to retain her composure in this dire situation, felt compelled to go all the way and politely replied, 'Just old clothes that belonged to Oliver's wife.'

The sergeant, fully expecting to find Marcella hidden inside one of the closets, began opening each. As he did, Oliver felt for his revolver, and Nellie, so protective of Marcella, held the handle of the knife, ready to strike when the discovery was made. When the sergeant went to open the last door, each braced themselves for the inevitable struggle that would follow. To their amazement and disbelief the closet revealed no more than clothes hanging on a rack. Marcella had vanished, but to where? How did this naïve island girl manage to escape with four mounted police stationed, one on each side of the house and keeping watch?

While the search continued, Oliver and Nellie exchange glances that told of their angst and fear that Marcella would be found somewhere else in the house. When done, the three officers, together with Oliver and Nellie, assembled in the dining room where the sergeant acknowledged that the girl had escaped, but also asserted the matter was not closed and that they would be back. When the police had ridden from sight, Thruppence helped the heavily concussed Seamus to his feet, and together they came to the house, where they joined Oliver and Nellie in the search for the mystery escapee. They soon found her in Oliver's office, sitting quietly at his desk. On seeing her, Nellie was the first to let go of her emotions, holding Marcella close like a precious doll. Oliver, beaming with admiration, followed with a hug that reassured Marcella he loved her. Thruppence just stood with a silly grin on his face. Seamus, holding his throbbing head, sat on the cast-iron chest, largely oblivious to the surrounds.

When the joy settled Nellie asked, 'How did you do it?'

Marcella, not thinking she had done anything special, explained that she could not bring herself to hide in the confined space of a cupboard so, while the mounted police officer guarding her side of the house busied himself lighting his pipe, she had, on hearing the sergeant approach her bedroom, simply stepped through the open French window to the veranda, took the few steps to Oliver's office and stepped through that window and into his office. Fortunately, the police had already searched that room and did not bother to return.

At that moment, all in the room marvelled at the ingenuity of this modest girl's daring and the calm with which she conducted her escape. While it should have been time for a celebration, Oliver, knowing this to be just the beginning of Marcella's evacuation and that it would be dangerous, kept a tight grip on his emotions.

Following the police raid, Oliver wrote a hurried note to Reg Brixton and dispatched it via Seamus who, though still very ill, saddled a horse and left at a canter:

> Dear Reg,
>
> Yes, I'll take the deal.
>
> The police raided my place this morning and, by a stroke of luck, missed the girl.
>
> When is the earliest you can ship her out?
>
> Best if it's done under cover.
>
> Oliver

Seamus sat in front of Reg's office while waiting for his reply that read:

> Dear Oliver,
>
> I have a schooner *Aquarius* that can accommodate her. It leaves No 4 wharf at 11:00 pm tomorrow.
>
> I will make arrangements with the captain. Can Seamus arrange for Fanny to be go-between with the transfer? She knows the police and their movements.
>
> Reg

Oliver received the reply, gave Seamus further instructions and, before breakfast the following morning, Seamus saddled a fresh horse and delivered Oliver's answer to Reg:

> Dear Reg,
>
> Yes, Seamus will speak to Fanny when in town this morning.
>
> Both Seamus and I will be there for the delivery.

The girl's name is Marcella. Will bring her on board just before castoff.

Many thanks,
Oliver

After leaving Reg's office, Seamus visited Fanny and told of the police raid and the proposed evacuation. She expressed relief at hearing that Marcella was to be sent away and said, 'Yes, I'll set up lookouts. Just drive the sulky along the decking.'

Oliver met Seamus at the stables on his return and finalised arrangements for the evacuation.

Oliver took Nellie aside and told her of the plan to evacuate Marcella. Of all that Nellie had endured since being at Sorrento, this news was the most devastating. She looked at Oliver blankly, unable to understand how he could turn Marcella away. Marcella had brought joy to the household. Everyone loved her. For Oliver to suddenly send her away would be a denial of all that had occurred since Marcella's arrival. Nellie fumbled with her apron, fighting back the tears, pleading in an unspoken way for Oliver to reach out and put Marcella at the forefront of his life. If she could not have Oliver then Marcella, with her youth, good looks and love, could fill the void in his life.

Something of this silent plea resonated with Oliver. He, for the first time, took Nellie into his arms and comforted her while she sobbed and, for the first time, Nellie told how she loved him. The love shown by Marcella and now Nellie touched his heart. He hugged Nellie dearly while speaking softly, expressing his true feelings and the depth of his love for both her and Marcella. When Nellie looked up at him, he brushed aside a wisp of hair spilling from beneath her bonnet, gazed into her hazel eyes and pressed his lips to hers. When settled, they discussed the situation further and, at Nellie's insistence, agreed on a compromise whereby Marcella would return to Sorrento when the way was clear. No matter that Nellie would never consummate her love for Oliver. The love the threesome shared would always bind them together.

Nellie found Marcella in her room, fiddling with one of Ivana's rag dolls. *How can I tell her?* thought Nellie as she watched Marcella playing a game of fantasy with the small effigy of a white farm boy. When she came close, Marcella looked up briefly and then turned her attention back to the doll, believing that Nellie, as she had done in the past, would join in the game with Marcella's imaginary friend.

Nellie gazed down on this loving child for a few moments and then interrupted. 'Marcie, I have something to tell you.'

Nellie sat beside Marcella and, trying as best she could to hold back the tears, explained the reason for the police raid and that Oliver was sending her away for a short time till things settled down. Marcella, with the same stoicism that she was to show later in life, listened to all that Nellie had to say and then asked, 'Why?'

Nellie burst into tears, took Marcella into her arms and cradled her till she was able to continue. Marcella, mystified but not tearful, accepted what was said. The only assurance she sought was a promise that she would be brought back to Sorrento.

'Yes, darling. You *will* come back to Sorrento,' said Nellie, catching Marcella's trusting look.

Nellie and Marcella busied themselves, selecting the best from Ivana's wardrobe and duchesse and packing it into the limited number of cases that Oliver allowed.

Oliver kept to himself in his office, brooding about what would become the most significant event in his life.

Thruppence had not been informed of Marcella's departure and became upset when Seamus told him while they penned the goats that evening.

At the appointed time of 8:00 pm, Seamus loaded Marcella's cases onto the sulky in the half dark and stood ready to help Marcella and Oliver to board.

Nellie was the first to give way, streaming tears and, in a reversal of commitment, made Marcella promise she would return.

Thruppence hung back, standing by a rail till Marcella called his name and then went over and hugged him.

They covered the ground in good time and, not wanting to be ahead of time, hid in a backstreet till Oliver said to Seamus, 'This is it.' Seamus, with the grey horse distinguishable in the nightlight, came into Queen Street and proceeded to the wharf. Both Oliver and Seamus, cautious but not expecting trouble, kept a sharp eye till suddenly the unmistakable silhouette of Rusty the hunchback slipped across an alleyway. Both men stiffened. Oliver drew his revolver and Seamus took a rifle from beneath the seat. The hunchback disappeared into the shadows as quickly as he had appeared, leaving only the fall of the horse's hooves on the wharf decking as a sign of life. Well down the wharf, they saw a light burning on the *Aquarius* and crewmen loosening the mooring ropes. As they passed the Mariners Inn, Oliver cast a sideways glance at the inn shadowed in darkness. He knew that Fanny and some of the boys would be there, hiding, ready to leap into action if needed. The first sign of trouble came when Seamus heard the click of a rifle bolt being closed. He reached across Marcella's lap, tapped Oliver's arm, and indicated by pointing a thumb. At this moment, Marcella realised that this was no ordinary manoeuvre, that they were being watched. Although not fully understanding the seriousness of the situation, she sensed the fear gripping both men. The grey horse, wary of the planking with gaps in between and the water beneath, balked and then snorted when a loose plank shifted underfoot. Seamus spoke in a whisper to calm the horse and flicked the reins to push him forward. Seamus, a horse whisperer, understood the grey and believed that the horse was signalling more than fear of a loose plank.

At that moment, an armed trooper stepped from the dark and confronted them. 'Stop! You're under arrest!'

The sight of a policeman confronting them drew Seamus' ire beyond the point of self-control. He lashed the reins across the grey's rump, sending him forward, and the grey, understanding his master's command, charged ahead, trampling the officer and dragging the sulky wheels across his body. All hell then broke loose, with cracks of rifle fire from the police being returned by Fanny and her trusted gang of men. In the chaos, the grey held his head, heading for the beacon light on the *Aquarius*. Oliver had jammed Marcella to the floor in front of the seat, giving some protection from the scatter of bullets going both ways. The calamity worsened when Sergeant Briley and a contingent of mounted police came from behind. Their horses, nowhere near as savvy as the grey, took fright on the shaky planking, with some shying and causing a break in the ranks. Briley's curses were heard by many when his horse stumbled and fell, landing Briley heavily on the rough timbers. He scrambled to his feet and, in a blind rage, gave the order to charge and fire at will. Fanny, with Sassy by her side and both with rifles to their shoulders, picked their mark. Fanny, driven by revenge, sighted Briley, pulled the trigger and watched with disdain as the mongrel fell to his knees and begged for mercy.

'Let him die a slow death!' she shouted to Sassy when Sassy swung her rifle barrel to finish him.

Sassy, with that fire in her eyes, called back, 'He's yours,' and then, without a flicker of hesitation, brought another trooper within her sights.

The cracks of the crossfire lit the wharf, with seamen on berthed ships arming themselves. Although they did not know the identity of Oliver and his accomplices, they knew which side to take and began firing at the police.

The sound of the shots creased the night sky, alerting the police at the local station that this was no normal arrest, that a full scale melee had broken out. One officer galloped along Queen Street, streaking past the gaslight lamps in a desperate rush to get reinforcements. The others at the station scrambled to arm themselves and then raced towards the wharf. Flashes of light from musket and rifle barrels lit the precinct like cracker night. From the wharf and from the decks of ships, and from windows of traders' buildings, the peppering continued, with several police lying dead or wounded, and a few defenders wounded. The grey, now driven to a crazed state, reared and kicked, making it impossible for them to continue on board the sulky. Oliver lowered himself down one side, while Seamus lifted Marcella from the floor and slid her into Oliver's arms. He then leapt to the ground and shouted to Oliver, 'Go. Take the girl aboard. I'll cover you!' Oliver, with his ammunition spent and heaving for breath from the strain, grabbed Marcella's hand and dragged her towards the waiting ship. Marcella, now utterly confused, followed Oliver's lead, holding his hand as they struggled through the pall of gun smoke now hanging overhead. Seamus caught a glimpse of a hunchback urging the police forward. Infuriated by the sight, he stood, exposing himself to gunfire as he took aim and then, with Rusty firmly in his sights and without a prayer, he squeezed the trigger. He watched as Rusty fell to the ground, suffering a mortal wound.

The captain of the *Aquarius* met Oliver and Marcella at the gangplank and shouted to his crew to cast off. When the captain reached for Marcella and Oliver went to release his grip, Marcella would not let him go. 'Oliver!' she shouted. 'Come with me! Come away with me!'

Even though the roar of gunfire continued, that moment in Oliver's life passed by him in slow motion. Never before had he experienced such a tranquil moment. He could hear Marcella's voice urging him to board ship, to go away with her, but he was drifting into another world. He had sustained a bullet wound and, unknown to Marcella, was dying. His grip of her hand weakened, and when it slid away and he sank to his knees, the captain realised what had happened. He took charge, pulling Marcella away from Oliver and to the deck. Marcella looked back and, seeing Oliver holding his chest and struggling for breath, she lost control. She screamed and fought against the captain's hold of her as the crew cast off and set sail down the river.

The smell of gunpowder still hung in the air the next morning when the police searched ships and waterside premises, interrogating dozens and arresting many for offences ranging from affray to murder. Public involvement and comment soon followed, with the community split as to who was responsible for the bloodshed.

The fracas stirred the halls of parliament. The newspapers took sides, with some blaming the mariners and others damning the government and police force for unconscionable conduct. An inquest followed, with the witnesses called giving conflicting evidence. The judge presiding over the hearing concluded that, since those who fired the fatal shots could not be clearly identified, no charges could be laid. The blood that had been spilt inflamed both the police and the mariners, resulting in decades of unrest on the waterfront.

Oliver's funeral followed two days after the affray. Seamus and Thruppence dug a grave beside Ivana's, while Nellie baked for a wake to follow the interment. Fanny, Sassy and a dozen of Oliver's loyal supporters attended the graveside funeral, conducted by a Methodist minister who mentioned that, unknown to anybody else, Oliver had given him regular donations to help the poor. It seemed that Oliver's lust for money was driven by the power that riches can bring rather than wealth itself.

Another surprise came when a letter arrived from a solicitor advising that he was executor of Oliver's will and to call at his office. Nellie and Seamus, who had been wondering what their future held, were exhilarated when told that Sorrento and everything thereon had been left to Nellie and Seamus in equal shares. The residue of Oliver's wealth was left to his only surviving relative, a sister who lived in England.

Seamus moved into the homestead with Nellie, and Thruppence formed a lasting relationship with a part Aboriginal girl who was happy to live in the shed and help with the goats.

As to Marcella, her name was often mentioned and, at times, Nellie went to the window when she thought she heard Marcella's voice calling.

PART TWO
Slaving on the Sugar Plantations

South Sea Islanders crushing sugar cane. Mackay, Queensland, Australia, 1870s

CHAPTER 9

Marcella lay on a bunk in the captain's cabin, unable to move. For three days she refused food and lay almost motionless with her mind trussed with grief, fear and confusion. She had no clue how long she would be at sea, where she was being taken or what the future might hold. As a frightened, lonely child in a foreign land with no one to turn to for guidance, she struggled to comprehend the situation. If it had not been for the comforting sound of the ocean sweeping against the hull of the schooner as it sliced through the surf Marcella would have surely gone mad.

She roused from the torment of her thoughts when, on the fourth day, she heard the sound of the swell of the open sea give way to an inshore calm. This message from the sea drew her curiosity, and soon she stepped from the doorway of the cabin to the open deck where, for the first time, she saw the ship and its crew in broad daylight. How different it all seemed, with memory of the gunfire and smell of gunpowder of that black night now replaced by tranquillity and blazing sunshine. For the next hour she watched with interest as the seamen carefully tacked their way between the sandbars to enter the mouth of the Mary River. Now free of the morbid confines of the cabin and with a fresh breeze blowing through her hair, Marcella began to come to terms with the carnage and grief that surrounded her departure from Sorrento. At moments she even thought that Oliver might have survived the gunshot and would soon come and take her back to her family at Sorrento. The crew, seeing Marcella in her fullness for the first time, cast admiring glances her way. The captain, sensing a reprieve from the damnation that Marcella had endured, came forward with an offering of a hand of ripe bananas and a jug of water. This, together with his engaging smile, drew her acceptance, and before long she began peeling and eating the fruit. Marcella's expectations grew as each turn in the river revealed more of the colourful river traffic. When they finally approached the busy riverside port of Maryborough, the sight of dozens of men at work brought further relief to her troubled soul.

The ship docked for two nights while tons of mining equipment, destined for the Gympie goldfield, was unloaded. Surprising to Marcella, no restrictions were placed on her movement. She could have gone ashore but chose to stay on board where she felt secure.

They cast off at midnight on the third night and sailed down the river to be in the open sea before the south-east winds began rolling the waves landward. The crew, though affable and polite, knew their place and, in spite of some being smitten by her presence, reserved their comments to little more than courtesies. In the days ahead, Marcella spent most of her time on deck, studying the passage of the sun as it arced across the sky and mapping in her mind the rugged coastline she could see to the port side. At night she sat alone on the deck till late, plotting the ship's course by the stars. She established that they were sailing north but could not coordinate her points of reference sufficiently to determine how far away or in what specific direction lay her island home of Lifou. She did, however, deduce that, given the size of the ship, the nature of the crew and the amount of provisioning, they were not bound for the South Sea Islands.

Sleeping arrangements in the captain's cabin remained simple, with each having a bunk and no night-time intrusions by the captain. For meals they sat together at a bench table fitted with a stool. The captain said little beyond mundane conversation that told Marcella nothing about his personal life or where they were headed. A bunch of dried heather flowers, tied with a dainty bow and half hidden beneath a bundle of scrolled charts, aroused Marcella's curiosity. Though she could not read the accompanying note, the feminine sweep of the lettering caught her attention. She imagined, rightly or wrongly, that they were from his lover. Having experienced what she thought to be love at Sorrento, she respected his position, and during the seven days and nights it took to sail from Maryborough to Port Mackay she kept her fantasies to herself.

Entry into the Pioneer River proved more difficult than expected. They became grounded on a sandbar and scrambled to move cargo to ballast the ship against a list that threatened to swamp her. Marcella, a strong swimmer, showed her worth when she stripped and dived overboard to assist crewmen securing lines to an anchor that had been cast to starboard. Once the saving lines had been secured she boarded with the help of those still on board. Without as much as a blink she stood, shook herself free of the salt water and then dressed before those on deck. This was the island way where modesty did not extend to nakedness. Some crewmen wished she would stay on board for the return journey, and then, if not at sea, they would seduce her soon after docking at the next port. The captain, though moved by the explicit show of femininity, kept his thoughts to himself.

After mooring at the wharf and directing the crew to discharge the cargo of farming equipment and tons of food provisions, the captain sent a letter via a messenger, addressed to Andrew and Atlanta Rushmore. He palmed the young messenger a shilling piece and told him that if he returned with a reply within a few hours he would be rewarded with a further shilling. The lad, an underfed urchin barely fifteen years of age, mounted his donkey bareback and sank his heels into its ribs as though his life depended on returning the dispatch in good time.

While the unloading continued, Marcella dwelt on the journey thus far and wondered whether she would be offloaded as part of the delivery. She thought that if she approached the captain he would tell but, fearing the answer, she stayed aft of the ship and brooded.

The young messenger pushed the donkey as hard as he could and managed a fast trot all the way upriver to Rosewood plantation, where Atlanta Rushmore met him with a frown. After he explained his mission she took the envelope lightly between her fingers so as not to soil herself with grime from the scruff of a child.

'Ma'am,' he said when she was about to turn away, 'the master of the ship says that the letter is urgent and I am to wait for a reply.'

'All right,' she said in a vexatious manner, adding, 'Take that donkey from my garden and wait outside the gate.'

Atlanta hurried inside, brushing past Lucille, her twenty-one-year-old daughter, in her haste to reach the office where she picked up a letter opener, slid the blade beneath the cover, cracked the seal and removed the letter. She brimmed with joy when she read:

Dear Mr and Mrs Rushmore,

As per your request to Reg Brixton, shipping agent of Brisbane, I have available a well-credentialed young lady able to fill the position of housekeeper.

The previous employer vouches for her diligence, obedience and good nature and is prepared to let her go to your employ for the sum of £25.

I am presently berthed at the wharf with the lady in my company and, as I wish to sail tomorrow evening, would be pleased if you would call to assess if she is suited to your requirement.

If commitments do not permit your attendance then you might wish to take her sight unseen.

If so I can arrange for her conveyance to Rosewood tomorrow morning.

She is most comely and would easily fetch the asking price if transferred to another.

If the latter arrangement suits then please send the money in a sealed envelope via the messenger.

Yours faithfully,
Anthony Borthwick,
Captain of the *Firefly*

After glancing through the letter Atlanta called, 'Lucille, come quickly. This *is* important!'

Lucille, a vivacious lass with sharp eyes and a quick wit, promptly entered the office, took the letter from her mother's hands and read the message.

'What do you think?' asked Atlanta, hardly able to contain her joy at receiving the offer.

'It's a lot of money,' said Lucille, coming straight to the point.

'Not if it's for my son's benefit!' hit back Atlanta, implying that nothing was too good for Saxon, her twenty-seven-year-old son.

Lucille waved the letter before Atlanta and cautioned, 'Maybe, but we'll have to interview the woman and decide upon her suitability. We can't afford to have another disaster.'

'Disaster?'

'Yes, Mother. You can dress it how you like but the last one was an absolute disaster.'

'Let's not dwell on that. We have to put Saxon first and foremost,' said Atlanta after a moment of reflection.

'Well, he's your son,' shot back Lucille.

'And I remind you, your brother,' countered Atlanta.

Lucille had her own opinion of her twenty-seven-year-old brother and her mother's plan to find him a wife but, rather than have another argument with her mother, met her insistent glare with an indifferent smile.

'He is a worthy man and don't you forget that,' continued Atlanta, reaffirming her support for her only son.

Lucille reread the letter and then asked Atlanta, 'Do we go to the bother of dressing and getting the stable hand to gather a horse to harness and then travel to town to interview the girl in the public glare at the wharf, or do we invite her to the home and conduct the interview in private?' She then added, 'I think it's only fair that the girl comes to the house and sees for herself before accepting.'

Atlanta, the self-appointed matriarch of Rosewood plantation, not wanting to demean herself by being seen in conversation with a commoner at the wharf suggested, 'Maybe you can go?'

'Me!' retaliated Lucille, revealing the rivalry that existed between mother and daughter. 'You're the one who wants to fix Saxon with a wife. Best you go, and preferably on your own.'

'Now, now,' cautioned Atlanta. 'You know that the town is no place for a lady like me to be seen unaccompanied.'

'Then what about me,' cut back Lucille.

'You're young and unattached,' declared Atlanta, drawing a distinction between the social statuses each held.

Rather than reply and infuriate her mother further, Lucille agreed to go to town and meet with the prospective housemaid.

The messenger, though disappointed he was not offered a piece of cake by the 'old girl' as he called her, was nevertheless grateful when he receive the second shilling from the ship's captain.

Harold, the English stable groom, assisted by Massan, a shiny black Islander, hitched a quiet horse to a sulky and sent Lucille on her way with the usual caution of 'drive carefully'. The Islander, a loyal servant and a favourite of Lucille, waved his felt hat upon her departure and watched till she disappeared from sight behind a field of green sugar cane.

The fifty minute journey passed quickly as Lucille conjured images of who would replace the last housekeeper, one of a string of housekeepers over the past few years who had failed to meet her mother's expectations as a suitable wife for her son or who had fled once realising the implications of their appointments.

Lucille, clean cut, pretty and with purpose in her stride, called to those she knew as she approached the ship *Firefly*. It seemed that all the crew wanted to be in her company and, within moments of boarding, the captain appeared from a hold to greet her. Lucille had seen the barefoot island girl aft of the vessel but, thinking her to be the 'captain's special', paid her no attention. She was surprised when the captain waved Marcella forward and offered her. Lucille, with a liberal and open mind, quickly put aside any colour prejudice and, in English tradition, shook Marcella's hand. Marcella, still knowing nothing of the purpose of the interaction or its consequences, complied with a warm handshake and a smile. During the conversation that ensued between Lucille and the captain, Marcella gleaned she was to be taken away by this girl to be put to work, as she had at Sorrento. As the discussion progressed, Lucille increasingly included Marcella by referring to her directly and asking for her comments. Marcella's fear of the unknown was soon replaced with an intuitive trust in this person she had met only an hour ago.

Lucille then sealed the deal by asking Marcella directly, 'Marcella, would you like to come with me and live on my parents' sugarcane plantation?'

Marcella, with no idea what to expect and with no time to think, followed her gut feeling and replied, 'Yes.'

The captain, holding the £25 payment in his hand, watched as the two mounted the sulky and drove off, sitting shoulder to shoulder on what he thought might well be an odyssey.

After they wended their way through the horse-drawn traffic of River Street, the main thoroughfare of the town, and as the horse clopped its way homewards, Lucille outlined the situation. She described the family homestead, Marcella's quarters, together with their large sugarcane plantation and sugar mill that was manned by 100 Islanders and supervised by white overseers. She said little about Marcella's duties, except that she would be engaged in general housework. Upon entering the main gate to the homestead, Marcella caught a fleeting glimpse of a white woman watching and then disappearing inside. The stable groom and Massan were pleased to see their young mistress return safely, and equally pleased to see her accompanied by a young, presentable mixed-race island girl. The girls carried Marcella's bags of clothes from the stables and, when on the veranda of the homestead, Lucille called, 'Mother, we've arrived.'

Atlanta, dressed in semi-formal wear and with her hair piled high on her head, made a gracious appearance to impress the new help. At first seeing Marcella alight from the sulky and realising that she was part Islander, shock and panic had beset her mind but now, seeing her up close and her companionship with Lucille, her emotions steadied sufficiently to, at least, give the girl a try. After all, the purpose of the appointment was to secure a wife for Saxon and, given his rejection by other women to date, a mixed-race might suffice.

Marcella breathed more easily when Lucille introduced her to Rosie, the Islander housemaid. Rosie and her husband Abraham lived together in a weatherboard cottage not far from the homestead. They, like most of the other Islanders on the property, were part of the indenture system where Islanders were procured to work in the cane fields by labour-hungry plantation owners who paid a pittance for their services. Some, like Marcella, had been kidnapped but, once stationed in frontier districts and away from close scrutiny, mingled anonymously with those who had been recruited under the indenture system.

Marcella settled into a small cottage behind the homestead and the accommodation suited her fine: running water from a storage tank up the hill, outdoor bathroom and earthen closet, a kitchen-dining room, a bedroom and a small porch with a view.

She bathed and dressed nicely for dinner, wearing a neat skirt and a colourful blouse. At hearing Lucille's call, she stepped along the paving stones to the rear door where Lucille invited her inside to dine with the family. Andrew, Lucille's father and head of the house, presented himself in true colonial style, dressed in collar and tie. Saxon took less interest in his dress and entered late, wearing an open-neck shirt and cuffs rolled to the elbows.

During their introduction to Marcella, Andrew showed interest, commenting on her neat appearance and asking if her living quarters were suitable. Saxon feasted his eyes on her body and guessed her age before welcoming her with a few words and sitting by her side.

At the tinkle of a crystal bell by Andrew, Rosie Solomon brought in a servery tray topped with a roast leg of lamb. She then brought a gravy boat and a large platter of roast vegetables as an accompaniment to the meat. Marcella and Rosie exchanged glances, telling each other in silent island code that they would talk later. During the meal Marcella, with the glow from the chandelier above lighting her expression, kept everyone engaged, telling them of her past and impressing them when they learned she was an island princess, fathered by an Australian ship's master.

During the next few days Lucille made a special effort of introducing Marcella to the white overseers and some of the dark-skinned Islanders, explaining that they worked on the plantation and in the sugar mill, as well as managing a herd of cattle and a flock of sheep. Marcella also spent time with Rosie, being introduced to the kitchen and other household duties. Rosie explained Marcella's obligations to her by simply saying, 'You and me share the housework.'

Rosie, like most of the Islanders, had an island name difficult to pronounce in English so, for convenience, she and others were assigned new names. In some instances the names reflected something about the individual's appearance, personality or their island of origin. Others had been given English names by missionaries prior to leaving the islands, while the planters sometimes showed their ugly side with names like Tarbucket, Frogface and Midnight. A few were named after members of the planter's family or their plantation, particularly in situations where mixed-race children were born to family members. Rosewood held its own secret. Saxon had fathered a child to an Islander female, with Atlanta and Saxon refusing to acknowledge the child. While Andrew remained noncommittal, Lucille, not blinded by racial prejudice, had, till now, continued to provide support. She worked in collusion with Rosie, smuggling food and clothing to the child and her mother.

Marcella began to get the measure of those about her. Andrew, a man moulded by hard work, rose before the sun, ate breakfast alone in the kitchen, and then set to the daily task of managing 100 plus employees, attending to

560 acres of sugar cane in various stages of growth and a sugar factory where cane stalks were crushed and the juice processed to produce sugar crystals. In addition to this, the horse and bullock teams necessary for the heavy work needed care. Beyond this his responsibility extended to keeping supply lines open to service the activities of the plantation and those living on site. With this weighty workload and demanding responsibility, it was no wonder that he devoted little time to family matters.

Atlanta, a former socialite of Sydney, spent her time shoring up her pretence as one of the elite; always insisting on the best and portraying herself and family as members of the landed gentry. She remained oblivious to the fact that, without the cheap labour from the South Sea Islands, the Bank of New South Wales would foreclose and the family would be turned out on the street. The two children born to her resulted from miscalculations and, while she expressed love and admiration for Saxon, she saw Lucille as recalcitrant and wilful. She wished for the day when Lucille would find a wealthy husband and leave home.

Saxon's schooldays at The King's School, Sydney, had been a failure. He never settled, learned near to nothing, was expelled when he strangled a kitten in front of other students, sought no purposeful vocation and by the time he and his family took up residence at Rosewood he had become an alcoholic. His father, believing that hard work makes the man, set Saxon to work on the plantation. He struggled with Saxon's indolence and addiction till, finally, he declared him useless. So hopeless was Saxon that, at times, Andrew wondered if he was the boy's father.

Lucille was the antithesis of Saxon: boisterous, charming and always willing to work. During the past year she had relieved Andrew of the arduous task of ordering and checking the arrival of goods. She wrote the cheques which he signed. Andrew now saw her as his successor and had given thought to rewriting his will. If this happened, and if Atlanta became aware, then his life's work might be torn apart.

Marcella, having experience of housework at Sorrento, soon settled into the daily routine, with Rosie doing most of the cooking and Marcella cleaning the house and washing the family's clothes and linen in a copper boiler.

She enjoyed the outdoors and, when not busy, spent time with Massan, the nineteen-year-old roustabout. Though he originated from a different island than Marcella, both understood Pidgin and could communicate fluently. She helped him milk the cows, feed the horses and care for the lavish gardens surrounding the homestead. Massan had been recruited as a sixteen-year-old by deceptive means and, since being taken away three years ago, had pined to return home. Now, with Marcella as a friend and, hopefully, one day his lover, he let go some of the thoughts of home. They did such a good job of training the trellis vines, weeding the garden beds, trimming the hedges, keeping the lawn tidy and supplying the family with produce from the vegetable garden that Atlanta set aside some of her jealous intent for her son and allowed the couple to sit together on the homestead veranda. On starry nights, Massan looked across from his room in the stables to Marcella's cottage, dreaming of holding her in his arms.

Marcella visited the island workers' accommodation and observed their lifestyle, peeping into their grass huts, built in traditional style by the river where they bathed, drew water, fished and attended to their gardens on the rich alluvial soil. She showed interest in how they sorted themselves by island of origin, family lineage and friendships established since arriving, and joined with them some evenings when they sat by their fires or went fishing. Sunday feasts were special, with fish, wildfowl, pig, goat, taro, yams and other vegetables cooked in pit ovens, with tropical fruits laid out on thatched mats. She came to know that, although impoverished and with little to look forward to, her people, who the white overlords referred to as Kanakas, had adapted well and remained cheerful much of the time. Apart from food, shelter, clothing and limited medical attention, all they would receive for their three-year indenture term was wages totalling £18 and a return ticket to their island of origin.

Smoke from the brick chimney of the sugar mill, together with the grinding noises and toots from the steam whistles within, drew Marcella's curiosity. At times she ventured upstream from the Islander's village to where the mill stood and studied what she could of the activity from a safe distance. She wished to go close, even pluck sufficient courage to investigate the strange clouds of steam and eerie noises coming from the factory. Some of the more superstitious of the workers referred to injuries and deaths caused by machinery and spills from cauldrons of boiling sugar syrup and attributed these mishaps to the work of evil spirits. Rumours frequently circulated about the mill being a place where white men practised sorcery. Marcella could have approached the factory on her own, but thoughts of the dire consequences that had been expressed by others kept her at a distance.

No Islander dared enter the barracks occupied by the white overseers. If sorcery was practised then the barracks was the home of the sorcerers. On occasions when Kanakas had to deliver a messages they stood at a safe distance and called the overseer's name. Marcella had been warned by Atlanta not to go near the white men's quarters and she wondered if this was to protect her from sorcery. Still, the barracks, set well apart from any other housing, drew Marcella's inquisitive nature and, from time to time, she spied on the men's movements from the cover of a thicket of trees.

The whirling blades of a windmill, set in a grassed paddock where draft animals and milking cows were pastured, fascinated Marcella. Though Rosie had explained that the windmill put water into the storage tank on the hill, Marcella remained confounded as to how a long rod thrusting up and down from behind the fan of the mill could get water into the tank—must be magic?

With Rosie attending to housework six days a week, Atlanta allowed her a long lunch break to take a meal to her husband Abraham, the ganger who supervised the field workers harvesting the sugar cane. To ease Rosie's workload, Marcella offered to deliver the lunch and, before long, made the daily run to where men and women were harvesting and transporting cane to the mill. Not having seen organised labour before, Marcella marvelled at the unity shown by her fellow Islanders as they toiled beneath the burning sun. As a gang of about forty they presented a colourful parade, with the men dressed in loin cloths or trousers and the women wearing brightly coloured garments. The leading men, lean, bare chested and with sweat dripping from their brows, swung broad-bladed knives, felling the stalks and topping the heads. The women, also barefoot and with a sweat rag to mop their faces, followed along, stripping trashy leaves from the stalks. As the horse-drawn carts arrived both men and women bent their backs, lifting heavy bundles of cane and heaving them into the carts. Most times an overseer riding a horse stood watch with a rifle holstered under his saddle flap and a coiled whip hanging from his shoulder. Marcella, never thinking they could be used as instruments of punishment or death against her people, thought the rifle and whip must be for their protection in the event of an attack by wild animals.

Marcella woke to the crowing of roosters, lay in the comfort of her bed till the morning sun broke over the brow of the hill, washed in the bedside basin, tidied herself before the mirror, dressed and entered the kitchen as Andrew picked up his hat to leave.

'Good morning, Marcella,' he greeted.

'Good morning, Sir,' replied Marcella respectfully and then added, 'Busy today, Sir?'

'Yes, I have shipments of bagged sugar to send downriver. It will take three days, loading and offloading the punt.' He hesitated and then added, 'Would you like to come with me and see it being loaded?'

This brief intimacy, the first shown by Andrew since her arrival, met with her enthusiastic reply. 'Sir, I would love to but Rosie will be here soon and today is wash day. Maybe another time?'

'Certainly,' replied Andrew with a hint of interest in his voice. 'Maybe tomorrow. We'll be shipping for the next three days.'

Marcella's heart leapt with joy at being included in his thoughts. She had noted that he and Atlanta slept in separate bedrooms and that he would probably welcome her as company.

Marcella toyed with this thought till she heard the patter of Rosie's feet on the veranda decking.

Rosie remained unusually quiet during the morning, and when it came time to prepare Abraham's lunch Marcella asked, 'Everything all right?'

Rosie, near to tears, sniffled. 'Abraham, he sick. I want to take him to the white doctor downriver.'

Marcella, still flush with Andrew's kind offer, suggested, 'The Master is taking sugar downstream. Abraham could go down on the punt, see the doctor and come back.'

Rosie turned aside as though dismissing the idea.

Marcella, buoyed further by what she thought to be Andrew's private feelings for her, put a hand on Rosie's shoulder and confided, 'I know the Master would do that for *me*.'

The meaning behind the suggestion became lost when Rosie explained, 'Abraham frightened of white-man doctor. He see the medicine man here at Rosewood but no good. He still lose weight.' She added, 'He's scared to lose work.'

'Why scared?' asked Marcella.

'Because if no work then the Master turn us out to live in the town with no hut or food. I say I work but Abraham no trust them white men in the town. Say they will use me.'

Marcella, grateful for the support Rosie and Abraham had given her during the past three months and now determined to save them, hugged Rosie and said, 'Don't you worry. The Master *will* let you stay!' Without divulging what she thought to be Andrew's interest in her or her plan she helped Rosie prepare Abraham's sandwich and, with a reassuring smile, whisked away to find him in the field.

Unknown to Andrew, and to Marcella's consternation, Saxon's wandering hands had not been idle. When moonbeams lit the landscape and Marcella sat in the cane chair on her porch gazing at the stars, Saxon made visits. Though innocent at the start, with him sitting on the top step and drinking rum, he soon ventured further. One night, when the lights of the homestead were turned low, he rose to his feet and, without notice, moved behind Marcella and began massaging her shoulders. Marcella, mindful that Saxon was the Master's son and that she depended on his family for food and shelter, lay her head back, accepting the attention without giving thought to possible consequences. Two nights later he called again and, within a few minutes, put his rum to one side and moved to win Marcella's favour. What she thought would be another massage soon extended to his slipping a hand to her cleavage and then her breasts. As his intentions became clear she tried to remove his hand but deferred when he squeezed a nipple as a means of coercion. No thoughts of sharing with him had ever occurred to Marcella, and when he undid the tie of her sarong, fully exposing her breasts, she pushed his hands aside and folded her arms. He persevered, trying to seduce her with words, till Marcella stood and covered herself. Saxon, knowing his mother had positioned Marcella for him, thought time to be on his side and, if not tonight, he would get his own way sometime soon.

CHAPTER 10

'Ma'am, there's a man at the front gate,' said Marcella as she approached Atlanta.

Atlanta, seated in a rocking chair on the back veranda, left off filing her nails and asked, 'Who is it?'

'Don't know. Never seen him before.'

'Black or white?'

'An Islander like me.'

'And you've not seen him before?'

'No. Never.'

'Did he ask for me?'

'Yes, said he has a message for the Missus.'

Atlanta, whose heckles raised at the mention of the word 'Missus', replied, 'Tell him to wait at the gate.' Then, in a show of childish retribution, she kept him waiting till she had finished rounding the nail.

Marcella, aware of Atlanta's insistence that she not fraternise with the men, relayed the message from the veranda. The young man, barely twenty years of age, barefoot and wearing only canvas pants, seemed unperturbed by the delay and stood patiently till Atlanta joined Marcella. As a measure of her authority, Atlanta took time to straighten creases in her long dress and brush curls from her forehead before saying, 'Ask him to come in.'

The messenger unlatched the garden gate, came to the bottom of the steps and announced, 'A message for you from the Missus of Savannah plantation.'

Marcella descended a step, took the envelope and with a sweep of her arm handed it to Atlanta, who opened the envelope and read:

Dear Atlanta,

With the weather pleasing and so much of interest happening, I thought, if the timing suits, that Florence and I could call tomorrow for morning tea.

Yours sincerely,
Antoinette Rousseau,
Savannah Plantation

Atlanta signalled for the lad to wait while she went to the office and wrote a note on the bottom of Antoinette's letter, confirming the arrangement.

After lunch, Atlanta took Marcella aside and, after referring to tomorrow's morning tea, said, 'Marcella, you are the only young island girl in the valley. All the others are older, married women who came here with their husbands and have papers. The sea captain who brought you to Australia had no papers for you so if the police find out you could be in big trouble.'

Marcella, with memory of the melee on the wharf still vivid in her mind, took this to mean that she might be shot on site by a man in uniform. Her mind rushed with fear of the possible consequences of being discovered.

Atlanta watched Marcella squirm with the thought and then, as though the idea had just occurred to her, offered a way out. 'If you were to marry an Australian there would be no trouble, especially if you have children.' Atlanta's cruel and conniving mind went further. 'I mention this because Mrs Rousseau might ask questions tomorrow.'

'I will stay in the cottage,' protested Marcella.

'That will not do because word of you will, if it has not already, spread throughout the district. Marriage is the only sure solution.'

While Atlanta knew that disclosure might implicate her and Andrew as accessories to the kidnapping and bring a jail term, her obsession was such that she was prepared to take the risk if it meant securing a wife for Saxon and producing offspring in the family name, even though they be mixed-race children.

Marcella brooded over Atlanta's words for the remainder of the day, retired to bed early, and lay awake till late, wondering if there was a subtext to Atlanta's suggestion of marriage.

Next morning Marcella rose early, helped Rosie in the kitchen and then, with Lucille's help, began preparing for her first formal engagement. After a good scrub and shampoo, Lucille brushed and braided her hair. They chose an island theme and, after rummaging through the clothes Marcella had brought from Sorrento, selected a form-fitting sarong, made of white cotton cloth, printed with red hibiscus flowers.

Atlanta almost went into a rapture when Marcella paraded before her in the dining room; particularly when Lucille made the observation that Marcella looked more Caucasian than Melanesian.

Rosie, speaking from the kitchen door, added her own touch by suggesting a frangipani lei.

'Where from?' asked Atlanta with a rare sparkle lighting her eyes.

'From our village. There's plenty there in bloom,' replied Rosie, already lifting the hem of her long dress to run the distance.

Atlanta, who seldom visited the worker's village, thought it a wonderful idea and sent Rosie running with the words, 'A garland of flowers. Yes, a garland of flowers for the one to be.'

Massan, the footman appointed to assist with guests' arrivals, took his footman's uniform from a trunk in his room at the stables and watched as Rosie pressed the white shirt and trousers with a hot iron in the kitchen. He then sat quietly on a stool in the garden while Rosie trimmed his youthful beard. Massan asked after Marcella, and when Rosie told him that she looked like a beautiful princess he could hardly wait for the guests to arrive and an opportunity to glimpse her.

Rosie had told Abraham of the event and, wanting his wife to look her best, he suggested she borrow a good dress from one of her friends. After some indignation and words to him about his own appearance, she slipped away and returned in a one-piece dress with an open bodice and full-flared skirt. Though Abraham thought the scarlet dress more suited to a young woman on the prowl, he readily gave it his blessing.

A glorious morning greeted Antoinette Rousseau and her sixteen-year-old daughter Florence. With the harvest proceeding in the cool of winter, the faint rumble from the sugar mill crushing the sugar cane, the homestead garden in full bloom and everyone cheerful, the morning tea would be a grand occasion to show all and maybe exchange some gossip. Massan, who had been watching expectantly, raised the alert when he heard a whinny. Under a cloudless sky and with wisps of dust rising behind the sulky the guests arrived, with Antoinette at the reins and Florence leaning forward in anticipation.

Massan, so pleased to be considered part of the household, nodded a greeting and held the horse while the guests alighted. Antoinette, dressed in a pale-green skirt and no need for a corset, carried herself with grace as she removed her driving gloves and thanked Massan. Florence wore breeches, hunting boots and a cap especially for the sulky ride. Atlanta, somewhat overdressed for the occasion in a crinoline dress heavily endowed with frills and flares, introduced Marcella, being sure to refer to her as a house guest. They then made their way to the west wing of the broad veranda where Rosie stood in waiting.

Fine linen and china, elegantly prepared food and silver service, together with gentile etiquette, epitomised the character of these landed gentry who captained the colony's plantocracy. Marcella, revelling in the thought of having been introduced as a house guest, and also being invited to join those at the table, modelled herself on the other women, taking tea with as much dignity and courtesy as her experience allowed.

Following tea, Antoinette suggested that Marcella show Florence about the garden while, as she said, 'The ladies discuss things that are too delicate for a young one's ears.' Florence, an easy-to-please teen, made light of her mother's comment and accompanied Marcella to the back garden. Lucille, who had come to the table late, excused herself and returned to the office to complete a stores order and then ride to town to catch the mail boat before it sailed mid-afternoon. As the sun filtered through the mauve flowers of the wisteria vine screening the veranda, casting shifting dapples of light across the cloth, Atlanta and Antoinette exchanged notes about recent events in the valley and the planter's personal lives. In answer to a comment made by Atlanta about the Rosewood's workforce, Antoinette, having heard some gossip, asked, 'How long do you expect Marcella will stay?'

Atlanta, caught a little off guard, paused and then replied, 'Oh, indefinitely. She has taken an interest in Saxon and might stay on.' She then set to fabricate a cover by explaining, 'She's the daughter of a seafarer who married an island princess. They lived in the islands till her mother recently died, and now he wants to settle her in Brisbane. He will be at sea for a while longer and, through an agent, placed her with us. He thinks it's best for her to start on a plantation where she is close to her own kind. She's here as a house guest, has the cottage to herself and helps about the house.'

Having heard Atlanta's story Antoinette, being a guest, smiled pleasantly and enquired no further.

Meanwhile, Marcella and Florence engaged in lively conversation. Marcella was enthralled by Florence's cultured voice, and Florence envied Marcella's simple Pidgin English. They even began tossing words about and practising each other's linguistic expression. Friends they would surely be, and when Marcella took Florence to her cottage and they sat together on the side of her bed their empathy strengthened, with each confiding closely guarded secrets. Florence told of her love for island people, and that one day she planned to marry an island boy who had a handsome body. In turn, Marcella told that Saxon had been making advances, that he was heartless and that she hated him. Each had compromised themselves for, if the secrets were divulged, their futures might be jeopardised.

Florence, the only white child at Savannah and following her fetish for island boys, had studied books about the South Sea Islands. She referred to a children's book titled *The Coral Island* which related the adventures of three shipwrecked boys and their escape from pirates and cannibals. Marcella listened intently, and when the boys finally returned home safely she asked if the book had pictures.

'Yes, I can give it to you to read if you like.'

Marcella became sad and dejected and looked to one side.

Florence in her gusto quickly followed with, 'You can read, can you not?'

Marcella looked back at Florence and shook her head in shame.

The realisation that Marcella could not read brought wells of tears to Florence's eyes. *How foolish, how stupid*, she thought. *All the shame should be on me*. She instinctively reached for Marcella who, likewise, stretched forth and took Florence into her arms. After a few words of apology and wiping away tears they slid from each other's arms, bonded by a new understanding and acceptance. They then planned how Marcella would visit Savannah and be taught to read.

Antoinette declined the invitation to stay for lunch, saying that those at Savannah would send out a search party if they did not arrive home soon. One call to Massan brought him from the stables, leading the horse, and when it came time to mount the sulky Florence kept her promise to Marcella by asking Atlanta, 'Can Marcella come to Savannah? I will teach her to read.'

Atlanta, not wanting to let Marcella out of her clutches, replied, 'It's too far to walk and she can't ride.'

Not to be outdone, Florence shot back, 'Massan can bring her over in the sulky.' She then turned to Massan. 'Do you know the way?'

Massan, while trying to hide his glee, looked directly at the group and said, 'Yes, Miss. Anytime, Miss.'

To deny Marcella the opportunity to learn to read would seem wholly unreasonable, so Atlanta had no alternative but to agree.

CHAPTER 11

✧

The evening meal started badly when Saxon entered the dining room partly drunk and shifted his chair away from Marcella. While Andrew and Lucille felt the hurt that this caused Marcella, Atlanta became angered by the move and, in her paranoid state, blamed Marcella for the show of separation. *What had Marcella done? Had she refused her son? What is to become of the planned union of the two?* These thought occupied her mind during the meal and afterwards till Andrew, at a vacant moment in the awkward dinner conversation, turned to Marcella and said, 'I'll be inspecting the plantation and visiting the mill tomorrow. Would you like to come along and see how sugar is made?'

This most unusual offer of the Master, inviting the coloured housemaid to be seen with him without the company of others, drew everyone's attention.

While Lucille kept her thoughts to herself, Saxon, who despised his father, made a snide remark, saying in a jocular tone, 'Every day brings something new.'

Atlanta, turning more crimson by the moment, dumped her napkin on the table and, with her voice trembling with rage, chastised Andrew for what she thought to be his lapse of judgement. 'Don't you think it's Saxon's place to show the girl around the property!'

Having pre-empted the response and ready to take a stand against the domestic browbeating he had endured for years, Andrew replied, 'Saxon has not offered.'

'How do you know?' shot back Atlanta with growing agitation.

Andrew, tired of his son's disrespect and philandering with the island women on the plantation, put the question directly to Saxon. 'Have you?'

126

The messy exchange, if allowed to continue, might expose Saxon further so, to clip the conversation, he answered, 'It's up to Marcella. I'll take her if that's what she wants.'

'Haven't you more to do than show people the factory,' interjected Atlanta, renewing her attack on Andrew and flexing her authority. 'As it is we are behind with filling sugar orders.'

Lucille felt compelled to intervene for, every time a dispute arose, her mother set to embarrass Andrew by referring to the financial difficulty besetting the plantation. Lucille understood this and the need to modernise the factory but also that, whenever spare cash became available, Atlanta lavished the funds on nonessentials like the recent extension to the homestead. She sided with her father and promptly took a swipe at Atlanta. 'If Saxon would put his shoulder to the wheel we would not be in this mess!'

'How dare you! The gall of you to speak to me like that!' spat Atlanta. She followed with, 'I don't see you working in the fields or the factory!'

Not satisfied with ridiculing Andrew and Lucille, Atlanta turned to Marcella. 'Well, what do you intend to do?'

Lucille, outraged by the unwarranted aggression towards Marcella, pounced on her mother's words. 'Mother, leave Marcella alone. She's done nothing wrong.'

'We'll see about that,' replied Atlanta, now in a fluster.

Saxon, who had initiated the furore by moving his chair away from Marcella, created more havoc. 'If father wants to show his princess around let him do so.'

The pointed inference infuriated Andrew, bringing him to his feet. He shouted, 'Saxon, leave the table!'

Lucille feared the worst when Saxon scraped his chair back and stood to challenge his father. She had seen them brawl on two previous occasions but that was almost a decade ago. Since then Saxon had grown strong and Andrew had aged. As quick as a cat she moved from her side of the table and positioned herself between the two. Atlanta watched intently till the moment of crisis passed and then washed her hands of the argument by leaving her place at the table without excusing herself and stomping off to her bedroom. Saxon, who had always followed his mother, soon disappeared outside with a bottle of rum in hand.

The dispute left Andrew shaken and pale. His good intentions had, as on so many occasions before when Atlanta interfered, left him wondering what the future held, not only for members of the family but for Rosewood, the property he had dreamed of owning since a child.

He accepted Lucille's comforting words and, when settled, confirmed with Marcella that she would accompany him to the plantation the next morning. Though the ordeal seemed bizarre to Marcella, the behaviour of those involved gave her a better understanding of the family hierarchy and where loyalties lay.

Next morning Marcella woke before sunrise and, upon seeing lamplight shining through the kitchen window, quickly slipped into a sarong and skipped along the paving stones to the homestead. Without knocking she opened the door and entered the kitchen to find Andrew with the stove fire lit and a pot of porridge coming to the boil.

'Good morning,' he said with a cheery smile.

'Morning, Master,' replied Marcella, realising she had not brushed her hair and sweeping strands from her forehead.

'Sorry about last night,' he said by way of apology.

Marcella saw no need to apologise and, feeling sorry for him, and given they were alone, she put an arm about him and reassured him with a hug.

They breakfasted together over bowls of porridge, and when Andrew had laced his boots and placed his hat on his thick head of hair they quietly left by the front door, careful not to wake the others.

During the night Marcella had thought of Andrew, his position in the family, his rude wife his downfall, his lazy, pernicious son and Lucille, his devoted and loyal daughter, living as a family in a household which, to an outsider, appeared as a bastion of harmony and success but on the inside was rotting as a carcass rots from the inside out.

As they walked to the brow of the hill overlooking Rosewood plantation, Marcella stayed a little behind to admire this man whom she respected and even thought she loved.

Throughout the morning he showed he cared, taking time to talk about the felling and burning of the forest, the land preparation with horse and plough, the cutting and planting of cane stalks, the weeding of the young crop by use of the hoe, the harvesting, with the people cutting and loading the cane into horse-drawn carts and delivering it to the mill. Everywhere she saw evidence of Andrew's hand. What's more, he told his story with pride. No matter his wife who spurned him as a failure and his reckless and indolent son, he had Lucille and now Marcella for support.

After having spoken to the overseer supervising the harvesting in the field, Andrew took Marcella to the river where they drank water from the palms of their hands and rested in the shade of a weeping willow. Marcella waited, wanting, knowing of Andrew's solitary home life and expecting him to take her into his arms. She knew that he and Atlanta slept in separate rooms and, from Atlanta's attitude towards him, any lovemaking between them would be a distant memory. Marcella wanted to fill this void, to give him what he deserved and, while he sat propped against the tree, she lay beside him, picking straws of grass and throwing them into his lap as a tease. Andrew dwelt on her kindly expression, smiling each time she tossed a suggestive smile, reading what could be. He so much wanted to hold her close, to feel the warmth and, in return, give of himself. Their intent, the willingness of both, their near encounter was suddenly thwarted when a small sailing boat glided past and the boatman, well known to Andrew, shouted 'Ahoy'. The boatman, having come across something that would certainly excite the gossip circles, waved a cheeky greeting and then proceeded downstream. Marcella realised the implication and, feeling guilty about having compromised Andrew, got to her knees and began to apologise. Andrew would have none of this and, after tossing a tuft of grass her way, took her by a hand and pulled her to her feet. Their gazes brought them close but not close enough and, after a light-hearted quip about being sprung, Andrew led the way downstream towards the sugar mill.

The rumble from the mill grew louder, and when they turned the corner of a riverside field of mature cane the mill came into full view. Before them lay a spectacle reminiscent of the earlier slave days in the Caribbean, where coloured people worked under the direction of white supervisors, processing sugar cane in a most primitive way. The tall brick chimney, the only monumental structure, stood central, with adjacent sheds made of timber and iron housing the equipment used for milling and processing the crop. Horse teams, hitched to carts loaded with freshly cut cane, queued patiently by the mill intake, while a team of bullocks, straining at the traces, approached slowly with a load of wood to fuel the furnace.

With some encouragement from Andrew and greetings from workers, Marcella followed Andrew as he did a round of inspection, which was also designed to introduce Marcella to factory life. To demonstrate the fury of the furnace, Andrew asked the attendant to open the furnace door and toss in a stick of wood. Sparks flew and tongues of fire leapt from the open door, convincing Marcella that this was indeed the dwelling place of evil spirits. At seeing the cane intake, where several men took cane from the carts and fed the sticks into the jaws of a huge three-roller crushing mill, Marcella held back and shuddered at the thought of a worker being crushed to death. The steam engine driving the mill possessed power unimaginable, and each time it hissed a cloud of steam her heart leapt to her mouth. As Andrew continued showing Marcella around he ducked under hot steam pipes and brushed dangerously close to machinery as though safety was of no concern.

He gave a running commentary on all the processes, from the crushing mill to the lime tank till, eventually, the juice entered the boiling room. This steam bath of hot fumes, with the stickiness of spilt sugar syrup under bare feet and the workers exposure to spills from the boiling cauldrons of sugar juice, fitted a description of hell on earth. The fifteen men engaged in boiling the juice to evaporate the excess water laboured strenuously, stirring the juice with paddles till, eventually, after ladling the content from one to another of four consecutive cauldrons of thickening liquid, they then ladled the viscous syrup into large pots that were left to cool and granulate into clusters of sugar crystals. Once the crystals formed, two men lifted each pot, poured off the waste liquid and then emptied the contents to a long bench, where the clustered masses of sugar landed with a thud. Other men followed along, breaking these clumps into smaller pieces that were then placed in perforated baskets to dry. The baskets, dependant on the weather, were dried in the sun. The final product, known as *rock sugar*, was then shovelled into hemp sacks and the openings securely stitched.

While in the boiling room, Andrew told Marcella of the problems besetting the mill. While handling of the cane and juice up to the boiling room stage was satisfactory, the boiling room processes were antiquated and, if Rosewood was to survive financially, more modern equipment must be installed. Plantations in the Caribbean had, during the past decade, begun replacing their witch's cauldrons with vacuum-controlled vats, switched from using pots to installing one large crystalliser, and installed centrifuges to separate the crystals from the liquid. These measures improved the amount and quality of sugar, sped up the process and freed some of the labour requirement by replacing manual labour with machinery. Although they harvested all year round, weather permitting, the throughput remained insufficient to be viable. A few other planters in the district had adopted these improvements and, if Andrew did not soon follow, he could be left behind and in dire financial trouble.

Though Marcella understood very little of what Andrew said regarding this problem, she gauged that the concern kept him awake at night and that explaining the intricacies to her was a way of thinking aloud, bouncing his thoughts off her and back to himself. Apart from being his friend and maybe eventually his lover, she filled the role of a neutral party he could rely on to listen to his thoughts without seeking to influence. It became apparent to Marcella that, apart from Lucille, Andrew had no one in whom he could confide about Rosewood's business. His overseers had neither the ability nor interest to provide meaningful input, and while those of his household complained of the shortfall in productivity, only Lucille actively participated in exploring possibilities and making suggestions of how best to raise the capital needed—particularly in their present situation when the bank had threatened foreclosure. It was in this frame of mind that he stood, till near noon, telling Marcella about his problems and listening to the echo of his own voice. With his thoughts reinvigorated by passing them by Marcella, and her emotions stirred by their earlier interlude, they made for home with a fresh spring in their step.

Rosie and Marcella struggled to close the lid of a hamper basket, with Rosie pushing down hard on the lid and Marcella trying to pin the latch.

'You have too much,' said Marcella, drawing away and standing up.

Rosie, not one to accept defeat, forced the lid tighter and insisted, 'Here, try now. I have squashed it some more.'

The girls kept their voices low as they prepared to smuggle food to Narisse, the Islander mother of Kabbau, Saxon's eight-month-old son. Ever since Rosie had helped deliver Kabbau by moonlight down by the river she had provided continual support by secreting food and other supplies to Narisse, who lived with her husband Kaipan in the village. The three of them originated from the island of Guadalcanal and, bound by close ancestral ties, Rosie filled the role of grandmother, doting on the half-caste child as if it were her own. Most of the villagers knew that the child had been fathered by the son of the Master and understood the strain this placed on Narisse's marriage to Kaipan and the broader social implications. So far Atlanta had brushed aside any suggestion that the baby was Saxon's. To those who enquired she replied that an overseer was the culprit, and even went as far as naming one of the overseers. The names of the mother and son were never mentioned in the household and, on one occasion, Saxon threatened violence when an overseer made a passing reference to the child. Fortunately for Rosie, she had become a favourite of the planter's household and, while they suspected that she stole food for Narisse, nobody challenged her. While Atlanta and Saxon remained in denial, Lucille, a close confidant of Rosie, was complicit in assisting Rosie and Narisse. Lucille had visited Narisse occasionally and, having held her nephew in her arms, would not abandon the child. Kaipan, Narisse's husband, while accepting the child in accordance with island tradition, had not forgiven Narisse and swore vengeance against Saxon. Although Narisse had given an assurance of her future fidelity, she feared that Kaipan might, in a jealous fit of rage, kill her. At times her dark thoughts extended to imagining that Kaipan could, after butchering her and the child with a machete, attack those at the big house. Narisse wished to return to the islands but feared that a request might be met with outright rejection because it might draw the attention of the police and expose the whole dastardly affair to the wider community. Since the birth of Kabbau, and with Saxon having received an anonymous death threat, he and Narisse had not spoken. The villagers gossiped among themselves, watching

Narisse's every move and, in some instances, fabricating sightings of Narisse and Saxon meeting in secret by the river. Kaipan's close friends informed him of this innuendo and, in return, Kaipan confided that he planned to murder Saxon. If any of this talk reached the ears of those at the big house swift action would result. Kaipan and Narisse would be evicted from the plantation. The police might possibly intervene and imprison them both. Alternatively, if Kaipan did murder Saxon, revenge by the whites would be wholesale, with plantation Kanakas disappearing as a result of retribution, or being taken away in chains in police custody. Conceivably, all or a large slice of Rosewood's labour force could be dispersed, resulting in a labour shortage and the disbandment of the plantation. Rosie, in spite of being a favourite of the household and given the liberty of taking food, could, if she overstepped the mark, find herself and Abraham evicted on the grounds of theft. Though living in fear of this possibility, Rosie continued her regular visits and, as she had done on many occasions before, and now with Marcella as an accomplice, prepared to slip out the back entrance, through the orchard and down to the village, where Narisse would be waiting. Saxon had a lot to answer for, but so far had taken no responsibility for his actions.

As they walked down the slope toward the river and the village, Marcella carried the heavy hamper and Rosie a hessian bag that held a leg of smoked pork she had snatched from the smoke house at the last moment. Wisps of smoke rose above village huts, and voices could be heard as they came closer. Though the workforce toiled six days a week, there were always some villagers left at home, either sick or attending to domestic duties. On entering the village perimeter, Marcella noticed a Kanaka woman sitting on a stool under a tree, smoking a pipe and looking at them intently. Rosie noted the attention and, with a sideways glance, said to Marcella, 'No look at her.'

Marcella replied in a whisper, 'Why?'

'She's Saxon's new girlfriend. Cause plenty of trouble.'

Marcella, drawn by curiosity, stole further looks as they passed by. The woman, still watching, followed their every step and, in particular, glared at Marcella. The woman, apparently not working, carried the hallmarks of one on the take and being well compensated: clothed in a new and colourful sarong and a linen head scarf, several strands of shiny beads hanging about her neck, a silver armlet, an expensive pipe hanging from her mouth and a full plug of tobacco by her side. The woman, jealous of Saxon and Narisse's past affair, had attacked Narisse three times, scratching and biting. Rosie took Marcella by the arm and led her away, slipping between huts, around gardens and by clumps of banana plants.

Narisse's pole hut, with a high-pitched roof and clad with thatch, showed that Kaipan had provided well in anticipation of he and Narisse having a family. However, after trying unsuccessfully for years, Narisse suddenly gave birth to Kabbau. Kaipan had an inkling about Narisse and Saxon but, thinking it not possible that Narisse would deceive him, had brushed aside the gossip. Upon the birth of the half-caste child, Kaipan was not only shattered by the discovery but also demeaned by thoughts of what others might be thinking. He confronted Narisse who admitted to the adultery but, although she promised that it would never happen again, suspicion continued to plague Kaipan's mind, causing him to sneak home during working hours to check that Narisse remained faithful.

Marcella and Rosie entered the hut and exchanged greetings with Narisse and then, as Rosie unpacked the hamper, Marcella cast about the single-room dwelling with its earthen floor and hessian drape fitted to the doorway. Push-out windows, made of tin and propped open with sticks, provided ample ventilation, while a vent in the roof allowed smoke to escape when cooking inside during rainy weather. A single timber bunk in one corner indicated that intimacy still existed between the two. Close by the bed, baby Kabbau lay asleep on a stretcher covered with lamb's wool. A cord line for hanging clothes stretched across the room, and wooden crates served as storage compartments. The table and two chairs where Rosie and Narisse unpacked the hamper stood central in the room.

Narisse gleamed with delight as the items were spread across the table and, between her expressions of gratitude, Rosie managed to get a word in, asking about the baby.

'He's good, drinking plenty of milk and getting stronger by the day,' said Narisse, before leaving the biscuits alone and reaching for Kabbau. Rosie loved Kabbau as her own, and after a big hug and some kisses she swirled around the room, singing to him in her native language. Marcella's turn came next. She hugged the little mite and blew bubbles on his chest to make him laugh. With the smoked pork being a must, Narisse took a carving knife and sliced some for them to have with bread for lunch. During lunch, Marcella sat on a crate that Narisse had pulled into place as an extra chair and listened while Narisse chattered, telling Rosie of the latest news of who was doing what in the village. Afterwards, when Narisse began talking secretively to Rosie, Marcella excused herself, stood and moved about the room, inspecting items of interest. In a corner at the rear she spied a cache of bows, arrows and spears. Though made in the traditional way, some added features drew her attention. She picked up a fire-hardened spear, felt it for weight and balance, and then inspected the forged steel tip. She next took hold of a four-foot bow made from local timber but of island design, drew the twined sinew bowstring to its fullest and released it with a twang. The bundle of arrows, all tipped with shards of steel pocketed from the blacksmith shop, tempted Marcella to take one, slot it to the string and draw back to gauge the smoothness of the draw. She bent to take one but suddenly stopped when Narisse called in a loud voice, 'Don't touch!'

Marcella, shocked at the tone of voice, turned, seeking an explanation.

Narisse, realising her raised voice was out of order, hastened to say, 'Sorry, but please don't touch the arrows.'

Rosie, struggling to understand Narisse's abrupt and terse intervention, touched Narisse's now trembling hand and asked, 'What is it? It's only an arrow.'

Narisse began to tremble more, and when Rosie rose to her feet and put her arms around Narisse's shoulders she broke into tears.

Rosie glanced at Marcella with concern and then turned her attention back to Narisse. 'Narisse, what is it? You can tell me and Marcella.'

Through the tears Narisse pointed to the arrows and said, 'Poison. They have poison tips.'

Rosie and Marcella froze because they knew that on the islands arrowheads were only poisoned for killing people. For wild game and fish no poison was needed nor was it safe, but for humans, if the person did not die from the trauma caused by the impact of the arrow, the resulting septicaemia from the pathogens on the tip would ensure the victim died a slow and cruel death.

'How? What for?' asked Rosie hurriedly, fearing that someone was about to be murdered and that the repercussions might cripple village life.

After regaining some composure Narisse explained, 'Kaipan do it. He rub the points into rotten meat.'

'And?' asked Rosie, pressing Narisse for a full answer.

'He want to kill Saxon. Say that if he kill Saxon the evil spirit will leave us alone. We be family again.'

The revelation shocked Rosie and Marcella. Believing in evil spirits and the need to appease them, they looked about the room for any evidence of their presence. They dwelt on the arrows momentarily and then, to avoid their influence, both women moved to Narisse's side of the table.

After recovering from the shock, Marcella took the lead and suggested, 'Narisse, maybe I can talk to the Master and he will move you and Kaipan to another plantation. I know someone at Savannah who might be able to help.'

'No, that will not work,' said Narisse, beginning to cry again. 'Saxon will kill me. He say that if I tell anyone he drown me in the river.'

Marcella scrambled for words to put to rest Saxon's threat. 'I can tell the Master to stop him.'

'No! No!' shouted Narisse, now in a panic. 'You leave alone.'

Rosie took Marcella aside and told her to leave it alone and that she would visit Narisse tomorrow. Marcella agreed and, after consoling Narisse as best they could, they left, with the woman smoking the pipe following their every step.

The next morning Rosie sauntered to the village. She had worried all night and, after speaking to Marcella in the kitchen earlier, decided it best if she go alone. Kaipan would be away felling forest trees as he had been doing the day before, giving Rosie private time with Narisse. When partway through the village, she spotted Saxon's girlfriend sitting on a log, picking her fingernails with a piece of shell. She wore a loin cloth only and, from the look of her shapely breasts, Rosie guessed she was childless and probably barren, just the kind of woman Saxon and other men covet. *Bitch!* thought Rosie, after exchanging a glare with the woman, who appeared much younger and more attractive than herself.

Rosie became alarmed when she approached Narisse's hut; the dusty ground around the hut had been swept clean by Kaipan the previous evening and, no doubt, would have been checked by him this morning for any signs of intrusion by a sorcerer. Also, the doorway drape remained drawn across the entrance. Something nasty must have occurred since her visit yesterday. The mere mention of sorcerers struck fear into the hearts of Islanders so Rosie, steeped in island belief, stepped lightly for fear of awakening these devils that prowled by night. At the entrance she called the Pidgin greeting of 'Halo', and when Narisse did not answer she drew the drape to find her seated at the table with Kabbau asleep in her arms. To allow for fresh air and to let a flood of light in to keep lurking spirits at bay, she pulled the drape to one side.

Normally the sight of Rosie would excite Narisse, but today she sat listless except for a faint smile.

'Here, my turn for a nurse,' said Rosie, taking the baby into her arms and trying to put some cheer into the otherwise morbid surrounds. Rosie cradled Kabbau and, when he was roused from sleep, she sang an island lullaby till he dozed again. Taking a cue from Narisse, she lay Kabbau on the lamb's wool and sat on the chair opposite.

Island people converse in island time which, unlike the conversations of Caucasians which get straight to the point, can be a roundabout of thought and words that gradually evolves into a conversation. This morning Narisse's thoughts were particularly slow to formulate, and Rosie, apart from a prompt here and there, listened patiently while Narisse laboured to tell what had happened since Rosie's last visit.

'That woman who sleep with Saxon, she come here after you go yesterday and cause trouble. She say that Saxon no want Kabbau, that he want her baby. She make a lot of noise, wake Kabbau and when I go to pick him up she try to grab him. Rosie, I only small but I go wild and hit her with a chair, tell her get out of my hut. She want fight, but when I hit her hard again she get the story and piss off.'

Rosie, having seen the measures taken to protect the hut and those inside, knew there was more to the story and asked pointedly, 'You think she go away now?'

Narisse crossed her arms, looked around and said in almost a whisper, 'She say witch doctor come along and cast spell on us.'

A deathly silence filled the room as the two women contemplated the worst. Even this far from the islands, many inexplicable deaths had occurred and, although the sorcerer remained anonymous, they believed, without a doubt, that he walked amongst them by day and cast spells by night. There were Woibi, Niu and Sorso, healthy men who suddenly became sick and, for reasons that the doctor could not diagnose, wasted away to mere shells of their former selves before closing their eyes, never to reawaken. This belief in sorcerers and evil spirits that had dogged the Melanesian people for millennia threatened to tear Narisse and Kaipan apart, and maybe destroy Rosie in the process. Rosie wanted to burn the hut and all its contents to exorcise the spirits, but Narisse pleaded she not strike a light till she spoke with Kaipan. Rosie stayed till Kabbau woke, and when Narisse had settled him on her breast and assured Rosie that she would be safe till Kaipan came home, Rosie stroked Kabbau's hair for a few moments and then left.

She purposely backtracked the way she had come and, upon finding the demon woman still sitting on the log, she picked up a stick and attacked. With a mighty wack she struck the half-clad woman across the head, knocking her from the log to her knees. She struck again and again till the stick broke in two. The woman, bleeding from the head and in a blind rage, charged at Rosie, knocking her to the ground and kicking into her with her bare feet. Rosie managed to grab a foot and, with a twist and thrust, sent the woman tumbling to the ground. Though battered, Rosie scrambled to her knees and lunged at the woman. Island women can be brutal, and as the two scratched, bit, gouged and kicked, onlookers came close to witness what was a typical island brawl. Rosie gained the upper hand and pounded the now naked woman relentlessly till she cowered and signalled defeat. Rosie stood above her, delivered a mouthful of abuse and, for good measure, gave her one last kick. She then, without giving the bystanders a glance, stumbled from the village and back to the homestead.

To avoid awkward questions she skirted around the homestead to Marcella's cottage, where Marcella helped her inside. Though bloodstained and in pain, she refused Marcella's suggestion of calling Atlanta or Lucille— disclosure of the incident would expose Saxon's involvement and could have unimagined consequences. Rosie rested for a couple of hours and, when she was able to move, Marcella escorted her through the nearby orchard that screened Rosie's cottage from the homestead and stables. Marcella managed to bluff her way through lunch with only Atlanta and Lucille home, but found the evening meal more challenging, having to substitute for Rosie in preparing the meal and making excuses for her absence.

CHAPTER 12

As the ganger for the sugarcane harvesting, Abraham Solomon carried much responsibility, not only to satisfy the plantation owner but also to care for the island workers. The workers' wages, fixed at £6 a year, represented only a fraction of that earned by their white counterparts. Rations often fell well short of that needed for heavy labouring, and housing consisted mostly of leaky grass huts. As bonded servants they had no bargaining power to negotiate improved wages or conditions and, in the event of disobedience or having absconded, they were heavily penalised. Under the terms of the indenture agreements, which were considered illegal by opponents of the trade, these men and women of the South Pacific were effectively enslaved.

Since Abraham's arrival two years ago and his promotion to ganger he had gained insight into the labour force of Rosewood and the expectations of the Rushmore family. Prior to the present financial hardship facing Rosewood, Abraham enjoyed a cordial relationship with Andrew and the field overseer. Andrew had stopped for a chat with Abraham every couple of days and also conversed with the overseer, who spent a few hours each day overseeing the harvest. Abraham took instructions from the overseer and, with the benefit of being an Islander and fluent in Pidgin, he ably managed the workers, being sympathetic to their needs while keeping a steady flow of cane to the mill. However, this arrangement began to founder when Andrew, in need of cash to satisfy the bank, insisted production be increased. Everyone, from the field workers to the mill hands, had felt the strain and the mounting resentment. So strained had relationships become that Andrew now seldom spoke to Abraham, preferring to pass messages to the overseer. The overseer, knowing that his ongoing employment depended on meeting the required quota of cane sent to the mill, became more involved, shouting at field workers rather than leaving it to the quietly spoken Abraham to manage. Of late the situation had become almost intolerable, with the overseer barking at individuals and threatening to use the lash. The situation so affected Abraham that he slept little at night and, as Rosie had observed, was losing weight. In earlier times Abraham could have walked from his cottage to the homestead, sat with Andrew on the veranda and discussed problems, but now he thought he would not be welcome and had not visited for weeks.

Crusoe, a mild-mannered man and a good worker, had taken ill but, wanting to pull his weight, had forced a crust of dry bread down his throat for breakfast and arrived late. The overseer, mounted on a horse as usual and armed with a rifle, a revolver and a whip, rode up to Crusoe and chastised him for being late. Abraham noticed and, although busy organising the crew of about forty with the cutting, trashing and loading of the wagons, he spared time to pass by Crusoe occasionally to check. By mid-morning Crusoe weakened, with barely enough strength to swing the cane knife, and when he stumbled and fell, narrowly missing the sharp blade, Abraham went to his aid, helped him to the shade of a nearby tree and handed him a canvas water bag.

'Stay here. I'll send you home on the next cart,' said Abraham, signalling to Crusoe that he would be confined to the village until well again. The overseer, behind with his weekly quota and having told Abraham to work the crew harder, took exception to what he saw. Soon after this another cutter, suffering exhaustion from working twelve hours a day in the hot and humid weather, sat in the shade of the tall cane. The other cutters, sweltering in the heat, spoke amongst themselves and then, in a show of defiance, set their knives on the ground. Before Abraham could run the distance to the men, the overseer spurred forward, unravelling his whip as he came. At seeing the overseer, all the men except one took up their knives and began cutting. Topey, a sturdy man, a full axe-handle width across the shoulders, stood firm, brandishing his cane knife and ready to confront the man and horse careering towards him. When within a few paces, the overseer reefed his mount to a halt and, in the same movement, swung the rawhide whip wide and drew it back for the coil to roll to the end and crack like a rifle shot.

As the overseer wielded the whip a second time, Abraham, out of breath and still at a distance, yelled, 'No! Leave him alone!'

The overseer could have cut the whip coil short but let it fling to its full extent and strike Topey on his bare chest. Topey, now primed beyond reason and not caring about his bleeding chest, raised the two-foot-long knife above his head and charged the horse. The horse, in a state of blind panic, swung to one side, just avoiding the flashing blade, and when Topey lunged forward again it swept further away. Without any thought of consequences, the overseer drew his rifle from its holster, raised it to his shoulder and took aim. In his rage he did not hear Abraham's pleas for him to stop and, as his finger touched the trigger, Abraham grabbed him by the thigh, pushing him off balance and sending the shot wide. Abraham, by no means a small man, then shook him by the torso, threatening to pull him from the saddle if he did not stop the shooting. Fearing that he might be mobbed and beaten to death if shoved to the ground, the overseer heeded the caution and rested the rifle across the front of the saddle. If it were not for Abraham's intervention, Topey would have been either shot or pursued the horseman till outdistanced.

The overseer, realising that his action could cause a general strike and jeopardise the future of Rosewood, spoke with Abraham, trying to pass the incident off as a misunderstanding. Abraham, who had been loyal to Rosewood and the planter's family till now, listened to what was said but deep down in his heart knew that, while he could probably persuade the men and women to return to work, the trust had been broken, never to be repaired. As a result of the disconnect, harvesting would be slowed. Once the overseer had said his piece, he gathered the reins and rode away to report to Andrew. Relief spread across the faces of those in the field. Abraham had saved them for the present.

Word of the incident soon spread amongst the villagers and those of the Rushmore household. Rosie, upset by the implications for her and Abraham, asked Marcella to serve the evening meal and then hurried to her cottage to be with Abraham.

As the setting sun cast lengthening shadows along the veranda, Marcella set the dining table, placing the silverware and arranging the napkins. So much had happened since arriving at Rosewood: the first meal with the Rushmore family, the warm welcome; and then, with the passing weeks and months, the growing acrimony she witnessed; and, of late, the open hostility shown between family members.

Saxon had continued visiting her cottage drunk, messing with her breasts and inferring that if she did not yield to his wishes she could find herself living in the village and labouring in the mill. In recent times, Atlanta had been cold and stony towards her on occasions and, although nothing had been said, Marcella sensed that Atlanta would side with Saxon if his imposition on her became an issue.

On the other hand, Andrew had always been kind to her, and particularly so since their moment of near embrace down by the river. Lucille also sided with Marcella and, in the event of a dispute regarding her, the support of family members would be evenly matched.

Marcella set these thoughts aside when Andrew entered the dining room, having bathed and dressed in his usual collar and tie and carrying a carafe of red wine. Atlanta, wearing an expensive evening dress and with her hair in ringlets, presented herself soon after, taking her seat and helping herself to a glass of sherry from a crystal decanter. Lucille had just returned from riding and, after offering an excuse for attending the table in her riding breeches, sat quietly till the meal was served. Saxon arrived late, dressed in grubby clothes, partly inebriated and with a bottle of rum in hand. He made no apology for his lateness or state of dress and cussed about the day as he plonked himself on the chair beside Marcella. The others, having waited half an hour for him to appear, were partway through their meals. He ignored Marcella's offer to get his meal from the stove warmer, not bothering to look her way and answering with no more than a grunt. Instead, he leant across the table, took a wine glass and proceeded to fill it with rum.

Andrew, having before seen the result of Saxon drinking spirits straight, went to pass a water jug but was rebuffed. Saxon brushed his hand aside and said, 'I'll manage my own affairs.'

The ongoing antagonism that had existed between father and son for years resurfaced, with Saxon seizing on today's event and adding, with a twist of malice in his voice, 'There should be more of the lash. It's the only language they understand. There's nothing wrong with laying the fall of a whip on a black man's back!'

While the attitude of each family member could be pieced together from private conversations held in the past, this open declaration at the dinner table went too far.

Andrew, who did not condone whippings, became enraged by Saxon's blunt assertion. He straightened in his chair and shouted, 'If you can't be humane then go! Get off the property!'

'You can't do that,' said Atlanta, coming to Saxon's defence. 'What he says is true. They must be made to work.'

'My dear wife,' replied Andrew, speaking in a low tone, 'let me manage the property. What has Saxon ever done for Rosewood?'

'He's our son, our heir. He's my flesh and blood,' she replied, repositioning herself as Saxon's devoted mother.

'Your son maybe but—' He cut short what he was about to say. The recriminations had gone far enough. Any more would only foment disunity. Further talk would only tear Rosewood apart.

Lucille, picking up on her father's reason for refusing to discuss the matter further, set to defuse the situation by saying, 'Arguing will get us nowhere. Let's talk about it tomorrow,' and with that offered to serve sweets.

Saxon, without as much as a 'Goodnight' to his mother and father, followed Lucille to the kitchen and took his meal to the back veranda. Lucille and Marcella spoke quietly between themselves as they dished the desserts in the kitchen. Upon re-entry to the dining room they found Andrew and Atlanta not on speaking terms and soon excused themselves to attend to washing the dishes. When retiring, Marcella stepped lightly along the paving stones to her cottage, hoping that Saxon would not see her by the moonlight and visit. She shut the door and undressed in the dark so as not to arouse his lust.

The words that had passed across the dinner table troubled Marcella. Though unaccustomed to the ways of white civilisation, Saxon's suggestion that her people should be whipped to make them work plagued her throughout the night. *What sort of man is he? Does he hate Islanders? Had Rosie been telling the truth when she said that Saxon had beaten a man to death and others had mysteriously disappeared? What will he do to me if I don't let him have his way?* What had been a nagging thought in recent times now loomed as a dire necessity. She must get away from Rosewood before Saxon beat her into submission. With her only contact in the outside world being Florence, she conspired how best to make contact and ask for help. She broached the subject with Rosie but, after a few words, realised that Rosie, fearing for her own future at Rosewood, was reluctant to make any suggestions. However, whatever avenue she took would have to be finally approved by Atlanta the matriarch and, now convinced that Atlanta had brought her to Rosewood for Saxon's pleasure, any request would be denied. Maybe she could seduce Andrew and, in the process, persuade him to make representation on her behalf or simply make the decision himself. She toyed with the idea for the remainder of the day and, at an opportune moment that evening, she spoke with Andrew when alone and made suggestive remarks.

Next morning Marcella rose before Andrew and had the fire lit and the water heating when he came into the kitchen. Andrew, buoyed by Marcella's approach the previous evening, jollied about in the lamplight, talking more than ever, referring to when he was young and alluding to private thoughts of long ago. Marcella seized the opportunity, came close, put her arms around him and lay her head on his chest. Andrew needed no further encouragement and instinctively put his lips to hers, holding the embrace for a few moments. Any thoughts of fidelity or respect Andrew might have held for Atlanta in the early days of their marriage had long been buried beneath her sexual abstinence and continual nagging. He fumbled Marcella's hair and shoulders and then put a hand to her breasts, caressing her through the fabric of her sarong. With playful ease their lips joined again, reaffirming their affection. Marcella, captivated by the Master's touch, put a hand to her cleavage and pulled the sarong down, exposing her breasts. Within an instant she felt the squeeze of his rough hands and then his wet lips sucking her excited nipples. He ravished her, biting hard in his lust and causing discomfort, but Marcella, wanting to be taken, did not resist. Andrew, now unrestrained and blinded to possible consequences, tore at Marcella's sarong, stripping it from her hips and leaving her naked. He feasted his eyes on her body, slim and bronze, believing this to be the magic moment he had dreamed of since Marcella's arrival. He had in his arms a young maiden, as he thought her to be, who would fulfil his pressing desire. Marcella fumbled with trembling fingers, unbuttoning his shirt as his hand slid between her legs. With little experience and not really knowing what to expect, Marcella accepted his rough handling, holding her position and allowing him to grope her crotch. The urgency of Andrew's need drove him with such ferocity that he soon forced entry with his fingers, pressing deep and causing so much pain that Marcella's ardour cooled and she became concerned as to what would come next. She felt some relief when he eventually withdrew his hand, but became anxious again when he undid his trousers, dropped them to his knees and displayed his bolt-upright erection that surpassed anything she had seen at Sorrento. His rough handling continued. He took her by the hands, pulled her to the floor and lay her on her back. All the care and affection that Andrew had shown previously had gone, leaving a man driven by base instinct. Without asking for approval, not even speaking a word, he spread the legs of her beautiful body, straddled her and, with a firm hold of his penis, set to take what he thought to be his entitlement. Her whole body stiffened with fear as she felt him enter and then penetrate deeply, without any consideration of her or her capacity to take what he delivered. As a slave girl being molested by her Master, she lay passive as Andrew rasped away without making eye contact. The feel of his body against hers, the engagement which she had yearned for earlier, turned into a repulsive invasion. She wished for him to cease hammering her and stop hurting her inside but, being the victim of a master-servant relationship, she lay powerless, treated with no more respect than the plantation's livestock. The further he went the harder he shoved and, when she thought she could take no more, he let loose, groaning loudly while pumping her full of spunk. Marcella lay wide eyed as he rested on her and then breathed relief when he rolled aside and rested on his back. After a couple of minutes she glanced his way to be sure he had finished and then rose to her feet. She stood looking down on him, bewildered as to how the man who had been so kind to her could treat her this way. Andrew slowly stirred from his state of bliss, opened his eyes and, when he began gazing at Marcella's body, she picked up the sarong and wrapped it around her waist. With blood now trickling down her legs, she went to leave but was startled when the back door suddenly opened and Rosie appeared. Andrew was similarly shocked and jumped to his feet still fully exposed. Horror stricken and in disbelief, Rosie shot each of them a piercing look before closing the door to hide what she had seen and running back to her cottage.

Andrew quickly pulled his trousers into place and turned to Marcella. Marcella, fearing that he was about to impose on her again, pulled the sarong across her breasts and stepped to one side. He then, showing no sign of concern or regret, took Marcella into his arms again and said, 'Darling, that was perfect. We'll have to do it again.'

Marcella avoided expressing her true feelings and, instead, just nodded. Andrew took this response to mean that she approved and therefore would keep the matter confidential. He paid Rosie's discovery little heed because she would understand that if she divulged it to others Abraham's position on the plantation would be in jeopardy. Though the first rays of dawn were beginning to light the kitchen and a family member might enter at any moment, Andrew again put a hand to Marcella's breast. Real fear gripped Marcella, not only at the prospect of Andrew violating her again, but also the ramifications if Atlanta caught them fornicating. She squirmed at the touch of his hands to her breasts and, when he lifted the skirt of her sarong, she pushed his hand aside, scrunched the sarong tightly about herself and turned to leave. Andrew called after her, offering words of apology, but the damage had been done. What could have been a loving embrace with more to come in the future was now finished. Marcella ignored her Master's call and left by the rear door.

For the next few days, Marcella's disgust with the men of the household burned deep in her mind. While she could understand Saxon's racist attitude, she would never have believed that Andrew could be painted with the same brush. She came to realise that so long as she stayed at Rosewood she would always be considered a slave girl and treated as such, and while confident of fending off advances by Andrew, she believed that Saxon would eventually have his way. Now determined more than ever to free herself from the demeaning and dangerous situation, she approached Lucille with a view to arranging a meeting with Florence.

'Hello there. Come in,' said Lucille when Marcella came to the office door.

Marcella entered, took a seat beside Lucille and, after fumbling for words of introduction, she found her stride and told of her concerns about Saxon. To Marcella's surprise, Lucille understood and replied by relating past events where Saxon had behaved badly. She told about the string of housekeepers that had preceded Marcella. How they had been hoodwinked into accepting the position and, once at Rosewood, Atlanta's attempts to match them with Saxon and then her turning them out like common curs. The last three had been dismissed for various reasons. The first, who Atlanta had anointed to be Saxon's wife, was sent packing when Atlanta discovered she was already married and that she had pocketed jewellery. The one who followed, a firebrand who came without credentials, sought to take over the household, fought with Atlanta, and was summarily dismissed when she abused Atlanta during an evening meal. The most recent, a small, timid woman who Saxon described as 'dry as an old crust', proved unsatisfactory for his purpose and, when he declared that he would rather 'fill a nigger', Atlanta sent her on her way.

In the discussion that followed, Marcella intimated that she would like to visit Florence, and Lucille, picking up on the suggestion, said she would speak with Atlanta. Lucille concluded by saying, 'Leave it with me. I'll ask mother and get back to you after lunch.'

Lucille joined Atlanta at the dining table and at an appropriate moment broached the subject. 'Marcella has asked about Florence's offer to teach her to read.'

Atlanta, a little piqued that the housekeeper would make such a request, put down her cutlery and said with a commanding voice, 'Her place is here, keeping house. Not scooting about the countryside.'

'Yes, but let's think ahead, Mother. If Marcella and her children are to carry the Rushmore name then it is important they are literate. Not only for plantation purposes, but for social reasons. She could even be swayed away from Pidgin and learn to speak correctly.' Lucille then tossed in a softener. 'I'm sure Saxon would appreciate it, particularly with the children.'

'Children!' said Atlanta with a start. 'I'm beginning to wonder if she's capable. What, five months now and not a sign and, I add, no indication that she wants to secure a place at Rosewood. Other women, let alone part-breeds, would give their eye teeth to have a man like Saxon.'

'That's my point, Mother. She wants to learn to read so she can be a good mother to Saxon's children. I think she is being very thoughtful—learn to read and write and then have children.'

'Think so?'

'I know so,' replied Lucille, inferring that she had spoken to Marcella about the prospect and wheedling her way into her mother's ambitions, if not her heart.

'I'm not sure if I want her subjected to outside influence. As it is she is a cleanskin and can be moulded to our ways.'

'That is so but, once again, think of the children. They will need to be worldly, and with Saxon working most of the time they will be left in their mother's care.'

'Well,' said Atlanta after a pause and resigning herself to the idea, 'I suppose a half-breed can be taught to read and write.'

'Then I can tell Marcella that she can go!' chipped in Lucille at this crucial moment.

Atlanta, mindful of Saxon's past and that her treasured son might not do any better for himself, reluctantly agreed. After discussing plans, Atlanta went to the writing desk in her bedroom and wrote to Antoinette Rousseau:

14th August 1871

Dear Antoinette,

Ever since your visit I have endeared myself to the thought of Florence offering to teach Marcella how to read.

You may have noticed during your visit that, as well as having a soft and caring nature, Marcella is also very intelligent.

She and Saxon have become close and, as it is expected that Marcella will become a member of the family, this makes Florence's offer all the more important.

If Florence is still agreeable to tutoring Marcella then next Sunday would suit, say 10:00 am.

Please advise by return mail if this arrangement is suitable.

Yours cordially,
Atlanta Rushmore,
Rosewood

Marcella listened while Lucille read and then reread the letter to her and, after exchanging devilish grins, they hurried to the stable to arrange its delivery.

The stable groom, while happy to oblige with the delivery, took note of the hour and suggested Massan ride to Savannah the next day rather than risk losing his way and having to travel home in the dark.

Lucille would hear none of this. 'If Massan is not allowed to go then I will saddle my own horse, go cross-country and be home before the sun sets on the yard rail!'

Massan, an inexperienced rider, feared the dark but, while he would have preferred to wait till the next day, he was prepared to risk all if it brought Marcella close to his heart.

What at first seemed a good idea became a worry for Marcella when Massan had not returned by sunset and the night fell into total darkness. Being frightened of the dark herself, Marcella imagined Massan, alone in the dark, and how he must be shivering with fear about the possible appearance of evil spirits. Yet he had done this for her and, as she sat on the top rail of the horse yard, anxious and frightened, she realised that he must love her. There could be no other explanation, because Islanders feared the dark and its prowling spirits more than death. When she heard the clopping of the horse's hooves her heart leapt and, when the horse halted and Massan dismounted to open the enclosure gate and all went silent, she feared the worst and murmured, offering herself to the spirits in return for sparing Massan. She began to sway on the rail, believing that the spirits had accepted her bargain and come to get their lot, when, suddenly, the clopping restarted and, to her utter surprise, the horse, with Massan sitting on top, came to her side.

'Have you got it?' she whispered to Massan as though not wanting to wake the spirits.

'Yes, the Missus write and give to me.' He pulled the sweaty envelope from his pocket and pressed it into her hand.

'You frightened?' asked Marcella.

'Yes, plenty.'

'Me too,' she replied, reassuring Massan that he was not alone. 'Come with me. We see Lucille and she read the paper.'

Marcella found Lucille in the dining room making a leather belt by lamplight. When she was told that Massan was at the door she invited him inside. As Lucille opened the envelope with a knife, Marcella's eyes lit with expectation, and Massan doted on Marcella's profile by the soft glow of the lamp.

'Here, let's see what they say,' began Lucille, turning the single page letter to catch the light:

14th August 1871

Dear Atlanta,

Ever since our visit Florence has been asking me to write and invite Marcella to Savannah and I must apologise for being remiss and not corresponding earlier.

Louis has been very busy with the harvest, and last week Sir George and Lady Hamilton stayed for two nights while Louis showed Sir George over the plantation. Hopefully, the submission Sir George puts to the House of Assembly will be enough to curtail the draconian measures the Government intends legislating to appease the Abolitionists. Lord only knows what we will do for labour if the trade is emasculated, and I pray constantly for common sense to prevail. The colony has enough problems without the reformers demanding better terms and conditions for the Kanakas.

I imagine Marcella will be travelling by sulky and chaperoned by a driver. Both are most welcome, and if they wish to stay overnight then Marcella can have the bed that Sir and Lady Hamilton slept in, and the driver can bunk in accommodation according to his station.

Marcella appears to have inherited her father's qualities, whoever he may be, and carries herself with, dare I say, commendable pride. Florence has no other company her age and so I, personally, would like to foster the friendship. Maybe she could visit each Sunday.

Florence is excited about the visit and we are looking forward to Marcella's arrival next Sunday.

With blessings,
Antoinette Rousseau

Atlanta had retired to her bedroom and, to be sure of gaining her full support, Lucille suggested that she wait till morning to present Antoinette's letter.

'After breakfast is the best time,' she explained to Marcella as she folded the paper.

Marcella arrived at the kitchen early the next morning, hardly able to wait for the final approval. She told Rosie who expressed concern, citing examples of similar requests to visit the township of Mackay having been denied. She supported her view with the comment, 'Ma'am no like that. Frightened they come home no more. Two go downriver last year with the sugar boat and not come back. Policeman bring them back in chains and they made to work, stirring the juice in the boiling room at the mill.'

'That's silly, Rosie,' said Marcella, trying to hide any doubts. 'Lucille read the paper and it say all right. She show Ma'am after breakfast.'

'Then best you turn that bacon before it burns,' replied Rosie, pointing to the pan and not wanting to blunt Marcella's enthusiasm.

Soon after breakfast Lucille handed the letter to Atlanta and received a less than enthusiastic reply. 'I'm not comfortable with this, and particularly the suggestion of staying overnight. Who knows what mischief those girls might get up to if left alone? They're at that age.'

'Mother, be realistic. The Rousseaus are God fearing, and nothing of the kind would be allowed,' countered Lucille in a vexed tone. 'Why, they even hold monthly church services at Savannah, and if the reverend visits this weekend Marcella might be invited to attend. A little Christianity wouldn't hurt. Could even be useful if we have christenings in the future.'

At mention of the word 'christenings', Atlanta conceded that there could be some good in the girl, particularly if she could be persuaded to switch from voodooism to Christianity.

Atlanta could be easily led, and Lucille, to strengthen her point, canvassed other reasons to support the visit. She sat beside Atlanta and began by saying, 'Mother, we must be mindful of the Rousseaus' position. In the past they have helped out when Rosewood has experienced labour shortages. And with the state of our mill, it could break down at any time and we would have to depend on the Rousseaus to crush what they could of our crop. As it is, they're crushing Rory Bullimore's cane.'

While not denying that what Lucille said was true, Atlanta's envy of Antoinette and Louis's success always drew a rebuke. 'It's only because they have capital behind them. Antoinette's parents have a stake in the Cardiff docks. Without that they would be no better off than us.'

'I agree,' concurred Lucille. 'If we had the money we could put in a second set of mill rollers, vacuum pans, a crystalliser and centrifuge, but the reality is that we do not have the money and the bank will not extend our credit. Rosewood is one of the first mills in the district and is trying to make do with outdated methods and antiquated machinery.' She finished with, 'Best we stay friends with the Rousseaus.'

The stark reality, as put by Lucille, struck home to Atlanta and, rather than be left destitute and without social standing, she agreed, adding the rider that she would leave all the arrangements to Lucille.

To be free, to be away from Rosewood for a day, would be bliss, and with only three nights till Sunday Marcella could hardly contain herself. Those of the household were reminded continuously by Marcella's not so secret excitement about her first outing since coming to Rosewood. Atlanta remained aloof, acknowledging the pending visit but not giving overt support. She feared that, once Marcella had a taste of life elsewhere, she might reject Saxon altogether, leaving no prospect of a clutch of children. Time was running out, with Saxon showing less interest in Marcella and becoming more dependent on the bottle. If the scales tipped too far Atlanta would have to revisit the past and replace Marcella with another unfortunate bride to be. While Andrew knew well his wife's obsession with finding a wife for Saxon, having witnessed the debacles of the past, he thought that, eventually, she would have to come to terms with the reality that Saxon was hopeless and that he would choose the bottle in preference to a woman every time. No doubt, any arranged marriage would fail, with the wife fleeing from Saxon's abuse and possibly leaving one or more children for Atlanta to raise in later years. Andrew and Atlanta had, at various times, discussed the prospect of Saxon finding a wife and marrying, only to disagree on the manner of procurement and the likelihood of the arrangement being successful. Andrew remained noncommittal but, if the truth be told, he wished Saxon would leave and that Marcella would stay. Marcella, thinking the approval of her visit to be unanimous, chatted openly, telling of her plans and asking questions about Savannah and its people. Rosie set Marcella to scrubbing and cleaning to settle her ardour, only to find that Marcella could scrub and talk at the same time. Marcella reminded the stable groom constantly about the upcoming event by visiting daily to make sure the horse and sulky would be ready. He had chosen an aged mare that would be quiet enough for Massan to handle, yet strong enough to make the journey to and from Savannah in one day. Massan hardly slept, dreaming about Marcella and what the day might bring.

On the morning of the visit, Marcella rose at sunrise, and soon after breakfast she put a few items into a calico bag, said goodbye to those in the household and joined Massan at the stables. To Massan's delight, Marcella presented herself fresh and breezy, dressed in a flowing skirt and with her hair braided. He too had made a special effort, dressed in white shirt and trousers that Rosie pressed for him. The old mare took to the sulky shafts readily and headed down the track, winding between stands of aged gum trees that towered above a grassy understorey. Wallabies hopped away when startled by the surprise appearance of the sulky, and a flight of cockatoos, emblazoned in white against a blue, cloudless sky, squawked their alarm at the intruders. They watered the mare at a creek halfway to Savannah and then continued on, with the mare maintaining her pace.

At the entrance to Savannah plantation they were greeted with a slab of hardwood mounted by the gateway with the words 'Savannah Plantation' chiselled into the flat surface. While neither Marcella nor Massan could read the words they knew, from Massan's previous visits, that Savannah homestead would soon be within sight. Upon seeing the sulky approach, Florence roused those at the homestead with rallying shouts. Antoinette came to the veranda railing, neatly dressed for the occasion. Three Islander domestics joined her, holding their skirts. The homestead roustabout and the stable hands downed tools to see the girl Florence had spoken so much about. Massan, proud to have navigated the dusty road and arrived with all intact, drove right to the garden gate, where Florence stood with the gate wide open. After calls of greeting,

Marcella stepped down and the girls hugged as if they were sisters who had not seen each other for ages. Antoinette joined them and, although joyous to see Marcella finally at Savannah, she, in accordance with accepted protocol, took Marcella first by the hand and then into her arms for a light embrace. Massan had not been overlooked and was surprised and almost overcome when Florence called and introduced an island lad that came from Tanna, the island of Massan's birthplace. After a brief round of talk in Pidgin between them and Marcella, the lads led the mare to the stables.

Antoinette smiled when, barely ten minutes after their arrival, Florence said she had something important in her bedroom that could not wait and whisked Marcella off to share her secrets. Florence's large bedroom with high ceiling, and walls made of red-cedar panelling, held all the things one would expect to find in the bedroom of the only child of rich colonials: a sturdy cast-iron bedstead covered with a Georgian velvet bedspread, cupboards full of clothes that she hardly wore because there was no place to go, the learning material of blackboard, chalk and volumes of books, a desk where Florence sat and wrote to pen friends, a rocking horse with a tattered mane and tail that told of her childhood, a pile of fashion magazines filled with pictures that gave a clue as to Florence's aspiration to become a lady of note, several items of craft work hanging from the walls and displayed on her dresser … All evidenced that here in the wilderness resided a young lass of immense talent.

Florence tripped over herself, showing Marcella all her treasures, sharing her private life with an outsider for the first time. So enthused was she that she did not notice Marcella beginning to sweat across the forehead, and when Marcella wiped her brow she opened the wide double doors to the veranda. This open space, across the floorboards to the garden, to the picket fence and beyond to the virgin woodland, connected two worlds—Florence's inner sanctum and the untamed wilderness. While Florence had everything in the material sense, she lacked the company of girls her own age, leaving a void in her heart, a place that needed to be filled. Round-table discussions had been held with a view to Florence's attending the Presbyterian Ladies College in Sydney. However, after much consideration, a decision had been made to continue her home schooling.

Florence had selected some of her favourite story books, and soon the girls sat on the bed, with Florence reading and Marcella enthralled with the storyline and pictures. They shared a common interest in story-telling, and soon Florence found herself pointing to words and spelling them with a clear emphasis on the phonics. For Marcella, this was the experience of a lifetime and, as the tutoring proceeded, she began tracing the words with a finger and repeating them. More surprising was that this girl who had, till less than a year ago, heard virtually no spoken English, was reciting the syllables almost word perfect. Florence looked at her in wonder when, after only an hour of tuition, Marcella picked up a book with a colourful picture cover and sounded the first two words of the title. The reading occupied most of their time till the lunchtime gong rang, at which time Florence bundled a few books containing both writing and pictures into Marcella's calico bag for her to take home. With a gleeful look, Marcella thanked her and promised to return the selection when she had 'read' them all.

On the way to the dining room, Florence showed her new friend about the lavish homestead, going down hallways and corridors, visiting all from the spacious bedroom occupied by her parents to the nooks and crannies used for storage. In the dining room Marcella found herself surrounded by unbelievable opulence. Painted portraits of family members going back three generations adorning the walls; the polished floor almost covered with a Persian rug of intricate design; the maple dining suite with its polished grain, glistening gold in the filtered light; the silver cutlery and china plates, together with starched napkins; the crystal chandelier with a family history. All this and more captured Marcella's imagination, turning her into a disciple of English culture and sharpening her desire to read to be able to learn more about these people who came from faraway.

Florence took pride in introducing her father, Louis, when he entered the room, standing close to him and revealing the empathy between them. Louis, a fifty-year-old with an affable personality, greeted Marcella with a courteous handshake and words of welcome. He then served the meal and, after grace was said, they enjoyed a meal of cold meat and salad. Most surprising was the late entry of a white woman about thirty years of age and plainly dressed. Before any introduction was made Marcella gauged her to be a forthright and determined woman.

Louis stood up from his chair and introduced her warmly. 'Jane, this is Marcella, our guest for the day.'

'Hello there,' called Jane across the table.

Marcella replied with what she thought to be politeness. 'Me too. Pleased to meet you.'

During lunch Louis, who did most of the talking, informed her that Jane was the plantation nurse who cared for the workers at their hospital. He went to explain further but was interrupted by Florence butting in and saying, 'Jane is also my tutor. She came as the nurse, but is so good at reading and writing that she has taken over from Mother.'

Jane engaged Marcella as they ate, gauging her personality and capacity to accept colonial life, and by the time they had finished, Jane had decided to offer Marcella a place in her 'school', as she like to call the tutoring program. At the mention of this, Marcella dropped her cutlery to the plate with a clatter and burst into tears. Never in her life had she dreamt that people could be so kind. Since being kidnapped and living with white people she had secretly wanted to be part of their community and realised that to achieve this she must be able to read and write. Now, with an opportunity presented across the lunch table, the unbelievable had come true. At that moment, all at the table knew they had in Marcella a winner, and each in their own mind resolved to help where possible.

After lunch, Jane invited Marcella to see the hospital and, together with Florence, the new 'school trio' followed a pathway that meandered through an extensive botanic garden. Louis, as a member of the Royal Acclimatisation Society, had sourced exotic plants from as far afield as South America and cultivated a botanical forest where people and wildlife found food, shelter and joy. Since Jane's arrival three years ago she had worked closely with Louis and the island workers to add another acre of plants and seedlings that would entice more wildlife to forage, rest and raise their young. She stopped partway along the path and cocked an ear. A deep 'oom' sound from a bronzewing pigeon filtered through the forest, calling to a mate. There again and only a few steps away a repeated 'oom, oom'. With a finger to her lips, Jane stepped forward, signalling for Marcella to follow. As stealthily as a cat, Marcella followed a few paces till Jane stopped and pointed to a patch of brown leaves on the forest floor. With a hand on Jane's shoulder to steady herself, Marcella lifted herself on tip-toe and saw the pigeon nestled amongst the leaves. A more beautiful sight she had never seen. This dove-like native of the forest, with its iridescent bronze wings and soft brown feathered chest clearly visible in the dappled light, looked back at her, trusting that Marcella, like the other girls, was a friend who would cause no harm. The girls lingered for a short while and then, so as not to distress this messenger of peace, Jane indicated with a nod that they should move on. This memory of peace stayed with Marcella, and often when Jane, during the tutorials that followed, became quiet and reflective she was reminded of that image.

Beyond the forest and hidden from sight of the homestead stood the hospital, a long shed with a tin roof, weatherboard walls and a wooden floor. Before entering, Jane explained that the sick and injured were hospitalised here in her care because there was no hospital at Mackay and, in urgent cases, the doctor from town was called to attend. Marcella was overcome with the expansiveness of what the family had referred to as the sick bay. Light flooded in through the large windows that were propped open to their fullest extent. The walls to the high ceiling were all whitewashed with lime, and the floor was so spotless that Marcella thought she could eat from the bare floorboards. The bedding, similarly in good condition and free of any grime or stains, evidenced why three domestics serviced the household. While Marcella knew nothing about the prevention of disease and infection, the obvious care gave her hope that this was a place of recovery. Five men lay on stretchers, gaunt and listless, and Marcella wondered if they would live or die.

As Jane spoke more about the hospital, Marcella's thoughts wandered to her experience at Rosewood and what Rosie had told her. Since Marcella's arrival three had died on the property without a mention of their passing being made in the household. If this was not frightening enough, Rosie said that in the two years she had worked for the Rushmores nine had died out of about one hundred Islanders. When asked why, Rosie blamed accidents caused by the white man's plantation, the food being bad for Islanders, some taking their own lives due to homesickness and, most perplexing, some that disappeared without explanation. Further to this, she had never seen the Rushmores treat those in need. The sick and injured stayed in their huts, being treated with traditional island medicine. According to Rosie, one in twenty died each year and were buried unceremoniously beside a swamp on the property where the ground was easy to dig and too wet to grow cane. Most grave sites were unmarked, and the few that could be identified were simply marked with logs or rocks placed by relatives or friends. When asked about what happens when a white man dies Rosie bit her lip and said, 'White man have own resting place in town but no black man allowed to be buried there.' As a warning to Marcella, she also advised Marcella not to speak of the graves or visit the swamp because it could bring bad luck.

Marcella admired Jane for doing her best under difficult conditions, and when told that Savannah buried their dead with dignity and provided numbered steel markers forged at their blacksmith shop to identify those interred she began to doubt the integrity of those at Rosewood.

Marcella was further impressed when shown about the property; seeing the herd of Clydesdale draught horses, all fit and well and, in the distance, smoke billowing from the tall mill chimney, signalling that the mill was operating at full capacity. During afternoon tea on the veranda, an air of goodwill prevailed, unlike Rosewood where it seemed that Atlanta and Saxon conspired to sour what was supposed to be a time of togetherness at evening meals.

Marcella so enjoyed the outing that, when it came time to say goodbye, she became misty eyed, not wanting to return to Rosewood.

CHAPTER 13

Thus began a weekly sojourn, with Marcella and Massan driving the sulky to Savannah early each Sunday morning and returning home late that evening.

While Sundays were supposed to be days of rest and religious contemplation, Marcella found the Sabbaths to be crammed with activity from start to finish. The order of business began with a church service in the small chapel at the rear of the homestead. The wooden building, built with Islander labour, glorified the Rousseaus' devotion to God. The district's Protestant clergyman called once a month, arriving on horseback Saturday evening, joining with the family for the evening meal and enjoying convivial conversation by the open hearth before retiring to the guestroom and settling himself in the comfort of the four-poster bed where state dignitaries had rested their heads. On the Sundays that he was elsewhere saving souls in his bush parish, Louis ministered the service, taking his place at the pulpit and giving sermons that sought salvation for the colonists and the 120 Islander souls in residence at Savannah. In addition to family members and Jane and Marcella, Islanders who had turned to Christianity attended. When the chapel filled to overflowing they sat on stools outside, holding umbrellas to shade them from the blistering sun. All listened to the readings from the bible, trying to fathom the Lord's meaning or, for those who spoke only Pidgin, trying to decipher the words as they were spoken. When singing the hymns, the strong melodic voices of the Islanders could be heard drifting to the stables and beyond. Marcella associated Christianity directly with the success she saw at Savannah and thought that, if this is what Christianity could provide, then she must follow the teaching. Jane, a lay preacher who had previously ministered in

New Caledonia as a missionary, visited the plantation's Islander community regularly to teach religious instruction with a view to converting these pagans to Christianity. Louis and Antoinette, equally passionate about spreading the Lord's word, played their part in this crusade by supplying Jane with material that the listeners could take home and hang in their grass huts. Florence had not escaped the influence of the teachings and, of late, had begun accompanying Jane to the village to preach God's word.

During the two hours following the church service, the girls sat at a table on a screened veranda with Jane tutoring them. While Jane taught Marcella reading and writing, Florence immersed herself in reading novels like *Jane Eyre, David Copperfield* and *Wuthering Heights*. As an avid reader she skipped through these and boxes of other titles as quickly as Antoinette could ship them in. Jane knew she had a literary prodigy in the name of Florence Rousseau but, for Florence's protection and, it must be confessed, Jane's love for Florence, she left it unsaid. When Antoinette first drew this to Jane's attention she acknowledged Florence's gift but qualified her comment by saying that it was not anything out of the ordinary, particularly nowadays with public school education becoming more available. Since then Antoinette had broached the subject with Jane several times, advocating that Florence be sent to Sydney to give her the best opportunity, only to be dissuaded by Jane who made veiled references to the sins that filled the dark corners of some supposedly reputable girls' schools. Though Jane had never told Antoinette about the molestation she suffered while in one of these institutions of learning, Jane vowed that, under her watch, Florence would never enter a boarding school. No one had ever openly questioned why Jane, an attractive miss in her early thirties, had never married. No one gave any thought to her possessiveness of Florence.

One Sunday, when Marcella, Jane and the Rousseaus finished lunch, Marcella handed her empty plate to an Islander housemaid named Mabel and said, 'T'nk you.'

The maid smiled broadly, took the plate and said, 'T'nk you, P'incess.'

At being addressed as 'Princess' Marcella held the woman's attention and asked, 'Where you from?'

'Loyalty. Loyalty Islands.'

'Which one?'

'Mare.'

Marcella, a native of Lifou, the largest of the Loyalty Islands, switched from speaking the universal language of Pidgin English to conversing in a dialect known only to the natives of the cluster of islands known as the Loyalty Group. Though the others at the table did not understand what passed between them, they watched, following the facial expressions and hand gestures, trying to fathom what the women held in common. Jane, who understood a word here and there from her missionary days, listened intently for giveaway words that would provide a clue to what was being said. Antoinette and Louis exchanged glances, for they had often spoken about Marcella in private and thought that, prior to being kidnapped, she, as a beautiful and intelligent mixed-race woman, would have held a high position within her island community. In expectation that all might now be revealed they sat quietly hoping that, via this animated interchange, something of Marcella's past might be revealed. Florence, fluent in Pidgin from spending time with the Islanders in the plantation village, thought that, with her flare for linguistics, given enough time she would unravel whatever had been unleashed by Mabel's reference.

Word of Princess Marcella, granddaughter of King Jacques, the ruler of Lifou, had filtered to the large contingent of Loyalty Islanders stationed at Savannah, and now that her status had been confirmed, she would be revered within the village community. When Mabel returned to the kitchen, the focus fell upon Marcella, obliging her to explain to the others the reason for Mabel's excitement and, in the process, disclose her full identity. Marcella willingly revealed her past and, after she had been showered with compliments, Louis raised his cup of tea and spoke for all there when he said with pride, 'Welcome, Princess Marcella. Welcome to Savannah, a place you can always call home.' This surety meant more than just words for, unknown to those there, Marcella planned to abscond from Rosewood and seek refuge at Savannah.

Marcella made regular visits to the hospital with Jane to attend the sick, and one Sunday a man in his forties, greying and lying on a stretcher, called to her. She hesitated, waiting for Jane, but, when he called again in a frail and anxious voice, she left the linen cupboard and came to his side. His eyes followed her every move as she looked down on his wasted body with its knobbly knees and elbows, skin tightly stretched across his exposed ribs, hollow cheeks and sunken eyes. She wanted to return to folding the linen, but when he took her by the hand and held tightly she knew that what he needed most of all was comfort. Her smile brought faint recognition to his eyes, lighting them for a few moments when he told her that his name was Moses. Without any nursing experience, Marcella did what she could, lifting Moses' head and putting a glass of water to his lips. After he took a few sips she repositioned the pillow and lay him down. She then sat beside him on the bed, held his hand, and spoke about life back home. The talk rallied him and, without needing to be prompted, he murmured the name of his village on Malaita Island and asked if Marcella would promise to return his remains to his village. Marcella knew well the belief that if an Islander's remains were not interred according to custom then their spirit would remain in a state of spiritual limbo and not return to its rightful place with their ancestors. At hearing this, Marcella felt a shiver pass over her because, according to superstition, all deaths, including those from old age, resulted from retribution by the spirits for some misdeed or neglect occasioned by the person during their life. This notion, once implanted in the mind, plunged the victim into a state of depression, causing them to waste away till overcome by death. Worse, if the remains were not interred in accordance with tradition, the unfortunate spirit would be locked into a state of damnation, never to reunite with their ancestors. With this foremost in her mind, Marcella promised Moses that she would fulfil his wish. Having set in place the final arrangements for life in the mortal realm, Moses sighed and closed his eyes in rest. Seeing him lying motionless and hardly breathing, Marcella, thinking he was about to die, panicked, put a hand to her mouth to muffle her scream and turned for help. Jane, hearing and then seeing Marcella's distress, came quickly and checked Moses' vital signs. She told Marcella that, while he would survive the night, his time was near. Marcella had attended the funeral rites of villagers in the past but never been so close to the moments before death. The complexity of island culture where worship revolved around the cosmos and the spirits of ancestors remained a mystery to the colonists. Even Jane, who had spent five years working amongst them in New Caledonia, could not fully comprehend their beliefs. The two women stayed by the bedside till Moses drifted into a deep sleep, with Marcella trying to relate death to her spirit world and Jane seeking salvation by praying to her God.

During the following week, Marcella brooded, wondering if Moses was still alive and, if not, how she would fulfil her promise to him. Those of the household at Rosewood would not be interested, and with Massan having only a casual interest this left Rosie as the only person in whom she could confide. Rosie did express sympathy but, with Abraham still losing weight and thinking he might also be infected by a bad spirit, she said little for fear of offending the spirits. If Marcella could send a message to Jane and enquire, a reply either way would satisfy the angst besetting her mind. She did broach the possibility with Lucille who, while sympathetic, thought the request to be one too far and, after noting that Sunday was only a few days away, suggested she wait till her next visit.

Upon arrival at Savannah the following Sunday, she asked Massan to drive directly to the hospital building where she jumped from the sulky, ran to the front door and dashed inside. A quick glance revealed that Moses' bed had been taken by another patient and that Moses was nowhere to be seen. The poignant realisation that Moses must be dead tore at her, spilling her into an emotional mess. She cried and shouted his name, hoping that, by some chance, he was tucked away somewhere close. Those at the homestead heard and Jane, guessing the cause of the upset, rushed to meet Marcella as she raced towards the front gate. Marcella's discovery that the kind, gentle man she had nursed and comforted was now gone crazed her mind, rendering her hysterical and uncomprehending. Jane, having had experience with traumatised patients, flung her arms around Marcella and held tightly to stop her from self-harming. Others of the household became involved, assisting Jane and offering Marcella assurances that she was in good hands, that all would be all right. Needless to say a solemn church service was held and all other activities for Marcella cancelled for the day. Of all those present, Marcella responded most to Massan, whose kindness she turned to in this time of grieving. Massan understood island belief and, in this time of need, Marcella turned to one of her own kind for comfort. All the way home Marcella leant on Massan's shoulder, sobbing while he held her with one hand around her waist and the other holding the reins.

Those at Savannah thought that, with Marcella so grief stricken, she might not visit next Sunday, but their hearts filled with joy when along they came with Massan in the driver's seat and Marcella waving a scarf for all to see. Sundays from that day onwards followed much the same routine, with church, tutoring, attendance at the hospital and Florence and Marcella capping the day with a horse-riding excursion like that of today.

As usual Massan had the horses saddled and ready to go when Florence and Marcella entered the gate to the stables. When mounted they looked like an odd couple, with Florence sitting high on a well-bred hack and Marcella astride a gentle pony named Pixie.

'Push him out,' said the stable overseer to Marcella, wanting her to dig her heels in harder to break the horse into a trot to be sure it would behave, before opening the stable gate and letting her loose on the plantation. Massan so loved Marcella, and all through the past weeks of visiting Savannah he had felt privileged to be by her side. Those at Savannah had found him to be a respectful lad and were left in no doubt regarding his affection for Marcella. The riding breeches Marcella wore had been made by Antoinette, and the riding boots loaned by Florence. Marcella dared not take the breeches home to be washed because to do so would certainly inflame Atlanta's jealousy of Antoinette. The only information Atlanta received about the outings were sketchy accounts given by Marcella when questioned. To tell that she went horse riding and thoroughly enjoyed herself would raise Atlanta's ire. She would discredit the practice by saying that horse riding was dangerous and to ride astride unladylike. In truth, Atlanta's objection would arise because Marcella would have contact with stable hands, and who knew what might eventuate. As for Massan, she had long suspected that he was making mischief with Marcella and intended curtailing their visits.

Massan wished the girls well and sat on the rail of the yard, watching till they disappeared from sight behind a field of sugar cane. He would still be there watching when they returned and greet them with a shout. Though cheery on the outside, Marcella concealed a grieving heart and, for the first time, asked to visit Moses' grave. They passed by broad fields, lush with stalks of cane higher than anything Marcella had seen at Rosewood. Where the young cane grew, workers were stretched across the field in a line, chipping weeds while singing island songs. Never had she heard laughter or song from field workers at Rosewood. They reserved this for their own time in the village. The oxen ploughing the fields and horses pulling carts of cane to the mill were in good condition, not like Rosewood where the animals showed their ribs. Even the wildlife, the natives of the land, were fewer at Rosewood due to rifle shot and traps, unlike Savannah where all God's creatures were respected and allowed a place on his blessed land.

The girls rode past all of this and into the bushland, winding along a narrow track accessible only on horseback or by foot. *Is this the way, the only way to the graveyard?* thought Marcella, thinking that a body would have to be carried rather than transported in a cart. *Why so far? Why not the sunny slope facing the breaking dawn they had passed earlier? Who will know that this hidden site ever existed when the sugar fields are gone and the land reclaimed by native trees and grasses? Will these shackled workers be forgotten forever?* Marcella's thoughts returned to the present when Florence's horse stopped in front and Florence beckoned her forward. They sat still and quiet for a few moments in reverence for the dead and then dismounted, hitched the horses to trees and looked across the open space. The graveyard, set in a clearing and dotted with steel peg markers, stood as a stark reminder of the lowly status given to the Islanders.

'Which one?' asked Marcella, timidly taking a pace forward.

'Over here.' Florence pointed to a fresh grave on the far side.

Florence led the way, skirting around the rows of pegs and then along one side till they came to the pile of fresh earth that marked where Moses had been interred.

'Here it is, *Number 32*. We keep a register of the burials in case the government inspector comes asking.'

'Who came to the funeral?' asked Marcella, feeling the loneliness.

'Oh, not many. Jane and I and a few of Moses' friends who dug the grave. We stayed while it was filled in and said some prayers.'

In island culture, Moses would have been given an elaborate funeral with colourful funeral rites that lasted two days and a day-long feast to follow. Marcella stood bewildered by the undignified end to Moses' life—so cold and unceremonious. Further to this, if Moses' remains were not returned to his homeland and interred with his ancestors, his spirit would remain in exile, never to be reunited with his ancestral spirits.

Florence, seeing tears falling from Marcella's cheeks, realised she had been brash and to make amends put an arm around Marcella and whispered, 'Sorry. He was a good man, one of the best.'

This only went part way to consoling Marcella, and to shield herself from a rebound of the trauma that beset her at first hearing of his death she asked to leave.

Back in the cane fields she heard song drifting across an open field and realised that Moses was not really alone because his friends would visit the peg marked *Number 32* and communicate with him in the spirit world.

From here they passed by the mill where women stripped the remaining trash from the stalks of cane before men fed them into the crushing rollers to extract the juice. Marcella compared this mill with that of Rosewood and, although she understood little of the process, the attitude of the workers, the cleanliness, and the large shed full of bagged sugar told her that things at Savannah were far superior to Rosewood. They followed with a jaunt alongside the river where they swam naked and, when clothed again, teased each other's wet hair to ensure it would be dry by the time they arrived home.

CHAPTER 14

With the passing of each winter came the risk of fire, and while all planters in the Pioneer River basin faced the danger, Rosewood, locked into a valley surrounded by spurs from the main mountain range, remained the most vulnerable. Year after year fires lit by careless settlers or lightning strikes threatened the planter's crops and livelihood. If a crop were burnt out then the planter would forfeit any further income for that year and, in addition to this loss, would have to cover the cost of their workforce cutting and dumping the burnt cane and then finance the worker's upkeep till the cane regrew for next year's harvest. If a planter was unable to finance this it could lead to closure of the plantation. Rosewood, with its precarious financial position, could not meet such a challenge and would, undoubtedly, be disbanded or sold.

With the landscape drying and the leaves of the cane turning rusty brown, Andrew remained vigilant, scanning the ranges for smoke or flame. His habit of lifting his hat and replacing it low over his forehead to cut the glare seemed like a quirk till, while standing on the veranda of the homestead at midmorning on a hot day, he spotted smoke spiralling from a heavily wooded forest. With the prevailing drought conditions and no plantations between Rosewood and the fire, Andrew panicked, thinking his worst nightmare might materialise. He shouted to Saxon who came to his side, and together they determined that Rosewood could be burnt out. They set out to mobilise the Kanakas to confront what threatened to be a fiery onslaught. Andrew took the side gate to the stables to saddle a horse while Saxon ran out front and careered down the slope to alert the mill workers, field hands and those in the village. Rosewood had fought fires in the past, losing fifty acres of mature cane one year when a fire jumped the fire break and roared through the field like an inferno. Fortunately, the adjoining fields had been harvested, and through the gallant efforts of the Kanakas the fire was arrested before it swept through the remainder of the plantation. With a brisk breeze blowing today's fire towards Rosewood, the threat bore all the hallmarks of that frightful day when all was nearly lost. Andrew galloped to the far corners of the plantation, marshalling workers and directing them to assemble at the mill in readiness to fight the fire.

By three o'clock dense smoke blanketed the sky, hawks circled above in search of fleeing prey, and smoke filled the nostrils of those standing ready to battle the blaze. With only empty sugar sacks and branches torn from trees to beat the flames, success or otherwise depended on the willingness of the Kanakas to face a wall of fire. Back-burning was suggested, but with the risk of a spark floating overhead and into another field the idea was discarded, leaving the 110 contingent of men to fight the flames almost bare handed. The fire gathered pace, consuming all in its way as it approached Rosewood. Flames, forty feet high, scorched the heavens as the tops of gum trees ignited and burst into fireballs. Andrew conferred with Saxon and the overseers and all agreed that if wind conditions did not change, the Kanakas would have to be called into retreat and make a stand to save the mill and village. Andrew also considered the homestead which, though positioned well away from the forest, could come under direct threat if the wind changed direction. The women there, unaware of this possibility, watched from the veranda as the troop left the mill to position themselves where first contact was expected to be made.

By five o'clock the fire front had leapt forward to within a mile of the plantation and the cordon of men now stationed ready to fight. The Kanaks could have refused to assist, but with no provision in their indenture agreement concerning the taking of risk and believing that any disobedience would be met with severe punishment, they banded together as a tribe without any thought of being obstructive. They would do as instructed and fight the fire as servants of the Master, without concern for their personal safety. The plantation had acquired a persona of its own where *it* was Lord and Master over all, including Andrew and his family. Its demands took precedence, controlling the lives of everyone in residence. In effect everybody, for one reason or another, had become a slave to Rosewood.

One overseer, an Irishman from Killarney, held open prayer, asking for forgiveness and that the evening breeze come early and steady the fire. Some other overseers revealed their belief by joining in the prayer and crossing themselves. Andrew, a non-practising Protestant, suddenly found a need for God and stood respectfully while the prayers were said. While the Kanakas made no visible signs of ritual, their moments of contemplation, brief as they were, served the same purpose, asking their ancestors for strength to fight the fire. The sky darkened as if night was falling. The roar of the fire filled the men's ears and smoke choked their throats.

Marcella stood on the homestead veranda with Atlanta and Rosie, watching the men confront the fire, exposing themselves to danger. Marcella feared that, apart from the loss of the crop, the mill and the village, there would be multiple injuries, with some dead and others critically injured. She set aside all thought of racial differences, thinking of them all as brave men, placing their lives in jeopardy for the sake of the plantation and its residents. She gripped the railing when a freakish gust of wind swept the fire through the tree tops and lit the sky above the firefighters' heads. By the firelight she clearly saw the men as they flung themselves forward to plug this gaping hole in their line of defence. With flame swirling overhead they did the unbelievable, standing their ground as a unified garrison, prepared to fight to the last man. Marcella gasped when an eddy of fire obliterated her view, leaving what she thought to be the men engulfed in flames. Though no screams could be heard from where she stood, she imagined them writhing on the ground, hairless and gasping their last breath. Atlanta and Rosie screamed at seeing this, thinking their spouses had been taken by the firestorm. Only Marcella dared to keep looking as the menacing flames twisted and turned on another gust, shooting high into the sky and leaving a mass of black smoke in their wake. A curtain had fallen, separating Marcella from the men's lives, leaving her horror stricken at the thought of what was happening in the darkness of the moment. Nothing would be spared, all would be taken asunder. A hideous scenario appeared before her, a vision of her and others picking through the bodies, helping those who had survived and trying to identify the dead. A sense of helplessness and dread descended on her, causing her to shake with fear of what would be revealed. She stood as a lonely soul, shrinking at the thought of the destruction till, suddenly, a cool breeze sprang up and played on her back. She felt it first on the nape of her neck and then across her cheeks as the breeze strengthened. She stayed in this vague state of mind till realising that this was not a cross-current caused by the thermal heat of the fire, that it was a sea breeze sweeping up the river. She remained statue still, transfixed, watching as the breeze gathered strength, ruffling the leaves of the fields of unburnt cane and beginning to lift the pall of smoke. She followed the rising cloud of smoke intently till, in the greying of dusk, she saw movement where the cordon of men had been stationed. There again, another gust, clearing more of the smoke and revealing dozens of men regrouping to attack the flames. She stood in awe of these brave men for a few moments and then, seeing the other women with their heads in their hands, shouted, 'They're alive. Looks like all of them, swinging their sacks!' Atlanta and Rosie looked across the fields and, upon confirming Marcella's sighting, collapsed, crying uncontrollably.

The breeze, having reached the men, brought the same realisation, that all was not lost, that if every man pitched in they could beat the odds. With that and a command from Andrew, the Kanakas and colonists marched against the flames, beating every lick of flame that came before them, smashing hard so every spark would be extinguished, sparing nothing of themselves to beat the peril of fire. By nine o'clock the women saw only the occasional flare of bright light, and by midnight not one spark lit the landscape. Unity and strength of commitment, together with prayer from their Irish friend, had halted what would have been the catastrophic end of Rosewood.

The next day, Andrew saddled a horse and rode back to where the men had fought the fire and marvelled that no lives had been lost. The blackened earth, right to the firebreak, stood as a stark reminder of how close Rosewood had come to being destroyed. Now aging and tiring from the rigours of colonial life, he sat in the saddle overlooking the plantation, assessing his situation, casting back to the past and considering the future. The monthly correspondence received last Friday contained two letters from the Bank of New South Wales: one a letter of demand and another, dated subsequent to the first, giving notice of foreclosure. Though Andrew had tried to conceal previous correspondence, Lucille, who collected the mail monthly from Mackay, had read the content in private and not told Andrew. Atlanta would have brushed the concern aside, telling Andrew that he must work the Kanakas harder. Saxon had never taken responsibility for anything, could not care and seemed destined to living life as a drunk. Andrew's previous letters to the bank, telling them that a fire sale would not recoup enough to cover the debt and, therefore, please grant an extension of time, had met with muted responses.

Andrew looked across the plantation with a heavy heart, unable to see a way clear. The vista before him: a patchwork of fields all suffering from drought, the Kanakas weary from being overworked and the mill falling into ruin. Only last week Andrew discovered a crack in one of the three cane-crushing rollers. If this were to fracture then all production would cease and, with procurement of a spare in the colony being unlikely and one ordered from England taking months to arrive, the bank would sustain an even bigger loss. Rosewood's indenture documents had been accepted by the bank as security and, in the event of foreclosure, the bank, to avoid the upkeep of the bonded Kanakas, would promptly sell the indentures to other planters, forcing the Kanakas to relocate and, in the process, fracture families and friendships. As for the Rushmores, they would leave with their suitcases and nothing more.

While these problems had been in the making during the past few years, things had become more strained since Marcella took up residence. Lucille no longer jollied about the house, fresh faced and fancy free. She focused on trying to balance the books, coming from all angles, accompanying Andrew on his field inspections and stretching her young mind, making suggestions that might improve efficiency of both the field work and milling. Though operational costs could conceivably be met, she had read Andrew's correspondence and was well aware of the pending demise. In her frantic effort to save Rosewood, she took Atlanta to task, asking her to curtail her personal expenditure and that of the household, but her mother would have none of it, insisting that funds were available and, if necessary, the bank would grant an extension of credit. Lucille felt sympathy for her father but, as yet, had not plucked the courage to disclose her knowledge of the bank's latest correspondence. To do so would surely embarrass him and possibly push him to suicide rather than admit defeat. She considered raising the topic on a few occasions but, knowing Andrew's unwillingness to discuss the distressed state of the plantation's finances, she had deferred, leaving the matter unresolved and Andrew carrying the burden. Of late this concern had become so acute that she became restless each time he left the house, particularly when he took a rifle.

Saxon's disservice to the family had worsened in recent months with him ignoring the urgent needs of the plantation and paying more attention to his personal interests. In past years he had been the plantation's marksman, slaughtering ten to twenty wild horses each time the herd came into the fields during the dry season to feed on the young cane. His routine of rising before dawn and surprising the animals had wakened everyone, both at the homestead and in the village, when cracks of rifle fire and the sound of galloping horses echoed around the ranges. However, this season not one shot had creased the air, allowing the horses to destroy several acres of cane. He drank rum till late, rose late and, by the time he sorted his inebriated brain, little time remained to do a productive day's work. Even then, these days were interrupted by his hiding rum and fishing lines in his saddle bag and spending hours fishing, drinking rum and fornicating with his Islander girlfriend by the river. Massan, who saddled Saxon's horse, knew of the deception and this, together with Massan's closeness to Marcella, led to Saxon's increasing contempt for Massan, at times bullying him with abuse and threats of violence. This show of the racial hatred he held for the Islanders was further exacerbated by Marcella's refusal to submit to his continued harassment for sex. His relationship with Andrew was finished, with the only resolution being one or the other departing the plantation.

Saxon had become more intimidating since Marcella's arrival, making uncalled for comments at the dining table and challenging Andrew with a view to embarrassing him in the presence of the others.

His snide remarks extended to all there, including Marcella. He inferred that everyone knew why she had been brought to Rosewood and that time would tell.

The strained relationship between him and Lucille reached breaking point when, one night, she told him, 'Shut up if you can't say anything nice.'

Before Saxon could respond Atlanta cut in. 'Saxon is free to say what he thinks. Why are you and your father so against him?'

This unwarranted support for Saxon drew Lucille's ire to fever pitch. 'What is it with Saxon? Why is he always right and I am wrong?'

Atlanta tossed her napkin to the table and confronted Lucille. 'Daughter, don't forget your place in this household. If you can't accept your brother then best you leave.'

This unprecedented attack riled Andrew. He turned to Atlanta and, with a threatening voice, said, 'Maybe Saxon should go!'

This provocation brought an immediate and savage rebuke. 'Maybe it is you who should go and leave it to Saxon to manage the property!'

The venomous reply by Atlanta flabbergasted Lucille who shouted, 'Saxon can go to hell!'

Atlanta, now in a fit of rage, picked up a fork and waved it at Lucille in a menacing manner. Lucille, having seen this behaviour before and knowing that Atlanta was now beyond reason, stood, glared at Atlanta momentarily and then, without excusing herself, left the table. Andrew soon followed, leaving Marcella at the mercy of the other two. To save herself she politely excused herself and went to the kitchen where she surprised Rosie listening with an ear to the door.

Andrew, the family man who had built Rosewood and now faced losing all, found himself in an impossible situation, with the plantation crumbling, the bank demanding settlement and his family disintegrating. In his darkest moments, thoughts never before considered possible crossed his mind. He felt shame at failing with the plantation, plunging Rosewood into debt with the bank, and bearing the cross of not being able to hold his family together.

Saxon had come to the stables early and waited impatiently while Massan caught his horse and proceeded to saddle the mount for the Master. As a stable hand for the past year, Massan had come to know Saxon's irritable personality, his mood swings and, at times, had borne the brunt of his verbal abuse and beatings. Last night Saxon had again been refused by Marcella, with the most telling moment being when she, out of sheer frustration, told him that she would never lie down for him. In his rum-fuelled state and anger he told her that the next time he called she would get it one way or another. The brief encounter ended when he flung his chair against the veranda wall and stormed back to the homestead. His aggression had become more threatening in recent weeks, and Marcella now feared for her life. She righted the chair and entered the cottage, closing the door behind. Ever since her arrival the front door had remained unlocked. The wooden slide that locked the door from the inside had been removed, with the door able to be opened at the touch of a finger.

'Hurry there, Boy,' shouted Saxon as Massan placed the saddle on the horse's back.

The girth strap needed to be lengthened. It was fiddly to undo the buckle and shift the pin a few notches in the leather strap. Massan fumbled to undo the buckle and then spent more time counting the number of holes he thought the strap needed to be lengthened.

'You ignorant nigger,' sneered Saxon, referring to Massan's limited ability to count. Then again, while stropping his trouser leg with a riding crop, 'Hurry or you'll get a bit of this.'

The threat made the situation worse. Massan's hands trembled and the horse, sensing the strife, fidgeted and moved away.

'You useless black bastard!' shouted Saxon when Massan dropped the girth strap and had to reach beneath the horse for another try. 'What is it with you niggers. Will you never learn!'

'No, Master, leather dry. Make it hard to find hole,' replied Massan, now sure he was about to receive another beating that would leave him bloodied and sore.

To Saxon's depraved mind black men and their labour came cheap, and if he happened to kill the 'boy' then he would simply have the Kanakas take him away in a cart early in the morning and bury him by the swamp. All so easy, buried anonymously and forgotten and, if he had any regret at all, it would be the loss of the labour the deceased could have supplied.

In the still of the morning, Marcella heard Saxon's shout and came to the porch of her cottage to see Saxon standing over Massan. Then, to her horror, she witnessed Saxon lift the riding crop high and whip it across Massan's back.

Massan fell to his knees, doubled over and cried out, 'No, Master, please! I try better!'

Marcella took hold of the hem of her nightdress, stumbled down the stairs and careered towards the stables, shouting, 'Stop! Stop!'

The women at the homestead heard and rushed to the veranda rail to see Saxon land another blow on Massan's back and Marcella in full flight, screaming for him to stop. In his rage and oblivious to Marcella's screams,

Saxon struck again and again, drawing blood from Massan's back and turning his white shirt bright red.

At the stable gate, Marcella swung the latch open, flung the gate to one side and stormed towards Saxon, yelling for him to cease, but her cries went unheeded. Saxon, firmly in the grip of his pathological state of mind, felt no shame, only the gratification his manic mind sought by causing pain to others.

Lucille had witnessed instances of this in the past, not only with Islanders but also animals. His psychotic mind had, time and again, resulted in unreasoned outbursts where he indiscriminately struck out in his lust to kill. Lucille knew the signs. After he had beaten Massan to death, he would take to Marcella and punish her in the same way. She leapt over the veranda rail, tore across the garden and raced forward without any thought of the consequences. Though he was supposedly her brother she, like Andrew, doubted his paternity. With no time to arm herself she ran through the gateway and to the fracas unfolding before the eyes of everyone present.

Marcella had shoved herself between Massan and Saxon, using her body to shield Massan from more harm. She stood defiant before Saxon's menacing look and spat in his face. 'Hit me! Hit me!' She challenged him to hit the woman he had been trying to seduce for months. Though Saxon was taken aback by her outburst, his unhinged mind recognised nothing of what she said. He had tasted blood and only a kill would satisfy his delusion. As Saxon raised his hand to deliver her a cutting blow she grabbed his arm and held tightly, trying to match his strength. In his fury he shook her free like a rag doll, and as she fell to the ground Lucille lunged forward, knocking him to one side. She then took to him with a ferocity and strength never before seen from this plantation girl. With fists clenched she hammered him about the head, smacking any eye and splitting his lip. If Saxon wanted violence then she had plenty to deliver, direct and hard hitting, without any concern for what he might do in retaliation. Saxon, having never believed Lucille to be his full sister, perceived her as sacrificial, one to be slain like others in the past. In his deranged state he lashed out, striking Lucille across the face and dropping her to the ground. Then, without a flicker of remorse, he turned to add her to the list of Islander people he had murdered on the plantation, all of which had subsequently been declared deaths by accident or illness by the administrators of Rosewood. If those in the graves by the swamp could speak, they could count amongst themselves several who had died at his hand.

Though neighbours gossiped among themselves about Saxon being a psychopath and related stories of black deaths at Rosewood, no one took any action to stop this hidden carnage. Information that passed to the police lay in files as sketchy notes, with not one instance having been properly investigated and no arrests. While all of this was committed in the name of the Rushmore family, blame lay at the feet of Saxon, the villain, and Atlanta his accessory. For years Andrew had covered for the misdeeds of these two, and when Lucille became old enough to understand, she sided with Andrew in concealing the truth of why Rosewood had lost an inordinate number of labourers over the years. A shroud of silence, like that over the graves of the deceased, kept hidden the truth of Saxon's heinous acts and disposal of the bodies.

As Saxon lifted a foot to sink his boot into Lucille's body, Marcella came from behind and wacked him across the back with a metal rake, sending him to the ground in agony. She, now also enraged to a point of no return, lifted the rake again to smash his skull but was intercepted by Rosie shouting in her ear, 'No! No! Marcella! No kill! We all get flogged!'

During Rosie's time at Rosewood she had seen the result of floggings; grown men severely injured, some maimed for life. To save those in the village she grabbed the rake and dragged it from Marcella's hands while shouting in her native dialect for Marcella to think of her people. The ring of Rosie's voice, the one Marcella respected as an elder, struck home, returning her to sensibility and staying her intent, which would have ended with Saxon dead.

The stable groom, having been alerted by the shouts and screams, rounded the corner of the stable and, seeing Saxon lying on the ground and groaning with pain, came to his aid. He lifted Saxon to his feet and helped him back to the homestead to be in Atlanta's care. Marcella, Rosie and Lucille assisted Massan to his room at the stables and lay him on a bunk. Massan, terrified and bewildered, cried and pleaded for Marcella to hold his hand. This she did while the others cut the shirt from his back. When Massan began to settle, Rosie and Lucille left him in Marcella's care. Before reaching the house, Lucille reminded Rosie of past events and that if word of this were to reach the police the workers at Rosewood might be flogged or sent to faraway places. Rosie understood and, as she had done in the past, pledged her silence for the sake of her kin.

That evening Marcella took hot soup to Massan and stayed the night, watching over him as he shrieked from night terrors. Lucille ate in the kitchen and then went to her bedroom without saying goodnight to the others. An argument erupted at the dining table. Andrew berated Saxon for his stupidity and Atlanta came to his defence while he sat passively without expressing any remorse. An uneasiness encrusted the homestead and stables for the remainder of the night.

During the night Marcella came to the conclusion that she must escape from Rosewood before Saxon sought revenge. However, when she took breakfast to Massan in the morning and he again insisted on holding her hand she realised that, for his sake, she must stay at least another night till he was able to cope on his own. She skipped lunch and, apart from speaking with Rosie and a visit from Lucille to apologise for Saxon's behaviour, she kept to herself in the cottage for most of the day. At evening time she again ate with Massan and stayed till late, before returning to her cottage. She changed into a nightdress by lamplight and, after snuffing the lamp wick, lay on the bed covers where she soon drifted to sleep. After a short while she woke, thinking she had been roused by a dream, but when she heard a creak of the floorboards she immediately sensed that this was no dream, that this was real. She lay still, not daring to open her eyes for fear of alerting the intruder, hoping that if she pretended to be asleep then whoever it was might take what they wanted and leave. The approaching footsteps gave no clue till, when they drew near to the bedside, she detected the unmistakable smell of rum. She cringed inside, knowing it was Saxon and that he came seeking retribution. The first she felt was his hand to her breast, and when she opened her eyes and tried to scream he slipped a hand to her throat, choking her. She froze, gasping for air, while he ripped her nightdress from her shoulders and dragged it full length till it slipped from her feet, leaving her fully naked in the moonlight flooding through the open window. Without a word he undressed and stood before her in full view.

She lay petrified, not game to scream as he straddled her body, spread her legs with his knees and, without any attempt at foreplay, thrust hard and deep, tearing his way into her crotch. His cruel and incisive rape lasted a few minutes and then, when in the throes of wild spasms, he jerked, filling her with spunk. After relieving himself he stayed on top of her, breathing heavily and nudging now and again. Marcella thought he was all done but, to her horror, she soon felt him firming again and, still without a word having passed between them, he set to butchering her for a second time. With warm blood now down her thighs and searing pain cramping her belly, Marcella could take no more. In a state of total distraction she unleashed a ferocious attack, sinking her teeth into Saxon's cheek, tearing the flesh and leaving a gaping hole. With blood streaming from his face and unbearable pain ripping through the side of his head, Saxon slipped from Marcella's body and fell to the floor, cradling his head in his hands. Marcella rose from the bed, picked up a water jug from her bedside dresser and smashed it across his head, knocking him unconscious. He made no movement and, thinking he might be dead, she fled naked from the house and into the darkness.

CHAPTER 15

Marcella ran blindly across the open grassland and into the forest with no thought or care, tripping and falling, picking herself up and careering forward with her heart pounding. On and on she went for miles, till her legs could carry her no further and she collapsed in a dry gully. How long Marcella lay there semiconscious she had no idea except that, by the time she rallied to full consciousness, her whole body throbbed. Though lost and confused, her understanding of the matrix of the stars and the angle of the shadows cast by the moon told her she must track in a northerly direction if she was to cross the road to Savannah. With the going rough and blackened stumps popping up like figures of the dead, she picked her way along the forest floor, hoping that each moonlit clearing would be the roadway. When she descended from a rolling ridge and felt silty soil beneath her feet, she knew she had entered the lowland, where the road meandered across the valley floor, but would her failing legs carry her the distance? Reaching the roadway would give her hope of being found. If Saxon had survived and came along, she would hide in the grass till he passed. With blood still weeping from her crotch, she worried she might fall unconscious and, if so, could fall prey to Saxon. She had last seen him motionless on the cottage floor, thinking he might be dead. When she came across a tree stump showing cut marks left by cordwood cutters who supplied wood to either the Rosewood or Savannah sugar mill, she knew the road must be close. A little further along she surprised herself when, coming over a rise, she stumbled onto the roadway. From previous trips to Savannah, Marcella knew that to get there she must keep the northern ranges on her right.

After travelling this road so many times with Massan driving the sulky, she could never have imagined a situation where she was struggling on foot and fearing for her life. With blood splattered across her thighs and down to her feet, and parched for a drink of water, she pushed ahead, hoping to find the creek crossing where Massan often stopped to water the horse. The road became more familiar the further she went, and when a tree line of dense forest loomed ahead she realised that the creek was near and licked her lips in anticipation.

The moon had sunk low to the horizon and now, making her approach, and with the thick canopy of trees crowding out much of the moonlight, fear of the dark replaced fear of the possibility of being surprised by Saxon. The threat posed by the eerie darkness replaced any thoughts of Saxon galloping her way. Marcella hesitated, torn between the fear now possessing her and the need to drink. She moved forward timidly, looking around with wide eyes for any signs of evil spirits that may be lurking in the shadows. When knee deep in the running stream, she knelt down, drank and then splashed water across her face and down her front. The blood that had gone unnoticed till now caught her attention and, feeling the discomfort, she took sand in her hand and scrubbed, washing from the waist down. This cleansing brought relief and, for the first time since escaping, Marcella thought that help might be within reach, even though Savannah still remained miles away. Swayed by the gentleness of the stream, Marcella lay down, immersing herself in the cool water, feeling life returning to her body and limbs. With the moon waning and the surrounds deepening in darkness, thoughts of the marauding spirits of her beliefs returned, and when a mopoke owl called from a nearby tree her spine stiffened. According to traditional belief, wherever Marcella went these demons of the past would pursue her, waiting for an opportunity to strike at her heart, seeking revenge for some wrongdoing perpetrated by one of her ancestors in a time gone by. There could be no escape. She would eventually be entrapped and here, in the loneliness of the dark, presented the perfect chance. There again 'mopoke, mopoke' echoed along the river, confirming her fear that her time had come, that she would be struck dead in a land far from home. Gripped by panic, Marcella rose from the water and rushed recklessly to the sandy bank and then down the road in the hope of leaving behind the damnation of the past.

The sulky ride from the creek to Savannah normally took at least an hour, and reaching there in the falling darkness without being hounded and taken down by the spirits seemed an impossibility. The muscles of her legs burned hot, sweat poured from her body; she was failing, and before long would be crawling on hands and knees. Time and again she fell, only to pick herself up and press on through the graveyard hours of the early morning. The moon had now disappeared, leaving her enveloped in a shroud of darkness. If not for the light colouring of the roadway and her bare feet able to feel the rills of soil left by sulky wheels, Marcella would have been trapped in total darkness till dawn. Islanders are tough, tough as boot leather, but this ordeal surpassed anything that Marcella could have envisioned, alone and scared out of her wits. If she had a horse and sulky she could draw some comfort from the company of the horse and have confidence it could find its way in the dark.

Oh, if only Massan could be by her side! His courage and steady hand would see them through. Then there was Grandpa, her guardian and mentor since birth. If only he could appear and lead her from the dark. Lucille at Rosewood and those at Savannah came to mind. She could hear their voices, bringing comfort and offering to guide the way. These distractions were all that kept Marcella on her feet, otherwise she would have crumpled to the roadway and, as she had seen happen to others of her kin, given up all hope and willed herself to death; dying alone, and later found cold and stiff on the roadway by a passer-by.

Her loss of blood, together with exhaustion and the fear of dying, reduced her mind to a mire of confusion. She was unable to gauge progress or the distance that remained to Savannah. Time and space became blurred, with no end in sight, yet she battled on, guided by thoughts of others and an inner strength inherited from her parents. Those steeped in island superstition would not believe how Marcella could have defied the spirits and come this far. Somehow Marcella had broken through a psychological barrier. If she persisted until dawn broke she might live to see Savannah.

She continued on and, when reduced to a crawl with dust filling her mouth from falling face down in the dirt, something miraculous happened. A warm lick to her cheek came like the touch of a guardian angel. She looked up and, against the first rays of dawn breaking over the brow of the ridge, she saw Sapphire, the Rousseaus' Irish setter, standing by her side. *Could it be? Am I saved?* Marcella's clouded thoughts struggled to comprehend and believe that Sapphire, whom she had cuddled so many times in the past, had come to her aid. Sapphire understood and continued licking, telling Marcella that she was now safe. Marcella went to speak but her lips, cracked from the dryness and the dust, garbled only a few words before her swollen tongue prevented her from saying more. The last Marcella remembered before falling unconscious was Sapphire licking the dust from her face.

Sapphire stayed by Marcella for a while, and when Marcella did not rouse she left her lying by the entrance to the plantation, raced to the homestead, scampered around the veranda and whimpered at Florence's veranda door. She listened for Florence to stir, and when no one stirred she stood on her hind legs, clawing at the door and barking.

Florence jumped from her bed at hearing the commotion, opened the double doors and, after asking Sapphire what the matter was, followed her through the garden gate and down the driveway. At seeing a naked body by the main entrance Florence hesitated, not knowing the gender or origin of what appeared to be a dead Islander. Then, with Sapphire's excited yelps to lead her forward, Florence took courage and followed, tripping on her nightdress. When close she recognised the naked body to be Marcella and dashed forward, screaming for help.

Seeing Marcella lying at her feet, and thinking she was dead, Florence shouted Marcella's name. When there was no response she turned and fled back to the homestead. Louis and Antoinette rolled from their bed at hearing Florence's distressed calls, and Jane came running from her cottage.

'It's Marcella,' she cried, 'down by the gate. I think she's dead!'

While Louis and Antoinette wanted to hear more, Jane took control, calling for Louis to help her with a stretcher from the hospital, and Antoinette and Florence to go to Marcella. Florence and Antoinette arrived first and rolled Marcella onto her back. Antoinette was patting her cheeks when the others arrived with the stretcher. Jane knelt beside Antoinette and slapped Marcella's shoulders while shouting her name. She repeated this over and over till, eventually, a movement of Marcella's arm and a groan brought calls of 'hurry' amidst their tears of joy. With the four of them each holding a corner of the stretcher, they trotted up the incline to the homestead, and then a little further to Jane's cottage, where they lay her on the bed in the spare bedroom. By now Marcella was beginning to rally, moving her head and trying to focus on those surrounding her.

'Florence, pour a glass of water. Antoinette, a sheet please to cover her. Louis, open all the windows and doors!'

Jane, with boarding-school regimentation and knowledge of nursing, took charge, issuing instructions while propping Marcella's head up ready to give her water. Marcella took one sip and then another. When she took a big gulp Jane exclaimed, 'She's back with us! She's going to live!' The room filled with joyous reverence as Louis led them in prayer.

Though Marcella's eyes were still shut, she heard the voices and the prayer and lifted a hand in response. Florence began to cry, holding her hands to her face and sobbing. Antoinette put her arms around her, held her close to her bosom and reassured her that Marcella would be all right. If Marcella did die, the bond between her and Florence would be broken and, as an only child, and with Marcella as her best friend, Florence would be crippled now and into the future. Jane understood this, and when the situation settled and the others needed time to go wash and have a cup of tea, Jane insisted that Florence stay by Marcella's side. She would bring tea and toast for Florence.

During the day Marcella rallied to a point where she could sit up in bed and take tea with toast and jam. Florence had not left Marcella's side, and when her bed time came she hugged Marcella and promised to return at first light.

Alone with Jane, Marcella began to fidget and look around the room anxiously. Jane, knowing the signs of panic and fearing that Marcella might lose control if left alone in the dark, reassured her. 'I won't leave you. I'll bring the couch in and sleep beside you.' While this went a long way to settling Marcella, Jane had not realised the full extent of her trauma and sat in a chair beside Marcella till Florence relieved her at dawn.

The night had been horrendous, with Marcella repeatedly insisting that Jane check all doors were locked. Also at Marcella's request, Jane hung a hessian sack across the window to block the outside world. The worst moments were when the lamp burnt out. Even though Jane kept talking while she refilled the lamp, Marcella clawed at the sheet, trying to hide herself and screaming. By morning Jane was totally exhausted and, having received words of appreciation for her effort in 'bringing Marcella back from the dead', she was relieved when Florence and Antoinette took turns in attending to Marcella's needs and comforting her.

As instructed by Jane, Marcella was not to be left alone to brood and imagine that evil spirits hovered close by. This disturbed state of mind remained for days till the visiting reverend, in the presence of the others, exorcised the cottage of any harmful spirits. From the church services that Marcella had regularly attended on earlier visits she had accepted the idea of Christianity and, believing God's powers to be superior to that of island belief, she believed she was now safe in the hands of the saviours at Savannah. Nevertheless, it still took another week before Marcella would venture to the cottage deck, and another week before she would move from the security of the exorcised cottage.

The trauma that Saxon had inflicted on Marcella, both physical and mental, was unforgivable, and Louis and Antoinette agreed privately between themselves that under no circumstances would Marcella be allowed to return to Rosewood. The possibility that Marcella was with child to Saxon had been discussed by the adults, and all agreed that Jane would monitor Marcella's condition. If it came to pass that she was with child, they would then deal with the matter. While every child is a gift from God, each wrestled with their own conscience concerning what should be done if that situation arose. Unknown to each other, the three adults had concluded in their own minds that Savannah was Marcella's home, and the plantation would also be home for the child.

The next month saw Marcella make good progress, engaging in household and hospital duties, becoming more outgoing and, of course, spending time playing with Sapphire on the lawn each evening. The white overseers had been told of the situation in broad terms and directed to challenge Saxon or anybody else from Rosewood; to turn them away and, if necessary, evict them by force. Louis and Antoinette did discuss this matter. While unsure how the Rushmores would respond, they fully expected repercussions. Marcella was never to be left alone when away from the house; a member of the household and Sapphire were to shepherd her at all times. Louis felt so strongly about the possibility of an attempted abduction that he sought counsel from God through prayer and received conditional approval to do whatever was necessary to preserved Marcella's safety and integrity. This man of peace was prepared to take up arms in God's name to protect Savannah's princess.

Jane pulled a pleat straight in Marcella's dress, stood and said, 'You look beautiful. Have a look in the mirror!'

Antoinette had finished sewing Marcella a new dress that morning and now, having pressed it with a hot iron, Marcella stood in her bedroom of the cottage she shared with Jane. She looked this way and that in the full-length mirror, admiring both her pretty dress and shapely body. Jane also took notice, and when Marcella glimpsed her in the mirror Jane's expression mellowed even more, revealing the depth of her affection for Marcella. Without any indication of what was to come, Jane stepped forward, took Marcella in her arms and held her in an embrace, while fondling her hips and buttocks. Marcella, a cuddly person by nature, took this to be a show of affection and nothing more. The possibility that Jane might be in love with Marcella and might want to go further did not enter her mind. As always, Marcella followed her emotions, feeling rather than thinking, and allowing things to take their course.

Jane's experience in life had taken a different course, and while she remained loving and compassionate, memories of her abusive past had foiled attempts at reaching out for the comfort of others. The boarding-school janitor, who denied molesting her, had been believed by the school principal. With years of unblemished service at the college and the authority that an adult male has over the word of a fifteen-year-old student, he was believed over Jane and she was discredited. The female principal even went as far as writing to Jane's parents, expressing profound disappointment at Jane's accusation. Worse still her parents, and in particular her father, also disbelieved her story. Her father, a clerk who saw Jane's attendance at the prestigious school as a means of gaining social status, became so inflamed that he took to Jane with a strap, belting the stripes of the Union Jack across her legs and behind. This lack of trust, this acceptance of the word of a despicable predator over that of their only daughter had, since that day, remained unresolved in Jane's mind. She was forcibly returned to the school as a boarder and, from the day she walked through the hallowed gates of that school till the day she finished her schooling two years later, she always carried sharp-pointed scissors beneath her uniform, ready to stab the vile man if he ever attempted to touch her again.

Like most children, Jane yearned to be part of her family and, after leaving school, she stayed at home, trying to forget the past, but the damage had been done and, for her own state of mind, she slipped away unannounced before her next birthday, never to return. She trained as a nurse and, when boarding in a small tenancy, men, some worthy and others nothing more than trash, made overtures but, close as some relationships became, she could never fully embrace any of them. She found more in common with women and fell for what she thought was a likeminded nurse at the hospital. This failed and, after being rejected and ostracised by others of the staff, she turned her back on the colony and joined a missionary service in New Caledonia for a few years. She eventually became restless and, after reading an advertisement in a copy of the *Brisbane Courier*, advertising for a live-in nurse at Savannah plantation via Port Mackay, she applied for the position and was accepted.

While the past few years at Savannah had satisfied most of her needs, there remained a void that only intimacy with another woman could fill. Since her arrival she had watched Florence mature from a girl with budding breasts to one now able to fill a mature woman's bodice, and she had, in recent months, found difficulty withholding her feelings. With Marcella now sharing the same cottage and unattached, the situation might change, but for better or worse Jane could not be sure.

As part of Marcella's rehabilitation, Florence took her to the stables most days, where they groomed horses and went riding in the open air. This outdoors activity proved to be of value, with Marcella being reintroduced to the outside world through her love of animals. The girls held common interests, visiting the village and talking to those there, passing the mill with its billows of smoke and clouds of steam, riding by the fields and drawing rein to stop and watch the colourful parade of island workers labouring under the hot sun and, as had become a regular event, visiting a secluded pool in the river where they stripped and swam, frolicking without a care. Any initial modesty they might have felt, particularly Florence, dissipated after the first few outings, leaving them bare in front of each other's gazes and open to temptation if they so desired. They became so comfortable with this routine that they stayed longer at the pool. So casual had they become that one day when Marcella shook her head, scattering droplets of water in the bright sunlight, Florence remarked, 'Don't bother to dry it. Just plonk your hat on and let's go before it gets too late.' Apart from the joyous smiles and enlivened chatter between them each time they returned to the stables, sight of their wet hair evidenced their nude swimming and conjured thoughts in the minds of the stable hands helping them unsaddle. What mischief had occupied the girls while away, and would they be willing to share?

This immodesty had not gone unnoticed by Jane and, apart from it being a departure from accepted protocol, she had her own reason for disapproving of Florence and Marcella's swimming together in the nude. She lay awake at night, able to hear the rustles when Marcella stirred in the bedroom next to hers. She entertained wild thoughts of the girls having fondled and maybe having gone further down by the river.

She had begun grooming Florence soon after her arrival. She truly loved her and, by some means, had intended making them a couple. Now, with the entry of Marcella and the possibility of her and Florence falling in love, her thoughts were awry, visualising scenarios that were simply not true. She feared a love triangle in which Jane loved both Florence and Marcella, Florence possibly loving her and, to her distorted perception, the certainty that Florence and Marcella loved one another. Fiercely loyal to Antoinette and Louis, Jane found herself in an unbearable situation. She was unable to openly express her feelings. Evening meal times were the worst when all sat at the dining table for dinner and Louis said grace. How could she, herself a minister of religion who had dedicated her life to doing God's will, think of her own tangled love affair when she was supposed to be offering thanks to God? Yet she did. Night after night she sat in their company, accepting their generosity while thinking the unacceptable. This conflict dragged her down to a depth so low that she would either break down and openly declare her position or leave Savannah without ever expressing her love for everyone there.

So passionate was Jane about mankind that she loved all, including the villagers living a traditional life by the river. In her darkest moments she thought she would quietly leave Savannah and retreat back to New Caledonia where she had spent time as a missionary. Day after day this conflict remained unresolved and began taking an increasing toll on one of the most beautiful women God had ever put on earth.

'Marcella, we have a man from the government staying tonight,' said Antoinette, looking up from her embroidery.

'What man?'

'He's from the Lands Office. Savannah is an agricultural lease, and once a year a man comes to check that we are doing things like clearing enough new land and making other improvements.'

Marcella, with a collection of new dresses that Antoinette had made for her saw this as an opportunity to dress nicely. 'Do you think the white cotton or lemon chiffon?'

Antoinette, as she had done so many times since Marcella's arrival, put down the embroidery and gave Marcella her full attention.

'I think the chiffon is much more ladylike. As an accompaniment, I'd suggest Florence plait a thread of lemon ribbon into your braids. As for shoes, the white ones go with almost anything.'

Antoinette had accepted Marcella as a daughter, a surrogate for the second child she had so badly wanted but was unable to have after Florence's difficult birth that nearly claimed Antoinette's life. She believed that Marcella was a gift from God, sent to fulfil the lives of her and Louis and be a sister for Florence. Marcella had been welcomed unconditionally and, now being a member of a wealthy planter family, she could look forward to a fulfilling future.

Antoinette finished the conversation by saying, 'He's been here before, a nice young bachelor man, about thirty and well mannered. I'll seat him beside you. Remember that his name is Oscar.'

Tingles of expectation warmed Marcella's cheeks as she thought about what to wear at this dinner, her first formal engagement, her first opportunity to sit as an equal in mixed company. Marcella laid out her dress and shoes and spent the morning washing her hair, filing her nails and admiring herself in the mirror. She involved Jane, taking her into her bedroom to approve the selection of evening wear. As always, Jane showed interest and suggested that, since

Marcella had well-rounded hips, she should wear the waistband that accompanied the dress to show the best of her island figure. By mid-afternoon she sat on the deck of the cottage like a true princess, with Florence drawing the strands of her wavy hair and plaiting long braids with the fine lemon ribbon woven in as a highlight.

As evening fell, she watched from the cottage as the young man rode up the driveway, said hello to Antoinette and then proceeded to the stables, where the groom took charge of the horse. As he strode to the homestead with a case in one hand and a bag in the other, Marcella stroked her hair, wondering if he would at least glance her way.

By the time the housemaid sounded the dinner bell, announcing that dinner was about to be served, Marcella had been introduced to Oscar and sat close beside him at the table. Like a maiden on her first outing, Marcella felt unsure of herself. Was she dressed nicely? Would he notice? She glanced Oscar's way, seizing on his cufflinks, bold and beautiful, and his strong hands with well-kept nails. When passing the gravy jug she ventured further, glimpsing his blue eyes and exchanging a smile.

During dinner Oscar's cultured accent and charm captivated Marcella. She was besotted by his every word. Each glance of adoration he passed her way was met with her wide brown eyes flooding with want. Marcella wanted to be everything English and, here with Oscar by her side, she saw an opportunity. Even though she had shared his company for only an hour, she thought she knew everything about him. In her heart she believed that to be part of his life would bring love, glory and riches, just like the Rousseau family. She became so obsessed with what she imagined him to be that she directed all her attention his way rather than to the others. So smitten was she with lust for this man she had just met that to touch his cufflinks would bring unimagined joy.

Never before had anyone at the table seen Marcella so effusive, touting for Oscar's courtship with hurried words and leaning forward, spilling over him. Antoinette, though deeply religious, understood the ways of women and, seeing Marcella looking so beautiful in her chiffon and braids and pursuing Oscar with such passion, wiped tears from the corners of her eyes. Louis, God's caretaker at Savannah, toyed with his napkin while watching, hoping that Marcella would remain virtuous. This was the first flirtatious encounter

Florence had witnessed, and she secretly wished that Antoinette had sat Oscar by her side. Jane, with her jealousy of Marcella piquing, squirmed at the thought of them lying together.

Nothing of Marcella's ardour had settled by the time family members began to excuse themselves. For Jane the evening had been a poignant reminder that her love for Marcella remained unrequited, that maybe the two might never be united in secret liaisons where words of love would be exchanged. With pain in her heart and a distressed mind, she excused herself from their presence and retired to her room at the cottage where Marcella, with or without company, would eventually return.

Marcella's amorous gestures towards Oscar embarrassed Louis and, to avoid what might happen next, he said goodnight soon after Jane and went to pray in the bedroom where he and Antoinette regularly enjoyed the same passion from which he now wanted Marcella to abstain.

Florence's undue attention to the couple remained unabated till Antoinette, wanting to foster the courtship, suggested that, since it was bedtime, she and Florence should say their prayers and go to bed.

When the candles of the chandelier burned low, Marcella took the liberty of cupping Oscar's hands in hers and leading him to the veranda, where she pulled two deck chairs close, sat in one, and patted the seat of the other for Oscar. The moon beamed with brilliance across the fields of sugar cane that stretched from the homestead to the river and to the unspoiled woodlands. The sight spiked Oscar's thoughts of one day becoming a planter, with hundreds of acres of tall sugar cane, a huge workforce and a sugar factory that produced more raw sugar per day than any other in the valley. This grand vision of riches and power occupied his mind, competing with Marcella's attempts to win his affection. Time and again she slid a hand across his on the chair rest and, in her fervour, ventured further by rubbing his shoulder and putting her lips close to his ear while whispering about the South Seas and what life could be if they were to share.

Oscar's charm had drawn other women in the past but, invariably, each time a women spoke of sharing a life together he had turned aside, fearing that marriage might interfere with his ambition of becoming a member of the plantocracy. He envisioned establishing himself and then marrying a genteel lady who would serve him by having his children to continue his name and perpetuate a family dynasty. To father a child to a mixed-race Islander would bring shame and a rebuke from the planters, jeopardising all, and so he decided to satisfy himself by toying with Marcella but abstaining from intercourse. With this in mind, he followed Marcella's lead, fumbling her breasts, stroking her thighs and feeling further, lifting her to heights never before experienced. Marcella could hold back no more and, riding high on her passion and arousal, she asked him to take her to his room and make love. At this Oscar restrained his advances, pulled back and, to Marcella's heartbreak, suggested that, since it was late and he had to ride to Rosewood tomorrow, he should get some sleep. The stark response, made in cold and uncompromising language, bit at Marcella's emotions, reducing her to tears. She then, as a last resort, knelt beside his chair and implored him to take her into his arms. The unbelievable happened when Oscar rose to his feet, took her outstretched hand and kissed the back of it with stoic formality. He followed with a few words of apology, wished her well, and then excused himself without turning back. Marcella lay on the hard veranda boards, distraught and sobbing, unable to comprehend the situation. She had laid herself bare, prepared to accept this man in love and bear his child, only to be spurned.

Antoinette, having watched the interplay at the dinner table and concerned about the outcome, lay awake brooding and praying for Marcella. On hearing the whimpers from outside she slipped from Louis's side, quietly opened the bedroom door to the veranda and went to Marcella's side. The first Marcella knew was Antoinette kneeling beside her, taking her hand and whispering. In near hysteria, Marcella rose to her knees, wrapped her arms around Antoinette and held her 'mother' as does a child when distressed. With the moonlight flooding the floor space, they remained locked in a caring embrace, sharing the love of God. Time slid by, the moon gradually dimmed and, when Marcella felt able, Antoinette ushered her to the cottage where she tucked her into bed and kissed her goodnight.

Marcella brooded for days, yearning for Oscar and unable to understand how he could have been so gracious and then treat her so badly. She raked through the tangle of her emotions, trying to come to terms with what she thought to be love. Over and over the thoughts tumbled in her mind as she cried into her pillow at night. Those of the household remained supportive, listening and trying to dispel her obsession. The fixation possessed her till the third week, when some semblance of normalcy began to return. Through the haze of the emotional cross-currents that had fobbed her mind she gradually came to realise that her intense feeling was infatuation rather than true love. Within the next two weeks she regained full control of herself and had become a wiser person.

CHAPTER 16

Soon after sunrise on the morning following Marcella's rape, Rosie entered the kitchen at Rosewood to find Saxon sitting at the kitchen table holding a bloodied towel to his face.

'Aah!' she exclaimed, shocked at the unexpected sight. 'Saxon! What have you done?' Rosie hurried to his side and lifted a corner of the towel to see his face.

Saxon, with stale blood caking the towel and dry blood down to his wrists, winced with pain while saying, 'I have a piece taken out of my cheek. Get Mother and hurry.'

Knowing better than to ask for an explanation, Rosie patted Saxon's shoulder by way of reassurance and then raced through the dining room and down a hallway to Atlanta's room.

'Ma'am, Ma'am!' She hammered the door with the palm of a hand. 'Quick! It's Saxon! He's hurt!'

'Won't be a moment!' Within a count of five Atlanta pulled the door wide, revealing a greying woman dressed in a frumpy nightdress. 'What's happened?' she asked with a tremor in her voice.

'It's Saxon. In the kitchen with a towel to his head and blood everywhere!'

Atlanta's aging cheeks paled at hearing the news that her precious son had been hurt.

'How bad?' Her voice trembled. Without a moment to lose, she gathered her crumpled nightie beneath her sagging breasts, pushed by Rosie and fled down the hallway.

Rosie ran behind and, upon entering the kitchen, saw Atlanta in a flood of tears and reaching for Saxon.

'Saxon! Saxon ...' Atlanta's lament could be heard throughout the household. She clutched Saxon about his shoulders and nuzzled her face into his bloody hair in her frenzied state.

'Mother, please, I need a doctor,' said Saxon softly through quivering lips.

Both Andrew and Lucille were aroused by Atlanta's shrieks and came running, bumping into each other at the kitchen door. Rosie, aghast at the bloody spectacle unfolding before her and beginning to suspect how the teeth-mark injury occurred, stayed clear, pressing her back against the kitchen bench.

Andrew, with his hair tossed in a mess, didn't care about his appearance as he forced Atlanta from Saxon's side and took charge. He spoke to Saxon with a firm voice, asking him to remove the towel and turn his head to the side. After a fleeting inspection of the wound and realising the most probable cause of the jagged wound he asked, 'How did this happen?' When Saxon refused to say he shouted, 'Tell me, son! Is it Marcella? Have you interfered with Marcella?'

Saxon, fearing his father's wrath, acknowledged the question by lowering his head and nodding.

At that moment Lucille, as she had done on a previous occasion at the dinner table, stepped in front of Andrew, braced herself and appealed for calm.

Andrew, unable to contain himself any longer slammed his fist on the table and shouted at Saxon, 'You're finished!' He then turned, leaving those in the kitchen to care for Saxon, and rushed to Marcella's cottage.

He charged up the steps, through the open door and into Marcella's bedroom, where he found blood-stained bed linen and a trail of blood leading to the doorway. In a blind rage he dashed to the stables, gave directions to the head groom while saddling his horse, and left at a gallop to where he thought he might find Marcella. The groom, as instructed, set off at a canter to visit the village and the plantation's work gangs and enquire if anyone had seen Marcella. Though Marcella had rejected Andrew's advances subsequent to his imposing himself on her in the kitchen, he still hoped that, with time, he could regain her trust and rekindle their friendship.

Atlanta had been reduced to a blithering heap, sitting on a chair with head in hands and sobbing inconsolably. With Saxon unable to help himself, Lucille set about doing what she could to dress the piece of flesh she had seen hanging from his right cheek. She set Rosie to work, stoking the embers of last night's fire, putting a kettle of water on the stove to heat and getting more towels. When done she asked Rosie to go to the stables and tell Massan to ride full speed to Mackay to summon the doctor.

To Massan's questioning, Rosie said in brief that Saxon was hurt and she thought Marcella had fled. 'Keep an eye open for her along the way. She might have gone to town!' said Rosie as her parting words. Now outside the house and away from Atlanta's sobbing, Rosie realised the implications of what had happened and looked towards Marcella's cottage with deep concern.

During the agonising wait for the doctor, Lucille wiped away what blood she could and bandaged a pad across the wound. Atlanta's hysteria eased and, at Rosie's suggestion, she sat on the veranda, with Rosie encouraging her to take a cup of tea. For Rosie, a nightmare had just begun. All the nurturing she had put Marcella's way, all the love she had given, would end in despair if Marcella had been killed or had taken her own life. Knowing Marcella's strength of mind she soon dismissed suicide and, given the improbability that she had met with a serious accident, Rosie came to the conclusion that Marcella had most likely found her way to Savannah. Accepting this as the most probable outcome, she settled and returned to the kitchen to wait for the doctor.

The doctor arrived in good time and, on examining the wound and being told how it had been inflicted, he told Saxon to take another swig of the rum he had been drinking and to grip the chair tightly. Saxon could be accused of many things but one thing was sure: he was tough and showed no emotion apart from a grimace each time the doctor slid the needle through his flesh to make a stitch. The doctor prescribed the use of diluted carbolic acid to swab the wound several times a day to, as he said, guard against any contamination from the mouth of the attacker. He put aside Saxon's suggestion that the alcohol in his overproof rum would be as effective.

When the doctor left, Lucille visited Narisse at the village, enquiring after Marcella and asking her to keep watch and to advise of anything she heard regarding Marcella's whereabouts. After leaving Narisse she searched elsewhere, including the river bank and the graveyard, where she thought Marcella might go to connect with the spirits of the deceased.

Lucille, like the others of the household, soon learned that Marcella had fled to Savannah and lived there in the care of Louis and Antoinette. She considered visiting Marcella but, as she said to Rosie, 'It's best to let sleeping dogs lie till the dust settles.' Rosie, wanting news of Marcella, had reminded Lucille, but to date she had given excuses for not visiting.

For Massan the days were long and the nights longer. He remained fixed in time, unable to let go of the memory of Marcella sitting on his bunk and holding his hand on that fateful night when she was raped and fled. Time and again he was tempted to steal a horse and ride to Savannah, but fearing that the Rousseaus would send him back and that he would be flogged or, worse, be beaten to death, he instead burned with revenge and plotted to murder Saxon.

Atlanta's paranoia had become intolerable, to the extent that she now imagined Marcella would return, wed Saxon and they would happily live together in the cottage. So driven had she become that she swept the cottage each week and on occasions put a vase of fresh flowers on the dining table as a welcome home. The bats in the belfry of her mind even extended to her enlisting Rosie's help to decorate a corner of the bedroom as a nursery. 'For when the babe arrives,' she told Rosie.

Saxon's thoughts were otherwise. He spent more time parading about the village hand in hand with his girlfriend. With a shiny black body, a loin cloth around her waist, strings of coloured beads dangling about her bare breasts and smoking a pipe, she fancied herself as Queen of Rosewood and gave to Saxon whatever he wanted to ensure she retained that crown.

Since the night of the rape and the confrontation the following morning when Andrew threatened to bash Saxon, father and son had not spoken. Neither did it appear that the difference would ever be reconciled. Saxon's relationship with Lucille had become tenuous. They only spoke to each other when a need arose. More so than before, Saxon skipped evening meals, staying out late and sometimes not returning till early morning. Atlanta's greatest fear was that he would visit the village one day and not return. She tried to persuade him to stop seeing the girl.

She confronted him one morning as he crossed the veranda with a bottle of rum in hand and asked, 'Where are you going?'

'To the village,' he replied offhandedly.

'To see *that* girl?' she asked with a strained voice.

'Yes.'

'Wouldn't it be better if you stayed home more?

'What for? There's no company here.'

'There's me.'

Saxon glanced at her aging frame and withering body and then, with ridicule in his voice, said, 'Mother, there are some things you can't do for me.'

The inference that Atlanta compared less than favourably with his girlfriend drew a hostile response. 'You've no right to speak to me like that! I've sacrificed everything for you!' She added, 'Can't you see there's no future with that black tramp?'

'You don't know the woman,' said Saxon, stiffening his stance.

'Know her! I've seen her, unbathed and a pipe glued to her mouth. How could you carry on with such a hag?'

'She's not a hag. I'll bring her to the house and you can see for yourself.'

Atlanta objected vehemently. 'She will never set foot inside the gate as long as I'm here. You seem to have forgotten your breeding.'

To which Saxon replied, 'What about my breeding? Is there something I don't know about my pedigree?'

'Please,' said Atlanta, realising her blunder and trying to cover the secret she had held since Saxon's birth.

On an impulse Saxon blurted, 'Is Andrew my father? I've heard talk to the contrary.'

Atlanta, on the verge of confessing that Andrew was not his birth parent, just shook her head rather than speak the words.

'Well,' said Saxon with a note of derision, 'my dear mother rolling in the hay with a lover. Tell me who is he?'

'Don't, please don't,' pleaded Atlanta, fearing that knowledge of her having cheated on Andrew in the early days of their marriage would be the last straw.

Saxon stood silent and unmoved, looking at her with the cold and distant look of a psychopath before uncorking the bottle and guzzling a large slug of rum. Atlanta had seen this transformation before and, frightened of what he might do, turned to leave.

'Not so fast,' taunted Saxon through his wet lips. 'I've something to tell you. The girl is pregnant and we intend living together.'

'What?' said Atlanta in total disbelief.

'Yes, I've told her we can move into the cottage.'

The words stormed Atlanta's mind. She stared at the son she had devoted her life to and then, unable to contain herself any longer, shouted, 'Over my dead body!' These few words, though spoken in a moment of rage, could become prophesy if Atlanta did not tread lightly.

'Don't push me!' replied Saxon with a twist of menace, before turning his back on his mother and swaggering down the slope towards the village.

Lucille entered the kitchen a few days after Saxon had threatened Atlanta to find Rosie sitting alone and forlorn at the table.

'Hello there,' she greeted, trying to put some cheer into the gloomy surrounds.

Rosie smiled as Lucille stepped forward and took a seat opposite. Rosie had become Lucille's soul mate, so much so that Lucille shared more with her than she ever had with her mother.

Lucille had no memory of Atlanta ever having given her a kiss let alone a hug. Nor had Atlanta ever fully opened up to Lucille, confiding or expressing affection. To Lucille, Atlanta appeared to be a woman who harboured regrets about having brought her into the world. On the other hand, Rosie, though taking a simplistic view of life, involved Lucille emotionally, bringing her into her company and providing support.

When Lucille enquired as to Atlanta's whereabouts Rosie replied, 'She's at the cottage. She go there all the time and just sit, sittin' and doin' nothin'.'

'Yes, I know,' replied Lucille with a sigh. 'She has hardly spoken a word for days, lies in bed till late, comes to breakfast in her nightdress and hardly eats.'

Rosie agreed. Then, speaking in little more than a whisper, she revealed her thoughts. 'She be sick from a bad spirit. Someone in village cast a spell.'

'Who?' asked Lucille.

'That woman of Saxon's. She no good. She cast a spell.'

'But why would she cast a spell?' pressed Lucille, wondering if Rosie's words were founded on superstition, premonition or fact.

''Cause I hear Ma'am and Saxon talk the other day. They fight about the black woman.'

'You mean Saxon's girlfriend?'

'Yes.'

'What did they say?'

'Saxon say he bring that woman to live in the cottage.'

'Here, with us!'

'Yes.'

'What did Mother say?'

'She say "Over my dead body".'

'And then—?' asked Lucille hurriedly.

'He stare at her with a deadly look, say leave alone then go off to the village.'

'And what about mother?'

'She frightened. She crying and shaking and go to her room.'

At hearing this, the colour drained from Lucille's cheeks. She remained silent, locked in fear of Saxon committing the unthinkable. The dark thought of her half-brother killing her mother was too much to comprehend. She remained speechless, in the grip of her chilling despair, and began to sweat. The homestead was taking on the persona of a house of horrors, with nobody, including Rosie, being safe.

At Rosie's prompting, Lucille eventually steadied enough to tell of her fear and for Rosie to watch her step. They talked on, swearing each other to secrecy and vowing to do all they could for Atlanta. Before Lucille left for the cottage to speak to Atlanta, they reassured each other with a hug and a promise to work together.

Before going to the cottage, Lucille circled the garden, trying to sort her mind. Rosewood had enough problems with plantation failures and the notice of foreclosure issued by the bank, without a member of the family going mad and possibly murdering one or more of their own. Action needed to be taken now, but should the responsibility for making a decision to abandon Rosewood be initiated by her or left to Andrew? Since Marcella's departure, Andrew had continued his routine of leaving the house soon after daybreak and being away most of the day but, from sightings made by Lucille, it had become increasingly evident he had lost heart in managing Rosewood. As to the other two, neither Atlanta nor Saxon had ever taken an interest in the property, freeloading on the efforts of Andrew. In recent years they had also depended on Lucille, who attended to the plantation administration. There seemed no way out other than for Lucille, Andrew, Rosie and Abraham, together with Narisse and a selection of trusted Islanders, to pack their bags and depart in the middle of one dark night. Though Atlanta had been less than a devoted mother, Lucille, obliged by a sense of duty, included her in the list she compiled in her mind while walking the garden.

The cottage stood in eerie silence with the front door closed as Lucille made her way along the paved walkway and up the steps. As a courtesy she knocked on the front door and called, 'Lucille here.'

Following a long pause, she heard a muffled reply, 'Is that you, Marcella?'

Thinking that Atlanta may have misheard or been asleep she called loudly, 'It's Lucille!'

Following another long pause, Atlanta replied, 'Marcella, I'm here in your room.'

There could be no mistake this time. Lucille had almost shouted the words. Aware of Atlanta's paranoia, she let herself in and went to the room where she found Atlanta sitting on the bed, gazing aimlessly through the open window.

'Mother, it's me, Lucille.'

Atlanta turned Lucille's way, looked at her wistfully and said, 'Oh, I thought it was Marcella.'

'Why did you think that?' asked Lucille as she came to Atlanta's side.

'Because Marcella is coming back. She is having Saxon's baby and they are to be married.'

'Are you sure?' asked Lucille.

'Yes, she promised. She promised she would marry Saxon and live in the cottage.'

'Is that why you're here?'

'Yes, I want to be here when she arrives to settle her in. She is the dearest child and deserves the best. Just like Saxon, they both deserve the best …'

Atlanta spoke on, telling Lucille that the baby would be a boy and how wonderful it would be to have a grandson to carry on the family name. She had even selected a name and asked Lucille what she thought of 'Saxon Bernard Rushmore', adding that Bernard was the name of her brother and that it would be nice if the family called the child by that name to avoid confusion with Saxon's name.

Lucille, thinking that Atlanta might snap out of the fantasy if jolted, mistakenly said, 'But Saxon already has a girlfriend.'

This brought an unexpected response. Atlanta began to tremble and look about anxiously. 'Is he here?' she asked with apparent nervousness.

Lucille wanted to ask more to gauge if her reaction was to Saxon's earlier threat, but realising that this might send her into a state of total despair she digressed, commenting on the nursery that Atlanta and Rosie had decorated in the corner of the room.

To ease Atlanta's anxiety, Lucille sat beside her for an hour, listening to her ramblings. She then excused herself. When she rose to leave, Atlanta remained motionless, sitting stiff and frigid, devoid of any emotion. Lucille became misty eyed and realised that Atlanta's problem was not of her own making; that, unfortunately, she had been born with a mental condition and that eventually she might be confined to an asylum. This recognition pushed aside her earlier belief that Atlanta was a self-centred and loveless mother. She now saw her as someone who had lost her way and needed care. For the first time in her life, Lucille put her arms around her mother and held her tenderly while whispering words of love.

Atlanta's disturbed state went deeper than Lucille had observed. Atlanta plotted to bring Marcella back to Rosewood, no matter what the cost, even if it meant tearing up her marriage certificate for the sake of her son. Nobody else now mattered. Her deranged mind perceived Saxon to be the only person worth living for and, driven by this obsession, she sat at the duchesse in her bedroom and penned the following letter to Antoinette Rousseau:

12th December 1871

Dear Antoinette,

I write to you concerning Marcella.

I have been informed that she is staying at Savannah and ask that she be returned to her rightful place here at Rosewood.

As you will appreciate, family disagreements sometimes occur and the parents have to intervene for the benefit of the younger ones. Marcella is young, and with time she will come to realise that being married to Saxon is a privilege seldom granted to a mixed-race of island descent. Plans are for Saxon to take over management of Rosewood in the not too distant future and to eventually inherit the plantation. This chance of a lifetime will benefit both Marcella and her children.

I am led to believe that she is pregnant, in which case it is all the more important that she be reunited with Saxon as soon as possible.

I am not sure what Marcella has told you about her departure but, as you know, Islanders often cannot be believed. However, all of us here at Rosewood are very fond of her and are prepared to overlook any misrepresentations she might have made.

I look forward to Marcella's return and remind you of the agreement between planters, whereby anyone absconding will be promptly returned to their rightful owner.

If Marcella is reluctant to leave then please remind her that she is the property of Rosewood and that we have the right to retrieve her.

Please convey my fond thoughts to Marcella.

Trusting that you will honour this request.

Yours in good faith,
Atlanta Rushmore.
PS. Please send a reply with the messenger.

When the messenger presented himself at the Savannah homestead with the letter in hand, one of the dark housemaids asked him to wait while she summoned the lady of the house. Antoinette soon appeared and, after the messenger explained his mission, she asked him to wait while she went to the office to read the letter. She broke the fresh wax seal, took out the letter and read the content with concern. Atlanta's request was no small matter, requiring discussion with Louis before a reply could be dispatched, so Antoinette instructed the messenger to tell Atlanta that her letter would be considered and a reply sent in due course.

While Antoinette and Louis had expected a response from Rosewood, the bluntness of the request and the threatening tone of the letter reinforced their determination to protect Marcella. They decided to keep the matter to themselves and not mention it to Marcella, Florence or Jane. During the next two days they revisited the content of the letter, discussing salient points and formulating a reply. The suggestion that Marcella could be pregnant was farfetched, given Marcella's account of the rape and the amount of blood she had lost. Further to this, Marcella had made no mention of any changes and she was certainly not showing. She often wore form-fitting dresses that clearly confirmed this, so there was no doubt that Atlanta was using this as a ploy to gain control. Equally offensive was Atlanta's claim that Marcella was the property of Rosewood. Antoinette and Louis both knew that Marcella had been kidnapped from the islands and on-sold to Rosewood. If the police or members of the Abolitionist Movement were informed of this then, under Imperial law, Andrew and Atlanta as joint tenant owners of Rosewood could face jail terms. They dismissed this assertion as another clumsy attempt to fetch Marcella back to Rosewood. They did comment on the absence of Andrew's signature and doubted he was aware of the approach. The second night after receiving the letter, they decided that Antoinette would reply in the morning with a short note declining the request. The letter, written on letterhead paper and placed in a sealed envelope, read:

14th December 1871

Dear Atlanta,

I am in receipt of your letter of the 12th instant and reply as follows.

Marcella has given her own account of why she left Rosewood and we have no reason to doubt the integrity of her version of events. Given this and in the interests of her safety and welfare, Savannah will not be returning Marcella to your property.

Marcella has settled well and is making a valuable contribution to the household as a housekeeper.

She is living in one of the plantation's cottages, dines with the family and has freedom of the house.

I trust that this explanation fully addresses your concerns and satisfies your enquiry.

With God's blessing,
Antoinette Rousseau.

Since Marcella's escape to Savannah, Rosie had continued her regular visits to Narisse, taking hampers of food for her, Kaipan and baby Kabbau. Not only was Kabbau now walking, but Narisse was expecting again, with her tummy bulging into late pregnancy and gossipers in the village speculating whether the babe was fathered by Kaipan or whether Narisse had met with Saxon again. Kaipan had become more anxious in recent weeks and convinced himself that Saxon had again filled Narisse's pouch. Rosie, aware of the innuendo surrounding the pending birth, spent more time with Narisse to keep her spirits high and to be there if Narisse were to fall into the trap of prenatal depression. Narisse had remained true to Kaipan, but with his believing otherwise the arguments between them had become more frequent. Rosie believed Narisse's word, and if she could hold the couple together till the baby was born and the truth revealed then Kaipan would be accepting. These thoughts occupied Rosie's mind as she approached Narisse's hut with a hamper in one hand and a bag of toiletries in the other. When close to Kaipan's vegetable patch she heard his raised voice inside the hut and shortened her step to listen before reaching the open doorway. To Rosie's shock, Kaipan was not only accusing Narisse of having slept with Saxon but was also threatening to go out and kill Saxon that day. As Rosie had discussed with Narisse on previous occasions, if Kaipan were to murder Saxon then, not only would he be hanged for the crime, but the whole village would suffer reprisals. Without a moment to spare, Rosie stepped into the hut to confront Kaipan about his foolish threat.

'Kaipan, what are you saying?'

Kaipan, surprised by Rosie's entry, spun around and said loudly, 'I kill!'

'No, Kaipan, you no kill. Saxon is the Master's son.'

'No matter. He mess with Narisse so he die.'

'Kaipan, please, please listen to me. Narisse not telling a lie.'

Kaipan interjected, 'Yes, she got his baby inside.'

'Why do you think that?'

'I hear talk in the village. He come when I'm at work.'

'Who say that?' demanded Rosie, becoming angry at Kaipan's lack of trust.

'Some people whisper.'

'Whisper! Who whisper? Who say that?' challenged Rosie.

'That woman!'

'What woman?' retorted Rosie, becoming riled.

Kaipan, dressed in a loin cloth only and sweating profusely, shook his fuzzy head of hair, making himself look fearsome, and then, with the whites of his eyes showing in the low light of the hut, shouted, 'That other woman Saxon pucking!'

This show of disrespect for Narisse drew a hostile reaction from Rosie. 'You pig!' she screeched, reaching for a chair and flinging it at him.

Kaipan dodged the chair and then yelled loud enough for his near neighbours to hear, 'You like the rest of them in the big house! You think you a big woman! You forget your people!'

Rosie spat back at him with, 'You talk rubbish. You got the brains of a pig!'

This reference, the most degrading insult that can be said of an Islander, inflamed Kaipan's already disturbed mind. He picked up a machete, swiped it in front of Rosie in a threatening manner, and then rushed through the doorway and charged out into the sunlight.

Rosie chased after him through the village, shouting for him to come back, but he outpaced her and soon disappeared from sight. When Rosie halted and took stock of herself she realised that the eyes of the villagers were upon her. She hurried back to Narisse, who was weeping inconsolably. Rosie stayed till lunchtime and then, after promising to return later in the day, went home to prepare Abraham's lunch.

By early afternoon the temperature had risen to breaking point, with the workers floundering to stay on their feet in the fields and the dry, trashy leaves of the sugar cane buckling and cracking from the heat. With the whole plantation suffering in the summer sun, the plantation took on a sleepy appearance, with little movement except for the flow of the river passing by. This was the hottest day this summer, and even Andrew retreated to the shade of the homestead, where he sat in a squatter's chair on the veranda, looking out across the parched fields. Atlanta and Lucille rested in their rooms with the doors to the veranda wide open. Saxon had left early in the morning on horseback and had not yet returned.

Andrew woke from his doze and, as was customary, cast an eye across Rosewood that stretched across a panoramic view from downstream of the mill and village to upstream of the furthest field and beyond to the outer reaches of the estate. The first tell-tale appeared as a small wisp of smoke from a field known as Riverside. *Maybe a villager cooking a meal of fish on an open fire*, thought Andrew, but as the black smoke gathered in intensity and spiralled higher, panic took hold. Rosewood was on fire!

Andrew leapt from the chair and dashed around the veranda, calling to Atlanta and Lucille. Then, as he ran towards the stables, he shouted for Rosie and Abraham to come fight the fire. After a quick word to the stable groom and instructions to Massan to stay and watch the horses, he and the groom raced across the open pasture, shouting as they went, raising the alarm to everyone within earshot. The villagers had seen the smoke soon after Andrew and scurried about, arming themselves with hessian sugar sacks, preparing to stamp out the fire before it took hold.

While Abraham joined the brigade of firefighters, Rosie went directly to Narisse's hut, where she found her holding Kabbau on her lap with one hand and her head in the other, crying.

'It's Kaipan,' she blurted when Rosie pulled her hand from her face. 'He's set Rosewood on fire!'

'Are you sure?' Rosie felt both Narisse's pain and the implications of losing Rosewood.

'Who else,' said Narisse through quivering lips. 'He's done what he said he'd do. Everything will be burnt to the ground!'

'Easy, easy,' consoled Rosie before taking Kabbau from her lap. In the wake of the catastrophic news, Rosie prioritised, putting Narisse, Kabbau and the baby-to-be at the forefront of her concerns. Although Narisse insisted she would be all right and for Rosie to go fight the fire, Rosie refused to leave her side.

All other able men and women, including Lucille, who followed Abraham, rushed to the fire and stood defiant as a wall of flame approached their position. Atlanta, confounded by her own mental problems, had told Lucille to go ahead and then stood on the veranda in a dazed state, not fully comprehending the seriousness of the situation.

Andrew and the overseers spoke hurriedly, deciding how best to fight the gathering inferno. To take on the fire as a front from where they stood would be hopeless so, to reposition the workers, Andrew shouted, directing them to race down a headland to a place where they could back-burn.

To the sound of shouts, rants and whip cracks, Andrew and the overseers herded the Islanders along the narrow headland that tracked between the cane fields. The Islanders, being compliant and, strange as it might seem, loyal to Rosewood, raced ahead, pushing aside long sheaths of cane that hung across their path.

Nobody thought of Saxon. As usual he was missing in action, not to be relied on in a crisis. He had been riding amongst tall timbers on a ridge when he noticed the melee erupting in the fields below and now, sitting high in the saddle and looking from his commanding position, he noticed a flare of flame rise from another part of the burning field. Suspecting sabotage, he sank his spurs deep into his horse's hide and galloped to investigate who was responsible. Upon rounding the headland near the site of the new fire, he spotted Kaipan with a handful of dry trash, lighting the cane as he moved quickly, brushing his lighted flare against the dense trash hanging from the stalks of cane. The first Kaipan knew of Saxon's presence was the sound of galloping hooves. He saw Saxon charging towards him at full gallop. With nowhere to go except inside the standing crop of cane, and with Saxon now only a few yards away and brandishing an unfurled whip, Kaipan ducked into the field. He heard Saxon try to force his horse into the field, but with the cane above the horse's head it baulked and reared, refusing to enter a field that already burned brightly.

Kaipan would have to come out of the field or be burned to death, so Saxon, after shouting abuse, galloped off towards the stables to get a rifle, with the intention of returning to kill Kaipan when the flames forced him into the open. His horse, with sweat dripping, flanks heaving and blood running from spur cuts, held firm under Saxon's weight as he forced it up the steep incline to the stables.

Massan had his own problems managing the horses, with those in the stable going crazy and those in the railed enclosure outside whinnying and milling about in the gathering smoke. The plantation's horses were vital to Rosewood's operations, particularly the prized stud stallion. Massan fought to manhandle the stallion in a corner stall of the stable. Though scared out of his wits, Massan kept hold of the halter lead, ducking and swerving to avoid being kicked or crushed within the confined space. He could save himself by simply opening the stall door and letting the stallion loose, but his loyalty to Master Andrew was such that he was prepared to risk his life.

Shouts coming from outside the stable alerted Massan to Saxon's arrival and, with the memory of the beating he had received at Saxon's hand, and now hearing the scream of Saxon's voice, he panicked. He opened the door of the stall and, as the stallion leapt clear and careered down the laneway between the stalls, Saxon appeared at the entrance. Like a lunatic on the loose, Saxon stood in defiance of the approaching horse, believing he could stop a horse in full flight. The stallion, possessed by fear and oblivious to Saxon wielding a whip, held its pace, trampling Saxon as it charged past. Massan watched, thinking Saxon was dead, but when Saxon scrambled to his knees, Massan knew he would be the next to cop the madman's wrath. With no outside entrance at his end of the stable, he ducked into the stallion's stall and pulled the door closed.

'You rotten, mongrel nigger. Try to kill me by letting the stallion loose!' Massan heard Saxon call. Then more, 'You're done this time, you black nigger!'

Massan took up the pitchfork he had been using to clean the stall and, when Saxon pushed open the door and stood fully exposed, Massan braced himself for a fight. Like his forebears when confronted by the enemy, he drew strength and courage from his ancestors' spirits and stood ready for combat. Saxon, with a blacksmith's hammer held high above his head, rushed at Massan in an attempt to smash his skull. He swung once, and then twice, narrowly missing Massan who managed to avoid the crushing blows. When he moved to strike a third time, Massan lunged forward, thrusting the pitchfork into Saxon's belly and then following through, holding his weight behind the handle and crashing Saxon to the ground. Now possessed by the power of his belief, Massan dug the fork right through Saxon's body and pinned him to the ground. Saxon, though a big man, could not match the strength of Massan, who held tightly to the handle of the fork as Saxon struggled to free himself. Driven by the will to live, Massan held his grip of the pitchfork till it ceased to wobble and shake and Saxon lay dead at his feet. The shock of having killed Master Andrew's son left Massan shaking. He had underestimated the strength his ancestors had given him. He stood, frozen in time for a minute, and then pulled the fork from the body and flung it aside as he left the stable.

From where he stood in the horse enclosure the situation appeared chaotic. In the distance and beneath a sky filled with billowing smoke, he saw flames leaping skywards from the burning fields and a string of workers racing about with lighted flares, dipping their torches of fire into the cane in a desperate attempt to back-burn before all was lost. The hilly woodland, upstream from the mill and village, a section that had not been burnt by the bushfire earlier in the season, had also caught fire, with clouds of grey smoke rising and mingling with the dense black smoke sweeping from the lowland cane fields. If a gust of river breeze were to suddenly spring up, the hillside fire might gather pace, cross a ravine and threaten the stables and nearby homestead.

Spellbound and gripped by confusion, Massan tried to gather his thoughts. He held no doubt that he was a doomed man who, if captured, would be beaten to death for killing Saxon. On the other hand, he had been charged with marshalling the horses and keeping them safe for the Master. As the sound of the fire intensified and the cries from those fighting the fire became louder, he struggled between absconding to save his own life and staying to save the horses. He remained undecided, standing by the milling horses, until his favourite mount came forward and nuzzled his hand. Massan looked into the anxious eyes of his equine friend, stroked his forehead and then, without hesitation, went to the gate and opened it wide, allowing the horses to gallop to the safety of the mountains.

After watching the horses cover the open ground and disappear into the untouched hinterland, his attention turned back to those risking their lives, attacking the blaze with no more than sugar sacks, now threadbare from thrashing the flames and hot ash. To go and help would expose him to capture, particularly if the fire came close to the stables and those defending the building discovered Saxon's body. He found himself once again torn between duty and self-interest—to stay and die or run to live for another day? Suddenly, through the smoke haze against the stable wall, he saw a vision of Marcella with her hands outstretched, beckoning him to come into her arms. He knew then and there what he should do and, after a last look at the conflagration consuming the fields of Rosewood, he turned and ran down the dusty road towards Savannah.

Across the fields the approaching flames created an image of hellfire, with the workers paling into insignificance as masters of the landscape. Nature had returned with all its fury, consuming everything mankind had fashioned by hand, cleansing the earth in readiness for a renewal of what was once a pristine forest. Be that as it may, these men and women, like possessed souls, still pitched themselves against the apocalypse that raged before them. Nothing could match the fear that consumed their minds as they fought, with their bodies glistening by the firelight.

Try as they did to quell the leaping flames, floaters of lighted trash spiralled from the field on thermal currents to settle further afield, igniting fresh fires that burned indiscriminately and spread in all directions.

From where the workers back-burned, the flames were soon drawn by the heat of the fire Kaipan had lit, curling into turrets fifty feet high and forcing the men back. As they began to retreat with singed hair and blistered feet, hideous screams erupted from within the field, telling the damning story of a man trapped between the converging walls of fire. They all recognised the voice as that of Kaipan and, although crippled by exhaustion, they turned once again to challenge the inferno in an attempt to save him. Some men tried to push through the wall of fire to reach him but were pushed back by the searing heat.

Andrew, realising the situation was out of control and, with himself and Lucille and the white overseers and one hundred island workers at risk of being burned to death, yelled to the overseers to take command and force the workers to flee. Most took notice and fled, while the few that remained, trying to rescue Kaipan, were man-handled and forced to run the gauntlet of the fiery pathway to a clearing. The Islanders, frightened and confused, murmured amongst themselves in native dialect till an overseer shouted, 'Boss, the fire's switching direction and heading for the mill and village!'

Andrew, though struggling to stay on his feet, shouted a call to arms and led the way to defend the vital infrastructure. Lucille, similarly fatigued, spurred herself forward with unbelievable doggedness, tripping and falling to the ground, only to pick herself up again and follow in Andrew's footsteps. The Islanders and white overseers, with any class distinction now buried deep beneath the urgency, lumbered behind.

At seeing the mill and village still standing, Andrew sooled the workers forward, organising a bucket brigade from the river and the issue of fresh sugar sacks for them to man the grassy perimeter surrounding the mill and the village. These workers, though haggard and red eyed, wet their new-issue sacks and formed a human chain, ready to beat the life from any flame that came within reach. White and black bonded for the fight of their life for, if the factory buildings were to catch fire and the village huts ignite, the estate would be finished. The black chain of Islanders, dotted with a white man here and there, held firm, shouting encouragement down the line as they stood defiant before the approaching flames. Time and again a man yelled and fell back after being burnt, only for the gap to be filled by two or three others putting themselves in harm's way for the sake of the estate.

After an hour of fierce defence the wind changed again, with a slight breeze drifting up the river, pushing against the fire. Although just enough to form tiny ripples on the surface of the river, all there took it to be a good omen, a change of fortune. With renewed faith the Islanders began to sing in unison to bolster their determination while swinging their sacks. By a remarkable feat of endurance, manpower and unity they held their post till the fire front was finally extinguished.

When the pall of smoke dissipated on the breeze and the homestead and outbuildings could be seen a new horror appeared. A floater had drifted uphill from the fire and lit the dry grass in the horse paddock near the homestead.

Andrew stood stunned and disbelieving, unable to comprehend as he saw his personal possessions and life's dream crumbling. The homestead, Marcella's and Rosie's cottages, the stables and the overseers' barracks all aflame. In his worst nightmare he could never have imagined a demise where everything he had worked for could be taken away by the strike of a match. How the blaze had ignited in one place and then another very soon after he had no idea, except that Kaipan's screams suggested he might have deliberately lit the fires and been trapped when the workers back-burned.

Lucille stood shaking and sobbing, cradled in the arms of an island woman who, though fighting tears of her own, shielded Lucille from the sight of the homestead which had been her home for most of her life.

Some of the overseers, followed by groups of straggling Islanders, scrambled up the slope as fast as they could in a bid to confront the ravenous flames but, on arrival, could do nothing with their bare hands to save the structures. They stood back from the glare of the blaze and watched as the last of Rosewood's stately home burnt to the ground.

So far little thought had been given to the whereabouts or safety of Atlanta, Saxon or Massan. The general consensus was that they would have escaped the fire individually or together and, when the firestorm passed, they would emerge to tell their story. However, when the fire settled and all that remained were red embers and wisps of smoke, those present began to question why none of the three had emerged to account for themselves. Thoughts and then suggestions evolved into gruesome possibilities, with attention focusing on the smouldering remains of the buildings. With Andrew's permission, two of the overseers crossed what used to be the garden and entered the charred timbers of the homestead. They searched by the floor plan, inspecting all sections of the house, but found no human remains. Maybe those missing had sought shelter in the stables, so the search party crossed to there and entered the enclosure, with Andrew and Lucille praying that no bodies would be found. The men searched the ruins, and from the farthest stall one shouted, 'Here, there's a body!'

'Who!' came Andrew's harrowing cry.

The man standing by the body took a moment to find his voice and then called, 'It's Saxon!'

'Dead!' shouted Andrew in disbelief.

'Yes.' When Andrew went to move forward the man issued a caution. 'It's best you not see him.'

Andrew ignored the plea. He pushed aside the man holding him with gentle restraint, went across and stood over Saxon, staring at his burnt remains. The island woman who had comforted Lucille earlier held her by the shirt collar, saying, 'No good for you go see.' Lucille, in a state of emotional collapse, complied, allowing herself to be led away.

The unexpected discovery of Saxon's body shocked Andrew beyond his capacity, locking his mind to the extent that he could not speak, leaving it to the overseers to go and search Marcella's cottage. Within moments they discovered the body of Atlanta in what used to be Marcella's bedroom. The sight of the matriarch, incinerated almost beyond recognition, brought tears to the eyes of some men while others cleared their throats. Andrew, with vivid memory of thirty years of life with Atlanta, could not bear the trauma of seeing her corpse and instinctively turned to Lucille. The island woman who had comforted Lucille before, now herself in tears, hugged Andrew and, when he embraced Lucille in grief, the woman held them both in her arms.

A search of the remaining outbuildings found no trace of Massan and nobody had seen him at the fire. The most widely held supposition was that, since none of the horses had perished in the fire, he might have saddled a horse and herded them to a safe place in the ranges and, if so, he could return at any time with the prized working stock.

As darkness approached some semblance of order returned, with the villagers returning to their commune while Andrew and Lucille, together with the overseers, camped in the sugar storage shed at the mill. Andrew and Lucille lay side by side on sacks on the ground, and each time Lucille began to whimper during the night Andrew reached and held her hand.

Few people slept that night. Those in the village sat by fires, recounting the horrors of the day and attending to the injured as best they could by applying traditional balms to burns and, for the seriously injured, reassuring them they would receive proper care when the doctor and police arrived early next morning. A message did reach the police station in Mackay, but the officer in charge said he would not saddle his horse and ride through the night to, as he put it, 'Sort some Kanakas.' The doctor had been called elsewhere but, given his devotion to serving people irrespective of their colour, he could be expected to arrive by first light.

The new dawn revealed sad tidings, with the blackened landscape taking on the appearance of a funeral shawl spread across all of the plantation except for the mill and village. The eerie stillness, with no bird calls or sounds of workers going to work, cast the plantation as a place mourning. Never, within living memory, would this event be forgotten and, for generations to come, the story of the devastation of Rosewood estate would be passed down and, in the telling, would be a reminder of the harsh days upon which the colony was founded.

Massan's escape, though undetected, would not be without consequences. He raced down the road like an escapee believing his captors were in hot pursuit. At every turn he imagined that, around the corner, a mounted policeman would be waiting to trample him to the ground and drag him to Mackay in chains. He paused for a few moments at the creek crossing to gulp water and then took flight again, careering towards Savannah. He became delirious, with the shrubbery on the sides of the road appearing as images of Saxon's face, demonising him with sadistic looks. Pools of blood, Saxon's blood that he had let with a thrust of the pitchfork, puddled on the road ahead, only to disappear as he approached. His mind, bereft of reason, could see no way out, only the darkness of death. As he staggered through the main entrance to Savannah, Sapphire, the Rousseaus' dog, roused those at the homestead with loud barks. The Islander housemaids came to the veranda railing first, followed by Antoinette and then Florence, Marcella and Jane. Massan, totally spent and disorientated, stood petrified, staring blindly at the figures on the veranda.

'It's Massan!' shouted Marcella, surprised and exhilarated to see him for the first time since leaving Rosewood. Antoinette acted swiftly, taking stock of the situation, calling Sapphire to heel and then running to the garden gate. Florence and Marcella followed quickly to help, while Jane stood alone with mixed feelings. She had observed the closeness between Massan and Marcella during their earlier visits and wondered if his stay would be brief.

Not knowing why he had come alone and on foot, and anxious for an explanation, Antoinette and the girls gathered around him.

Antoinette spoke first. 'What is it? What's happened?'

Massan muttered, 'The Master, his cane burn.'

'How much?'

Massan just shrugged his shoulders.

'Massan, tell us how much cane burn?'

'Dunno, fire burn high and I let the horses go.'

'You let the horses go!'

'Yes, Ma'am.'

'What did Mr. Rushmore say?'

'He no see. He at the fire.'

'And the others?'

'They all at the fire.'

With mounting frustration Antoinette asked, 'Why didn't you go to the fire?'

'Because—'

'Because what?'

'Master Andrew would beat me for letting horses loose,' replied Massan, struggling to find an answer.

With Massan in a state of shock and one side of his face twitching, Antoinette thought it best to let the matter lie for the moment. She turned to Marcella and said, 'Take Massan to the stables and let him settle. Maybe he'll talk to you.'

At dinner time, Marcella entered the dining room and reported to Antoinette, Louis, Florence and Jane that Massan was too frightened to speak, and that from the little he had told her the plantation was well alight when he left and all the men were fighting the fire. After returning to the stables with a meal each, Marcella endured an agonising night, talking with Massan and trying to console him through the dark hours. Amongst other things Massan confessed to killing Saxon, saying that he struck him with a pitchfork in self-defence. Marcella kept her word and the secret would never be revealed to others.

After Florence and Jane had gone to bed, Louis and Antoinette stayed at the dining table till late, discussing what might have happened at Rosewood. Knowing the dire financial situation facing the Rushmores, would the property now be for sale? They set a plan and, after Louis advised two of his leading hands that the three of them would be leaving for Rosewood before sunrise, he and Antoinette slept till the chiming clock struck 3:30 am.

By the first glimmer of dawn they entered the high ground of Rosewood, where they reined to a halt to view the desecrated remains of a plantation that, if financed and managed properly, would complement Louis's home property of Savannah. An overseer saw the three approaching on fine thoroughbred horses and, knowing it was Louis, counted this as a blessing, because if anybody could recoup the losses sustained by Rosewood, it would be the quietly spoken Louis Rousseau. Louis joined Andrew and Lucille and, after sharing a cup of tea and expressing his condolences for the deaths in the family, he and Andrew moved aside and entered private conversation as to the future of Rosewood. Andrew confessed that the estate owed the bank £105,000 and that foreclosure was imminent. During the two hours of discussion that followed, they addressed detail pertinent to the property, including a transfer of ownership. Settlement of the bank debt figured prominently, and when Louis agreed to a sale price equal to the debt the men shook hands on a gentleman's agreement. Without disclosing the source of his finances, Louis knew that the dividends from Antoinette's family holding in the Cardiff docks of South Wales would be enough to meet the amount owing to the bank. As to preliminary planning to resurrect Rosewood, they agreed that: Andrew and Lucille would stay as managers, the indentured workforce would be transferred to the Rousseau name, construction of a new homestead and outbuildings would commence immediately, the mill would be upgraded with modern equipment and the field workers would resume work as of tomorrow. As Louis said, 'It's to nobody's benefit to have manpower standing idle when there's work to be done.' Fortunately, the food storage shed adjoining the mill had been saved and held enough stores to feed everybody on the plantation for the next month.

The events of the past twenty-four hours had been tumultuous for Andrew: the annihilation of most of Rosewood, the loss of his wife and son, the agreed sale of the property, and funds committed to settling the bank's debt. Out of sheer gratitude, Andrew shook Louis's hand again and, in so doing, confirmed the deal.

The doctor arrived soon after Louis and, not one to waste time on courtesies, made his way directly to the village where he moved from hut to hut attending to the injured. No additional deaths were reported, and most of those treated were back at work within two weeks and willing to meet the new challenge.

The sergeant of police arrived later in the morning with three constables to assist him with assessing the situation and to gather information for an inquest that would be held to determine the cause of death of Saxon and Atlanta. He spoke with the overseers and some of the Islanders, and then Andrew and Lucille. The consensus of the verbal witness statements was that Saxon had been trapped when he went to save the horses from the fire and Atlanta, being panicked by the fire, left the homestead when it caught fire and sought refuge in the cottage, rather than escaping to the open bushland. Nobody mentioned Massan because it was presumed that he had herded the horses to the ranges and would return with them later in the day. This evidence satisfied the sergeant who, when leaving, said to Andrew, 'That about wraps up this mess. I'll submit my report to the Mackay police magistrate who is acting coroner for the district. You and some others will be called to give evidence at the hearing but, by all accounts, it should be an open-and-shut hearing.' He then, with apparent insensitivity, added that his men had wrapped the bodies of Atlanta and Saxon in canvas and were taking them to Mackay on a buckboard. To add further insult he followed by saying, 'Suppose you want them buried in the town graveyard. I'll hold the bodies in the lockup but expect you to make the burial arrangements and have them buried by the day after tomorrow.' As an afterthought he said, 'You can find the black fella in the cane field and dispose of him.'

While the men attended to the business of the plantation and the disposal of Kaipan's body, Lucille visited Narisse's hut to share her grief at losing Kaipan and to offer help. She found Narisse lying on a bunk, trying to rest to avoid miscarrying her baby. Kabbau slept close by, and Rosie, tired and drawn, sat at the table where once Kaipan had sat for meals. In the gloom and sorrow of the steamy hut, Lucille first hugged Rosie and then sat beside Narisse, holding her hand. She had brought food from the storeroom and, sensing that neither had eaten since receiving the terrible news, she lit the outside fire and cooked oats to have with goat's milk she scrounged along the way. Rosie, in her grief, referred to Kaipan's death, telling of his threat to destroy Rosewood only minutes before the fire took hold. Following further discussion, Rosie and Lucille came to the conclusion that Atlanta, driven to distraction by her son, had probably committed suicide by being in Marcella's bedroom when the fire consumed the cottage.

Rosewood was blessed when, soon after the fire, thunderstorms gathered and, with flashes of lightning crazing the sky and rolls of thunder rumbling in the mountains, the rain fell by the bucketful, replenishing the landscape and lifting the spirits of all those residing on the plantation. Andrew and Lucille camped in the sugar storage shed with hessian hung from the rafters to divide the space into rooms. The overseers slept on makeshift bunks under the mill roof, while Rosie and Abraham cared for Narisse at her hut. Louis sent thirty of Savannah's Kanakas to help, setting them up in a camp on the river bank and working in teams at Andrew's direction.

Dozens of men and several women spread across the fields, cutting and removing the burnt stalks of cane so the cane could reshoot. Another gang laboured hard, milling timber for the new homestead and outbuildings.

219

Horsemen from Savannah mustered the horses that had been let loose by Massan, and cattle that had broken fences and escaped when the fire raged. Louis worked behind the scenes, attending to the transfer of the property and the indentured Islanders. As for the mill, Louis ordered £23,000 worth of equipment from Glasgow to upgrade the factory to a standard that could efficiently process all the cane Rosewood could grow. Although the rainy season of January, February and March of the new year hampered progress, nobody complained because all knew Rosewood's future and their livelihood depended on a good crop of cane and a reliable mill.

By August the new equipment had been installed in the mill, and cane on the more fertile soil was mature enough to begin harvesting. The 'first crush', when the first stalks of cane were fed into the new mill, marked a milestone, and to celebrate, Louis and Antoinette invited those at Rosewood to observe as Louis and Andrew slid the first stalks down the chute and into the 'jaws' of the new crushing mill. To repay everybody for their fine effort, Louis and Antoinette hosted a feast at the village where a bullock was roasted. Marcella and Massan were invited but declined because, unknown to Louis and Antoinette, Marcella did not want to meet with Andrew, and Massan feared retribution by Saxon's spirit.

Thereafter the crops grew well. The mill performed better than expected, producing quality crystal sugar and tripling the number of trips the barge made down the river loaded with sacks of sugar to be shipped to faraway places. Those at Rosewood became so proud of the quality of the sugar they produced that they branded the sacks *Rosewood, Port Mackay, Australia*. The administration by Louis and Antoinette, and the close supervision by Andrew, lifted the estate from its previous quagmire to the extent that they could boast that Rosewood's rate of throughput of cane bettered any other plantation in the valley except for Savannah.

Rosewood achieved the crown that Andrew had always dreamed of and now, with Louis and Antoinette giving him full credit for the accomplishment, he, in spite of previous failures, saw himself as a success. He and Lucille lived in the new homestead with its view across the fields of green. The column of smoke rising to the sky was a reminder that the wheels were turning the crop into sugar, and he spent much time sitting in the squatter's chair on the veranda.

Lucille now partnered with a seafarer who came and went and, although there could be no certainty, the prospect of marrying and having children was never far from her mind.

Narisse had overcome the trauma of losing Kaipan. She lived in the same hut in the village, raising Kabbau and her second son who, by his appearance, was fathered by Kaipan and not some loose arrangement with Saxon. Rosie and Abraham lived close and, by the grace of the Rousseaus, Rosie cared for Abraham, who could no longer work, and Narisse with two young children to raise. Abraham continued to waste away and, although the doctor diagnosed a heart condition, Rosie still held to her belief that Abraham had succumb to the spell of an evil spirit. Sadly his health deteriorated more rapidly than expected and he passed away soon after the new mill was commissioned. Many people, including those from the Rushmore and Rousseau households, attended the funeral and, at Rosie's request, he was buried in a grove of woodland that overlooked the cane fields where he had been ganger in charge of the harvesting. Marcella and Massan did attend, but Marcella stayed clear of Andrew, even to the extent of avoiding eye contact.

CHAPTER 17

The storms that had drenched Rosewood soon after the fire also reached Savannah plantation, bringing welcome rain and signalling the end of the dry season. With thirty of Savannah's workers having been seconded to Rosewood for the reconstruction, those left behind found themselves more engaged than ever to meet the orders of bagged sugar that Savannah had agreed to prior to the debacle at Rosewood. Even Massan was sent to work in the fields, leaving Florence and Marcella to take his place at the stables. The girls, sharing a love of horses and able to handle livestock, undertook the duty with gusto, shrugging off comments that stable work was not women's work.

Though Marcella shared the cottage with Jane, and Massan slept at the stables, they still found time to be together. Marcella was able to excuse herself after the evening meal and go to the stables to bed down the horses. Although polite when excusing herself, her unmistakable body language and rush to be gone left no doubt that she and Massan were canoodling and probably engaging further. Jane, while taking exception at first, gradually accepted that Marcella would partner with a man and put behind her any expectation of sharing a bed with her. Antoinette wanted only the best for Marcella and, by her silence on the matter, gave tacit approval to the blossoming romance. Florence, the same age as Marcella and encouraged by Marcella's openness, thought she would soon approach a young Islander farm hand she had been admiring since his arrival a few months earlier. Louis, not wanting to dwell on any impropriety that Marcella might entertain, made light when comments were passed across the table. However, he did believe that if God had chosen Massan to be Marcella's husband then the choice should be respected. His only difficulty was accepting that they were keeping such close company without being married.

Everyone kept watch for signs that Marcella might be pregnant. The rainy season passed without any signs, and people began to wonder what was really happening at the stables late at night. However, in June Marcella confided to Florence that her belly was getting big and she thought she was going to have Massan's baby. The revelation brought joy to the household. Antoinette hovered about like an expectant grandmother, trying to dissuade Marcella from doing heavy lifting at the stables. Marcella's assurance that 'island girls work hard till the day the baby is born' did little to alleviate Antoinette's concern.

When Marcella felt the baby kicking and invited all to put a hand to her tummy, everyone crowded around, spoiling her and opening their hearts for Massan to join with the family. During this time Massan learnt more about life, loving and family than he had in his entire life. Their acceptance and welcome opened his mind to the joys of living. This youth who began work at Rosewood as a virtual slave could now see a bright future, sharing with the girl he had fallen in love with at first sight.

Unknown to the others, Marcella secretly wished members of her island family could be present at the time of the birth. When alone she sometimes felt a yearning to return to her island, to hear Grandpa's voice, to put flowers on her mother's grave and to keep watch for the day when her seafaring father would fulfil his promise of returning to Lifou. While those at Savannah provided love and care, her spiritual connection to Lifou called. At times she imagined she heard the sound of the conch horns, relaying messages or summoning everybody to assemble for an important announcement or a traditional feast. So much had been gained by being kidnapped—being taken to Sorrento, and then Rosewood and now Savannah—but so much had been left behind. In moments of solitude, she wondered where she belonged.

Marcella kept pace with Florence, pitching hay and handling unruly horses, always by Florence's side, until one afternoon Florence came around the corner of the stable to find Marcella on her knees and clutching her belly in pain. She shouted for help and, with Antoinette and Jane lending a hand, they took Marcella to a bedroom at the homestead. Louis and Massan each reacted differently when they returned from the field at dusk and were told of the pending birth. Louis, raised in the stoic Victorian tradition, found excuses for not visiting the room, while Massan, in a whirl of excitement, rushed to Marcella's bedside where he knelt and held her hand. Marcella, now heavily in labour, acknowledged his presence by turning her head his way and managing a smile. When Massan wiped the tears from his cheeks she squeezed his hand, reassuring him she had the strength to bear the pain and deliver their baby. By 8:00 pm the contractions had become stronger and longer, prompting Jane to take charge and prepare for the delivery. She asked Massan and Florence to leave the room so she and Antoinette could attend to Marcella in private. Massan, having no knowledge of childbirth and overcome with anxiety, refused to leave till Florence wrapped an arm around his shoulders and coaxed him to the veranda. The labour stalled. Jane and Antoinette exchanged worried looks. Jane had delivered many babies both at the Sydney hospital and the islands and lost some, but to lose Marcella's baby or both mother and child would be more than she could endure. Although Marcella was now partnered with Massan, she promised herself that she would love both Marcella and baby as if they were her own. With Antoinette sponging Marcella's naked body and Jane giving Marcella instructions about when to breathe and to push, they persevered, with each hour casting more doubt on a successful delivery. Louis, who had stationed himself at the far end of the veranda, found Marcella's shrieks unbearable and went to the stables where he prayed to the Almighty for a safe outcome. Massan, by nature a gentle and kind person, put his head in his hands each time Marcella screamed and, if it were not for Florence holding him in her arms, he would have become hysterical.

'Try! Try!' encouraged Jane soon after midnight. 'You must try, Marcella. One more try, please. Push, push as hard as you can.' Through the pain and emotional turmoil, Marcella heard Jane's guiding words and, after taking a deep breath, squeezed with every fibre of her body. 'It's coming!' called Jane, and when the newborn slipped into her hands she shouted, 'It's a boy. Marcella, you have a baby boy!' At hearing this, Massan rushed through the open door, fell to his knees again and, through sobs of joy, praised Marcella for delivering him a son. At hearing the announcement, Louis looked towards the heavens and thanked God for saving his treasured 'child' and her son. When Massan settled and order returned, Florence came forward and, with wonder and admiration in her eyes, bent over Marcella and whispered, 'Well done, my sister.'

Marcella was soon on her feet, breastfeeding and wanting to return to work at the stables. To the many objections raised, Marcella replied, 'Island girls take their babies to work. Baby always stay with mother.' The carers lost the battle to contain Marcella's enthusiasm and, within a week, she returned to work at the stables with her baby close by in a bassinet. Between the two girls, no more than a couple of minutes passed without one of them checking on baby Massan Louis. Marcella and Massan chose the names themselves, paying tribute to Massan the father and Louis who made everything possible.

Life at Savannah rolled along in a happy and orderly fashion, with the weeks becoming months and Christmas approaching. Christmas, one of the most anticipated days on the Christian calendar, was celebrated with gift giving, prayer at the chapel, a hearty luncheon and relaxation during the afternoon.

During the rainy season following Christmas, Louis and Antoinette built a new cottage for the young couple, with the front porch so close to the main residence that some believed Antoinette had positioned it there so she could hear when the baby cried. Though those seconded to Rosewood to help after the fire had been returned to Savannah, Marcella and Florence continued working at the stables while finding time to attend Jane's school lessons. Antoinette, the self-appointed grandmother, now cared for Massan Jr when the girls were working or being schooled. With Antoinette considering Massan Jr to be her own grandson, she had, in addition to the nursery at Marcella's cottage, decorated a room in the homestead as a nursery. She and Marcella shared young Massan, with Antoinette taking charge during the day and Marcella and Massan Sr having him at night.

Antoinette was changing the youngster's nappy when a housemaid came to the door mid-morning and said, 'Ma'am, there's a man out front asking for you.'

'What man?'

'Don't know. He's young and riding a horse.'

Antoinette finished pinning the nappy, gave the baby a kiss, and then handed him to the maid, saying, 'Here, it's bottle time. There's one warming by the stove.'

The young messenger waved and rode closer when he saw Antoinette come to the veranda. Antoinette, not having seen him before, went to the gate rather than invite him inside and offer a drink.

'I have a letter for you,' he said, nudging his horse closer.

Antoinette took the envelope, inspected the seal and return address on the back, and then asked the lad to wait while she went to the office to read the content. She opened the seal, removed the letter and was astonished when she read:

Mr and Mrs Rousseau.
Savannah Plantation.
Via Port Mackay.

5th May 1873

Dear Sir and Madam,

I have been engaged by a client to enquire about the whereabouts of his daughter.

The client, who wishes to remain nameless for privacy reasons, fathered a child on the island of Lifou nineteen years ago and, due to unforeseen circumstances has, till recently, been unable to return to claim her.

Information he has provided indicates that she could be the mixed-race girl I sent to Rosewood plantation in early 1871. The transfer was a hurried matter, without me sighting the girl or getting much detail.

The girl's original owner is now deceased, and enquiry with those still on his property near Brisbane has met with a denial that the girl ever existed!

In the absence of their assistance I wrote to Rosewood and received a short note saying that no mixed-race females reside on the plantation.

I am aware of the fire that nearly destroyed Rosewood and wonder if, by chance, she has been transferred to Savannah.

I add that the client is a reputable seafarer who, had he not been shipwrecked and suffered financial difficulties as a result, would have returned to Lifou in that same year.

My client confirms that he is prepared to pay for the girl's release upon confirming that, indeed, she is his daughter.

As this matter is attended with some urgency, please send a reply with the messenger.

Yours in confidence,
Reg Brixton,
Shipping Agent, Brisbane

Antoinette began to sweat around the collar as she reread the letter. The implications of a strange man coming to claim Marcella was almost too much to comprehend. Though she was usually placid, this threat riled her, such that the stern face she held on the second reading turned to bright red on the third. To her mind Marcella and her family belonged at Savannah, and under no circumstances would she let them go—no amount of money could ever buy Marcella's soul. To avoid going to the garden gate and possibly invoking a scene, she went to the kitchen and directed the maid to go and tell the messenger not to wait for a reply.

With the lunchtime meal being a casual arrangement whereby Antoinette, Louis, Florence and Jane helped themselves from the kitchen and Marcella and Massan prepared their own meal at the cottage, Antoinette easily found an opportunity to discuss her concern with Louis. Before Louis had removed his boots Antoinette briefed him on the unwanted news and, after snatching a quick bite at the kitchen table, they retreated to the seclusion of the office. Antoinette could hardly contain herself while Louis read the letter, and when he placed it on the desk and looked her way she babbled as never before, spilling forth her worries.

'What if he is an imposter!' She was frustrated by Louis's lack of expressed concern. 'He could be anybody, particularly being a seaman, roving the seas, picking up women and then dumping them. And Brixton the agent. We all know about his conniving! Anything to make a shilling.'

Louis made no comment as Antoinette rattled on, trying to deride what she firmly believed was crooked business where slave girls were targeted by unscrupulous dealers chasing after a quick quid. She referred to Jack Marshall, the ex-Jamaican planter who lived in the hills, with his bonded labourers living in subhuman conditions and black women at his beck and call.

'I've heard that Reg Brixton has dealt with Marshall, supplying him with young island girls and moving them on when he has finished with them. What plans has he for Marcella? Is this mystery man just a go between with plans to sell Marcella downriver or to some perverted colonist elsewhere?'

Antoinette became so passionate about the rights of black women that Louis, surprised at the outburst, just sat, listening to his wife's tirade. Though he agreed with her argument, the depth of contempt she expressed for the likes of Marshall revealed an inner hatred of slave traders, and maybe hatred for the whole system of procuring South Sea Islanders. As a deeply religious man Louis believed in the rights of the individual, but when it came to manning his plantation he, somehow, justified the procurement by believing that the practice bettered the lives of the Islanders as well as introducing them to Christianity.

Antoinette, having had her say and now nearly in tears, checked herself and, by way of apology, said, 'Sorry, darling, for a moment I forgot my place. Please understand that I love Marcella and baby Massan and no one can take them from me.'

Louis patted Antoinette's hand and, speaking for the first time, replied, 'I understand and agree that under no circumstances will Marcella be surrendered.'

He then referred to the letter, setting aside any emotional bias and dealing with the specifics. On paper the request seemed plausible and, as such, should be considered in a positive light. He then elaborated, discussing the proposal at length, weighing the likelihood that this unknown man could be Marcella's father. The evidence presented about Marcella's island of origin, her mixed-race status and age lent support to the claim that Marcella was indeed the daughter of the enquirer. Further, there was nothing to suggest that the letter was not genuine or that it had not been written with sincerity. After an hour-long discussion they concluded that for Marcella's sake they should at least explore the possibility. They drafted a letter written in Antoinette's hand. The reply read:

Mr Reg Brixton.
Shipping Agent
Brisbane.

28th May 1873

Dear Mr Brixton,

I am in receipt of your letter and reply on behalf of myself and husband Louis.

Yes, we do have a young mixed-race island girl employed on the plantation.

Further, my husband and I have considered the request and welcome your client to visit.

We ask that your client be mindful that Savannah cares for all employees and that any discussion must be bona fide.

We also insist that prior notice of the date of visitation be provided.

While no guarantees can be given we look forward to the meeting with a spirit of goodwill.

Yours faithfully,
Antoinette Rousseau.

Louis read the letter while Antoinette addressed the envelope. When handing it back to her he said, 'It's in the Lord's hands now.' Further to this, they agreed not to tell Marcella or the others so as not to raise what could be a false hope.

Antoinette remained unsettled, to the extent of often looking down the road, expecting the stranger to arrive unannounced. The suspicion raised in the letter scripted by Brixton's hand became an obsession, plaguing her thoughts by day and causing nightmares at night. Night sweats, something never before experienced, alerted Louis to her distress and, although he tried to allay her fears, she could not shake off the prospect of some ogre charging into Savannah and demanding to take Marcella and the child. Even Louis's assurance that they had the means to deal with such a man brought no resolution. Her angst betrayed itself to the others by way of omissions in her daily routine and a reluctance to discuss her upset. Each time she heard movement outside or Sapphire bark she hurried to the door to check that the man, possibly armed and accompanied by a cohort, had not burst his way into the heart of Savannah. She marked the calendar and checked off the days, with each new week being a fresh reminder that every day that passed brought the arrival day closer. Baby Massan, only eight months old, detected the anxiety and reached with his arms each time Antoinette leant over to lift him from the cot.

Midway through the fourth week, the same lad who had delivered the letter from Brixton visited with a note for Mrs Rousseau. After unfolding the note and glancing at the content she called to a maid to give the lad a shilling and then hastened to the office to consider the short message that read:

Mrs Rousseau.

Thank you for your letter about my daughter.

I have sent this note with a messenger today and will visit you the day after tomorrow.

Yours sincerely,
Mark Richards

The simplicity of the note, written on a piece of scrap paper by an uneducated hand, turned Antoinette's thoughts into a mire of confusion. She had expected a bold letter, written by an assertive hand, and maybe a statement claiming ownership of Marcella. If the writer was not someone with a cavalier approach, who could this person be? To what station in life did he belong? He could be a vagabond, a hobo, a person with no worthy credentials and no means of supporting Marcella and the baby. Her focus turned from one of protecting Marcella from an ogre to protecting her from a malingerer or fool who would never have the means to provide for a secure future. Fortunately, Louis returned from the field early that day and together they sorted through the possibilities, assessing the situation and, in so doing, came to the conclusion that to prejudge could be harmful to Marcella and that, led by God's hand, they would wait and see.

On the day of the proposed visit, Antoinette busied herself with housework and Louis attended to the accounts till, soon after morning tea time, Sapphire sounded an alarm by barking loudly. Antoinette rushed to the veranda rail and sighted a man and sulky careering her way. The mare, obviously out of control, whinnied to the horses at the stables while pulling against the reins to join them. The driver, dressed in white and with his ponytail flowing, repeatedly shouted *Whoa* while struggling to bring the mare back to the roadway. Louis came to Antoinette's side and together they watched as the driver, who knew little about horses, eventually arced in a wide circle to bring the mare to a stop at the homestead gate.

'Hello there!' shouted the stranger in a cheerful voice when the mare halted.

'Hello!' returned Louis, relieved to discover that the mystery man was not the tyrannical overlord Antoinette had expected.

Antoinette, having turned to Louis and seen his approving look, also waved a welcome.

Sapphire, bred to be drawn to warm personalities, gave her approval by going ahead of Louis and Antoinette with her tail wagging.

Mark introduced himself, and one of the maids led the mare to the stables. Then the three sat by an occasional table on the veranda to discuss the purpose of the visit. What disarmed Antoinette most was Mark's appearance, with his sun-bleached hair, open-neck shirt, a whale's tooth hanging from a leather string about his neck, canvas trousers and bare feet. Further to this, his open face, broad smile and hearty laugh shone a light on his happy and engaging personality, swaying Antoinette his way before he provided any evidence of his paternity claim to Marcella. Louis led the way, interspersing questions in the conversation to establish Mark's bona fides. Mark confirmed Marcella's age and island of origin, and told of his brief love affair with Marcella's mother, Emile. With all this being able to be confirmed by Marcella, they crossed to the stables where Marcella and Florence were attending to the horse stalls.

Marcella, though having never seen her father and knowing nothing about the correspondence or the visit, before a word was spoken shared a knowing look with Mark that revealed a connection. When Louis introduced the visitor by saying, 'Marcella, this is Mark Richards,' they looked at each other briefly before rushing one another with open arms. They held each other tightly, with Marcella weeping and Mark murmuring, 'Marcella, all this time, all this time and not knowing.' He stepped back and looked at her in wonderment. After all this time, they were finally united.

'Yes, you are the image of your mother. Do you know that your name Marcella is the same as my mother's name?'

Marcella broke into the brightest smile. 'Yes, Grandpa told me. He told me to never forget.'

Mark and Marcella fell over each other in their excitement to confirm their relationship; describing her village at Lifou, Grandpa and the description Grandpa had given of the sailor with whom his daughter had fallen in love. When they moved out into the sunlight and Mark spotted the ring on Marcella's hand he choked for words. 'That ring, it's the one I gave to Emile!'

Marcella went to take it from her finger but before she did Mark said, 'Wait. I'll tell you what's inscribed on the inside: *Mark Richards 1813.*'

This caused a rush of blood to everyone's head as they waited anxiously for Marcella to remove the ring and hand it to Florence, who then read aloud, '*Mark Richards 1813.*'

They enjoyed an evening meal as never before, telling stories, gathering together more evidence of their connection, and strengthening the bonds between all at the table, including Jane, who found the revelation most wonderful. Mark recounted the story of his shipwreck in the Philippines, how he had been left financially destitute and how he had been unable to return to Lifou till recently. Mark stayed for two more days, getting to know them all, including Massan and the baby, before having to return to Port Mackay where his schooner, with a crew of three, was scheduled to set sail the following day.

The next six months proved to be busy and exciting. Though Mark's present cargo business serviced ports from Brisbane to Sydney, he planned to replace this southern run by extending northwards of Brisbane. He made two visits to Savannah, with the second bringing news that Marcella was again pregnant and a request he attend the marriage of Marcella and Massan, where he would escort her down the aisle.

Antoinette spent a small fortune placing orders with leading fashion houses in Sydney and eagerly opening the boxes as they arrived. The garden received special attention, with two gardeners watering and manicuring the lawn and Jane nurturing the extensive rose beds in the hope that all would be in bloom for the first marriage to be celebrated at Savannah. The farm manager put a spring into his step, directing farm hands to scythe the grass outside the garden fence and paint the picket fence with a fresh coat of whitewash. The carriageway leading to the house was to be made as smooth as if the Queen was invited.

Jane spent days slavishly adorning an evening dress with hundreds of bright sequins. Florence thumbed through the pages of women's magazines and eventually chose a pale-blue, slim-fitting dress made of chiffon, with a whalebone corset to accentuate her slim waist.

Antoinette arranged her and Louis's wardrobe in traditional style. She planned to wear a full-length crinoline, and Louis a three-piece suit and collar. Antoinette initially wanted to dress Marcella as an English bride, but with Marcella's quiet resistance and support from Florence and Jane they settled for a surprise which they kept from Massan and Louis.

Massan intended wearing a traditional loin cloth, no shirt and an elaborate island headdress; that is, until Antoinette got herself into a fluster. Marcella intervened and, with Antoinette's eventual agreement, persuaded him to wear a white shirt with the loin cloth and forget the headdress. However, Massan still planned to wear a small treasure he had brought from Tanna Island. The multipronged hair pin carved from black ebony wood represented a connection to his family and must be worn.

Neither Marcella nor Massan mentioned to Antoinette that he would be barefoot. Nobody knew what Mark would wear, and conjecture passed around as to his dress sense and the amount he would spend on attire for this once-in-a-lifetime occasion.

The housemaids showed more enthusiasm as the day drew near. They got down on bended knees and scrubbed the verandas, steps and walkway pavers of both the homestead and Marcella's cottage.

Word of the wedding spread amongst the villagers, with the women being curious to witness the ceremony. The women of the homestead pawed over the invitation list, preparing handmade invitations for Savannah's white employees, the Islander churchgoers and those at Rosewood. A general invitation, spread by word of mouth, circulated amongst Savannah's villagers, telling them they were welcome to attend but they must let Marcella know well before the wedding date for catering purposes. The parish reverend, who had been serving the parish for the past five years, graciously accepted the request to officiate, adding that he had only solemnised three other weddings since arriving.

Of most concern was whether Mark would be present on the grand day! Some of the women thought a lapse of memory might cloud his mind and he might not show. However, Louis explained that Mark must have an organised mind to be able to schedule his shipping and felt confident he would attend. As a contingency plan, he offered to stand in for Mark if, due to unforeseen circumstance, Mark could not get to the wedding on time. Louis, though he said little to the others, had come to regard Mark as a champion chap, a man of integrity who would meet his promise to be there for Marcella's big day.

If Marcella had not been pregnant, the women would not be in such a rush to arrange the marriage. Ever since Marcella had announced the news the girls, particularly Antoinette, had made it their business to have the couple wed as soon as possible. They fussed as never before, so much so that Louis was left wondering if Antoinette had secretly invited the Governor of Queensland. Louis had his own reasons for wanting the betrothed wed as soon as possible. Though Marcella was the daughter of a British subject, she had been born in the islands and needed proof of her British status, otherwise she might be considered an alien and deported. Massan, with no hereditary links to British ancestry, was definitely an alien and, although the colonies were flooded with illegal immigrants, he, having come as an indentured labourer, could easily be deported back to Tanna Island. To obviate these possibilities, Louis had previously, with a signed declaration from Mark, registered Marcella's birth certificate, identifying Mark as her father. Following the marriage, the marriage certificate would certify Massan as Marcella's lawful husband and make him a British subject. Rather than complicate matters, Louis planned to wait till after the wedding before telling them of his manoeuvres.

Antoinette and the girls were thrown into turmoil the day before the wedding when Mark failed to appear as promised. So frenzied had they become by evening meal time that Louis excused himself soon after and hid away in the office, attending to the accounting books to avoid being caught in the crossfire of commentary about Marcella's father. Next morning was no better, with worried faces and doubtful minds speaking amongst themselves, blaming Mark for ruining what would have been a marvellous day for all. Louis still refused to engage in the criticism and parked himself on the far corner of the veranda with a view towards the carriageway. A pleased smile crossed his lips when, in the distance, he saw a wisp of dust. As Mark and the sulky came closer, billows of dust spiralled behind. Louis left it to Sapphire to announce Mark's arrival, and when she barked all the women rushed out front to see for themselves. Louis watched as they crowded around the sulky and welcomed Mark as some sort of hero for having driven the mare at such a pace to arrive in time. Louis smiled again when he heard Mark telling some heroic story about battling high seas and skating his ship *Stormbird* across the foam-swept sandbar at the mouth of the river to dock in time. Though Mark was prone to telling tall stories, Louis loved his spirit of adventure and what he perceived as Mark's courage in time of need.

Lucille, Rosie and Narisse, with her two children, arrived soon after in two sulkies. Andrew decline the invitation to attend and, instead, sent a card wishing Marcella and Massan well. The reverend, also arriving late, jogged in on horseback. Antoinette took charge, directing people to rooms where they could dress and freshen their appearance and overseeing the maids assembling a scrumptious lunch on trestle tables on the shaded veranda. Mark spoke with Marcella and Jane about the ceremony before they retreated to their cottage. Massan was confined to the stables to be out of sight of Marcella—not a peep, Florence had said, when he suggested he come to the house for lunch. The stickybeak women wondered what Mark had in the two bags he unloaded from the sulky and took directly to his room. One bag had accompanied him on previous visits, so what did the second bag contain? Massan's best man, young

Turgy, did his best to contain Massan's curiosity by telling him that after today he would be able to see Marcella every day for the rest of his life.

Following the morning greetings and the din of conversation at lunchtime, the homestead quietened as people either rested or prepared themselves for the four o'clock wedding ceremony. Near to the time, Louis visited Mark's room to see how his nerves were faring and to refresh his memory of his role as father of the bride.

The churchgoing Islanders and some others from the village wandered up the slope to the homestead and positioned themselves in the shade of trees next to a tall poinciana, ablaze with clusters of bright red flowers. Massan and Turgy held back at the stables till the reverend summoned them with a wave to join him beneath the tree. When Antoinette, Louis and the others were settled, the reverend spoke a few words to indicate that proceedings were about to commence. Then, as a prearranged signal, he raised his bible and tipped it towards Marcella's cottage. All waited in silent anticipation till the cottage door opened and Mark and Marcella appeared, arm in arm, leading the way, with Jane the matron of honour and Florence as the bridesmaid following. Marcella, dressed in a full-length sea-blue sarong imprinted with images of coral, with her hair braided, a frangipani lei about her neck and white shoes, revealed the grace of a princess of high distinction. Mark, standing upright and elegantly dressed in a white cotton shirt and trousers and shiny new shoes, and with his hair falling freely about his shoulders, matched Marcella's deportment so well that the resemblance of father and daughter could not be denied.

With the tapestry of Savannah's bushland as a magnificent backdrop and the blessing of bright sunshine above, Marcella and her entourage walked gracefully forward, stepping along a pathway lined with a scattering of rose petals. Marcella paused when almost within reach of the reverend and then, at a prompt from him, came beneath the spreading poinciana where he stood with Massan and the best man in a space circled with poinciana florets that had been laid on the ground. The reverend then signalled for a senior Christian Islander to come forward to help conduct the ceremony. With everyone looking on attentively, the reverend began the service, introducing the bride and groom and proceeding accordingly. Vows were exchanged in loud voices so all those assembled could hear, and as Massan and Marcella each said their vows the Christian Islander repeated the words in Pidgin so his people could understand.

Mark held his emotions together till Turgy handed Massan the ring and the reverend told the assembly the story of how Mark had given the ring to Marcella's mother, Emile, on the island of Lifou. He fought the tears but, as Massan slipped the ring onto Marcella's finger, he could contain himself no longer and cried unashamedly. Those witnessing the coming together of these two young and proud people could do no more than wipe aside a tear and murmur well wishes. Antoinette, who was nursing baby Massan, felt a nearness to Mark that assured her that all would be well.

As the sun set on the mountains of the Great Dividing Range, the guests joined on the veranda of the homestead. Those who found it too crowded sat on wooden forms placed around the garden. Most set aside racial prejudice, mingling freely while helping themselves to the feast of pig-on-a-spit and other meats, together with salads, homemade bread, platters of fruit, and fruit juice punch. Conversations in English, Pidgin English, and some in a mix of these languages, drifted on the evening air, providing a unique moment in the history of colonial Queensland.

The reverend called everybody to attention for the formal part of the evening, when Louis and Mark delivered the main speeches. Louis dwelt on devotion to family, the importance of work and service to God. Marcella, he said, had earned the title of princess, and Massan had proved himself to be reliable and diligent and would soon be promoted to the position of ganger. He told how he and Antoinette were godparents to baby Massan. He kept till last his promise to Marcella and Massan that they and their family would always have a home at Savannah.

Mark surprised everybody by speaking so openly, telling the story of how he met Emile, the joy of discovering Marcella his only child, and that he had now established Port Mackay as the base for his shipping business. He welcomed Massan to the family and disclosed with gusto that his wedding present to the couple would be a visit to Lifou and to Massan's island home of Tanna. As a show of gratitude for all that Louis and Antoinette had done for Marcella, he then opened the second bag that had kept the women guessing and presented Louis with artefacts he had traded with the Islanders during his visit of discovery to Marcella's village at Lifou.

Late in the evening, after people thanked one another and made their way to bed, each lay awake, at least for a short while, casting back to the occasion and thinking someone must be watching over them.

CHAPTER 18

The birth of Marcella's second child brought great excitement. With Massan and Louis away working when the labour pains started soon after breakfast and the delivery made before they arrived home for lunch, the women were able to attend to the birthing without the distraction of menfolk, who understood little about the birth process. When told, Massan, as he had done before, found it difficult to comprehend that he had conceived a child, while Louis gave thanks for not having to endure Marcella's screams and bear the women's anxiety. When word reached Mark, he announced to his crew that the scheduled delivery of cargo to Townsville would be delayed till after he had visited his new granddaughter. He visited once, and then a second time for the christening, where the reverend explained that the child's name, Emile Antoinette, derived from Marcella's mother and the godmother Antoinette.

Marcella fell pregnant again, and after the third child arrived, time and space were at a premium, with a four and a five-year-old running rampant through the homestead and the baby demanding much of Marcella's time. Massan doted on all three, whispering in Pidgin to the baby and setting Massan Jr and Emile on the pathway to island tradition by teaching them spear throwing and basket weaving. Those that visited from plantations in the valley, and others from further afield, took home stories of the success of the blended family at Savannah.

Mark kept the promise of his wedding gift and sailed with Marcella, Massan and the three children to Lifou, where they met with Grandpa Jacques and visited Emile's grave. For a brief moment Marcella was overcome with homesickness and only left after Grandpa told her not to worry about him and insisted she return to Savannah, where the sun shone upon her and her family.

After leaving Lifou they sailed to Tanna Island where they spent a few days with Massan's family and friends. During the voyage, Marcella harboured the regret of not fulfilling her promise of returning Moses' remains to his home village on the island of Malaita. She had planned to do this on the trip, but when Mark explained that this meant sailing another thousand miles north she considered Massan and the children and quietly dismissed the idea. For the rest of her life she would have a recurring dream of his holding her hand in the plantation hospital, and her promising to return his bones to the land of his ancestors so his spirit could rest in peace.

By now Marcella had matured into a well-rounded adult, ably caring for her children and presenting herself as a commendable host to those visiting. Massan, with guidance from Louis, had become a ganger, adopting the Protestant ethic of hard work and fairness and leading by example. Jane, beginning to think she was destined to live life as a spinster at Savannah, continued caring for the sick and injured, as well as schooling the children.

Marcella became a religious zealot and, although she had three children to care for, she and Jane found time to take religious instruction classes in the Islanders' village. With many of the Islanders believing their beautiful princess to be a messiah sent by the gods, they readily attended the classes, which quickly swelled into a well-attended congregation. They all sat cross-legged beneath the shade trees in the village, listening to Jane preaching and singing hymns to the sound of an accordion. This led to the establishment of weekly clinics, where Jane and Marcella attended to the sick and injured, while Antoinette cared for Marcella's children. Though Jane was a skilled nurse and compassionate, the Islanders saw Marcella as one of their own and turned to her when very ill or dying. It became customary for them to request that she be at their bedside, where she held the hand of many as they passed to the next world. During the decades that followed, Marcella assisted hundreds of her people with medical and spiritual needs, as well as counselling those with personal problems. She became so revered that those returning to the islands of Melanesia spread stories of the *Princess of the South Pacific* and her divine gift. Her name became legendary and, even today, in small pockets where Islanders live a traditional life, mention is made of the Princess.

Florence had outgrown her fetish for island boys and now spent much of her time courting a courthouse assistant at Mackay. Antoinette and Louis, though having reached midlife, showed no sign of slowing in their mission of spreading the Lord's teaching and praying for salvation for all. The workforce remained reasonably contented, with more than ever before opting to stay at Savannah rather than return to the islands at the end of the contractual term of their indenture agreement. Contact with those at Rosewood remained regular, with Louis visiting to oversee operations and discuss management. Andrew, now realising that his strength lay as a supervising manager rather than owner of a plantation, fulfilled his role capably, keeping the level of production up to Louis's expectations. Lucille had eventually won the heart of her roving seafarer, anchored him as an employee of Rosewood and was expecting her first child.

Massan, struggling to understand and believe what Marcella told him about birth control, kept making babies and when, by year ten of their marriage, they had seven children running wild, Louis, at prompting from Antoinette, had an awkward talk with him. Apparently Louis did not press his point hard enough, and when the eighth child was born it was left to Jane, with the forthrightness of an experienced nurse, to take Massan aside and explain how having sex made babies. The birth rate then fell, with the couple parenting nine children during fifteen years of marriage.

Florence had married her courthouse sweetheart, given birth to four children, and lived in a cottage at Savannah. With Florence heavily engaged in management of the plantation and Marcella now almost full time assisting those in the village, Grandma Rousseau was run ragged caring for the younger children.

All this time Mark conducted his shipping business from Port Mackay and visited the family at Savannah. He had never married and, as some said, he was 'married to the sea'. The older children knew him as Grandpa, while the younger ones knew him as the man who brought the presents. Marcella, knowing the hardships faced by seamen and seeing Mark beginning to age, wondered how much longer he could continue as a seafarer. She mentioned this to Antoinette and felt relieved when Antoinette said, 'Mark can always stay with us.'

The colony of Queensland had progressed since Marcella first arrived at Rosewood. Land north to the tip of Cape York was being opened by gold seekers, pastoralists and agriculturalists. These frontiers people sweltered in the hot tropics, facing fire, floods and cyclones that could claim lives and destroy livestock, crops and orchards overnight. Yet they came, spurred by the promise of fortune. Like the Rousseaus, some achieved success while others either perished in the northern wilds or returned to the southern cities, broken and destitute. When women accompanied their husbands they had to contend with unimaginable deprivations and threats of attack by marauding Aborigines. These stout and stoic women stood by their men, struggling to survive while raising large families to carry their legacy into the future.

By 1888 much had changed in the valley since Louis and Antoinette established Savannah in the early 1860s. Tens of thousands of acres of virgin land had been cleared and put under production, with most of the new settlers acquiring relatively small acreages of sixty to one hundred acres. With these new properties being too small to warrant a mill on each holding, the owners banded together to finance centralised cooperative mills that crushed the cane from their properties. Only a few, like Savannah and Rosewood, continued to crush their own cane and, in some instances, that of growers with whom they held long-standing arrangements. In this respect, the likes of the Rousseaus were considered pioneers and icons of the industry. With Louis and Antoinette nearing retirement and Florence and her husband to inherit Savannah and Rosewood, the couple worked tirelessly to hold the estate together. Though the era of large plantations and the plantocracy were fast disappearing, they held to the vision of living the life of the wealthy gentry.

Tragedy struck when, one afternoon, Florence went to check on Antoinette who had been feeling unwell and found her in her bedroom, having died of a suspected heart attack. With the body having to be interred promptly in the hot climate, messengers galloped to all points of the valley, spreading the sad news and advising of the funeral to be held at Savannah. The funeral, held two days after the death, brought sympathisers from near and far, arriving in coaches, carriages, sulkies, riding astride on saddle horses and some even making the journey on foot. Everyone paid homage to a wonderful lady during the graveside service, which was conducted at the foot of a hill facing the rising sun. This loss traumatised the now aging Louis to such an extent that, if

Florence and her husband had not taken control, these legendary properties would have been sold off as small lots, destroying symbols of the hardy pioneering days when people challenged the frontier in search of fame and fortune. Louis never recovered from the grief and quietly passed away two years later, to be laid to rest beside his dear wife.

With the passing of each year, Mark found it increasingly difficult to man his schooner, and when he slipped on the wet deck and tore a ligament he sold the schooner and retired to a modest home on the outskirts of Mackay. Marcella tried her best to bring him to Savannah, but the old sea dog would not shift far from the smell of the ocean or sight of the ships plying the river and berthing at the dock. Marcella's oldest daughter moved to Mackay to care for him and, within a couple of years, two more daughters, wanting to experience town life, joined them. Though Mark loved his granddaughters and they devoted themselves to his care, he struggled with town life and died within five years of leaving the sea. The doctor diagnosed anaemia, but those close to him believed he had fretted for the sea and slowly wasted away. The family buried him in the Mackay cemetery, where a headstone erected by Savannah marks his grave. The house then stayed in the family for decades, providing a town house for the grandchildren.

Rosewood also lost an old friend when Andrew, against the advice of the stable manager, insisted on mounting a young horse in the stable yard. The young horse, nervous of the new rider, refused to move forward and, when Andrew slapped it across its wither with the bridle reins, it leapt forward and then bucked, throwing Andrew head first into a rail and leaving him unconscious on the ground. The doctor responded to the urgent call, arriving later that day and, after examining Andrew, who was still unconscious, expressed doubt that he would survive. 'Only time will tell.'

Lucille sat by Andrew's bed throughout the night, and when Jane arrived from Savannah mid-morning the following day they took shifts, watching over him and praying for a flicker of an eyelid or other movement. Day two and then day three passed without their prayers being answered and, when the doctor visited on day four and pronounced him dead, the curtains were drawn. Rosewood and Savannah sent messengers to pass the word to everyone in the valley and those at Mackay. Dozens attended the graveside service at Rosewood to pay their respects and say goodbye to one of the early settlers of the Pioneer Valley. Andrew's death left Lucille bewildered, and within six months of his passing she gave notice that she, together with her husband and only child, were going to Sydney to make a fresh start. Though the news came as a shock, Florence appointed one of the overseers to pick up the reins of management and take Rosewood forward.

Jane, feeling a need to leave the bush and return to civilisation, followed Lucille's lead and returned to Sydney. Florence, Marcella and their families accompanied her to the dock at Mackay and, amidst floods of tears, waved goodbye to the woman who had devoted three decades of her life to caring for and educating those at Savannah.

Savannah and Rosewood plantations encountered further difficulties when, during the 1890s, the trade union movement agitated to have the Islanders repatriated to the islands because they wanted to fill their positions with members of the union. On the other hand, Florence and other planters wanted to retain their cheap source of labour. Battles within the halls of power pitched back and forth till the formation of the Commonwealth of Australia in 1901. Under its *White Australia Policy*, the Commonwealth Government introduced the *Pacific Island Labourers Act* that decreed that most of the Islanders residing in Australia at the time be deported back to their island of origin. Although 62,000 Islanders had been brought to Australia during the previous forty years, most had either returned to the islands or died while in the country. Of the 9,000 remaining at the time of the Act, 7,000 were forcibly repatriated to their homeland and 2,000 allowed to stay. Those exempted from deportation were mainly the elderly and infirm who posed no threat to the policy of excluding Islanders from the workforce. No recognition was given to the fact that those deported and their predecessors had slaved on the plantations to clear virgin bushland and develop an industry upon which the planters, the economy and government depended. Many had settled into life on the mainland and wanted to stay, only to be evicted by the stroke of a pen. This reprehensible legislation, with the aims of racially purifying Australia and protecting white Australian workers from cheap labour, heralded the decline of the plantation era. Most of the workforce of Savannah and Rosewood were sent home, some after a decade or more of faithfully serving the Rousseaus. This racially based edict and the calamitous dislocation it caused to people's lives both within Australia and the South Sea Islands is a pockmark on the history of Australia and one of many examples of how Australia got it wrong when dealing with native affairs.

An eeriness engulfed the Islander village of Savannah as Florence wandered the lonely walkways between the grass huts, now empty except for the few occupied by those who had been exempted from deportation. The spirals of smoke from cooking fires, the chatter and the laughter were all gone. Only memories lingered to be recalled by those who had lived through the days of plantation life at Savannah.

The Sugar Worker's Union had gained a stranglehold on the industry from field work to milling; even to shipping, where they held ship's masters to ransom to leverage benefits for their members.

Plantation owners were again starved of cheap labour and, with the low sugar price, were forced to curtail production.

Savannah became a ghost of its former self, with some fields left idle, little cane being crushed and the bank account dwindling.

With Florence's husband now almost bedridden with an arthritic condition and only one of her four children having returned to Savannah after being educated in Brisbane, full responsibility of managing the plantations fell upon her shoulders.

A telling day occurred when a union representative visited Savannah and, after inspecting the property, presented Florence with a list of conditions applicable to white workers that, if not met, would result in her two plantations being black-banned by the union.

After fifty years of Savannah managing its own affairs, this intrusion, apart from the burden of additional cost, bit deep into the independence the family had previously enjoyed.

Since the establishment of the central mills where each crushed the cane of several small properties, Florence had received offers to purchase sections of both Savannah and Rosewood. However, she still held to her vision of preserving the properties as self-contained plantations and the dream of a dynastic succession for her children. With this in mind, she turned away the enquiries.

A turning point occurred when her husband's condition slipped to an extent where he needed constant care and the doctor advised that, for both their sakes, Florence would best be served by selling the properties and retiring to Brisbane.

Faced with the biggest decision of her life, Florence cogitated for months, seeking solace by wandering about what used to be fields of green and sitting by her parents' graves in the hope of receiving divine guidance. This indecision continued till her second son, the only child to return to the plantations, announced that he planned to join his siblings in Brisbane. This unforeseen and devastating news, the loss of her only hope for the property to continue in the family name, crushed all expectations and, to hide her distress, she slipped away unnoticed, went to Louis's grave and lay on the cold granite slab, where she sobbed and prayed for the Lord to make a decision. The Lord answered and, after he channelled Louis's advice to her, she rose up, straightened her back and returned to the homestead with a firm resolve to dispose of both Savannah and Rosewood.

With this decision made, Florence, without any mention to the union, dismissed all white employees. The few Islanders who remained on her plantations, those who had escaped deportation, she kept on as caretakers and promised to find them employment elsewhere before she departed. The two mills lay idle, looking forlorn as symbols of the waste caused by the greed of racist unions squeezing out black labour for their own gain. All livestock, apart from a team of wagon horses and some sulky and saddle horses, together with the farming equipment, was sold at auction. She then engaged surveyors and a selling agent to subdivide and sell both plantations as farms small enough to be operated without union labour. These farmers, along with others, would then supply their cane to the central mills operated as cooperatives. Within eighteen months the lots were selling and the proceeds being accumulated in the bank's care, ready for when she and her husband retired to Brisbane, where they would be close to family and the best medical care.

All this while Marcella, who still lived in her original cottage, together with Massan and two of her sons, shared Florence's pain by listening to her concerns and comforting her when she occasionally lost control. In the forty-two years since they first met as sixteen-year-olds, the bond of friendship had never failed them. They were always there for each other in times of need. Marcella, though fearing the wrench of leaving her home and crying herself dry when left alone, did what she could to reassure Florence and, at times, carry her through the turmoil.

When the time to leave Savannah drew close, Florence said to Marcella, 'I want you to come to town with me so I can make provision for your future.'

'Future?'

'Yes. I have a surprise for you and Massan.'

'What sort of surprise?'

'You'll see. Here, help me harness a sulky and we'll be off to town.'

Marcella, knowing little about providing for the future, imagined a new dress and matching shoes, so she was surprised when they stopped in front of the Bank of New South Wales and Antoinette hitched the horse to the bank's hitching rail in the main street. The clerk behind the counter said to Florence, 'Please wait,' and then disappeared behind a door.

'The lady from Savannah wants to speak to you,' he said, addressing the bank manager in a low tone. He then added, 'She has a black woman with her.'

Florence, knowing the manager well, introduced Marcella and then sat with her at the desk. After discussing progress of the land sales, Florence turned to talking about the move to Brisbane and how Marcella and her husband would settle in Mackay where they had an extended family. The manager hid his surprise when Florence said that she wanted to open an account in Marcella's name and deposit a substantial amount of money to help her settle in the town. The manager, thinking a deposit of a few pounds in gratitude for the years of service would be a nice gesture, gladly opened an account and recorded Marcella's specimen signature. He then asked Florence, 'How much would you like to deposit?'

Florence handed him a signed cheque. When he read the amount of £500 he took a second look at Marcella.

To cover for his surprise, Florence quickly added, 'It's to buy a house.'

Never before had the manager seen an Islander in possession of more than a few pounds, and to hide his astonishment he politely commented, 'This will buy a few houses in Mackay.'

Florence, anticipating the manager's concern that, in accordance with island custom, what belonged to one belonged to all and that the money would soon be frittered, set to justify the amount by saying, 'It's also for my nieces and nephews.'

The manager, knowing that Florence was an only child and that her children lived in Brisbane and would have access to money from the Brisbane branch of the bank, gave her a curious look, to which she replied, 'They're Marcella's children, but I'm their aunt!'

The seasoned banker had seen some strange bequests in his years in the bank, but to give £500 to an Islander was beyond the pale. He asked if any of the money was to be held in trust for the future, and when Florence confirmed that it was an outright gift the conversation extended to how best to protect Marcella from unscrupulous people dipping into her windfall. At the bank manager's suggestion, Florence agreed that all withdrawals were to be jointly signed by Marcella and the bank manager in residence at the time of withdrawals. Once done, the women took tea at a café, where Florence tried to explain further to the bewildered Marcella. Marcella, still hardly able to comprehend the significance of so much money, asked many more questions on the way home. Massan, illiterate and never having handled money, remained in blissful ignorance when told that the family was now rich.

Inevitably, the day came when Florence had to brace herself and begin packing the family belongings that had surrounded her since childhood. Where to start, what to take, what memories were to be left behind proved more daunting than Florence could have ever imagined. Furnishings, including a piano which had been purchased by Louis and Antoinette, and items collected by herself, asked to be taken and not left to the fate of falling into the hands of unknown recipients. With her mind muddled from the stress, she decided to partition the house, sorting one room at a time, but found that so many items and memories were interconnected with treasures elsewhere in the house that not a day passed without her throwing her hands up in despair. As for a helping hand from her incapacitated husband, he struggled to get through each day, let alone provide assistance with the task that was becoming more impossible with each passing day. Oh, if only he were well enough or her children would leave the comfort of their homes, sail north and help!

Most worrisome for Florence was the thought of leaving behind her beloved horses, Cherry and Beauty. She had helped with their births and nurtured them to become loving and dependable saddle horses. She breathed relief when a gentleman farmer on a sprawling acreage upriver offered to give them a good home.

The evening before departure from Savannah was, for Florence, the *last supper*. Never again would she sit at the dining table where she had occupied a seat for as long as she could remember. By the dim lamplight, she visualised the family all around, chatting and exchanging notes as they ate a hearty meal prepared by Islander housemaids. Everything seemed surreal: her ailing husband, her children a month away by letter, and the last of the household furnishings loaded onto a wagon, ready for an early start the next morning. Massan and his boys rose early and harnessed the sulky mare and the team of wagon horses, ready to make the last journey along what had become a path well worn by those who lived at Savannah. With Florence and her husband in the sulky, and Marcella, Massan and their two boys riding in the wagon, they set off with the sulky in the lead.

Goodbye Savannah, cried Florence in her heart as they passed through the front entrance of the estate for the last time. Never could Florence have foreseen that life would end this way, leaving behind her parents and everything they had created. With Florence managing the reins, the horse kept a steady pace till it almost halted at the turnoff to Rosewood. Florence, at the biggest crossroads in her life, almost swung towards Rosewood in the hope of delaying if not aborting her departure. However Rosewood, like Savannah, had been placed in the hands of a selling agent. There could be no turning back, and after a wistful glance down the road to the plantation she continued on to Mackay and the waiting ship.

The bustle at the wharf, as the last of the cargo was loaded to the ship and passengers began to embark, caused a storm of regret in Florence's mind. The full magnitude of the decision to leave home stared her in the face: *What have I done? Everything I have ever lived for and treasured now gone.*

With nowhere to turn and stricken with fear of the future, she fell into Marcella's arms. Some bystanders, recalling the thousands of Islanders that had been brought ashore at the wharf and put to work on plantations as virtual slaves, watched with disbelief as the former slave girl comforted her mistress.

The ship's captain, a former slaver with blood on his hands, searched his soul as he held from sounding the ship's horn for castoff. The police inspector and his officers were left wondering about their past conduct and self-worth. Time and again they had herded or dragged in chains recalcitrant Islanders to the magistrate's court in Mackay to be handed judgements they neither understood nor deserved. Businessmen felt guilt at having cheated Islanders of the pittance of a wage they received for breaking their backs from daylight to dusk to fill the planter's coffers. Other townspeople felt sympathy for the forgotten people who had been hidden away on plantations, with some realising, for the first time, that these living souls where no different to themselves and that they should have been more kind to them in the past—even a wave to acknowledge their existence.

An elderly Islander came forward and expressed his gratitude for all that Florence, Louis and Antoinette had done for him during his years of toil in the fields of their plantation. He stood proud before Florence, wanting to hug her as he would his mother, but the racial divide prevented him from reaching out to her. Florence, through the blur of tears that clouded her sight and mind, recognised him as a lad who, as a sixteen-year-old, had arrived with nothing more than the loin cloth about his waist. This recollection, the connection to the past and all the good Savannah had done for those in its care, blasted away the last remnant of Florence's restraint. She fell to her knees before him and, when he reached forward and lifted her up to be an equal, she lost control totally, wailing in strains reminiscent of the wails of grief she had heard drifting from the village from homesick recruits and those grieving the death of a loved one.

Marcella gave Florence a last, lingering hug, kissed her on the forehead and then turned to Massan who, though struggling to contain his own feelings, took Florence by the hand. Now in disarray and unable to help herself, Florence, without again looking Marcella's way, allowed Massan to usher her up the gangway, with her husband following. At castoff, the captain sounded the horn several times as a resounding farewell.

As the ship turned about and set sail down the river, Marcella came to the full realisation that she would never see Florence again. This slipping away on the tide, the last glimpse of Florence standing on the rear deck and now waving goodbye, was too much to bear. Marcella gave one final wave and then held her head in her hands, in a state of emotional collapse. A flood of memories cascaded before her mind: Being kidnapped by Oliver Morgan, raped by both Andrew and Saxon Rushmore; being united with her father; marrying Massan and raising a large family on Savannah plantation. All appeared fleetingly. The regrets of not having returned Moses' remains to his village in Malaita, and not being at Grandpa's side when he passed away, bit deeply. The help she had provided to Savannah's island community for decades as carer and counsellor, and being named *Princess of the South Pacific* for her compassion and dedication. These thoughts and more filtered through the haze of Marcella's grief, leaving her with head in hands and sobbing, while the crowd watched and felt sympathy for the island girl grieving the loss of her white mistress.

When the ship eventually disappeared from sight and those assembled began to disperse, Massan, assisted by his sons, helped Marcella to the sulky. He led the way, with the boys following in the wagon, as they proceeded along River Street and out into the bushland surrounding the town, where the family had bought acreage and a house with Florence's bequest money.

Florence's departure heralded a new chapter in Marcella's life. Her children, all nine of them, flocked around her and Massan to comfort them through the grief of leaving Savannah and the loss of Florence. Their home, a five-acre allotment set away from neighbours, became a halfway house for the shanty dwellers and destitute of her people. With zeal she put these people to work, growing vegetables, keeping chooks and herding goats in the nearby forest. She won the admiration of the townspeople and respect of the police. She became a go-between, liaising and negotiating with the police and local business houses for a better deal for her people. The government became a target as she led the Pacific Islanders' Association, fighting for equal employment opportunity and fair pay. She became recognised as a formidable foe by those of the white community who challenged her sense of justice. Time and again she stood before the magistrate as mentor for an accused Islander, exposing the hypocrisy of the law.

She managed Florence's financial bequest wisely, buying houses and establishing the boys and their families in business as market gardeners, saw millers and fishermen. The girls, having been raised at Savannah and educated, married well, with three taking reputable colonists as spouses, and the other two raising a family with their Islander husbands. All members of the family held to their strict religious beliefs and conducted their lives accordingly, attending church regularly and helping the needy, whether black or white. With the assistance of her daughters, Marcella conducted a Sunday School where, as well as receiving religious instruction, the children were taught to read and write.

Grief shrouded the family when Massan, in his seventies, took ill and passed away at home. Not surprisingly, the church service was well attended, with many in the congregation from the white community. Marcella, with the same stoic resilience she had displayed throughout her life, lived to be in her nineties. The Islander community of Mackay wept with her passing and, in their hearts, promised to carry on her legacy of bettering the lives of Islanders and their descendants living in Australia. Not a month passed without somebody placing frangipani, hibiscus or some other remembrance flowers on the graves of Marcella, Massan and Marcella's father Mark, who all lie in a family plot, where inscriptions on their headstones provide a lasting memory to this day.

Marcella's descendants continued to support the church and to assist within the community, becoming church leaders and advocates for change in what was still a racist society.

Much has been gained and today, with members of their extended family engaging with the wider community and acceptance being achieved, these previously maligned people are assured a bright and rewarding future.

Due to misinformation or a glossing over of the past history of Queensland some readers might find it difficult to accept that the *Labour Trade* portrayed in the story ever existed. Indeed, such a possibility may be beyond their comprehension. To remove any doubt as to the existence and savagery of the trade see the following newspaper extract.

Weekly Times (Melbourne, Vic. 1869–1954), Saturday 22 February 1890, page 20.

"Blackbirding" in the South Pacific.

THE RELEASED PRISONERS IN BRISBANE.

The six prisoners who have for the past few years been confined at the St. Helena penal establishment, in Moreton Bay, for atrocities committed in the South Pacific six years ago, and who were released by order of the Governor-in-Council, were brought to town to-day and were met at Toombal Wharf by Mr. Philp, member for Townsville, and others. They were escorted to the city in order to secure them lodgings. They appeared beside themselves when first questioned as to their regaining their liberty, but only said they were glad to be released, and asked that the past be forgotten. Interviewers failed to obtain any personal accounts from individuals. Sir Samuel Griffith, on being interviewed on the subject, expressed indignant surprise, but allowed that the Governor is entitled to use his prerogative of mercy. The convicts who have thus been released made themselves infamous throughout the world by their cold-blooded atrocities in the "labour schooner" *Hopeful*. Their vile record is without a single redeeming feature, and the cruise of the *Hopeful* was marked by a series of blood-curdling atrocities on the hapless natives. Mr. Millman, the Cooktown P.M., officially reported that at one place on the New Guinea coast the *Hopeful*'s crew shot thirty-eight natives; at another they shot two; at a third they forcibly kidnapped twenty-one, of whom two were drowned in attempting to swim ashore. At a fourth place they not only kidnapped, but brutally ill-treated and outraged a woman, shooting three natives in the fracas that followed. At Normanby Island natives who came out in their canoes to trade were chased and fired at, three shot dead, and nine captured alive. The record of these men was such that on reading it Sir Samuel Griffith declared his feeling was that every man of them should be promptly strung up to the yardarm of their own schooner. The trial showed that there were degrees in the murderous villainy of the men—the more actively bloodthirsty and fiendish of the six being McNeil, the second mate of the *Hopeful*, who at Harris Island deliberately shot, at five yards distance, a native boy who had innocently been offering from his canoe a sucking pig as "trade"—and Williams, the boatswain, who, finding some difficulty in overhauling a native that was diving and swimming vigorously in the effort to escape his would-be kidnapper, deliberately reloaded his rifle and blew the man's brains out. These two were sentenced to death, but popular agitation procured them respite, the plea urged on their behalf being that others had been as bad and that it was hard that they should be made scapegoats for all the murders in the Pacific labour trade. Shaw and Schofield [Schofield was a Government agent appointed to ensure humane treatment of the natives procured], two of the "Hopefuls", were sentenced to penal servitude for life, Freeman to ten, Preston and Rodgers to seven years, and now, after five years have passed, the Queensland authorities release the whole gang of murderers at once.

To learn more about the South Sea Islander experience see internet reference *State Library of Queensland Australian South Sea Islanders*.